Praise for
Donita K. Paul

"The writing is crisp and the setting imaginative. This series will speak to all ages of Christian readers, from preadolescent on up."
—*Publishers Weekly* review of the DragonKeeper chronicles

"Engaging characters, enchanting locales, and perilous creatures await the brave soul who enters the realm of Amara. Donita K. Paul's DragonKeeper chronicles will surely delight fantasy readers with the kind of story that allows a reader to escape into it, but its powerful message lingers long after the final page is turned."
—WAYNE THOMAS BATSON, author of The Door Within trilogy

"Donita K. Paul is amazing! *DragonLight* has the allegorical depth to satisfy the most discerning adult reader seeking spiritual depth, and yet it's fun enough to fascinate a child. This book will enthrall, uplift, and if allowed, change lives, as we are gently drawn to realize that each of us is flawed, that each of us must have patience with other flawed believers."
—HANNAH ALEXANDER, author of *Double Blind*

"*DragonFire* is a soaring adventure. But I wouldn't expect any less from Donita K. Paul, as she always gives us a delightful read: intriguing, challenging, and full of blessing."
—KATHRYN MACKEL, author of *Vanished* and *Outriders*

"Donita K. Paul never fails to satisfy the imagination and delight the soul. In *The Vanishing Sculptor,* she takes us beyond the boundaries of her beloved DragonKeeper chronicles and opens up vast new realms of wonder. The adventure of Tipper, the sculptor's daughter, will strike a responsive chord in the heart of every reader who has ever faced a seemingly impossible challenge. This is fantasy that truly illuminates reality!"

—JIM DENNEY, author of the Timebenders series

"Stunning beginning to a new series! Rarely does an author recapture the exquisite charm and the bold freshness first discovered in her initial series. Donita K. Paul fans are in for a treat as they uncover new wonders and enchantment in the world of Chiril. New readers will revel in the magical blend of mischief and mayhem woven with witness and intrigue throughout this engaging tale. From the zany disposition of Lady Peg to the spirited charm and wit of Tipper, her youthful daughter, *The Vanishing Sculptor* tingles our most fervent emotions of love, joy, and hope. It's an exciting compliment to the DragonKeeper series and a fantastical adventure for inaugural audiences of all ages."

—ERIC REINHOLD, author of the Annals of Aeliana

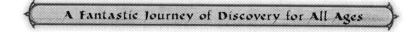
A Fantastic Journey of Discovery for All Ages

Donita K. Paul

A NOVEL

Dragons
of the Valley

WaterBrook
PRESS

DRAGONS OF THE VALLEY
PUBLISHED BY WATERBROOK PRESS
12265 Oracle Boulevard, Suite 200
Colorado Springs, Colorado 80921

ISBN 978-1-4000-7340-5
ISBN 978-0-307-45911-4 (electronic)

Published in association with the literary agency of Alive Communications Inc., 7680 Goddard Street, Suite 200, Colorado Springs, CO 80920, www.alivecommunications.com.

Published in the United States by WaterBrook Multnomah, an imprint of the Crown Publishing Group, a division of Random House Inc., New York.

WATERBROOK and its deer colophon are registered trademarks of Random House Inc.

Library of Congress Cataloging-in-Publication Data
Paul, Donita K.
   Dragons of the valley : a novel / Donita K. Paul. — 1st ed.
      p. cm.
   ISBN 978-1-4000-7340-5 — ISBN 978-0-307-45911-4 (electronic)
   1. Dragons—Fiction. I. Title.
   PS3616.A94D729 2010
   813'.6—dc22
                              2010021910

2010—First Edition

147429898

Dedicated to:

Jessica Agius
Hannah Johnson
Ian McNear
Rachael Selk
Rebecca Wilber
Joshua and Kayla Woodhouse

Contents

Acknowledgments

God is so good to give me pushers and prodders,
supporters and cheerleaders!

Mary Agius
Jessica Barnes
James Matthew Byers
Evangeline Denmark
Jani Dick
Jack Hagar
Jim Hart
Kathy Hurst
Heidi Likens
Joel Kneedler
Shannon Marchese
Shannon McNear
Carol Reinsma
Faye Spieker
Tiffany and Stuart Stockton
Case Tompkins
Beth and Robert Vogt
Kim Woodhouse
Laura Wright

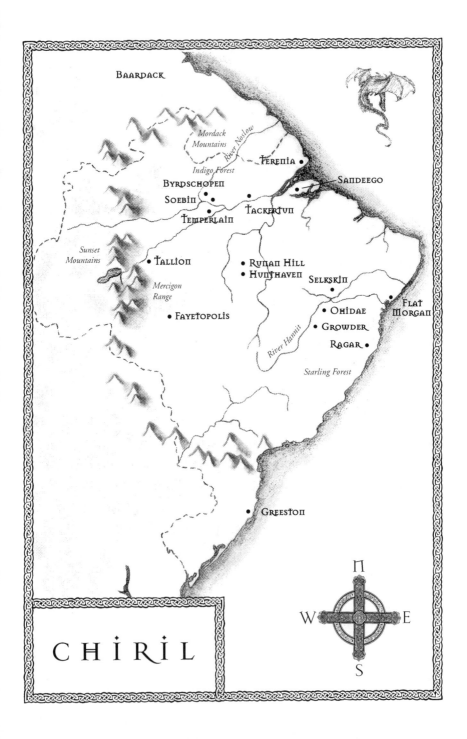

BAARDACK

Mordack
Mountains

River Noslow

Indigo Forest

TERENIA

BYRDSCHOPEN

SANDEEGO

SOEBIN

TEMPERLAIN

TACKERTUN

Sunset
Mountains

TALLION

RUNAN HILL

HUNTHAVEN

SELKSKIN

Mercigon
Range

OHIDAE

FLAT
MORGAN

FAYETOPOLIS

GROWDER

RAGAR

River Hannit

Starling Forest

GREESTON

N

W   E

S

CHIRIL

Theft

Bealomondore stood in the doorway of the darkened hall. Shadows hid the statue he'd been ordered to steal.

His heart told him to retreat. His feet wouldn't move. But the kimen, whose wildest flying lock of hair reached only to the tumanhofer's knee, insisted that the statue be stolen.

The artist cast the kimen a menacing look. The rude little man had startled him out of a sound sleep and proposed this ridiculous escapade. Bealomondore only wanted to go back to his chamber. In the middle of the night, the proper place for an aristocratic tumanhofer was his bed.

He had not had time to dress properly. He looked disheveled. He straightened his tie, but he couldn't do anything about his wrinkled shirt. He closed his fine dinner coat and fastened two ornate buttons.

Bealomondore resented the fact that the small creature had managed to get him out of his bed, dressed, and actually contemplating the theft. An apprentice stealing the work of his esteemed master? Ludicrous!

"Come on," said Maxon. His tiny hand pushed at the back of Bealomondore's leg. "We haven't got all night."

"This is ill-advised," said Bealomondore. "Those statues have just been reunited. Why would your Wulder want one stolen?"

"Not stolen." The kimen's disgusted look further aggravated Bealomondore. He winced at the high-pitched protest flung at him. "I told you, 'Removed from harm's way.'"

The tumanhofer surveyed his serene surroundings. Cool blue moonlight lay in lopsided rectangles on the floor before the ornate windows. Portraits hung mutely on the walls. An elaborate rug silenced footsteps on most of the marble floor. Not even a flatrat would raise a skittering noise.

His gaze returned to his companion. "We're in a guarded castle in a well-policed city with military posts all around. What harm could come to the statues here?"

Maxon crossed his thin arms over his wee chest. "I have my orders."

"I don't see why your orders are mine as well."

"You're needed." He backed up a step, placed his fists on his hips, and glared at the taller tumanhofer. "Are you going to turn your back on a call to service?"

Bealomondore nodded. "I think that's a reasonable choice."

The kimen sighed. "I was told this would be a difficult assignment."

They stood in silence. Bealomondore considered returning to his spacious chambers, warm bed, and pleasant dreams.

Maxon snapped his fingers. "Compromise!"

Bealomondore lifted one eyebrow. "We look out the windows, see if danger lurks, then forget this whole outlandish idea. That's the only compromise I'm interested in."

The kimen ignored his ill humor and tugged on the tumanhofer's pants once more. "Right! Let's go look at the statues. I want to see them up close."

"Looking is all right." Bealomondore smoothed the material of his sleeves and stepped into the hushed hall. "Taking is not."

His footsteps tapped on the marble floor as they approached the carpet centered in the hall.

"Shh!" said Maxon, who didn't make a sound as he glided toward the display of the revered sculptor Verrin Schope's famous *Trio of Elements*.

The three statues had been carved out of one stone, the brilliance of the artist depicted in the layered symbolism. The most obvious interpretation would be of morning, day, and night. But the trio also represented air, earth, and water. Kimen, emerlindian, and marione figures depicted three of the fourteen races that populated the world.

Recently brought to the attention of the royal court, the statues had not yet been expounded upon by critics. Bealomondore felt more symbolism would be exposed with time. Master sculptor Verrin Schope layered his work with meaning. With uncanny skill, he could almost coax life into the cold stone.

The craftsmanship alone made the art valuable. The depth of the imagery would place the art among the most famous classics. Bealomondore's pride in being under Verrin Schope's tutelage puffed out his chest. And he, a humble but aspiring artist, was privy to the backstory of these magnificent pieces. The history and intrigue surrounding the importance of the original stone… *That* would become the material of legends.

And perhaps humble Graddapotmorphit Bealomondore of Greeston in Dornum would be mentioned for his part in the fantastic quest. He patted his chest, a smile tugging at his lips.

As he and Maxon passed a pillar, the entire display came into sight. Bealomondore stopped and gasped at the vacant spot in the circle of three statues.

"One's already gone," whispered Maxon. "See? I told you we had to act quickly."

Bealomondore whipped his head around, searching the shadows, hoping to spy some thief tiptoeing out of the hall.

Nothing stirred.

"Take it," urged Maxon. "Take *Day's Deed* before the thief comes back for it."

"I don't understand your reasoning. I don't understand why I'm supposed to believe your Wulder would urge me to steal."

The kimen vibrated. His already shrill voice screeched up a notch. "Not stealing! Protecting! We can't let a wicked force get hold of all three statues. You don't want to be responsible for the evil consequences, do you?"

That caught his attention. The *Trio of Elements* had been rescued from the hands of a nefarious wizard. If someone plotted to steal all three, then having one in Bealomondore's possession would thwart the evildoer's plans.

"Why do we have to leave the city?"

"Because," answered Maxon, prodding Bealomondore closer to the two figures in stone, "we don't know who the perpetrator is, and getting as far away as possible is critical." Maxon turned away from Bealomondore, braced his back against the tumanhofer's leg, and pushed. "And if the thief is here in the palace, we won't be able to keep him from stealing another piece of the *Trio*."

"Fine!" Bealomondore picked up the statue of a marione farmer. "Where's that sack you brought along?"

Maxon jumped away and did a little skip. "Hollow. It's a hollow bag, given to our clan by your honored wizard friend, Fenworth."

"Friend? More like acquaintance. He's an odd man, and even after questing with him, I don't claim to know him well enough to say 'friend.'"

Maxon put his hand between the folds of his tunic and pulled out a limp cloth bag. He held it open as Bealomondore lowered the statue. The neck of the hollow bulged, but as the stone figure disappeared, the material returned to a flaccid state.

The kimen thrust the bag toward the tumanhofer. "You take it."

Bealomondore clenched his fists. "Why? It certainly is not too heavy for you to tote."

"My orders say for you to take it. Not me."

Bealomondore hesitated while Maxon thrust the empty-looking

sack at him. The image of a mercenary army marching through a gateway created by villains using the three stones made his stomach tighten. He had no desire to repeat that event in the near future.

He sighed and took the bag, rolling it into a tight cylinder, then stuffed it in his stylish shoulder satchel. "At least in this form the bulky statue won't ruin the lines of my attire." He looked down at his mismatched jacket, trousers, vest, and crumpled cravat.

The kimen's light laughter echoed in the hall. Maxon clamped his hand over his own mouth.

Bealomondore studied the little man's face. Bright, cheerful eyes twinkled at him. With wispy hair and no eyebrows, kimens always looked surprised. Their clothing was an odd substance, both beautiful and as disorderly as their topknot. In Chiril, the little people did not mix with the other six high races, and this added to their mystique. The artist in Bealomondore wanted to capture Maxon's expression of delight.

Maxon lowered his hand. "You wear very nice clothes. But we don't have time to pack a bag."

That statement jerked the tumanhofer out of any appreciation for the comeliness of his companion.

He growled his disapproval. "You expect me to travel to who-knows-where with only the clothes on my back?"

Maxon nodded vigorously. "Indeed, I do. But it isn't as bad as you might think. If I'm right, we'll be directed to a kimen village in the Starling Forest. They'll have adequate accommodations and clothing you'll admire."

"And if you're wrong?"

He shook his head, wild hair lashing the air. "You like to worry." He turned and headed for the far end of the great hall. "Come on. Let's sneak out and find our contact."

Bealomondore stepped softly behind the kimen, who moved with such grace that he appeared to be floating. No one challenged them as they skulked by the guard stations. The tumanhofer glowered at their lack of alertness. He wouldn't be stealing this statue if they were more conscientious in their duties.

He and the kimen reached the courtyard, lit with torches, and walked boldly to the massive gate.

Two soldiers stood sentinel. They saluted as the king's guests left the castle grounds at three o'clock in the morning. The tumanhofer nodded but disapproved.

After they entered the deserted street, Bealomondore whispered to his short companion, "Someone should do something about the lax security of the castle."

"Why?" Maxon turned quickly, with a puzzled air. "No one has challenged the king of Chiril for centuries."

"I seem to remember a wicked wizard and a delusional gentleman farmer attempting to take over the kingdom less than a week ago."

"Yes, that unfortunate circumstance disturbed our calm a bit. But you must agree that rebellion is a very rare occurrence and, once it has happened, is not likely to be repeated any time soon."

"The law of probability?"

Maxon nodded. "Exactly."

"I'm not sure that applies to nefarious deeds. It seems to me that once evil permeates the air, more evil mushrooms out of the dark recesses of society."

"But that proves my point. We aren't likely to have another paid army run by Chirilian madmen running amuck in our land. Odds are this is an entirely different foe we must look out for."

"I'd rather be on the lookout for spring showers, buds swelling to full blossoms, birds serenading the earth's renewal, and breezes ushering the fragrance of rich loam from the newly plowed fields."

The kimen stopped, again planted his fists on his hips, and tilted his head to look up at Bealomondore. "I thought you were an artist. You sound like a poet."

"I am indeed an artist. But the sensitive soul requires a more sophisticated language to express profound observations."

The kimen giggled and resumed his march to whatever destination he'd chosen. Bealomondore followed, fuming over lackadaisical guards, impertinent kimens, and the dubious honor of protecting a magnificent piece of art.

Just before dawn they reached a small cookery at the outskirts of the city. Wonderful aromas filled the air. Bealomondore's stomach rumbled. Red letters proclaimed, "Good Food—Cheap Cheep."

Maxon waved toward a big building down the lane. "This place opens the day by serving breakfast to workers from a nearby weaving facility."

The small print under the name of the establishment said, "Eggs and such for breakfast. All things poultry for noonmeal. No dinner served."

Maxon ducked down an alley and headed to the back of the bustling business. He spoke over his shoulder. "You'd like the work done at the mill, real art in cloth. Meals here at Cheap Cheep are included as part of the artisans' wages."

"I'm familiar with the quality of Ragar Textile." Bealomondore followed Maxon through the back door. He glanced down at his inappropriate attire and sighed deeply.

A marione wearing an apron over his plain clothes waved a ladle at them in greeting. "Maxon, you have kimens waiting for you," he said. "They're in the back room."

"Wait here," the kimen ordered Bealomondore and disappeared through a rough-hewn door.

The tumanhofer twisted his lower lip in displeasure.

"Hungry?" asked the cook.

"Starving."

The marione gestured toward a table. "Have a seat, and I'll bring you today's special."

In only a moment, he placed a steaming bowl of krupant and thick slices of bread in front of Bealomondore.

"Bring it in here," Maxon called from the doorway. "My friends want to meet you."

Bealomondore picked up the plate and spoon and ducked through the wooden door. He saw no lighting in the room other than the shine of the kimens' apparel. He counted five besides Maxon and nodded as he was introduced. They sat with empty plates before them, obviously having already enjoyed a hearty meal.

Maxon pointed to a chair made for a larger person, and Bealomondore joined them. He placed his food before him and considered taking his satchel holding the hollow bag off his shoulder. Between his feet below the table might be safe, but he decided to keep it on his person. The Verrin Schope statue would receive his wholehearted protection.

"I'm Winkel. We'll be taking you to our village," said the kimen sitting at the head of the table. She poured liquid from a large pitcher into a tankard and pushed it across the table.

"Thank you." Bealomondore took a swig and found the substance unfamiliar to him but very soothing to his dry throat. He dug into his meal with gusto as the little people talked among themselves.

The more he ate, the more content he felt. Winkel refilled his drink as soon as Bealomondore drained it.

Kimens were known to be courteous, friendly people, but it niggled at his brain that the depth of his comfort among them seemed unnatural. He was ordinarily cautious and observant, necessary skills in navigating the waters of high society, where friend could become foe with the turn of a phrase. In unfamiliar circumstances, he paid attention to detail and unobtrusively gathered information about strangers.

But as the tension eased out of his shoulders, he let go of all worries, and the high voices around him became a tune of good cheer.

He ate and drank and mellowed to the point of drowsiness. When he found he had to work to keep his eyes open, he caught Maxon watching him with an expectant expression.

An alarming thought rose to the top of his muddled mind as he sagged toward the empty plate before him. The kind kimens had drugged him.

Two Taken

Tipper Schope tiptoed through the wet, nasty tunnel. She stepped in a cold puddle and gasped. For a moment her eyes flashed from the little light dancing ahead of her to the uneven floor. She clutched to her chest a sack that looked empty but held one of her father's most interesting statues.

She hugged the limp cloth tighter, wishing she had a shawl or coat to wrap around her shoulders. She wiggled her toes. Her face scrunched in reaction to the repulsive squishy feeling of wet stockings in the heavy boots. Closing her eyes, she sighed and summoned courage. Her father had said to trust him, to follow his instructions precisely, and all would be well.

He'd told her to wear britches, boots, and a warm shirt and tunic. Perhaps she wasn't so much chilled as terrified.

The air stirred. She heard, rather than saw, the kimen approach. The small creature moved quickly, and the fluttering of her clothes sounded like bird wings beating the spring air. But this was no sunny day in a glade. Tipper shivered and opened her eyes.

The kimen cocked her head, a mixture of concern and impatience on her face. "Are you all right?"

Tipper's teeth chattered. "I'm cold but otherwise fine. Please don't go so far ahead of me, Taeda Bel."

The kimen's sudden bright smile dazzled Tipper. "I understand. I forget you don't carry your own light."

The tiny being bent at the waist in a bow that would have done a footman in Tipper's grandfather's castle proud.

Tipper giggled, partly from nerves but also because the very feminine kimen looked way too girlish for the formal masculine gesture. Her gleaming though ragged gown of delicate pink shimmered as the miniature guide moved.

Taeda Bel straightened with grace. The arm that had been swept before her bow extended high over her head in an elegant pose. She twirled and took off down the dank tunnel as if she danced across a ballet stage.

Taeda Bel flitted forward and then returned closer to Tipper. Tipper smiled at the kimen's consideration. Their passage through the underground corridor made Tipper's skin crawl. By her estimation, their mission was unnecessary. But she had promised to take the statue out of the castle.

What had her father meant about invasion? Of course, they'd been invaded, but Paladin and Wizard Fenworth had taken care of that. The villains had been vanquished. Paladin had disbanded the conscripted army. Under his watchful eye, the young men were sent back to their own lands.

"Paladin," she muttered under her breath. "What is he? Oh, right! He's tall and charming. His smile makes my knees wobbly. His voice plucks my heart like a lute. He sets me to singing, inside and out. What an embarrassment."

She stomped in the next few puddles. "It's probably best I'm off on this errand for Papa. Even Mother noticed I couldn't look straight into those blue eyes. Nobody should have eyes the color of cobalt skies."

She hummed a few lines of a song she'd made up about one man's eyes twinkling and a girl bubbling with joy. She caught herself and slammed her foot down in a puddle. The water drenched her leg, and she stumbled.

Taeda Bel appeared by her side. "Are you all right?"

"Yes." She shook her foot. "It was deeper than I thought."

"Be careful." Taeda Bel hopped in the air and floated down. "If you got hurt, it would be more than an inconvenience."

"Right. I'll remember."

The kimen took up her lead position, and Tipper dutifully followed.

Her mind still chewed on the enigma of the mysterious young man who had assumed a status of leader. Prince Jayrus, he had called himself, though he claimed no real kingdom. Her father and his friends called him Paladin, the leader of some foreign religion. Perhaps it would be good to be away from everyone so she could order things in her mind. Everyone respected Paladin, and she did too.

"More reason for me to be out of his way. If he is who he says he is, he doesn't need me around."

"What was that?" asked Taeda Bel without slowing her pace.

"Never mind."

Tipper clamped her mouth shut. This Prince Jayrus–Paladin person could stay behind and befuddle her grandfather's court. She was free and clear. She didn't have to puzzle out the mystery he presented.

He was a mixture of wisdom and social ineptitude. But she didn't have to think about it.

He knew which fork to pick up at a fancy dinner, but his conversation revealed he'd spent more time with books than with people. Who used *verisimilitude* in everyday speech? Who compared a sunset to a resplendent pennon? Who knew what a pennon was?

Paladin was back at her grandparents' castle, the Amber Palace. A good place for him to be, because she wasn't.

Tipper's untimely departure had separated her from the company of Paladin. Maybe she did want to know Paladin better, but that meant she'd have to listen to him explain the contents of Wulder's Tomes. That's what it would take to keep his interest.

Ha! He was way too busy to be interested in her. And she, of course, was going to be way too busy protecting the statue to even think about him.

Her father had not told her how long she and the statue would be banished from Amber Palace and the city. He simply said to follow the kimen.

Tipper splashed through another puddle, resisted the urge to groan, and kept an eye on the light in the distance. Taeda Bel had forgotten her promise to stay close.

Tipper picked up her pace and gained on the little kimen. Her friendly guide must have stopped to wait for her. When she reached Taeda Bel's side, a breath of warm, dry air greeted her.

The kimen's shine decreased. "We're leaving the caverns now." She stood inside the lip of the opening with her back pressed against the rock wall. "I won't use my light as we slip through the woods. There's almost too much moonlight for proper darkness to keep us hidden." Her voice trailed off as if she were talking more to herself than to Tipper. Taeda Bel looked sharply at her charge. "Can you keep up with me?"

"Yes."

Taeda Bel's dim glow extinguished.

The sudden darkness radiated with soft sounds. Tipper held her breath. She heard tree frogs, night birds, and the breeze rattling leaves in trees and bushes. Slowly she released the air in her lungs and took a step out of the cave.

She leaned to whisper in the kimen's ear. "There's something in the forest besides creatures of the night."

"I know."

"Do you know what or who?"

By the light of the moon, Tipper saw the kimen nod. "Who *and* what."

Tipper bit back a sarcastic reply. "Then tell me."

"A band of mariones and bisonbecks."

"Bisonbecks? The mountain tribe of renegades from the land of Mordack? They've never come to Chiril."

"And they wouldn't now except they come at the orders of King Odidoddex."

Tipper did a quick survey of her knowledge of the neighboring countries. The mountains of Mordack contained wild creatures, namely three of the seven low races—ropmas, grawligs, and bisonbecks. The region stood as a territory of unrest, with no government and no order. None of the bordering lands would claim it under their jurisdictions. Travelers skirted around the dangerous mountains. Only a few outlaws dared to hide with the crude rogues of the hinterland.

Tipper cocked her head. "Mariones from Mordack?"

"No, mariones under the rule of King Odidoddex."

Tipper scrunched her forehead, picturing the country tinged with brown and green on the map she'd seen as a child. "In Baardack?"

"No, in our backyard." Taeda Bel pushed through thick bushes, releasing the fragrance of sweet bumberlilies. "The Baardack army is still tramping through the mountains. They intend to capture Ragar and take over the throne on behalf of Odidoddex."

Tipper turned back to the dank cave. "My family!"

The kimen grabbed her fingertips. "Your family will be all right. Our task is to keep the villains from getting their hands on all three of your father's statues."

Taeda Bel stilled as if listening. Then her image faded so that even with the moonlight Tipper strained to see her outline. Had the kimen moved?

"Come," Taeda Bel commanded.

"There!" a harsh voice ripped the calm.

"Run!" Taeda Bel's light brightened just enough for Tipper to be able to follow.

Someone crashed through the underbrush behind them. Tipper

abandoned any attempt to move quietly and ran. Soon she heard exclamations from different directions. It sounded as if they were surrounded. Voices growled commands she didn't understand but assumed meant they were bent on capturing her and Taeda Bel. In a breathless race to escape their pursuers, Tipper kept her eyes on the kimen and hoped the small creature knew where to go.

Taeda Bel's thin voice sounded in Tipper's mind. *"Hide!"*

Tipper fell to the ground and scrambled under the bushes. The sound of Taeda Bel's voice in her head had hardly faded before heavy boots clomped by. Tipper started to inch out of her cover as soon as the soldier had moved on, but again her small guide gave a mindspeak command.

"Stay there!"

Tipper pulled herself into a ball and tried to make no noise. Her breathing sounded loud enough to herald her presence, and she wondered if anyone else could hear her heart thumping.

Two more hulking soldiers pounded past her hiding place. Shouts filled the air. The men realized they'd lost her. She heard them beating the bushes. She pictured their heavy swords slicing through the branches.

In desperation, Tipper tried to project a call with her own mind. *Taeda Bel?*

Did it work? Was she heard? Wizard Fenworth, Librettowit, and her father could mindspeak, but she could just barely understand the dragons when they spoke to her. Would the kimen hear her? *Taeda Bel?*

No response. Tipper heard the guards. They'd changed directions, coming back toward her hiding place.

This time she whispered the kimen's name through clenched teeth. "Taeda Bel?"

Again, no answer. Tipper winced as two men shouted. She crawled out from her refuge and crouched in the indistinct path. Her sense of direction had deserted her, but she knew the correct way to go was away from the noise made by the soldiers. Keeping low, she darted from one clump of trees to the next.

The darkness spooked her as branches reached out like arms and rustling leaves brought visions of soldiers waiting for her. But the commotion made by her pursuers grew distant. Perhaps she would escape after all.

A figure stepped out in front of her. She screeched and whirled to get away, but another bisonbeck soldier blocked her escape. He grabbed her by the arms and hoisted her over his shoulder.

She screamed and kicked.

"Wait," said a gruff voice. "Let's see what's in that thing she carries."

The man with a vise grip on her legs grunted. "Shouldn't we let First Speatus have the honors?"

A noise that blended a growl and a scornful laugh sent chills down Tipper's spine.

"Why should we give booty to him? If it's valuable, it's ours. No one need know." His voice came closer. "Dump her."

The huge man dropped her on the ground and put a boot on her stomach. Tipper gripped the hollow sack and struggled to breathe.

With one yank, the second soldier took possession of her father's statue, still hidden inside the nondescript bag.

"There's nothing in it," said the bisonbeck with a heavy foot on her middle. "Empty."

"Sometimes things of great value are very small. A diamond, for instance." He shook the bag and frowned.

Tipper tried to speak, but no words came out.

The rougher soldier, the one who seemed in charge, looked into the cloth sack, then stuck his massive hand inside. He hollered and threw the bag down. It landed on Tipper's face, and she shook her head to dislodge the obstruction to her view. Smoke curled into the air over the singed hair on the soldier's hand and wrist.

He growled, glaring at the other bisonbeck to cut off his subordinate's ill-timed laugh.

"Pick her up. We'll take the bag to First."

"Get ready to run." Taeda Bel's warning washed relief over Tipper's despair. *"Close your eyes."*

Tipper did as she was told, losing sight of the ugly brute as he bent to grab her. A flash of light surprised her. She saw only red through her eyelids, but the men grunted and stumbled.

"Now! Run!"

Tipper snatched the sack by her head, scrambled to her feet, and took off. Taeda Bel's light flitted through the trees, and Tipper followed. She heard her own panting. She felt her blood pumping within her ears. But she didn't hear anyone in pursuit. She slowed. The night noises of the forest had disappeared. She trudged toward the light. It grew dimmer.

Taeda Bel, wait!

Was that kimen deaf?

"Taeda Bel!" Would her hoarse whisper be heard? Could she safely call louder?

Something gripped her ankle. Had she stepped into a mess of vines? She needed light. She needed Taeda Bel. She stooped to untangle her foot, but as she leaned over, whatever held her captive jerked. She landed on her face and felt ropelike fingers knot around her other leg. She screamed, "Taeda Bel!"

"Shh!" came a voice close to her face.

Tipper peered into the dark but saw only intertwined vegetation.

"Gotcha," said another voice near her feet.

Whatever it was began to drag her.

"Taeda Bel!"

Someone pinched her shoulder. She saw only a mass of leaves and vines leaning over her, but this plant reached forward and pushed against her shoulders, aiding the efforts of whatever held her feet.

She took a deep breath to scream again, and a fistful of leaves pushed into her open mouth. Foul tasting. Choking. She bit down and heard only a wicked little giggle.

"Shh!"

"Gotcha."

They pushed and pulled her down an incline. She expected to come to a level place. No huge hills existed in any part of the woods scattered around the city.

Loose dirt replaced the air and forest undergrowth. Soil covered her legs and hips. The angle of the tilt steepened. Her back and shoulders sank into the ground. She was not going down a hill but under the earth.

"Please." The mangled word sounded nothing like a plea for mercy.

They kept at it, laughing a little with suppressed pleasure.

"We got 'er," said the one pushing.

"Gotcha," came the muffled reply.

The dirt surrounded Tipper's neck and chin. She tried to pull in a deep breath before her head went under. She inhaled a leaf, choked, and only barely heard the next comment from her captors.

"Knew we could."

"Gotcha, gotcha."

3

Invasion

Sir Beccaroon sensed the turmoil in the Amber Palace as soon as he landed on the roof. He shook his feathers, cocked his head, and tried to discern exactly where the commotion centered. Not the servants' quarters. Not the armory or the bailiwicks. Ah! The main hall near the gallery.

He strutted across the tiled roof to the circular stairs wrapping around the east tower. Perhaps the alarm had already been raised. That would be convenient. He really didn't want to be the one who broke the news.

Inside, he followed several servants scurrying toward the central part of the castle. On the walls and in alcoves, paintings and statues displayed timeless beauty and serenity. He recognized voices raised in discord as he rounded the corner. At the sunlit entrance to the gallery itself, the king, queen, Lady Peg, and Librettowit raged on about some difficulty.

Beccaroon paused to listen. The object of their concern was not soldiers stealthily advancing toward the castle. They argued about missing statues.

Not just any statues, but Verrin Schope's *Trio of Elements.* The problem of an impending attack was weighty enough on its own. The missing artwork complicated matters tremendously. Had Tipper's father shattered when the statues left their dais? Were cows and farmhouses falling into gaping crevices caused by the world's surface stretching?

The three statues had been carved from one stone. Verrin Schope had not known at the time that Wulder had used the marvelous piece of marble as a cornerstone for the world He created. As long as the statues were set up as originally designed, nothing went awry. But when separated, physical changes erupted in the countryside. And Verrin Schope also suffered. He literally came apart, his being dissipating and scattering, not horribly uncomfortable but very disorienting. And each fracturing and re-assembly took its toll on the artist's health. His parrot friend easily envisioned disaster if the enemy gained any of the powers associated with the stones.

"Awk!" Sir Beccaroon ruffled his feathers and moved more briskly down the hall, muttering. "Friendly foreigners bring odd ideas and unsteady shifts in what should be reliable nature. And now definitely un-friendly foreigners infiltrate our countryside bringing weapons and monsters of war."

Lady Peg glanced his way, and a look of relief smoothed her anxious wrinkles. "Here's Beccaroon. He'll know what this is all about and how to proceed."

King Yellat turned to him. "My granddaughter is gone, along with that tumanhofer artist. Apparently they've taken two of Verrin Schope's statues."

"Perhaps," said Beccaroon in his most diplomatic voice, "they discovered the statues stolen and are in pursuit of the thieves."

"See?" said Lady Peg. "I told you he'd have a sensible answer. The tumanhofer is after the scoundrels." Her face collapsed again into puzzlement. "I don't know why Tipper had to go along. I hope it's not a romantic entanglement. My daughter is not at all in the know when it comes to men."

The king lowered his chin and pinned Beccaroon with a fierce scowl. "In my experience, artists are not practical, not heroic, and more likely to keep their brushes in good order than the blades of their swords sharpened."

Lady Peg folded her hands in front of her. "Verrin Schope is an artist, and *he* is a noble man. He risked his life to save this country. My husband is practical and heroic, and he doesn't have any swords. But I do think he keeps his sculpting tools sharp."

"Your daughter"—Queen Venmarie's accusatory tone rankled Beccaroon's nerves—"has followed in the footsteps of her mother, engaging in a relationship with a ne'er-do-well."

Lady Peg's face went blank, a trait that often indicated her confused state. "That's unfair, Mother. Tipper isn't here, so she can't possibly be following me." Lady Peg glanced behind her to be sure. "And of course, my husband is not a ne'er-do-well. Everything he does, he does well. Thousands of people say so. Even the king, my father, has noted that he is an exceptional artisan. Although Verrin Schope says he's a jack-of-all-sorts, I've never seen him make candles or shoe a horse. I don't believe he grows wheat or fixes plumbing. I suppose it is bad of him to say he is a jack-of-all-that. Still, he is very accomplished at things that are not practical."

She ran out of breath and looked close to crying. Beccaroon went to her side. She rested her hand on the back of his neck, softly stroking his feathers. Her expression clearly suggested a deep turmoil developing.

"Bec," she whispered, "what is that jack-of-something?"

"Jack-of-all-trades."

Her countenance brightened. "Exactly. That is exactly what Verrin Schope is not." Her face lost its shine. "Bec, do you know where Tipper is?"

"No, milady, I don't."

Lady Peg straightened. "I'm going to find her."

She turned swiftly and strode off, her head held high. Tipper labeled her mother's dramatic exits "the regal departure."

Beccaroon shook his head. Where had that girl gone? The others in the room seemed to be more interested in the loss of the two statues. Beccaroon didn't blame them for that. But he was in the habit of looking after Tipper, and her disappearance brought her safety to the front of his mind. He could think of many traps the young woman could fall into.

Librettowit stood, scowling at the remaining statue. Beccaroon half listened to the king and queen squabbling. Had Tipper run off? He'd thought she was in danger of losing her heart to Paladin. Was it the tumanhofer who'd caught her eye?

"Awk!"

Librettowit looked at him and arched an eyebrow. Beccaroon strutted across the space between them, hating the way the rug captured his talons.

"Do you have any theories?" the grand parrot asked the librarian.

"Only another question. Why take two of the statues and not the third?"

Beccaroon detected the rumble of voices coming into this wing of the palace. "Paladin and Verrin Schope are coming. Fenworth too. Perhaps they will have answers."

Librettowit frowned as he peered down the hall. "Mumbling. I can't make out what they're talking about."

"Awk!" exclaimed Beccaroon. "They know of the foreign soldiers in the woods to the west of Ragar."

Librettowit's scowl deepened. "Some of the crew put together by the evil wizard Runan? I thought Paladin sent them all home."

"No, these men wear no uniform."

"Then why do you say soldiers?"

Beccaroon gestured with his wingtip. "The way they advance through the terrain indicates special training. They move with stealth and assurance. I'd say they are a strike force, meant to sabotage our peace in some manner or weaken our defenses before a full army appears."

"How do you know all this? Have you studied warcraft?"

"Yes, at university. And you?"

The librarian glanced toward the hall where his wizard friend walked with Verrin Schope and Paladin. Distracted, Librettowit mumbled, "Fenworth's library contains many books on military history, statistics, and strategy."

The trio of men entered the main hall.

Verrin Schope broke off his conversation with Paladin and spoke to those already assembled around the defiled art display. "We have unpleasant news." He stopped beside the king. "King Yellat, Chiril has a new enemy, one pouring into the country by way of the coastline northeast of here and the mountains."

"This is a threat from outside our borders?" The king swept a scorching gaze over the company around him. "Who dares assault us? We've been at peace for centuries, and now our safety is challenged twice in such a short time? Who? Who is behind this new threat?"

Paladin put up his hand to stop the angry flow of words. "Our information is sketchy, but three kimens have delivered an account of boats landing under cover of night along the rough shore below the port of Terenia and unusual activity in the Mordack Mountains. Kimen spies heard the men speak of weakening our defenses by striking barracks and weapon strongholds. King Odidoddex was mentioned."

King Yellat glared at Paladin. "I thank you for the report on rumors that have already reached me." He turned to stare at the two empty places where Verrin Schope's statues should have been standing. "Does the theft of these powerful statues have something to do with the invasion?"

Verrin Schope went to stand beside his father-in-law. "They were not stolen, your majesty. I instructed the kimens to escort all three statues out of the city and out of the reach of our enemy. It would not do to have such an effective instrument of transportation fall into the wrong hands."

"One of the statues remains."

Wizard Fenworth cleared his throat. "I can explain that." He patted his robes until he found the pocket he wanted. He reached in, his arm disappearing up to his elbow, and pulled out a dark shape. "I beg your pardon," he said to the disheveled figure as it stretched and grew lighter.

Fenworth turned to the others. "This fine young woman came to me last night, woke me from a sound sleep, and told me of some urgent business. I'm afraid I stuffed her in a hollow and went back to sleep. I do recall her saying something about the statue, prudent flight, and averting disaster."

The pouting kimen brushed her hands over her clothing as it shone with a red hue. "I told him to hurry, and he says to me, 'Morning is soon enough.' Next thing I know, I'm trapped in a dark place where things keep bumping into me."

Fenworth tilted his head. "What things?"

"How am I to know? I told you it was dark, and in that despicable place my lights wouldn't work."

"It's just that I am missing some belongings. Mislaid, you know. Like you were. I fear I'd completely forgotten about your visit. Or thought it was a dream. Whatever. I'm glad to see you again, and to make up for the delay in following through with your bidding, I will take you on a whirl. Some people get a little motion sickness, but I'm quite sure you are of a stronger constitution."

Fenworth crossed the room to snatch the remaining statue and then hurried to put his arm around Librettowit's shoulders.

"Oh no!" said the librarian. "I've no wish to go swirling with you."

"Whirling," corrected the wizard. "A slight technical difference."

"No," said Librettowit.

A rush of wind swept through, the noise of which assailed the occupants of the room without the evidence of anything being blown. One moment, Beccaroon saw the two men, a frantic female kimen, and the statue. The next, they were gone.

4

Where Are We?

Bealomondore groaned and opened his eyes slowly. Flowers canopied over him. He sat up, only to be repulsed by thorny branches that held grapelike clusters of purple blooms. He leaned back and tried to make sense of his situation.

He remembered the kimens in the tavern, and he vaguely remembered the name of this bush. Was it wild cascade? He shook his head and regretted the sharp movement. He swallowed an unpleasant taste in his mouth and tried to think. Details of what had happened between his head falling to the rough-hewn boards of a back-room table and this floral awakening eluded him.

"Sorry about the headache."

He turned toward the soft voice. "Maxon? What am I doing here?"

The kimen lay on his stomach, peering under the foliage. His pointed chin rested on his folded hands. His eyebrow-less expression made him look as surprised to find Bealomondore under a flowering cascade bush as the tumanhofer himself was.

"You drugged me."

A smile flitted across the kimen's face. "Technically Winkel drugged you."

"Why?"

"To get you here without your seeing how to get here."

Bealomondore's head pounded. "Wouldn't a blindfold have worked? A sack over my head? You could have just said, 'Don't look.' "

"The first two are worthy suggestions. I'll mention them to our leaders. The last is something that might not prove reliable for all our guests."

Closing his eyes, Bealomondore tried to relax against the pain, diffusing it. "You have lots of company, do you?"

"Not so much."

The tumanhofer put his palm against his forehead and tried to press away his suffering. Surely his brains had turned to coarse rocks and some imp had stirred them with a heavy lead pole. He heard vague rustling noises and turned his attention to his surroundings.

"Here," said the kimen. "I've got something for your pain."

Bealomondore squinted as he turned his head. Maxon held out a white egg-shaped object the size of the tumanhofer's thumb. It completely covered the kimen's palm.

"What is it?"

"A seedpod. Just pop it in your mouth and chew. You'll feel much better."

"It's not an egg?"

"No, it's a seedpod."

"It looks like an insect egg."

"It's a seedpod."

The tumanhofer wrinkled his nose. "What kind of seedpod?"

Maxon thrust the object closer to Bealomondore's face. "A medicinal seedpod. Do you want it or not?"

Bealomondore took it, slipped it between his lips, and crunched. The shell broke, and a sweet juice flowed over his tongue. The taste alone pacified his warring nerves.

"Umm, good," he said, then frowned at Maxon. "What kind of seedpod has a liquid center?"

"This kind."

"Is it raw?"

"Raw works best."

Bealomondore chewed and swallowed. He immediately felt the effect of the medicinal seedpod.

"Want another?" asked Maxon.

"Yes."

Maxon offered another egglike pod, this one a pale green. Bealomondore took it without question. This seed husk had a crunchy center with a tangy taste, leaving him fully alert.

Without the nagging headache and with his mind clear, Bealomondore conjured up a list of questions. He felt around his clothing, hoping to locate the hollow bag containing the statue. His movements brought him in contact with the thorny bush, and flower petals showered from above. He stuck out his lower lip and blew upward, dislodging a purple bud from his nose.

"Where is the hollow with the statue in it?" he asked Maxon.

"Inside your coat, in the breast pocket."

He sighed with relief when his fingers found the soft material of the collapsed bag. But every move he made was accompanied by pokes and scrapes from the surrounding bush.

"I want out of here," he said.

"Easily done." Maxon scooted backward. "I'll just get some helpers."

Bealomondore scowled at the situation. "If I can't move to get out, how did you move me to get in?"

Maxon's muffled voice drifted through the branches of Bealomondore's resplendent bower. "Don't panic now. Just stay still and let Roof and Door do all the work."

The ground bubbled below Bealomondore, the dirt churned, something beneath the surface reached through, and he felt himself carried out of the hedge by nubby, malletlike objects. Feet first, he rolled out from under the thorny cascade bush. As soon as he cleared the last branches, he jumped to his feet.

He whirled around and stared at the ground. The dirt looked like freshly tilled soil on a farm. Hairy fingers wiggled out of the loam. With disgust, Bealomondore realized these had propelled him out of the bower. Dirty palms pushed upward, then thick wrists, long arms, and shoulders. Between the shoulders, a round head perched and wobbled.

With hands pressing the surface at its sides, the shaggy creature hoisted the lower half of its body clear of the earth. The ground behind the first creature stirred, and another beast emerged.

"Step back," warned Maxon.

Bealomondore almost missed that the order was directed at him, but Maxon's powerful tug on his trouser leg emphasized the need to move.

Like wet dogs, both earth creatures squeezed their eyes shut and gave a tremendous shake of their bodies. Clods of dirt sprayed in every direction. Bealomondore and Maxon backed farther away.

The tumanhofer gasped. "They're ropmas."

"Yes." Maxon eyed the figures before them. "Are you done shaking?"

A low, rumbling chortle came from the two as they stretched and shook once more. Smaller bits of dirt, vegetation, even gritty pebbles flew from their woolly coats.

Bealomondore had never seen a ropma up close. One of the low races, they lived in forests, mountains, and other isolated areas. His fingers itched to pick up a pencil and sketch pad. He wanted a picture to capture the distinctiveness of the two.

Shaggy fur covered their muscular bodies. Dirt obscured the light color of their coats. They wore no clothing but looked natural and decent, like some huge house pet. In fact, Bealomondore decided the ropmas looked like friendly longhair cats. Big cats, standing on their hind legs.

Maxon pointed to each ropma. "This is Roof and his brother, Door."

The brothers exchanged looks. Then, once again, deep-throated chuckles tumbled out of their smiling mouths.

"All right then." Maxon grimaced and reversed the order as he pointed to each one. "That one is Roof, and the other is Door."

The ropmas continued their gravelly laugh and bobbed their heads.

"Thank you," said Bealomondore, "for getting me out of that hole."

The brothers dropped their smiles and looked at each other with concern.

"Hole?"

"Hole?"

They turned to Maxon for an explanation.

"He doesn't mean your hole." Maxon turned his bright eyes on Bealomondore. "They call their homes 'holes.' They're burrowing ropmas, and for them, the word *home* refers to a structure built above ground. So when you said 'hole,' they thought you thought you'd been in their home."

Out of the corner of his eye, Bealomondore caught movement. He turned his head to see the two brothers disappear under the flowering bush.

"They're shy," said Maxon. "They rarely stick around for a conversation."

"They talk?"

"Some."

Vague memories rose in the artist's mind. It would be a joy to capture the ropmas' lives on paper, to record their culture. But could he get close to them? "More than just one word at a time?"

Maxon looked up at Bealomondore. "What are you getting at?"

"I was told they were dumb."

"They are simple, not dumb."

Maxon darted away, forging a trail through the trees. Bealomondore followed, having more trouble than the small kimen.

He pushed branches out of his way and saw Maxon slip under another bush. "Wait up. And I meant 'dumb' as in deaf and dumb."

Maxon made no comment, and Bealomondore had to shove more aggressively through the thick brushwood to keep up with the little kimen.

"Where are we going?" he asked.

"To my village," answered Maxon. "It's not far now."

Bealomondore followed his voice. He could no longer see his guide. "Are there any ropmas in your village?"

Maxon laughed. "Only kimens and guests."

"Guests. You have very few guests, right?"

"Right."

A branch scraped across the tumanhofer's face, and he grimaced. "How long will I be there? And *why* am I going to be there?"

"I think you will be there a long time. Or maybe a short time."

Bealomondore stumbled over roots and growled. "Maxon, you are moving too fast. Slow down."

He blinked, and the little man stood at his knee.

"I am anxious to get home," said the kimen.

The tumanhofer pulled a handkerchief from his pocket and pressed it to the scratch on his face. "Why are ropmas who live underground named after things you would find in a house above ground? Why 'Roof' and 'Door'?"

"The story is that one day someone laughed at a group of ropmas and told them their houses were inferior because they had no floors, windows, doors, roofs, rooms, and all that. Ropmas don't usually understand when someone pokes fun at them. But they got the idea that they needed those things in their holes."

Understanding dawned in Bealomondore's brain. "So they named their children for the things they were lacking."

"Exactly," said Maxon and started through the undergrowth again.

Bealomondore followed quietly for a time. Maxon did a better job of guiding, slowing his pace so the artist could keep up.

Resigned to his unplanned visit to the kimen village, Bealomondore pondered his fate. Did kimens have beds to fit a tumanhofer? Would he have clothes to wear? What kind of clothes? After all, he enjoyed fine fashion and elegant garments. His sense of fashion got him accepted in the higher circles of society. At first it had been a tool to promote his art, but he had become accustomed to fine fabrics, a distinguished cut, and splendid colors.

The intrigue of experiencing life among the kimens overrode his sense of style and dignity. Would he be able to draw? Kimens had fascinating features, and he'd always wanted to capture their whimsical expressions.

He noticed his kimen was out of sight again. "Hey, Maxon."

Maxon popped into sight, right in front of him.

He jumped. "You startled me."

"You called?"

"What am I to do in your village? What am I to wear?"

The kimen waved his hand in the air as he turned away. "All taken care of. You'll be fine."

Maxon had just disappeared from view again when he whistled and exclaimed, "Uh-oh."

Alert and wary, Bealomondore cautiously parted the branches in front of him. Maxon stood with his hands on his hips.

Bealomondore bent forward and whispered. "What is it?"

"Our lost parcel." He pointed to a mound covered with old, moldy vegetation from the forest floor. "The ropma forgot where he delivered it."

Bealomondore squinted and peered over the head of his small companion.

Was that a pointed ear he saw sticking out of the dark, crumbling leaves?

5

Kimen Village

Bealomondore nudged the kimen aside and knelt beside the body buried in mulch. He brushed away the debris around the ear and uncovered a familiar face. "Tipper."

Using both hands, he cleared away the old leaves clinging to her hair and shoulders. He gently gripped her upper arms and shook. "Tipper!"

He cast a look at Maxon, who now hovered near the girl's other side.

"She's not dead," said the kimen.

"Her skin's cold." Bealomondore touched her throat and felt a weak pulse. "What's wrong with her?"

"Couldn't be drugged," Maxon murmured. "Door and Roof wouldn't be trusted with a potion. They consume anything that even looks like food or drink." The kimen pulled his hair. "Winkel ordered you drugged to keep the village whereabouts unknown. But this emerlindian came by a different route." He shook his head. "Odd, decidedly odd. Roof and Door were told to rescue her from being found by the foreigners."

Bealomondore glared at him. "Then what happened?"

Maxon leaned closer and sniffed. "Ah."

"Ah? What do you mean, 'Ah'?"

"She smells of awdenberry."

Bealomondore sat back on his heels and narrowed his eyes. "Tell me what awdenberry is and what it does." He stood. "Now!"

Maxon held his hands up in a placating manner. "Hold on. This is just an unfortunate circumstance. No permanent damage done. The ropma must have carried her through an awdenberry patch. The oil from the leaves would not have bothered them because of their thick, hairy coats. But many of the high races can't tolerate the soporific side effects of the fruit and foliage."

All the anger drained out of the tumanhofer. He'd grown fond of Tipper on their original quest. He found her exasperating, but he also found her tender-hearted.

Bealomondore stroked one finger down the sleeping emerlindian's cheek. "What do we do to wake her?"

"The scent of bogswart bark should do it. You wouldn't happen to have a piece on you?"

Bealomondore pressed his lips together and closed his eyes, holding his breath for a second before he answered. "No."

"Well then, we have two options." Maxon held up a finger. "We can carry her to the village, where I'm sure we can find some bogswart." He lifted a second finger. "Or I can run ahead and get a piece and bring it back."

"Will it take you long to fetch the bark?"

Maxon chortled. "A matter of minutes."

"Then go."

Maxon shook his head. "But it will be several hours after she whiffs the antidote before she can stand and walk."

"Then we'll carry her."

"She's rather long." The kimen moved away from Tipper's head and brushed forest debris from her feet.

Bealomondore contemplated her lengthy body. He could carry her weight, but her long limbs presented a problem. Her feet and hands would drag in any position he held her.

He frowned at his guide. "Do you have a suggestion that will work?"

"Of course." Maxon grinned. "I'll go get someone to help carry her."

"Ropmas?"

He shook his head. "Kimens." He turned and disappeared between the nearest bushes, then popped his head back through. "We ought to check if she still has the statue. It would be a shame if she lost it."

Bealomondore looked down at the princess, who, covered with dirt, still looked beautiful. He was not about to search her for the statue. Since it was probably in a hollow bag, he wouldn't be able to feel it. And it was just something a gentleman should not do.

"The statue will wait. Go get your helpers."

While Maxon went for help, Bealomondore rid the sleeping beauty of her forest décor. He cleared off most of the larger decaying leaves with his hand, then used his handkerchief to swipe off the clinging dirt and damp mulch.

Maxon returned with nine kimens in tow. They lined up on Tipper's sides and hoisted her onto their shoulders. Bealomondore followed, and very soon they stepped through a scanty hedge to find a narrow path.

The tumanhofer took his first unhindered step since waking in this dense forest. He looked down at his torn and dirtied apparel. "Too late for these clothes. I don't suppose the kimen village has shops and booteries."

"What was that?" asked Maxon from his position in the formation. He carried Tipper's left foot.

"I'm merely lamenting the utter ruin of a splendid morning coat, a stylish made-to-order shirt, and a very decent pair of trousers, not to mention the most comfortable walking shoes I've ever owned."

Without turning, Maxon waved his free hand in a dismissive manner. "My kin know you're coming. They've done all to make you comfortable. Clothes, a spacious habitat, supplies for your art. You will live in luxury until we receive orders as to what we are to do with the statues."

A warm glow settled in Bealomondore's middle. Luxury, leisure, painting kimens, ropmas, and the beautiful emerlindian. This jaunt to an isolated village might be just what his weary self needed. He agreed with the rascally Wizard Fenworth that quests were uncomfortable ventures. He'd had enough of gallivanting around the country, looking for statues and finding villains instead. Bealomondore grinned. If he'd been given the duty of holing up in obscurity with a stolen statue in his possession, he'd make the best of it.

They stopped in a clearing.

"This will do," said Maxon, and the ten kimens gently lowered the emerlindian to the ground.

"Where's the village?" asked Bealomondore.

Maxon gestured to their surroundings. "This is it."

With a hand in his trouser pocket, Bealomondore turned a full circle, inspecting every rock and tree. Nothing looked like a habitat. Then the side of a tree opened, and two kimens stepped out, obviously children by the size of them. Their fair hair stood even more wildly on their heads than the adult kimens' topknots.

Several vines slipped into view from the trees. Gliding gracefully down these vines, a dozen kimens joined those who were appearing from bushes, trees, and burrows in the ground.

Bealomondore gazed with amazement. His artist eye picked out the slight variation of features that made each kimen individual. No artist had ever been presented with such a wonderful collection of untamed beauty.

Many kimens clustered around Tipper. One spoke earnestly to Maxon. Bealomondore recognized the speaker as Winkel, the kimen responsible for drugging him.

Maxon nodded and left Tipper in the hands of Winkel and a dozen of her comrades. He approached Bealomondore with an excited expression. "I'll show you to the guesthouse. We'll have lunch, and you can try on your new clothes."

"Are you excited about lunch or my new clothes?"

"Both! You're going to be delighted. Kimens are wonderful hosts." He started toward the far side of the crowded clearing.

Bealomondore remained where he stood. When Maxon looked back and frowned, he spoke. "What are they doing with Tipper?"

Maxon looked puzzled. "Taking care of her."

"What are they going to do exactly?

"They'll hold a piece of the bogswart bark under her nose until she's had a good sniff of it. Her color will improve and her breathing will deepen. Then the lady kimens will help her clean up. You know, take a bath, wash her hair, put something pretty on. You know, female things. They'll feed her, and when she's ready, she'll join us. Probably tomorrow."

"I want to see her sooner than that. I want to see that she's all right."

Maxon gazed at him with serious eyes, then nodded. "I'll arrange it." He started to turn away but looked back. "Are you coming now?"

"Yes." Bealomondore considered the activity around his sleeping friend one more time. The kimens carefully, almost reverently, lifted Tipper. Reassured that they would treat her well, he followed Maxon.

A dozen steps beyond the perimeter of the clearing, a solid wall of vines blocked their path. Maxon reached into the foliage, twisted something, and pulled. A door made out of the vegetation opened. Bealomondore's eyes grew wide as he walked in. Whatever the walls, roof, floor, and furnishings were made of, they glowed so that the inside was brighter than the shaded forest outside.

He moved on to a second room, where a bed and clothing awaited him.

"My friends are bringing water for your bath. I'll come back and get you for noonmeal. We eat at the commons. I'll show you. You're going to like the food."

"I... I'm overcome, dear Maxon. This is perfect. Beautiful and the right size." He gestured to the bed and the door frame, including everything. "It's like a crystal palace."

Maxon shrugged. "It's only two rooms."

"It's magnificent." He ran his hand down the wall, marveling at the polished, cool, glowing substance. "What is this made of?"

"Oh, just a little something we whip up for guests. We, the family and friends and all, don't need all the trimmings. But we know those from beyond require a little pampering."

"I'm much obliged." Bealomondore picked up a jacket of material so smooth that he could not make out the weave. "I shall be spoiled and not want to go back to ordinary clothes."

Maxon chortled. "That is if you remember what you've seen when you return to your own towns and cities."

Bealomondore frowned and examined the little man's face. "Is there a likelihood that I won't remember?"

The kimen shrugged. "I wouldn't know. I've never been an outsider who's visited and then left."

"You're saying that your people will take away my memories somehow when it is time for me to go?"

"Only if they don't trust you. And I think they will find you trustworthy." He cocked his head. "What's that noise?"

Bealomondore opened his mouth to say he didn't hear anything unusual when the sound of a low whistle caught his attention.

A voice rumbled under a sustained whoosh. "To the left, I say."

Another voice sounded louder. "Land, for all the blinking stars in the heavens. Just land!"

"You'd have us in a pigsty."

"We aren't going to a farm."

"Well then, a prickly bush. You want me to just plop down in thorns, with maybe a smelly bristle bomber in residence, a hive full of buzzerbees, and perhaps a growly ginger bear?"

"My beard's all twisted inside out. Land!"

Maxon and Bealomondore started to the outer door to see what the commotion might be. As they crossed the first room, a whirlwind formed, knocking them back against the walls.

Wizard Fenworth, Librettowit, and a bedraggled kimen appeared out of the cyclonic wind. The swirl of air dissipated, leaving Fenworth and his tumanhofer companion on the floor, glaring at each other.

The tumanhofer librarian stood, straightened his clothing, and worried his fingers through his bushy beard, trying to tame its awful tangles. "That was a poor transportation, a poor landing, and a poor example of misused wizardry. I should pin you in a chair with *Margoteum's Book of Level One Mastery.*"

The wizard rose and gently placed the small creature he had been holding on the floor. The kimen crumpled into a heap and covered her eyes with her hands.

"Oh, bother!" said Fenworth. "Don't cry. I really get muddled when people cry. It mixes my thoughts up like a bowl of noodles."

"We don't want that!" Librettowit took off his hat and threw it on a table. "May Wulder protect us from such a dire circumstance. Imagine a wizard who operates in a state of confusion. The results might very well be disastrous."

The wizard produced a clean handkerchief and offered it to the distraught kimen. He pulled it back just before her hand closed on it and plucked a very small lizard from its folds. "I don't believe this fine young reptile would help you recover your equilibrium, my dear." He shook the handkerchief, then returned the uninhabited cloth to the kimen.

"You know," he said as she dabbed her eyes, "I don't believe we've been introduced. I'm Fenworth, bog wizard of Amara. This is my esteemed librarian, Trevithick Librettowit. He's been known to be in a better mood from time to time, but we must make allowances. He prefers a good book, a comfy chair, a plate of daggarts, tea, and a fire in the fireplace. Unfortunately, we are often called to adventure. Slaying damsels, rescuing dragons in distress, collapsing kingdoms, thwarting evil, purging plagues, that sort of thing."

He bowed with an elaborate sweep of his arm before him.

"A servant of Wulder, dear girl, at your service."

He straightened and looked around the room.

"Oh, see here, Librettowit. Not a growly ginger bear at all, but Bealomondore and a friend. See, you needn't have worried. We've landed precisely where I intended." His eyes inspected the walls and furnishings. "Bealomondore, good friend, exactly where are we?"

6

The Grawl

Vaguely aware of the fuss being made over her, Tipper tried to muster enough energy to protest. Her tongue didn't cooperate any more than her arms and legs. She managed to open her eyelids to a slit, but they closed before she could focus on the little beings that surrounded her.

Their touch soothed her. She wasn't afraid but definitely confused. Why would someone else be braiding her hair?

And they were singing. Tipper wanted to sing with them. She didn't know the words or the tune, but the music reached into her heart and made her want to sing, dance, do something to join in. Song had rescued her many times from despair and loneliness. She sang for herself, but she knew her talent lightened others' burdens as well.

The memory of hands grasping her ankles, harsh voices, and smothering dirt threatened her peace. The song grew louder, and unease melted into safe sleep.

"I'm staying here." Bealomondore's voice pierced the fabric of a pleasant dream.

A meadow full of colorful minor dragons slipped from Tipper's mind. An invasive question screamed, "Where am I?"

She opened her eyes and swiveled her head, taking in her surroundings. Kimens, two tumanhofers, and the o'rant wizard crowded the tent.

Sunlight diffused through the fine blue material. The walls and ceiling of this abode tinged everything in sight with a glowing azure light.

The one tall figure paced beside her couch. He hadn't noticed her, which was typical. She wanted some answers. "Wizard Fenworth!"

He turned toward her, his eyes sparkling. "So you're awake. Good, good. Need you to talk some sense into this stubborn tumanhofer. I mean to tell you, girl, tumanhofers have more than their share of contrariness. And he's an artist. You know what that means."

Tipper didn't know what being an artist had to do with anything. Her expression must have said as much to the wizard.

"Unpredictable!" He shifted his glare to focus on Bealomondore. "You would think a man who's undertaken the removal of a valued item from harm's way would be willing—no, not willing, *anxious*—to transport that valuable item to a place where it can do some good." He lifted one eyebrow and scrutinized Tipper. "Wouldn't you?"

Memories swelled like a riptide over her peace. She sat up. "The statues." She swung her legs off the couch.

"Exactly, my dear." Librettowit came to sit next to her.

Some measure of relief came with the wizard's librarian she had learned to trust. Often he was sensible when the others were merely loud.

"I thought we were safe here," she said.

He nodded. "Somewhat. We must sort out the myths and the truth before we decide what is to be done with the statues."

Librettowit pinched at his mustache with thumb and forefinger. "In Amara, tradition has it that kimens cannot be tracked." He looked around the room at the kimens assembled. "Is that true?"

The kimens nodded.

Maxon stepped forward. "Yes, it is, but we've had disturbing reports of an unusual warrior in an enemy camp."

A chair appeared next to the wizard, and he sat, taking off his hat and rubbing his hair. His hand dislodged several small creatures that ran down his robes and out the tent flap.

"We've met our fair share of unusual warriors," said the wizard and clapped his pointed hat back on his head.

Librettowit ignored him. "The description of this man is more like a beast than one of the seven low races, but he speaks and wears clothes."

Maxon cleared his throat. "He also growls and eats his food like a lion devours its prey, tearing the raw meat from the bone. He wears pants and a shirt, all right, but he also wears battle gear and carries a spear that he throws far distances with great accuracy."

Librettowit nodded. "These are facts, not myth."

Taeda Bel came close to Tipper and put her hands on the emerlindian's leg. The kimen's eyes rounded with fear. "He looked straight at me. He shouldn't have known we were there. Maxon, Hollee, and I scouted the camp. I think he saw us all." She shuddered. "They call him The Grawl. He's not like other creatures, high race or low. He doesn't belong in the animal kingdom either. He should not exist."

Tipper placed her hand on her small friend's back. She could think of nothing to calm Taeda Bel's dread. Instead, she swallowed and looked at the serious faces surrounding her. At times she had seen a group of kimens together on market day, but in this small tent, around thirty of the dainty people watched her.

"So who do you report to about the things you find out? My grandfather? His commander of arms?" The kimens looked at each other, and when no one spoke, Tipper asked again. "Who?"

"It is our nature to keep an eye on things, especially in the Starling Forest. If we are to tell someone, we find out later."

Tipper turned to Librettowit for an explanation.

The old tumanhofer shrugged. "In Amara, the kimens are very conscientious in their regard of Wulder. Here, they seem to take on the same duties without the close bond with their creator." He shook his head in puzzlement. "I must study them and probe their history to find out what their function is in His design for Chiril."

Taeda Bel's happy smile returned to her face. "Hollee knows a lot. Her family is the keeper of tales for the village."

"Who is Hollee?" Tipper asked.

The female kimen standing closest to the wizard stepped forward. "I am. I've been assigned to Wizard Fenworth."

Even in the solemnity of the meeting, a few snickers escaped. Tipper caught two kimens exchanging a look that included rolling eyes. She bit her lip to keep from smiling. Being assigned to the rascally wizard would be an arduous task for any of the fun-loving kimens.

Bealomondore shifted in his chair. Tipper's eyes widened as she took in the splendor of his garments. The cut of the clothing duplicated what he normally wore, but the clarity of color and the quality of material outshone anything bought in a shop. The kimens had apparently dressed him.

She looked down at her own gown. She could not stop her fingers from stroking the shining peach folds flowing over her knees. She'd never been particular about her attire, but she longed for a full-length mirror to see if she looked as beautiful as she felt. If the kimens had mirrors that were full length for them, she'd only be able to see the bottom of her skirt.

"We have business to do," said Fenworth. He began rummaging through his hollows. He pulled out a statue, *Evening Yearns*. A female figure danced over grass.

Hollee clapped her hands. "That's a kimen."

Maxon, Taeda Bel, and Hollee made a circle around the statue and trilled their excitement as they examined the craftsmanship.

"It's marvelous!" Hollee said as she grabbed the other two kimens in a hug.

"Oh dear, oh dear. I do hope you young people have not mislaid your statues. We must put them together so that Verrin Schope will not get discombobulated. And there is the added problem of how the lack of approximatation and balance of line causes disruption to nature in general."

"What's approximatation?" asked Hollee.

Librettowit scowled. "Something he made up, most likely. But he means they need to be close together and properly arranged or trees fall over and the ground sinks into deep holes and other disastrous anomalies occur."

Tipper and Bealomondore produced *Day's Deed* and *Morning Glory.*

"No room in here," said Fenworth. "We shall place them in the kimens' glen."

"Outside?" asked Bealomondore.

Tipper smiled. "My father's statues were hidden in Beccaroon's forest for years. They don't fall apart under the stress of a little weather."

The tumanhofer did not look pleased but followed the others out of his dwelling.

The activity of setting up the statues in their precise formation attracted the attention of many villagers. Songs and dance and storytelling invested the impromptu celebration with a merry, festive tone.

Fenworth found a place to sit and cheered the kimens on in their revelry. He even joined in a dance but soon had to rest. He pulled a container of daggarts out of a hollow and shared them. Tipper wondered how long they had been in storage.

With all the commotion, she had almost forgotten the importance of the *Trio of Elements.* Without her father's art positioned as a unit, the world and her father crumbled. Her father dissipated and reformed. But the ground, cracked and altered, never came back to its original state. Living things like trees lost their form, and the restructuring contained gross abnormalities.

Bealomondore interrupted her wandering thoughts. "If we are safe here, why move? The company is pleasant, and they seem at ease with our visit."

Wizard Fenworth cast the young artist a speculative glance. "You are pleased with the paints and brushes our hosts have provided."

"Of course I am, and they are agreeable to letting me do portraits. It's the opportunity an artist lives for." He gestured to the dancing villagers. "This scene needs to be captured on canvas."

Librettowit wrinkled his brow. "Your art will mean little in a country devastated by war."

"I don't believe the enemy can find us. The statues are safe here. We put them in peril by leaving this sanctuary."

Fenworth stood, dropping leaves and bugs. "I know exactly the course we should take at this time."

All eyes turned to the oldest and presumably wisest among them. He patted his lean stomach.

"Eat. Solid food. Nourishment. Where's the kitchen in this establishment?"

The Grawl crouched in the underbrush, sitting on his heels. He could remain in this position for hours. The small creatures called kimens had been a challenge to track, but he knew of no animal that could throw him off its trail. The three kimens never even suspected that he followed. And now he'd discovered their village, each structure obscured from the naked eye but clearly perceptible to his keen senses. Detecting each of their dwellings pleased him immensely. Listening to their debate raised a smile on his ugly face.

He watched the merriment with disdain. The villagers celebrated the statues with much fervor. Obviously their worth included something more than just artistry. He didn't know exactly what, but it would be something he'd investigate.

He frowned. He did not know if he could stomach reporting his find to First Speatus Kulson. The bisonbecks he traveled with were the best of Odidoddex's army—yet still inferior. They needed too much food, water, and sleep. To follow the orders of the fool who led the other fools made The Grawl's leathered skin crawl.

This venture had been of his own doing. The small creatures spying on the camp had intrigued him, and he'd tracked them for the fun of it. Why should he reveal his findings? Perhaps the information would be worth an extra payment if he waited until the right moment.

A mouse scurried through the tall grass. It paused, stood on its hind legs, nose quivering. Did it sense him sitting so still? With uncanny swiftness, The Grawl snatched the small animal. He tossed the mouse, whole and living, into his mouth and crunched down on fur and bones. Warm blood squirted over his tongue. He chewed a moment and swallowed.

Rising without a sound from his hiding place, The Grawl headed back to the camp. He'd get there soon enough, but it would be a while before he spoke of wizards, artists, and valuable statues.

7

Hollee's Joy

Hollee did a somersault in the air as she followed Wizard Fenworth. Finally they were going to do something. The week since the arrival of the four outsiders had been interesting but not exciting. One tumanhofer drew, the other wrote, the wizard slept, and the beautiful emerlindian investigated every aspect of the village. Hollee enjoyed going with Taeda Bel as she explained how things were done in the kimen village, but now that her wizard was awake and muttering, things would happen. She just knew it.

The other kimens joked about Hollee's attachment to the scatterbrained old man, but she thought the possibilities for fun and adventure abounded within his quirks and foibles. Taeda Bel enjoyed the emerlindian Tipper. Their personalities matched. Maxon would probably be stuck in the village, watching the painter paint. How boring. Fenworth would surprise her, and Hollee couldn't wait to see what he did next.

They crossed the village clearing and entered the woods, coming to the door of Bealomondore's specially designed quarters.

"Confound it!" said the wizard. "How do you knock on this thing? I don't suppose there is anything as practical as a doorbell."

Hollee stepped forward to help, but before she could rattle the branches, the door swung open to reveal the tumanhofer artist with a smock over his elaborate clothing and a paintbrush in his hand.

"I heard you," he said. "Come in, come in. I'll show you my latest drawings, all mere sketches but magnificent, and the painting I started this morning."

"Hurray! I want to see," said Hollee. She entered the bower abode, dancing forward on her toes.

"You work rapidly," Fenworth observed as he walked into the well-lit room Bealomondore had fitted out as his studio.

Hollee skipped around the room, examining the pictures and recognizing her friends. The wizard followed at a more sedate pace. With his hands clasped behind his back, he mumbled as he moved from sketch to sketch. Bealomondore kept in step with him, leaning close as if to catch a word or two from the wizard's incoherent muttering.

"You are wringing my nerves, sir." He hurried to block the man's progress to the next picture. "Are those positive or negative comments, Wizard Fenworth?"

The wizard turned abruptly and frowned down at the tumanhofer. "Eh? What? Tut, tut, man. Don't be in such a twitter."

"Do you like them, sir?"

"Like kimens? Of course I do. What's not to like about a quick, cheery, clever kimen?"

A grin spread over Hollee's face. She loved the wizard's way of saying things.

Bealomondore sucked in a long breath and let it out slowly. "The drawings *of* the kimens. Do you like them?"

Hollee sat down, directing her full attention to the conversation. A squirmy intuition in her belly told her this would be entertaining.

The wizard's frown deepened. "What do you care if I like them or not? Do *you* like them?"

"Well, y-yes."

"Good." He clapped a hand on Bealomondore's shoulder. "Shows you have good taste. These are excellent. Finest I've seen. You've been working hard. Time to take a break. Look at other things."

"I'm not tired at all. This project energizes me. And I haven't even started on the ropmas."

"Mustn't do it all at once. I have a job for you."

Hollee's head bobbed in anticipation. She knew the wizard's scheme, and she knew the tumanhofer would object. Which stubborn man would come out on top?

"A job?" Bealomondore backed up.

"Yes, you and I will go have a look at this enemy."

Hollee sat up straighter. This wasn't exactly what she expected. The wizard had been muttering all morning about a trip to Ragar to get more information from King Yellat and Paladin. He also planned to gather information on the way.

The tumanhofer went rigid. "I don't want to go anywhere."

"It will only take a day or so. We don't have to search for them. Hollee knows right where their camp is."

Hollee frowned. This dangerous mission might not be enjoyable. Still, The Grawl couldn't see her, and she found the intruders fascinating.

Bealomondore shook his head and backed up another step. "No, thank you. I am quite content to do what I do best. I am recording this culture for those who will never have the pleasure of living among the kimens."

Fenworth let out an exasperated sigh. "Librettowit."

"What?"

Giggling, Hollee explained, "The librarian is writing a paper to be published. On kimens. He plans another on ropmas."

"Tumanhofers!" The wizard took his hat off and rammed it back on his head.

Hollee frowned. She was sure the paper was on kimens.

Wizard Fenworth pulled his beard, and Hollee hopped to a different position to see what creatures fell out. She counted two beetles, a salamander, and a centipede.

Fenworth paced back and forth in the small area cluttered with the artist's tools and pictures. Bealomondore jumped to save an easel from crashing to the ground.

"Tumanhofers are infuriating travel companions. They can always think of a reason to procrastinate." Fenworth stopped in front of Bealomondore. "You're a hero, man. Act like one."

"No, I'm an artist. And I *am* acting like one."

"Weren't you with us on the quest? Yes, you were. I remember. We found the statues, vanquished insidious evil. The entire journey was great as far as questing and heroing goes. But you've just had a small taste of victory over disaster. Surely you long for more."

"Yes, I admit I had my bite of conquering villains, and because of it, I'm up to my gullet with the unpleasant business."

Hollee cringed. Would her chance for adventure be smashed by this reluctant tumanhofer?

The wizard sighed, flapped his arms against his sides, and nodded. "I don't really blame you. I hate questing myself. It's a most uncomfortable business." He grasped the lapels of his robe and laid his chin on his chest, frowning ferociously. "But I want to see this thing called The Grawl. Must be some kind of grawlig with a name like that, and grawligs are ornery, not particularly dangerous."

Wizard Fenworth reached inside his robe and searched his pockets. "Tut, tut, oh dear. Have I forgotten them?"

Bealomondore lifted an eyebrow and watched the other man with unbridled suspicion on his face. "What are you looking for?"

"Things."

"What things?"

"Ah, here's one now." Fenworth pulled a sword from a hollow just as he might pull it from a sheath. "A warrior's sword. Very handy." He held it out to the tumanhofer. "Hold this."

Bealomondore hesitated, then took the weapon. The weight of it pulled his arm down so the tip touched the floor.

Fenworth continued his rummaging. "Here somewhere. Tut, tut. What's this?" He brought forth a scrap of cloth. "I haven't the foggiest idea where this came from."

Hollee eyed him, wondering what fantastic thing he might do with that bit of material. He blew his nose on the scrap, took off his hat, and poked the makeshift handkerchief inside.

"Cleaning, Hollee. The hat cleans as well as mends." He replaced the hat on his head, then removed it again. He stuck his arm in the crown all the way up to his shoulder, then smiled.

"You found something, sir?" asked Hollee, trying to be still and not wiggle with anticipation.

"What? No. No, no. Just a touch of aches in the old bones. Elbow to be exact. The hat is certainly useful." He pulled out his arm, flexed the joints, and then dove into his inner pockets once more. "Here, here," he announced as he removed two limp pouches. He handed them to Bealomondore. "A bag of money. A bag of food."

The tumanhofer shifted the sword to lie across his other arm so he could take the pouches.

Fenworth grinned. "I've found the lot." He began loading Bealomondore's arms with packages and various items. "A tent, a blanket for when it's freezing, a cooling sheet for when it's unbearably hot, cooking spices, cooking utensils, eating utensils, maps, traps, wraps, and this thingamajiggy, a perpetual lamp, an antidote for most poisons, a hunting knife, a soldier knife, and a butter knife. That should do it." He patted his sides. "Oh, wait." He reached in one more time and produced a small brown paper bag. "Tea." He held up a finger again. "You'll need a garment to carry your belongings in. I'll mention it to Winkel."

The tumanhofer's expression changed from suspicious to outraged. "Are you giving this to me?"

"Yes."

"I don't need all this," Bealomondore sputtered. "I've never owned a sword, and I don't want to. And I don't need money and food. I don't need any of this. What are you up to?"

Wizard Fenworth held up a finger while he delved into his robe pockets with the other hand. "Oh, but you might go on a quest, and then you'd need them."

"I'm staying here." He looked around for a place to dump his armload of unwanted treasure.

"Yes, yes, I think that's it." Fenworth stopped examining his pockets and gestured to Hollee to come. "We're going to visit the enemy. Artist, are you sure you don't want to join us? A gruesome beast might make a good subject for a drawing."

Bealomondore shook his head slowly from side to side. "I'm staying here."

Fenworth opened the door and looked back over his shoulder. "Last chance."

Bealomondore's jaw tightened. He spoke through clenched teeth. "Have a good trip."

"Thank you. We will. Come, Hollee. I must say I like your name. I like the way it uses the tongue so aptly." He pronounced her name again with great relish. "Hollee. Hollee, it will be a pleasure scouting with you."

Hollee jumped up and skipped out. She pulled the door closed behind her and zipped to catch up to the wizard's long strides. He stopped short, and she just avoided running into the back of his legs.

"The statue. I must take *Evening Yearns* with us. We wouldn't want something to happen to it while we're away."

"But I thought they needed to be together."

"Yes, yes, quite right. But I took on the duty of keeping that statue safe. How can I keep it safe if I leave it here?"

"Will we be gone long?"

The wizard shrugged. "A day, a week."

Hollee thought the statues looked fine in the kimens' glen. A natural backdrop of trees, grass, and bushes with small animals and butterflies added to the scene. Fenworth yanked one statue out of the serene setting and maneuvered it into a hollow with Hollee's help.

"There now, ready to go." He marched off again, only to come to another abrupt stop with Hollee running into the back of his legs.

"I must have my walking staff." He looked up at the trees for a moment, and just before Hollee asked if she could help find the staff, he took off his hat and retrieved it from within.

"I put it in here to be fixed. Remember that, Hollee. Broken things should be put in the hat, left for mending, and pulled out when needed. Unbroken things should be stored in hollows. But you know all about hollows."

Yes, she did, and she had been in one of his. She remembered her night in his hollow while he slept instead of listening to her important message. She frowned for half a second, then brightened with the prospect of their journey. She wondered if her hollows were packed with the appropriate supplies for this adventure.

She skipped beside the man she was charged to guide, inform, and protect. A wizard would know what to pack. She wouldn't waste time worrying. Her duty would be easy and great fun. Winkel had said they deserved each other when she handed out the assignments. Hollee laughed and did cartwheels. Facing The Grawl would be nothing with a wizard by her side.

Misdirection

Hollee had lost Wizard Fenworth, but it didn't worry her much.

He'd been sitting very still while vines sprouted from his beard. His skin and robes took on the appearance of bark. After a long while, he looked just like the other trees. How could he spy when he'd turned himself into a tree?

She admitted the tree thing was a very good disguise, so much so that she tripped off to get a closer look at the bisonbecks. But then she'd seen The Grawl, and that sent her scurrying back to her wizard. To her momentary dismay, she couldn't find the Fenworth tree when she returned. The alarm lasted only until the marvel of being the assistant to a wizard popped back in her mind.

As soon as Fenworth moved, she'd find him. Was he asleep? Was he still spying? Probably asleep. Most old people took naps.

She climbed a tree and sat on a branch, comfortable in the knowledge that the beast wouldn't be able to see her if he came looking. From her perch on a limb, she could see everything that went on in the enemy camp, and she could see the part of the woods where she thought Wizard Fenworth hid.

The Grawl sat still, in control of every muscle in his body. He trained all his senses on the erratic movement of a kimen in the forest around the camp. The kimen presented no problems, but what had happened to the creature who had come with the kimen?

Around him, bisonbeck soldiers joked with one another as they prepared a deer carcass to butcher. Their chatter annoyed him. The smell of blood as they sliced the meat from the bone covered the other scents of the forest and made it harder to keep track of the kimen. She flitted about the forest in an irregular manner, and that brought a snarl to his lips. He didn't like unpredictable creatures.

He rose to his seven-foot height and glared at the three soldiers. Without a word, he stalked out of the camp. He would be able to hear their conversation long after he was out of their sight.

Brox growled, "What's the matter with him?"

The one named Gorse answered. "I don't know, and I don't much care. He makes me think of swamps, snakes, and those drooling quiss suckers."

"I've never seen a quiss. Have you?" asked Brox.

Gorse muttered, "No, but I thought about them a lot when we came in on the boat."

Kulson turned the conversation back to The Grawl. "He probably doesn't like the fact that we'll cook some of the meat and dry the rest. He prefers his dinner to be warm because he just killed it, not because it was spitted and roasted over a fire."

"Yeah," said Gorse. "I've never seen him do anything other than snatch up his prey and devour it."

A small smile tilted the corner of The Grawl's mouth. Perhaps these bisonbecks did understand how inferior they were to him. But he wasn't interested in the soldiers. He already knew too much about them from their travels together. Their odor almost choked him when in closed quarters. Wet goats smelled better.

He stopped and allowed his senses to center on the kimen. He didn't understand her movements. If she'd come to spy on them, why hadn't she hunkered down to do some observing? He focused on the other entity, the one he'd lost. The nerve endings in his skin quivered.

With heightened awareness, he shivered as he sought but could not find the powerful o'rant who had walked like an old man toward the camp.

The Grawl's nostrils flared as he detected the kimen. She'd returned to the same spot where he had lost the scent of the man.

The o'rant posed a problem. The female kimen would die with one well-placed smack, much like the swatting of a gnat. But the o'rant… All circumstances would have to be on The Grawl's side in order for him to win a fight with this o'rant. He wanted all the odds in his favor. The man had too many unknown qualities about him. It bothered The Grawl that he could not pinpoint the o'rant's position.

He circled the area where the kimen now lingered. She might provide a clue. But he moved warily. He did not want to come across the old man unexpectedly.

A whiff of the o'rant stopped him. With great caution, The Grawl turned his head, allowing his eyes to explore the terrain. The kimen sat on the limb of a tree, much like a bird, constantly twitching. Little birdies annoyed The Grawl. So did the kimen. But the o'rant… Where was the o'rant?

Again he purposefully ignored the small creature and tried to find the other. His nose picked up the faint citrus smell of an o'rant. A woody scent almost obliterated the telltale odor of the high race.

Patience while hunting was a necessity. His capacity to outwait prey made him a particularly successful hunter. The Grawl waited, alert and ready to act. He didn't want to engage this foe, but he wanted to know as much about him as possible. He didn't plan to hunt the man— unless he was offered a bounty, of course. But one as powerful as this o'rant might choose to hunt him.

The Grawl had not often been the subject of the hunt. Too many feared him. His lips pulled back in a soundless sneer.

A breeze stirred the long hair draping over his shoulders. It also carried a stronger fragrance of wood and citrus. The Grawl turned his head toward the scent. A tree caught his attention. The bark and leaves of the plant contrasted with the other trees, just enough for The Grawl to become wary.

Inch by inch, he examined the trunk. When he reached a height equal to his chest, he paused. Two holes where branches had broken off looked like eyes. He scoffed at himself. "Looked like eyes" did not make them eyes. Still he studied them, and as he stared, the holes looked more like eyes, eyes that stared back. And then one wooden eyelid dropped and rose again. The Grawl held his breath.

A wizard. He'd heard of wizards but never encountered one. Slowly he backed up. Now he could feel the power emanating from the tree. He could see that one part of the bark and leaves resembled a beard. His muscles tensed. This tree wizard could defeat him. The Grawl would be sure he never engaged this creature in a fair fight. No profit came from a fight. He was a hunter, and his skill brought him much reward. He left the slaughter of army against army to those who had no skill.

He clenched his claws into the palms of his hands and backed into a tangle of bushes that would hide his departure.

"There you are, Wizard Fenworth," the kimen spoke as she dropped to the ground. "I thought this was you." She giggled.

One more step back and The Grawl was out of the wizard's line of vision. He'd been careful. The kimen had never detected his presence. But not careful enough. The wizard knew. The Grawl turned and sprinted through the woods.

He wasn't running away. No panic surged through him. He was smart, prudent, and alive. The Grawl. The Hunter. Not the warrior. Not the hunted. The Grawl's pride in who he was vanquished the momentary feeling of inadequacy that fell upon him under the gaze of the wizard.

Hunger hurried his pace. He sensed a herd of deer in the valley.

Hollee watched as Fenworth stood, stretched, and shook the last vestige of treeness from his form. Foliage fell around him, leaving him in his somber robes of brown and gray, the apparel he chose for traveling. She liked his fancier colorful robes better.

"We've been visited, Hollee," he said.

"Sir?" Hollee glanced around.

Fenworth pointed to a spot near a bentleaf tree. "That creature called The Grawl stood just over there, watching us."

Hollee shivered. "He was that close? I never saw him."

"He's a hunter." The wizard chuckled. "Luckily, he wasn't hunting kimen."

"Oh, he doesn't see me."

"I beg to differ, Hollee. He doesn't want you to know that he sees you so you won't be prepared for him to attack."

She moved closer to stand where her side rubbed against his long robes. "Who was he hunting?"

"Me."

A gasp exploded from her mouth. "You?"

Fenworth chuckled again. Hollee didn't think the situation was funny.

"Don't worry," said Fenworth. "He was curious. He hunts for two reasons—to fill his stomach or his purse."

"Oh." Hollee peered past the bentleaf tree.

"We'll go watch him."

"Why?"

"For the same reason he watched us. To learn his ways. To gauge him as an adversary."

As he started forward, Hollee grabbed a fistful of Fenworth's robe. "I'm really not all that interested."

"I shall hide us. He won't see, hear, or smell us."

She screwed up her face. "I'm more worried about him touching and tasting us."

"He won't." Fenworth patted her on the head.

Normally being patted on the head irritated Hollee, but his touch made her feel warm and safe.

"You're covered now," he said and started to walk away.

Hollee skipped and caught up with no trouble. "Covered?" She examined her arms and torso, and then with a puzzled frown she stuck out a leg to see if anything clung to it. "With what?"

Fenworth waved his hand in the air. "With…whatever. I can't remember what it's called. It should be called the-cover-that-keeps-your-smell-noise-and-looks-to-yourself. That would be very accurate. But of course, it doesn't work on me, so it would have to be the-cover-that-keeps-your-smell-noise-and-looks-to-yourself-and-to-your-wizard. That's a lot to say when you can call it by what it is called if you can remember what that is."

"It's like a shield, huh?" Hollee reached out all around her to see if she could feel it.

Wizard Fenworth paused for a moment, cast her an appreciative look, and went on. "You're a clever kimen, as well as cheerful. It is a shield. That's the name I could not remember. It has another name in front of it. We'll have to ask Librettowit when we get back to the camp. It is the so-and-so shield, named after the wizard who invented it."

They moved through the woods rapidly, not bothering to be sneaky at all. Hollee would have liked to practice being sneaky, but Fenworth said it was unnecessary and a waste of time.

"Here we are," Fenworth announced and sat on a boulder that gave them a good view of the valley. "And there he is."

Hollee settled on the rock beside the wizard. "I don't see him."

Fenworth pointed. "There. It will be difficult because part of his craft is to blend into the scenery. He's very still, and it looks to me like he expects to have venison for dinner."

Hollee spotted the herd of deer immediately. "Oh, they're beautiful."

"They look good in a different way to the hunter."

"Oh, yuck. I don't think I want to watch."

"Do you see him now?" Fenworth pointed again. "Between the stand of rock pines and the stream, near that drab outcropping of flint?"

"Yes, I see him. He's intent on those deer. His leg muscles are rippling. Will he pounce like a cat?"

"You *do* have very good eyesight."

Hollee smiled. "We all do."

At that moment, The Grawl sprang forward. He covered half the distance between himself and his prey before the herd even knew of the threat. They scattered, but one half-grown fawn didn't move quickly enough. Its neck was broken before it toppled at the feet of The Grawl. The hunter hoisted the body in the air, turned around twice, stomping his feet, then brought his kill down to his face. He drew in a long breath through his nose.

"What's he doing?" asked Hollee with her hands covering her face.

"He's relishing his reward for patience and skill."

Hollee spread her fingers apart for a better look.

The Grawl opened his mouth and sank his teeth into the flank of the dead animal.

She squeezed her eyes shut. "Can we go now?"

"Most certainly." Fenworth scooped her up and put her under the flap of his robe. "Prepare to whirl."

"Where are we going?"

"To eat our noonmeal, of course."

"Where?"

"With that king fellow and Paladin."

"We're going to the castle?"

She didn't hear the answer. The wind whistled and mixed with disconnected sounds as the wizard transported them from the forest to Ragar.

The whooshing and whirling stopped just before Hollee gave up her breakfast. Her first experience of traveling with the wizard had made her a bit queasy, but this passage had been extra rough.

"Oh dear, tut, tut."

Hollee tensed for a moment, then scrambled to get out. She needed to see what had alarmed her wizard. As she moved, she felt Fenworth sit.

"Oh dear, oh dear."

She popped out of the folds of his robe and gasped. They weren't in Ragar. Hollee doubted they were even in Chiril. From their perch on a high cliff, an ocean stretched clear to the horizon. Gray waves tossed murky froth on a sandy shore to their left. And on the right, a small village of huts clustered among towering trees, the like of which Hollee had never seen.

"Tut, tut. That's what I get for thinking of tangonut crème pie while whirling."

9

Council Meeting

Beccaroon strutted through the elegant hallway, keeping to the side of the rug running down the center. His claws tripped him up when they caught in the pile of the beautiful carpet. Falling on his face didn't appeal to him at any time. Doing so now would damage his ability to present a convincing argument to King Yellat.

The time had come to act, but his past experience with Yellat prepared him to expect opposition. All the appeals he had made for Lady Peg during her husband's long absence had fallen on deaf ears. The king's stubborn refusal to reinstate his daughter in his court had lasted for more than twenty years. Only the scheming of two madmen had forced the estranged members of the royal family to work together and ultimately achieve reconciliation.

Beccaroon stopped to gaze out the window, but the beautiful view did not have the usual soothing effect. His scowl deepened. Verrin Schope had come back with a wizard and a librarian in tow. The wizard claimed that their success in defeating the masterminds of corruption had been through the influence of the god of his country. The tales of their Wulder intrigued Beccaroon, but he wasn't ready to dig deeper into this foreign concept.

He left the window and its beautiful view. Under the circumstances, having a powerful and omniscient god would be handy. He didn't care to call upon Boscamon to stick his finger in this pie. A capricious god was worse than no god at all.

Sir Beccaroon turned the corner and saw that the king waited for him at the end of the corridor. The grand parrot recognized the obstinate set of the man's jaw. As he approached the ruler of Chiril, he made his courtly bow.

The king nodded. "I just arrived myself. The others should be waiting for us in the council room. I trust your news is worthy of gathering them in such a hasty manner?"

"It is." Beccaroon flicked away the doubt that fluttered through his mind. He had no reason to suspect his information was false. His sources were reliable. But he did question whether or not this council, under the influence of a "wait and see" ruler, would agree with him.

A footman opened a carved wooden door, and the king and the great parrot entered a richly appointed chamber. Verrin Schope, Paladin, and three court officials stood and acknowledged the king. Only the three men from King Yellat's circle of advisors gave a full bow. The king went to his chair, which was larger and more ornate than the others. He sat and gave a signal for the rest to take their places around the oval table.

Then the king fixed his royal gaze upon Sir Beccaroon. "You called us together. You have information?"

Beccaroon inclined his head. "I do."

He strolled to the other end of the table, covertly studying those assembled, trying to determine their receptiveness to this meeting. Verrin Schope drooped in his chair. He examined a piece of paper on the table where he rested his hands. The three advisors to the king sat straight, giving the appearance of preybirds lined up on a branch, eying the field and eager to be the first to spot a morsel for an afternoon snack. Paladin wore his congenial but noncommittal expression. Beccaroon found this young man hard to measure. His face hid his thoughts.

A perch had been placed for him instead of a chair, but Beccaroon did not sit. He continued across the room to a map of the country. "I have received intelligence through a network of friends about each region of Chiril. My informants tell me that men from Baardack are gathering in small groups within our borders." He pointed to the map with a wingtip. "Here, here, and here, there are as many as two dozen congregated, evidently with no business to warrant their presence. Between these spots, smaller groups of a half dozen each are loitering in our country. If you draw a line through these localities, you can see they are strategically placed to interrupt trade and damage our supply lines."

Advisor Cornagin, an o'rant of noble birth, held up a letter and shook it. To Beccaroon, the fluttering pages sounded like wing feathers rattling as a large bird took flight.

"My subordinates," said Advisor Cornagin, "also noted an influx of strangers into the local guilds. Of course, they have met with resistance. Our people aren't happy to give up their jobs to foreigners."

Beccaroon nodded. He also had this news on his list. Cornagin, no doubt, wanted the king to know that he was doing his job. The three advisors were part of the king's inner circle. They probably chafed at having a meeting called by an outsider.

The marione advisor, Malidore, cleared his throat and shifted back and forth on his seat. "As quickly as the amazing story of the three statues spread among the populace, the disturbing news of the theft followed. People are alarmed that the rebellion led by Runan rose up with no one in our government aware of the threat. The tale is"—he glanced at Paladin and Verrin Schope—"that outsiders had to save our skin, so to speak. Follow that with the statues being easily lifted right out of the Amber Palace, and we appear to be a most inept government."

King Yellat ground his teeth. "For hundreds of years we manage to keep peace. At the first sign of trouble, before we are even given the chance to counteract, we are labeled buffoons."

The three advisors reacted with assurances that the king was still highly esteemed. Beccaroon tuned out the four-way conversation that pulled the men away from their business at hand.

Sir Beccaroon studied his old friend Verrin Schope. The parrot expected him to speak up at any moment and explain some of the unusual circumstances of the day. But he sat there, brooding. Paladin looked far more interested in the discussion than Verrin Schope did.

Chief Advisor Likens tapped his fingers on the table. A fine network of wrinkles crisscrossed his dark complexion, reflecting his age as an emerlindian.

Sir Beccaroon deferred to the man who was the oldest in the room. He waited a moment, knowing the advisor would have something of value to contribute.

"The harbor masters tell me a disturbing tale. Our traders are not returning from Baardack. Those who normally make monthly trips from our coastline to theirs went out but did not come back. I had thought it too early to be concerned, but with these other developments, I fear foul play."

Sir Beccaroon bobbed his head and moved back to the table, hopping onto the perch. "I, too, have unsettling reports. The correspondence from my district is sketchy. Whereas in the past, my constables have sent very lucid accounts, this last batch contained rambling, disjointed information. From what I could pull out of these notes, either discontent or a malaise has captured my countrymen. They either stew verbally about their lot in life, or they sit in a morose stupor."

Verrin Schope's head came up, and he looked directly into Beccaroon's eyes. "For some reason, the statues are no longer in line. I feel the effects as well."

The king made a scoffing noise and deliberately ignored his son-in-law. He placed his hands flat on the table and looked at each of the other men sitting with him. "We must first determine which of these threats is most dangerous. We'll prioritize them and set about making a plan to eliminate each menace."

A knock on the door interrupted the king. "Come," he called out in annoyance.

The footman appeared in the doorway. "An urgent message for Chief Advisor Likens, your majesty."

"Send him in."

A disheveled courier bowed quickly to his king, then hurried to pass a folded paper to Likens.

The emerlindian councilman dismissed him. "You may wait outside."

After reading quickly through the one-page missive, Chief Advisor Likens glanced around the table. "This is unconscionable. A citizen of Chiril has been tried in Baardack courts and sentenced to death."

"What's this?" asked King Yellat. "Surely they wouldn't throw our diplomatic relations to the wind."

Likens threw the paper he held onto the table. "There's more. The man is dead. And I probably wouldn't have been informed now except that Trader Bount was executed in Baardack and his body shipped home in a basket. A Baardack vessel sailed into Sandeego. The sailors dumped the basket and the merchandise Bount had taken to trade on the dock. A litigation pronouncement tagged the basket. Evidently, a Baardack citizen filed a grievance against Bount for a shady business deal. He was found guilty and hung."

The king exploded out of his chair. "Preposterous. How dare they?"

Advisor Cornagin leaned forward, one clenched hand resting on a stack of papers. "All foreigners must be isolated, returned to their homeland, and denied entrance in the future."

"On what grounds?" asked King Yellat. "We've good relations with all of our neighboring countries. If we treat their citizens with disrespect, the action will escalate this incident with Baardack."

"I'm more concerned for our countrymen who have not returned," said Chief Advisor Likens. "I recommend sending a delegation to

Baardack to make inquiries and, if necessary, lodge a protest with King Odidoddex."

"I agree," the king said and turned to the marione advisor, Malidore. "We must also lay to rest the notion that we are not in control of Chiril's destiny. In the same fashion that the first stories spread through the streets, let the people know that we have secreted the *Trio of Elements* statues to safety."

Paladin broke his silence. "I find it strange that the rumors of the insurgent army and theft from the castle spread so quickly."

"Yes," said Chief Advisor Likens. "That says to me that something beyond the normal dispersion of gossip is at play."

Beccaroon eyed the men in the room. Everyone but Verrin Schope followed the conversation with keen interest. The artist sat with his chin propped on his hand, still looking preoccupied.

Was he listening? Perhaps he dreamed about his stay in Amara and the intriguing tales of a god called Wulder who ruled above kings and queens. Would Beccaroon's old friend ever again be of any use to his people?

Paladin pressed on. "The morale of the people is also a cause for alarm. I agree that there is more at work here than the circumstances we can identify. And I am curious why, as Verrin Schope has suggested, the three statues are not together."

"I suggest," said Beccaroon, "that Verrin Schope, Paladin, and I venture out of Ragar and get a closer look at the unrest in the neighboring towns."

Paladin looked up and nodded, but Verrin Schope remained silent.

The king frowned at the quiet sculptor. "Verrin Schope?"

He looked up. "I apologize, King Yellat, but I must add to this gloomy scenario." He closed his eyes and remained quiet.

"Well?" roared the king. "What else darkens our doorstep?"

With a weary sigh, Verrin Schope opened his eyes and shook his head. "Our plan to take the statues out of the city succeeded. But the scheme to put them back together in a secure place has not. *Morning Glory, Day's Deed,* and *Evening Yearns* are still separated."

King Yellat stared at his son-in-law. In a subdued tone, he said, "So you say, but I don't understand why that is relevant to the dealings with Baardack. This is a local problem."

"Local? Yes, local. I am using all my energy to keep myself from disassembling. But a disheartened populace does not defend itself well. And a disgruntled populace is easily persuaded to be disloyal. I believe this local problem will affect the outcome of any hostilities with Baardack."

Beccaroon assessed his friend anew, this time without the shroud of condemnation he had allowed to impair his judgment. Verrin Schope did look pale. Would he scatter as he had before?

The artist continued. "I believe our original assessment that Odidoddex seeks to take over Chiril is accurate. However, with the three stones separated, we have the added danger of unrest among the people. It would seem that the power of the stones, which caused physical anomalies a few weeks ago, is now causing an illness of the spirit."

The feathers around Sir Beccaroon's neck fluffed out as indignation ruffled his usual calm. "Awk! It seems to me that this god, Wulder, who you think so highly of, has created a hideous situation. If this *being* is so wise, why did He design something that could be so easily broken? Why are we paying the price for your chipping away at one of His cornerstones? As a god, He is no better than the Boscamon fairy tales."

Verrin Schope sagged in his chair and shook his head, his expression one of great sadness. "We are responsible for the corruption. Wulder is incapable of doing wrong."

Sir Beccaroon hopped off his perch. "How very convenient for Him."

"You don't understand," said Verrin Schope. "It is because I am too inadequate to explain His Infinite Being. You will have to meet Him, Bec. It is the only way to truly comprehend."

"Whether He exists or not, we have problems to solve." Beccaroon walked back to the map. "I'm willing to meet your god, even entertain Him, as long as He doesn't interfere with the serious business we have at hand."

He turned back to glare at Verrin Schope, but his chair was empty.

10

Verrin Schope Disappears

"Well," said the king, "I am disappointed once again. Verrin Schope is as unreliable as any other artist I've ever met." He shook his head. "Gone, without a word."

Beccaroon dropped his irritation with his old friend and sprang to his defense. "This situation is caused by the statues being out of alignment. He didn't run away from this meeting. That's absurd. The Verrin Schope I know is as conscientious as he is brilliant."

The king's face twisted in disdain. Beccaroon realized he'd just implied that King Yellat's opinion was absurd. Not exactly a diplomatic move. He flapped his wings once, tamped down his frustration, took a deep breath, and attempted to reason with King Yellat and his council.

"When the news came in the middle of the night that foreign forces were sneaking into Chiril, Verrin Schope arranged to have the statues spirited away for the safety of the country. He knew how the dismantling of the display would affect him. I would hardly claim such a selfless act to be irresponsible."

A knock sounded on the door.

"Come," ordered the king.

A footman opened the door, bowed, and addressed the assembly. "Lady Peg has sent for Sir Beccaroon."

The king looked from the footman to the grand parrot. His eyes narrowed, his jaw clenched, and he nodded. "You may go."

Beccaroon swallowed the words that sprang to mind. *Glad to get rid of me.*

No need to add to the animosity. He wouldn't do any good here. The council was aware of the threat to their country. Let them stew on the ramifications. Endless discussion would most likely follow. Eagerness to find Verrin Schope and attack the problem on their own provided enough motivation for him to bow politely and excuse himself.

Although he rarely flew inside a building, the palace foyer offered ample room. He took wing as he came out of the council hall and landed at the top of the stairwell. He strutted down the common hallway and turned down the corridor to the private chambers.

Lady Peg stood in her doorway, wringing her hands and watching for Sir Beccaroon. She started talking before he reached the midpoint of the corridor.

"He's doing it again, Bec. Scared me. And scaring one's wife is not something he enjoyed doing previously. Although I'm not sure he enjoyed doing it this time, which doesn't excuse him for doing it. Because one minute he was not there, and then he was. And I didn't expect him so soon because everyone knows when one goes to a council meeting, everyone talks and talks and then everyone argues and argues, then they move into the pontificating stage, which lasts for hours.

"But Verrin Schope says he disappeared from the council room, which is sure to irk my father, and he reappeared in our bedroom. My husband, not my father. Having my father pop into my chambers would have thoroughly unnerved me. But for Verrin Schope to do so only caused me momentary alarm.

"He—my husband, not my father—is just sitting on the trunk that has that piece of wood from my closet, with a look on his face that shouts, 'Don't talk to me just yet, Peg!' "

She paused to pull in a breath of air. "And so I sent for you. Because if my husband can't tell me what's going on right now, you can." She pressed a handkerchief to her lips. "Bec, has Tipper returned?"

"No, milady, she has not."

"I'm not used to her being gone. I should like to leave the palace now and go home."

He put a wing around her back and gently guided her into her room.

Verrin Schope nodded in greeting, then rose to close the door. "Bec, it's clear that we must do something about the state Chiril has fallen into."

"Which state?" asked Lady Peg. "Was it damaged?"

Verrin Schope grinned at his wife. "No, dear. Why don't you pack? We're going on an expedition."

Her face brightened, and for a moment, Beccaroon saw the astonishing likeness to her daughter, Tipper. He sometimes forgot how much the two looked alike. Lady Peg's expression was often one of bemusement, whereas Tipper always looked alert and intelligent. The different attitudes toward life made a significant difference in their appearance.

Lady Peg came to her husband's side, gave him a quick kiss, then scurried into the adjoining room of their suite. She closed the door behind her.

Verrin Schope sat on the trunk once more and addressed Beccaroon. "I don't suppose the council came up with any brilliant ideas after I left."

The grand parrot's muscles relaxed with a sigh. He took a perch on the arm of a chair and settled his feathers. "In a few minutes? Awk. It will take a great deal longer than a few minutes."

"Are you game, old friend, to venture forth with me and Peg to see what we can do?"

Beccaroon clicked his tongue. "Yes, in fact, that is exactly what I propose."

A mischievous grin added a twinkle to Verrin Schope's eyes. "Really? You were going to propose an expedition to rout the enemy? An expedition that includes Lady Peg?"

Beccaroon refused to rise to the bait. "It will certainly disguise our intent to have the lady with us. But our concern should be for her safety."

Verrin Schope nodded. "With the two of us, she'll be safe. I wouldn't leave her here in the palace, nor would I send her home to Byrdschopen with only two servants there."

"I agree. Where do you propose we start?"

"At one of those locations where an influx of foreigners has congregated."

"Very good." Beccaroon hopped down. "I see no reason to wait. How soon can you have Lady Peg ready to embark?"

"Left on her own, it would take a day or so, but I'll help and have her down to the courtyard in an hour."

Beccaroon started toward the door. "I'll order a carriage and obtain maps." He paused as Verrin Schope came to turn the handle for him. "I'll ride with you some. My tail is giving me trouble, and you will want to tell me about this Wulder."

Verrin Schope clapped him on the shoulder. "You want to hear?"

"Not necessarily, but I know you won't be able to curb your enthusiasm. I figure our relationship will be less strained if I just give in and invite you to expound upon the deity of your choice."

Verrin Schope tilted his head back and laughed. "You won't regret it, my friend."

"We shall see." He marched through the open door. "The courtyard, in one hour."

"Yes, indeed," said Verrin Schope. "Yes, indeed."

11

A Visit

Tipper stretched and turned over in her soft hammock. It swayed danger-ously, and she balanced to keep from flipping over. She'd ejected herself onto the hard floor the first morning she woke up in her fancy blue tent. The floor, like everything else in her quarters, was lovely. But it was still hard.

The kimens were artisans of anything practical. They wove exquisite designs into their baskets. The scenes carved on the trunk for keeping her belongings looked fine enough to be in a museum. The tent material glis-tened as if coated with moon dust. The rug on the floor could have hung in a gallery.

In the three weeks since she and Bealomondore had arrived in the kimen village, Tipper had been royally spoiled. The clothing she wore floated around her and sparkled with lights. She would have to watch her attitude when she returned to the city. Everything would be coarse and dull in comparison.

The soft voices of very excited kimens stirred her from her lazy obser-vations. She swung her legs over the edge of the lofty bed and eased her feet into slippers before going to the flap that covered the tent's entry.

She listened. Fits of giggles disrupted the chatter to the point that she could hardly make out individual words. She grabbed a robe to cover her nightgown, cinched the belt, and plunged through her doorway.

"What's happening?" she asked six tiny kimen children.

They danced in a ring, holding hands, chanting, and circling closer to her. When they reached her skirts, they let go of each other and grabbed her hem. As they skipped around her legs, she had to keep up by turning in place or be hopelessly twisted in her clothing.

Their infectious gaiety had her laughing with them, and in a manner of seconds, she joined in their simple song.

A Don, ditty-don
A Don, ditty-don
Fumbee, fumbee, fumbee, fumbee,
Ditty-don-don
A donkey, a donkey,
Fumbee, fumbee, fumbee, fumbee,
Ditty-don-don

Breathless from the quick beat of the song, Tipper called out, "Scoot, scoot, I'm going to collapse."

The children scattered, and she sat down in a heap. They ran back to climb into her lap.

"Now tell me why we are so happy this morning."

Out of the chorus of excited voices, she caught one message. "Paladin is coming."

"Here?"

They nodded, clapped their hands, and chanted, "Today! Today! Today!"

"Oh my!" Tipper struggled to get up, moving the tiny sprites out of her way and shifting to a position so that she could stand. "I can't be dressed like this with company coming."

"Why?" asked one little girl.

Tipper stood, smoothed out her robe, and tried to push her long hair into some kind of order.

"Why?" the girl asked again, this time tugging on Tipper's hem.

"Because a lady doesn't receive visitors unless properly attired."

Tipper quoted her mother. " 'It's odd, but we don't admit to society that we become tired and sleep. We must give the impression that we are not tired, but attired.' " Tipper laughed as she headed toward her tent. "Never ask my mother about being retired. That one is beyond even me to decipher."

As she pushed aside the flap over her tent door, Paladin's voice stopped her. "I understood it. If one tires of doing a task and therefore takes a break, then returns to the job at hand only to grow weary again, then you have definitely retired."

Tipper whirled around to look at him. He grinned and winked. Her heart did the double-timed beat that only he could summon. She charged across the space between them and threw her arms around his neck. With a strong embrace, he lifted her off the ground and spun in a circle.

Her joy in their spontaneous greeting broke with the awful realization that she had literally flung herself at Prince Jayrus, Paladin, spiritual leader of Chiril. She knew he was something special even if most of the citizens did not yet understand his position.

She started to protest against being slung around like a child but realized both she and the great Paladin were spotted with bits of light. She giggled instead. The kimen children had flung themselves at Paladin as well and clung to her clothing as he spun them all around. The children squealed in delight, she and Paladin laughed, and their antics brought adults, who gathered in the commons of the kimen village.

Paladin gave Tipper one last squeeze and set her on her feet. Mothers and fathers called their children to their sides but did not chastise them for swarming all over their visitor.

Tipper watched the ease with which he accepted their homage. He looked even more confident than when she first met him. She noticed his skin had darkened. His hair too. She looked down at her own. She had matured, grown in wisdom and experience, but the change to her skin tone and blond hair was slight. She hoped that she would, with time, darken to the rich ebony that indicated her father had reached an older age in good favor. Her mother had not, but Lady Peg did not seem to mind.

Winkel came forward and bowed to Paladin. "We are honored to greet you in our village. Our kin in the Mercigon Mountains have kept us informed of your status. In fact, we have closely watched the unfolding history of the chosen princes throughout the ages. We are at your service." She bowed again, and all the other villagers and even some of the younger children bowed as well.

Paladin beamed at them, the warmth of his smile melting away Tipper's embarrassment. But at the same time, she remembered how important he was and how he treated everyone he met as if that person was important as well. So did he accept her very forward embrace because he treated all people equally? Or did he greet her in that manner because he felt drawn to her as she felt drawn to him?

She stood back, watching the villagers as each one came up individually or as a family to swear their allegiance to this prince and paladin. Tipper wondered if she should be affronted. Technically the villagers were subjects to her grandfather, King Yellat.

Eventually she ducked into her tent and got properly dressed. Taeda Bel came in later to announce a feast to celebrate the coming of Paladin. "And he's going to tell us more about Wulder."

Tipper dropped the braid she'd been winding around the top of her head. "More about Wulder? What do you know about Wulder to begin with? How could you know anything about Wulder?"

The dainty kimen plopped into Tipper's hammock and set it gently swaying back and forth. "We know the promise. The promise has been handed down for generations. And the promise is Wulder."

"I've never heard of a promise."

"It's for kimens." She tilted backward, then forward, to speed up the hammock's motion. Her voice took on the tone of someone reciting. " 'The One who creates, the One who assigns our task, the One who nurtures, the One who designs our path will send a man to speak words of understanding so that the hand of He Who Is will be close enough to hold.' "

Tipper picked up the braid and tightened the weave. She pinned it as a circlet around the crown of her head before she spoke again.

"Taeda Bel, what makes you think that this Wulder of Amara is the one you call He Who Is?"

Taeda Bel jumped from the hammock and glided across the floor to stand beside the tall emerlindian princess. "My heart, not my head, tells me it's true. Then my brain compares the points of prophecy to the actuality of recent events. There are too many coincidences to be...coincidental."

"So you *feel* that what Paladin says is true."

Taeda Bel's face glowed with assurance. "No, I *trust* that it is so because the messenger is trustworthy."

Tipper walked to her doorway and peeked around the cloth closure. Prince Jayrus, Paladin, sat with children on his knees, and others pushed against him. He spoke quietly, too quietly for her to hear his words. But the rapt expressions of the little ones told her what she wanted to know. This young man with no guile was trustworthy. She knew it in her heart, and she witnessed it in his manner. She would listen carefully to his accounting of the god known as Wulder. She rushed to finish her morning routine.

12

A New Friend

Tipper hurried out of the tent to find that the crowd had shifted to the commons. Her lodging sat on the edge of the small clearing, and all gatherings of the kimen village took place within yards of her front door. Unless the weather turned nasty, the kimens ate every meal together. The women now served breakfast.

Paladin sat among the people, eating and listening as the conversation centered on the history of their settlement. Tipper managed to get close enough to hear but not as close as she would have liked. After they'd eaten, the kimens abandoned their usual routines to listen to their honored guest talk.

Paladin told stories that showed how simple choices made the relationships between people good or bad. And when he described the connection all people could have under the guidance of Wulder, a chill ran over Tipper's skin. She clasped her arms around her middle and felt like her embrace was but a symbol of more powerful arms securing her in a place of safety.

After a time of storytelling, they ate, drank, danced, and sang. Nothing could be more spectacular than watching the fluid movements of the kimens as they expressed joy that stirred even Bealomondore and Librettowit.

The librarian could also sing. When he added his baritone to the sweet voices of the villagers, Tipper expected some visual display to spring out of the air in response to their harmony. She leaned back and closed her eyes, letting her imagination paint beautiful pictures that floated among the notes of music.

In the afternoon, Paladin again sat among the band of small villagers. He never seemed to make a point without using a story, and the stories never disappointed his listeners.

After a short rest in the afternoon, when both children and adults took a little nap, the citizens of the village came again to the commons and asked for more teaching about Wulder and His principles. Paladin obliged while the cooks prepared the evening meal. Librettowit invited Tipper to sing, and she did.

She sang with the chorus of kimens and with Librettowit. But she didn't feel that her voice melded with their pure tones. The experience left her dissatisfied when, usually, singing gave her a feeling of completion. That troubled her, but she lost the discontent as she enjoyed the music that followed. And then Paladin spoke, and his stories pulled her in. The more she listened to Jayrus today, the more she wanted to listen. Not just because he was attractive, but the words he used attracted her as well.

The long day ended with another wonderful supper. Kimens cleared away the last of the food, and mothers ushered their children to warm beds. Tipper strolled down one of the forest paths, too filled with bliss to enter her tent and calmly go to sleep.

Tipper sat on the edge of a tiny brook, breathing in the cool night air and the fragrance of moonflowers. The spicy-sweet scent burst into the air as the blossoms unfolded in response to the light of a full moon. Tiny sparkle bugs floated on the breeze, giving the air an astonishing shimmer. Drummerbugs supplied the percussion for an eerie insect symphony of trills and hums. As she sat, enjoying the sights, sounds, and scents of the night, the quiver of excitement mellowed into a warm contentment.

She heard footsteps and knew it had to be Paladin. The kimens rarely made noise as they moved. The tumanhofers clumped around. And Wizard Fenworth had gone off somewhere. She looked over her shoulder and smiled at his approach. He cradled something small in his hand against his chest.

"I brought someone to meet you." He sat down beside her.

She leaned forward to peer into his hand. She could only make out a glowing blob. "Someone?" she asked. The blob stretched, and Tipper made out a tail and head. "A dragon! He's so small!"

"There are several unusual things about him. He changes color, he's undersized, as you noted, and he has a remarkable range of abilities." Paladin ran a fingertip down the tiny dragon's back. "And he is weak."

Tipper almost asked if he would die but remembered that the small dragon could probably understand every word she said. "How did he come to be in your care?"

"He bonded with one of the Amber Palace servants. She found the egg in an old shed and kept it. Her name was Bretta."

"Was?"

"She died of old age."

"How old is he?"

"Twelve days."

"Oh, then he didn't live with her for long."

"I don't know for sure, but I think his frailty can be linked to bonding with Bretta when she was so near the end of her life and the sorrow of losing his person."

"What are you going to do with him?"

"Try to find him a new home." Paladin looked up from the small creature and caught Tipper's eye.

She recognized the sparkle for what it was. "Me?"

"You miss Junkit and Zabeth, don't you?"

"And Hue and Grandur." She touched the small body resting in Paladin's large palm. "My mother needs Junkit and Zabeth."

Paladin nodded but didn't interrupt.

"And now that my father is…back—I guess that's the best way to say it—and whole again, I can't get over worrying that everything will come undone. So I want Grandur there to help with his health. And Hue cheers Papa up."

"But you need someone too."

Her eyes darted to his face. How did he know? She had lost her place as the stoic daughter who kept things in order under trying circumstances. Her relationship with Beccaroon had shifted into something she couldn't identify anymore. She couldn't say he was her guardian, and he wasn't exactly a friend.

She shrugged. "I'm all right."

Paladin grinned. "You're more than all right. But that doesn't make your situation any less lonely. Would you hold my young friend for a minute?"

At her nod, he gently transferred the glowing dragon into her cupped hands.

The dragon stretched and rubbed his sides on her skin. He put his chin against her pulse and settled down. The glow of his scales dimmed until he looked a pale blue in the moonlight.

Tipper whispered. "He's so tiny."

"How does he feel in your hand?"

"Warm. Soft."

"And how do you feel?"

She held her breath for a moment and concentrated. Then she looked at Paladin. "It's going to work, isn't it? He's going to bond with me."

"I thought so, but one can't be presumptuous with a dragon." Paladin put his arm around her back, and she leaned against him. He rested his chin against her head.

"What's his name?" She gave a hiccup of surprise. "Oh! His name is Rayn."

Paladin leaned back and laughed. "Now we know for sure that this is going to work."

Tipper cuddled Rayn under her chin. When she lowered him to kiss the top of his head, she saw that he had again changed colors. Now he was green.

"Green?" She looked at Paladin. "Is he offering to heal me? I'm not hurt."

Paladin shrugged. "I think you've got the cause and effect switched. He turned green because he was healing you, not because he recognized you needed healing."

"But I don't. I'm perfectly fit."

He squeezed her shoulders, pulling her closer and laying his forehead against hers. "Sometimes healing doesn't involve the physical. Your heart is bruised."

Tipper pulled away. "It's not. I'm fine."

Paladin stood. "I'll walk you to your tent."

She stared up at him for a moment, then rose to her feet. She chortled. "I was about to protest that I'm not tired. But I really am. And now I'm relaxed enough to sleep." She gazed down the path to the village. "Jayrus?"

"Yes?"

"Do you like being the paladin?"

He nodded and took her free hand to nestle between his larger, stronger hands. A thrill skipped down her spine. Her toes curled inside her slippers. She forced herself to breathe evenly, hoping to calm her erratic heartbeat. With trepidation, she allowed herself to gaze into his eyes. Would he see how much she cared for him? Would he mistake it for the same type of adoration the young kimens showered on him?

"Yes, I like it very much." Jayrus wore a smile of satisfaction on his lips.

Her mind had wandered, and confusion covered her reasoning. Like it? Like her? Her throat closed around the question, causing a squeak. "It?"

He grinned. "Being the paladin. Yes, I like being the paladin very much."

"Why?"

He slid his fingers between hers and kept her close to his side as they walked toward the village.

"Suppose a caterpillar spins its cocoon, then bursts out to find itself in a turtle shell, moving slowly across the forest floor."

She giggled. "What a disappointment."

"Not really." He grinned at her. "It had always been a caterpillar, and it was used to moving slowly. It didn't know it was supposed to be a beautiful butterfly. It was used to the forest floor."

She screwed up her face and shook her head, then whispered to the tiny dragon cupped in her hand near her chin. "This is an unusual tale."

"We're not done. The turtle goes about doing the things that occupy a turtle. But something inside doesn't feel right. It is compelled to wrap itself in long vines and hibernate. When it emerges sometime later, it discovers its body has metamorphosed into a large, lumbering bird, one too heavy to fly and with wings too puny to be useful."

"He speaks of a most unusual animal," Tipper said to Rayn.

"But still," Paladin said, "the flightless bird is dissatisfied, and one day, it hunkers down in a deep nest of long shafts of prairie grass and goes to sleep. The bird is ill at ease, not because being a flightless bird is a bad thing, but somehow it is not the right thing for a caterpillar.

"It emerges again from the long sleep, and this time it is a bird, not too big, not too small, and a dull black."

"Can it fly?" Tipper asked.

"Yes, it can fly."

"So now it is content?"

Paladin shook his head sadly. He stopped walking and turned her to face him. "It will never be content until it finds the full glory of what Wulder created it to be." He held up a finger. "Once more the bird sleeps deeply and awakes with colors as beautiful as Beccaroon's plumage. The bird is light and can soar through the heavens. Its song is sweet, and it feels joy as it vocalizes."

"Now? Now is the bird happy?"

"What do you think?"

She took time to consider. "Caterpillars do not change into birds."

"That's right."

"So?"

"So the bird takes stock of its life and knows it should not be distressed. But still there is that something inside that dampens its pleasure. Something that says, 'Not yet.' "

"So it has to change again."

"One more time. And this time, at the end of its season of rest, it emerges as a butterfly."

"I think I know what you're telling me."

He lifted an eyebrow and waited.

"The caterpillar wanted to change. Something inside told it to seek something different."

Paladin nodded.

"But it kept emerging as the wrong thing. Not necessarily a bad thing, but not the right thing."

He nodded again.

"And until it became the form that Wulder intended, it didn't feel...peace?"

"That's right. And even though it gave up its beautiful voice and flights high in the sky, it was content." He gently hugged her. "When

I became the paladin, I knew Wulder was pleased. I am content to be the one who shares His love with people."

Tipper smiled. "I know what you've told me and maybe a bit of what it means. But I think I shall have to do some thinking before I know *why* you told me of this misguided caterpillar."

"Don't forget to bring Wulder into your musing. The life cycle of His caterpillar is only a symbol of what He wants for you."

He kissed her on the forehead. "I'll see you and Rayn in the morning."

He released her and walked away. She stood for a moment, stroking the tiny dragon with a fingertip. When she looked down, her eyes widened with surprise. Rayn's color had changed to gold, and he glowed with a soft radiance as he slept.

13

Tavern

The slim possibility of walking into a tavern and not being noticed rankled him. Sir Beccaroon did not often wish to be of another species, but spying and his unmistakable identity did not go well together. He sat at a corner table and asked for a bowl of water and the specialty bread of the Round Baker Inn.

"My pleasure," said the serving girl, who could not keep the awe out of her voice or expressive face. Obviously grand parrots did not visit the small town of Selkskin.

He nodded and cut off any further questions by turning his head to examine the other patrons of the inn. Most of the customers stared back with undisguised curiosity. Some ducked their heads when his gaze locked with theirs. Hopefully his appearance would cause such a distraction that no one would notice Verrin Schope and Lady Peg. Verrin Schope was intent on gathering information.

The couple sat on the other side of the room, enjoying a plain meal of traveler stew and round bread. Verrin Schope had engaged one of the locals in a conversation. Sir Beccaroon nodded to the young lady who served him and sniffed the savory bread. The aroma stirred his appetite, and the first bite reassured him that the stop at the tavern had been an excellent idea.

He had lowered his beak to the water bowl when everyone in the room ceased talking. He straightened and saw the cause for alarm. Three bison-becks and a seven-foot creature of unknown origin stood inside the front door. The burly men surveyed the room with a cocky arrogance that caused the grand parrot to snap his beak. The beast leaned against the door-jamb, looking bored.

The marione owner of the establishment hurried to confront the new customers. Young and strong, he didn't look like the round baker on the sign that hung outside. "I'll serve you in the back. We've an open terrace there where you can enjoy the fine weather."

The leader of the men sneered at the innkeeper. "We're not good enough for your main dining hall?"

The owner stood taller and looked the bully in the eye, although he had to tilt his head back some to do so. "Our best customers favor the outdoor dining. But I do not serve those who have not had the opportunity to wash in here. Many travelers are in the same circumstance. If you prefer, there is a bathhouse at the end of the street. You are free to use their facilities first, then return for your meal."

The leader's hand flashed forward and grabbed the innkeeper's neck. He lifted the man off his feet. "We prefer to eat now."

He pulled the man closer so that they stared at each other nose to bulbous nose. The unfortunate marione's face turned red, and choking noises could be heard over the stillness of the room.

A chair scraped across the wooden floor, and Verrin Schope stood. He strolled over to join the dangerous scene. Standing with his arms folded in front of him and looking completely at ease, he said, "Put him down."

The bisonbeck's intimidating glare fell on the dark emerlindian. "Why should I?"

"So often what is inflicted on another comes back to torment the offender." Verrin Schope smiled. "Don't you find that to be true?"

A puzzled look from the bisonbeck changed quickly to rage. He dropped the struggling marione and grabbed for his own neck as if to tear choking hands from his throat. The innkeeper scrabbled out of reach, then stood behind Verrin Schope.

The two other bisonbecks sprang forward, weapons drawn. Verrin Schope merely raised a hand as if to signal for them to stop. The ruffians clattered against an unseen barrier and bounced back. The leader of the group fell. Once on the floor, he no longer struggled to breathe. Evidently the grasp on his throat had loosened. The other two helped him to his feet, speaking excitedly in a foreign tongue.

The beast still leaned against the wall, but he no longer looked bored. His narrowed eyes surveyed all before him. When his eyes came across Beccaroon, the parrot saw a muscle twitch high on the creature's cheek. What was he thinking? And what kind of man-beast was he?

The strange creature turned and walked out of the inn. His comrades did not seem to notice his departure. They glared at Verrin Schope and the innkeeper, darting glances at the other patrons of the tavern. Clearly the situation didn't reflect the way they usually encountered people. The leader pulled his shoulders back, stuck out his chest, and said something to his men. With faces still hardened with anger, they turned and left the building.

The innkeeper bowed before Verrin Schope. "Thank you."

"My pleasure." He turned, and Beccaroon saw the serious expression on his face. "Those men are expecting to meet a man from their country. I would appreciate knowing when he arrives."

"Yes sir." The marione bowed again. "I'll do my best to spot him and let you know. Will you be staying at our inn?"

"Yes." Verrin Schope patted the man's shoulder. "I'm an artist, and I choose to paint the quaint apothecary shop across the square."

The man next to Beccaroon mumbled to his tablemates, "Artist? That man's more than a picture painter."

Sir Beccaroon sighed. So much for Verrin Schope and Lady Peg being inconspicuous.

The Grawl loped through the street to a stand of trees just outside the town. He crouched in the shade and took in his surroundings. He detected a few small animals and birds. Nothing to disturb him as he contemplated his next action. After knocking over several small toadstools, he picked at the bugs underneath. He liked the larger ones that crunched in his mouth.

Chewing helped him think. Crisp snacks satisfied the need to hear the pop and grind between his teeth. He moved a mossy stone and found a delectable selection of very small snails. He grunted and turned his mind to the problem.

Another wizard. He'd never heard of wizards in Chiril. Yet he hadn't been here a month and had run into two. If he'd been hired to find wizards and kill them, he'd do it. But to have to deal with their interference while he located strongholds in enemy territory was not in the verbal contract he'd made with King Odidoddex. One purse of gold before the journey and one when they returned, having sabotaged Chiril's defense, presented a reasonable business deal. He should have asked for more money just for the annoyance of putting up with three bisonbeck warriors.

A wizard. Two wizards. Time to renegotiate with Odidoddex.

He and the bisonbecks had come to town to meet the man who delivered pay and took back reports. The Grawl gritted his teeth. He'd challenge the messenger to guarantee a more lucrative deal. If the king had sent Groddenmitersay, the problem would be easily solved. The tumanhofer sat as the head of the war council and could authorize anything that struck his fancy.

The Grawl stood when he saw the bisonbecks emerge from the inn and come his way. They marched down the street, not in formation, but anyone watching would recognize the military bearing. The fools couldn't avoid trouble even when they were under orders.

Gorse bristled as he came near. "You deserted us."

The Grawl only gave him a cursory glance. His eyes went to the commander of their mission. The soldier quivered with resentment. He'd been beaten by what he saw as a scrawny foe. And there had been witnesses. The Grawl knew he'd be attacked, a substitute for the one who had really raised First Speatus Kulson's ire.

"You're under my command, Grawl. You don't leave unless I dismiss you."

The Grawl kept his gaze steady. He could stare down this petty tyrant, but it didn't serve his purpose to further humiliate the bisonbeck. "I was not hired to brawl in taverns."

Kulson took the easy way out. He swung around to attack his two underlings. "We're going to the bathhouse."

"What?"

Brox's expression of disbelief caused a snort of laughter to escape from The Grawl. Kulson didn't even acknowledge he heard.

"We are going back to the tavern. I want to keep an eye on that man."

That piqued The Grawl's interest. "The wizard?"

Kulson still didn't look at him. "Wizard? Trickster maybe. Wizards wear robes and have pointed hats. They don't come to the aid of insolent innkeepers."

The Grawl didn't answer.

Gorse wasn't that smart. "You know a lot about wizards, huh?"

Kulson backhanded the soldier. Gorse lay on the ground, nursing a sore jaw.

"We're going to get cleaned up. By the time Groddenmitersay gets here, we'll have a lot to tell him about a certain emerlindian." He strode away, not looking to see if his men followed.

Brox extended a hand. Gorse grabbed it, and after hoisting him to his feet, Brox followed their leader. Gorse marched along behind.

The Grawl grinned. He wouldn't be staying in any tavern, but he'd be close by. The right man was coming to gather information and dispense money. And The Grawl knew he could negotiate a better deal for himself.

14

Must Go

Bealomondore stepped back and studied his latest sketch. Done. And done well. On his canvas, three kimen children hung upside down from a tree, their legs hooked over a limb. The artist smiled.

"Come see." He gestured to his models.

They tumbled off their perch, landed lightly, and ran to see their picture. With exclamations of delight, they danced around the artist, then ran off to tell their friends.

Maxon strolled into the clearing. "You've caused a great deal of excitement. The village has never had a portrait artist before."

"You once told me that you rarely had guests. Now you've had Librettowit, Tipper, and me for almost two months. Paladin has come and gone, causing quite a stir while he was here. Have we irrevocably disrupted your daily living?"

Maxon sat on a stump. "No, no. We were made to glorify Wulder and enjoy Him. One of the ways we do this is to serve. We've come through a long, bleak period where our race did not have a focus. Now we do. Paladin has explained things that were lost in our history. Our customs and traditions make much more sense now that he has renewed our knowledge of the Creator, Wulder."

Bealomondore's response was a noncommittal, "Hmm." He didn't want to discuss Wulder.

He hunched a shoulder and turned to his art, adding a few more strokes to his sketch. He stood back, examined the effect, then added two more.

"I'm waiting for the ropmas to come," he said. "I had a promise from a young man named Handle. Of course, I realize that time is a nebulous thing for them."

"That's actually why I've come."

Bealomondore turned to study his kimen friend. The frown on his little face did not bode well.

"What's happened?"

Maxon's shoulders bunched up and fell as he gave a huge sigh. "The ropmas have seen The Grawl. They've gone so far underground that we haven't seen them at all today."

Bealomondore sat on one of the stools he'd brought out from his abode. "Well, this Grawl beast isn't after them, is he? Surely they're safe."

"Near here is a marione village where craftsmen fashion all sorts of knives, swords, spears, and arrows. The ropmas provide raw ore for the metals. They think it is a good deal, trading mud for fancy food like bacon. Ropmas are particularly fond of bacon. And ham. But it would be unthinkable for a ropma to slaughter an animal for its meat."

"Vegetarians?"

"Not really. Just squeamish." Maxon stood looking at the portrait of the carefree kimen children. "You have a great gift, Bealomondore."

"Yes, but I have no subjects for my next sitting." He rolled his piece of charcoal between two fingers. "Tell me the rest of the tale."

"The night before last, The Grawl led bisonbeck men into the village. The marauders destroyed each building in which weapons had been made and all the storage sheds. They torched some of the buildings, and fire spread to homes. Ropmas, especially burrowing ropmas, are terrified of fire."

"Was anyone hurt?"

"The raiding party didn't seem interested in hurting the mariones, but they thrashed anyone who came out to stop them, and several villagers were hurt as they put out the blazes."

Bealomondore put down his charcoal and picked up a rag to wipe his hands. "This is why we brought the statues out of the city. These men must not get hold of a powerful gateway."

"Exactly."

"Well, the two statues are safe in your settlement."

A cool breeze ruffled a stack of paper the artist had left on a stump. Bealomondore moved to put away his tools.

Maxon rested a hand on the pages to keep them in place. "Yes, but we have had a message from the palace, regarding Verrin Schope."

He stopped and focused on Maxon. "Surely it can't be too urgent."

"Only if you value the artist's life."

"What? Tell me this instant."

"He has returned to the unstable state that was cured when the three statues were reunited. And now Lady Peg, Beccaroon, and Verrin Schope have disappeared in the countryside. No one knows exactly where they are."

Bealomondore pondered this news. He looked up at the darkening sky and noted the threat of rain. Even in this forest he'd jokingly referred to as enchanted, the possibility of storms loomed. He turned back to his task of cleaning up. "We must come to his aid. But how?"

"You and Princess Tipper only have two of the statues. We need the third."

"But Fenworth left here to go to Ragar. We'll just send for him. That's no problem."

"If he had arrived, it would be no problem. But Wizard Fenworth and Hollee have not been seen or heard from since the day they left the Starling Forest."

"Fenworth isn't in Ragar?"

"No."

"Then he and Hollee have been missing for almost all of the two months we've been here? Why didn't the people in Ragar tell us?"

"Probably because they weren't expecting him to come and so didn't realize he was missing."

"Do you suppose this Grawl…"

Maxon shook his head. "We've been watching him. It seems his main function is to locate places that are key to the defense of our nation. He has also been hunting down persons of consequence."

"Persons of consequence?"

"Leaders in the military and local authorities."

"And what happens when he finds these people?"

"They disappear." Maxon fidgeted with his hair. "While you've been sequestered here in the Starling Forest, more than thirty individuals have gone missing."

"Could be the slave trade."

Maxon shook his head again. "Slavers want young people who have the capacity to work hard. And most often, the captives are taken closer to the shore. The missing persons are older and from towns and cities scattered across our eastern territories."

"We're in the East."

"And so is The Grawl."

Bealomondore tossed several brushes, pencils, and charcoal sticks into a box and closed the lid. "Does Tipper know of her father's illness?"

"Taeda Bel has gone to tell her."

Maxon hoisted a small tablet of paper to his shoulder and took it to Bealomondore's open door. The artist followed with his newest sketch and the easel.

The kimen folk reminded the tumanhofer of ants. They could carry objects that appeared to be too heavy or cumbersome for them. Between Bealomondore and Maxon, they toted all his belongings into the safety of his bower.

A light rain chased them into his enclosure with the last of his painting gear in their arms.

After storing his supplies, Bealomondore offered his kimen refreshment. He searched through piles of stuff. "I brought some daggarts back from lunch. If we can find them, we'll eat them. And we'll ask Tipper over for tea to see how she is doing."

Maxon grinned and began his own search.

A gush of wind fluttered the branches that made up his closely woven walls. A moment later, Tipper called from outside, "Let me in, Bealomondore. We must talk."

He sprang to the door and opened it quickly. A spray of raindrops flew in with the wind. He shut the door as soon as Tipper and Taeda Bel passed him.

Rain spots dotted Tipper's apparel. She shivered, and Bealomondore hurried to his bedroom and brought back a blanket to wrap around her.

"You heard about my father?"

Bealomondore nodded as Tipper plunged ahead. "We must do something!"

Maxon and Taeda Bel whispered in the corner. Bealomondore drew Tipper's attention to the two kimens with a gesture.

He patted her arm and turned to the little people. "Ahem, I think Tipper and I would like to discuss this matter in private. You will excuse us, won't you?"

Maxon looked surprised. "You'd turn us out in the rain?"

He chortled as he opened the door. "I've never seen a wet kimen. I assume you run between the raindrops."

The kimens laughed good-naturedly and bowed before they left.

Bealomondore reached for a chair and placed it next to his guest.

Tipper clutched the blanket closer as she sat. "Why did you send them away?"

"I don't believe they would be in favor of any plan we make."

"Why?"

"I am remembering the way we arrived in this village. Much care was taken to keep us from knowing the exact location. If we are to leave, they might impose some rigorous falderal to keep from revealing their secret."

"Then you think we should go to my father and mother?"

Bealomondore sat on a stool. "No, I don't think we should. We were charged with protecting the statues. We are safe, and therefore, the statues are safe."

Tears welled in Tipper's eyes. "Bealomondore!"

He held up a hand. "That is what my reason tells me. In truth, I don't see how we can sit securely in this sanctuary while your father is in peril."

"We'll go?"

"Yes." He slapped his palms down on his thighs and stood. "Fenworth left me a pile of useless goods. Useless if one is going to stay and paint pretty pictures. Now, I think it would be wise to pack this paraphernalia in that cape Winkel brought me."

Tipper moved to the side of the room, peering in and around the many stacks. "What color is it?"

"That's hard to say. It is made of moonbeam cloth."

Tipper turned abruptly, her eyes wide. "Jayrus has one of those. Well, not exactly. He has an outfit made by the kimens. Did you ever see it?"

Bealomondore grinned. "Yes, I have, and that may be one of the reasons I'm willing to trek all over the countryside with you. Imagine being invisible when you stand still."

Tipper reached behind a closed-up box. "Here it is."

"Let's fill the pockets." Bealomondore took the cloak as she offered it to him, then turned slowly. "I put it all in one place, so it shouldn't be hard to find. But that was months ago, and things tend to shift down to the bottom of piles as time goes by."

"I never would have suspected you to be so untidy." Tipper tsked as she nosed around the periphery of the crowded room.

"Disorder occurs only when I am at work. The more creativity I exhibit, the more clutter collects. Surely it is a sign of genius." He pulled a drop cloth off a pile. "Here."

Tipper knelt on the floor with the blanket still wrapped around her. Bealomondore spread the cape inside out with the hollow pockets available. They began packing.

"No, no, no, Bealomondore. Put all the things that are used together in one pocket. Put your art supplies in this one, eating utensils and the like in here, and we can use this one for weapons."

"And the last one?"

"Food and money."

"We don't have any food or money."

Tipper sat back on her heels. "I have some money. We'll have to get food in the first town we come across."

"Wait, I remember a bag of food and a bag of money that Wizard Fenworth gave me. We'll have to find that."

He began to search and found a bowl filled with crackers and a handful of daggarts. He also lifted up a plate of cheese and showed it to Tipper.

She wrinkled her nose. "Ew! How old is that? There must be an inch of mold on it."

"We could scrape the mold off. The cheese underneath is probably good."

"You scrape it off, and *you* eat it. I want to find the food provided by Fenworth."

He shrugged his shoulders, put the plate down, and transferred the crackers and daggarts to a small box. Tipper found the two bags they needed and poked them in a hollow.

After a few more minutes, he declared they were ready to go.

"I'll have to stop by my tent and get a few things," Tipper said.

"We'd best try to look as if we are not doing anything unusual. I'll go to the stream and wait for you. Perhaps no one will notice we're leaving." Bealomondore opened the door. "It's stopped raining."

He motioned for Tipper to precede him. She stepped through the door and stopped. Bealomondore managed to look around her.

Taeda Bel and Maxon stood on the doorstep with big grins on their pert faces.

"We're going with you," said Maxon.

Taeda Bel held up a flat bag. "I packed your things, Tipper."

Bealomondore frowned. "Who said you could come along?"

The kimens turned surprised faces toward each other and said in unison, "We did!"

Bealomondore and Tipper exchanged exasperated looks. Tipper walked out of the house and looked down at the two friends. "I don't—"

Winkel bustled into the clearing with a huge folded garment on her head. "I just finished it, Princess Tipper. Your moonbeam cape. You can't go questing without one."

"Oh," cried the pretty emerlindian as she reached for her gift. "Oh, thank you."

"Not a quest," boomed Librettowit as he arrived in the commons with a dozen kimens following. "I don't like quests."

More kimens, mostly children, scuttled out of the trees and from behind bushes.

"You don't need to come," said Tipper. "I know you'd prefer to finish your discourse on the kimen lifestyle. And you still have the ropmas to study."

"I know my duty, young lady. Your father would be most upset if his daughter went gallivanting around Chiril with a bachelor tumanhofer. I will go along as chaperone."

"I don't think—" Bealomondore began.

Winkel patted his leg. "Yes, dear. It *is* necessary." She gestured toward those crowding around the departing adventurers. "We've brought food for your hollows."

It took a few moments to store bread, cheese, jars of soup, dried berries and nuts, and bars of delicious yumber into their clothing.

"Take care," said Winkel, "and don't mess with that growling thing."

"We won't," said Tipper and leaned over to kiss the kimen matriarch's cheek.

That started a round of hugs and kisses and advice giving from the villagers.

Finally, Librettowit cleared his throat and made a pronouncement. "We're leaving now, before the sun sets and the moon rises. Any more advice can be forwarded through Chiril's excellent postal system. Thank you for your hospitality, dear kimens of the Starling Forest. I hope to return to finish my studies."

"There's just one more thing," said Winkel. She pulled out a large sack, presumably from a hollow in her clothing. She waved it at those about to depart. "Blindfolds."

15

Disappearing

A soft knock on the door brought a satisfied twitch of Sir Beccaroon's tail, or at least a twitch of the stump under the artificial contraption that passed for his tail.

He tilted his head and heard Lady Peg's muffled voice.

He called, "Come in."

The door opened, and Verrin Schope and his lady entered. Lady Peg carried a board and a jar of salve. Her husband carried a bucket and two sponges. Their four minor dragons fluttered into the room as well and proceeded to explore before taking up roosts.

"I'm sorry we didn't get here right after supper," explained Lady Peg. "We had to wait until the hall was clear, and a very improper lady stood outside her door for the longest time having a conversation with a gentleman. It is, of course, improper for a lady to talk to a man who is not her relative unless they are in a public place. I suppose the man could have been her brother, but I don't think so. Finally Verrin Schope had to suggest to the man that he was very, very thirsty, so he left. But don't ask me how my husband convinced him he was thirsty. He just did."

Verrin Schope placed a towel on the seat of a wooden chair and the bucket on top of the towel. He then put a heavy foot on one of the rungs underneath, and Beccaroon flew to perch on the back of the chair.

Lady Peg continued to natter on as both she and her husband used the sponges to soak the prosthesis, softening the special glue invented by Wizard Fenworth and his associates. When the rounded bowl disguised with feathers came off, Beccaroon gave his backside an undignified shake.

Grandur and Zabeth flew in to examine his irritated skin. They aided the two emerlindians as they soaked and peeled off the remnants of sticky glue. Verrin Schope unscrewed the lid on the salve, and both he and his wife dipped their fingers into it.

"I know you think this is beneath you, to have your skin taken care of this way," said Lady Peg. "But I want you to know that I like doing it. Your poor rump was injured protecting my daughter after all. You were so brave to fly in and attack her attackers, and those bug men at the Insect Emporium were clever enough to devise a tail. Actually I don't mean they were clever because I assume they are still being clever, so I should say are clever instead of were clever."

Verrin Schope cleared his throat. "We must be quiet, my dear. We don't want someone passing in the hall to hear us. It would be difficult to explain why we are in the room of the grand parrot. And it would be even more cumbersome to explain why we've de-tailed him."

If he could have rolled his eyes, Beccaroon would have. The mischief in his old friend's expression did make him laugh.

Lady Peg's eyes grew wide, and she whispered, "Verrin Schope, we certainly have a right to help our friend. And how can we help him if we aren't in his room?"

Verrin Schope smoothed the ointment over the tender skin, and Lady Peg joined in the ritual that kept Beccaroon's wound site free of the complications of wearing a prosthesis.

Beccaroon turned his head and peered over his shoulder. The dragons resettled themselves close enough to keep watch over the proceedings.

"But we are not supposed to know him." Verrin Schope winked at Bec.

Lady Peg continued her hushed meanderings. "Oh, now that's not right. We *do* know him, so you can't change that. What you must mean is that others we meet aren't supposed to know that we know him.

That's a big difference. It isn't logical to say we don't know him when we do, but it is possible to fool others into believing we don't know him."

"Just so," Beccaroon said. "A very logical point, Lady Peg."

She smiled at Beccaroon, then frowned at her husband. "And if some come to know we know Sir Bec, it won't be because of burrs in his feathers. Wherever did you get such a notion?"

Beccaroon tried to puzzle that one out but gave up with a shrug of his shoulders. Verrin Schope checked to see that his wife was not watching and mouthed the word "cum-*bers*-ome." Bec nodded his understanding. Lady Peg had moved on to "de-tailed."

After four of his self-appointed attendants left for their own beds, Beccaroon pushed a chair over to the open window and perched there to enjoy the cloudless night. The two healing dragons stayed. As he sat on the arm of the chair, his backside rested in the cushioned seat. Grandur and Zabeth curled up next to the tender stump.

From his window the next day, Beccaroon could see Verrin Schope in the town square. He'd set up his easel and dabbed paint on a canvas. He stood on a familiar piece of flooring. With the board from his wife's closet beneath his feet, Verrin Schope's body would dissipate and reform within the blink of an eye. No one should notice the phenomenon. Without the centering board that somehow connected with a portal to another continent, the artist could scatter to the corners of the world.

The wizard artist interacted with townspeople as they passed by him on their daily business. Bec knew Verrin Schope extracted more facts from their minds than he did from their words. Along with mind reading and subliminal suggestion, the wizard could delve into a person's mind as easily as flipping the pages of a book.

Lady Peg sat in a comfy chair confiscated from the inn. She wore a large floppy hat to protect her skin. Much to the delight of the children, the minor dragons frolicked in the grass and did tricks in the air. Beccaroon watched for a while, then turned back to his book.

Hours later, Beccaroon sat in the tavern with his tail restored. He enjoyed his evening meal and eavesdropped on the conversations at tables nearby. The urge to compete with Verrin Schope in the collection of useful rumors kept him attentive to all around him.

He picked up only a few nuggets of information. The bisonbecks had come to the inn weeks earlier and met with another foreigner. The region had fewer problems with kidnappings by slave traders this year, but the farmers had lost livestock to some marauders who left no tracks. They were fearful of blaming the bisonbecks. No one wanted to confront such brawny thugs. But the worst of the rumors he overheard was the disappearance of so many men in authority. Mayors, legislators, councilmen, magistrates, military officers, and powerful landowners had gone missing.

A local band set up to play at one end of the room, and Beccaroon decided to retire. He wouldn't be able to hear much over whatever music they played. He signaled for his waitress to bring the check, but instead the serving maid brought a marione over and introduced him as the local magistrate, Hopdin.

"Join me." Beccaroon nodded to the chair at his corner table. "I'm the magistrate in my region. We should be able to think of something to talk about."

Hopdin laughed as he pulled out the chair and took a seat. Three hours later, the two were fast friends.

"Tell me about these disappearances," said Bec.

"Ah yes. That is a sinister puzzle. Odd really. Those who disappear are those who have the responsibility of keeping order in one way or another."

Beccaroon clicked his beak. "If we could figure out who's behind these actions and what's achieved by this ploy, we'd be closer to putting our finger on the culprit."

"Or culprits."

"Indeed. Aren't these officials replaced as soon as it is determined they are more or less permanently absent from their posts?"

Hopdin nodded and sipped his ale before he spoke. "Word came from the palace this week that any foreign traveler is to be kept under surveillance and his movements cataloged and reported to Ragar. Obviously, the king thinks the influx of strangers has something to do with it. And the rumors of war brewing with Baardack make me think the disappearances are serving to disrupt our organization if a war actually breaks out."

"I concur." Beccaroon nodded toward the three men sitting around a table. "So you have someone keeping tabs on those bisonbecks?"

"That's right."

"And that creature?"

"The Grawl? His comrades call him The Grawl. He almost never comes into the village, and when he's in the woods, it's impossible to keep track of him."

"I'd like to know exactly where he came from and what he is."

Hopdin stood. "You and everyone else in this town." He pushed in his chair. "I've got to get home. It was nice meeting you, Sir Beccaroon. If you're staying a few days, maybe we can do this again."

Bec nodded, and the marione magistrate made his way to the door, speaking to several people along the way. The grand parrot glanced around the room and noticed that most people were on friendly terms with their magistrate. If they didn't call out a farewell, they gave a wave. All except the bisonbecks. They did not acknowledge his departure. But why should they?

Hopdin went out the front door.

Beccaroon studied the three bisonbeck men. He again noted their indifference, but this time a frisson of alarm chilled him. Their disregard appeared too pat, too studied. Beccaroon hopped down from his perch and pushed through the crowded tavern to follow his new friend.

Outside, he saw Hopdin approaching a corner, whistling as he walked. Beccaroon walked after him, listening to the tune that echoed the last one played in the inn. He came to the corner, but before he turned in the same direction, the cheerful whistle came to an abrupt end. Bec peered into the dim street. The main road behind him had lamps at intervals. This side street did not.

"Hopdin?" Bec's voice sounded loud in the still night air. No answer brought another call, louder than the first. "Hopdin?"

Beccaroon thrust out his wings and took to the air. He could see more from that vantage point. Above the buildings, he batted back an onslaught of despair. He saw more shadows and dark alleys than patches of light. Nowhere did he see the marione magistrate.

The Grawl stood in the shadows of a mercantile, his victim at his feet. He preferred to dispose of the body outside city limits, in the woods, but he could do it here. He spent a moment watching the circling bird, quite sure Beccaroon had not spotted him. The radius of the grand parrot's circle grew larger.

The Grawl pulled out a pouch from an inner pocket of his tunic. He frowned over the few capsules remaining in his supply. Groddenmitersay had ordered a new supply of the poison, and hopefully it would come soon. He could wait for hours to snare prey, but waiting for the tumanhofer's shipment did not sit well with him.

Beccaroon altered his pattern to a figure eight. The Grawl sneered. If the man at his feet was the object of this search, the bird would not find him.

The Grawl opened the pouch and fingered three oblong capsules into his palm. He used his foot to turn Hopdin over. The man still breathed, and that was essential. The Grawl had not yet made the mistake of outright killing his victim. The potion worked only when a heart pumped it through the body.

He leaned over and pinched Hopdin's cheeks, opening the marione's mouth. He put all three capsules under his tongue, then poured in a liquid from a flask. He then held the man's jaw closed. A bit of red foam dribbled out. The Grawl carefully avoided the liquid. After ten seconds, he released his grip and stood.

He sat on a barrel to count the remaining capsules. Eighteen. He looked down at the now dead and disintegrating man. He'd wait until the entire corpse dissolved, then scatter the sodden ash with his feet. By morning there would be no trace of Magistrate Hopdin.

Normally The Grawl wouldn't commit two assassinations in the same town, but the bird annoyed him. He'd learned two days before that the grand parrot was a magistrate. He wouldn't slay Sir Beccaroon just for being an annoyance, but he would do the deed for another gold coin. His hoard would weigh a great deal by the time he returned to his homeland.

16

Revelation

As Tipper changed her shoes for boots, she couldn't help but look with trepidation at the rocky slope.

Bealomondore leaned against a huge boulder, taking advantage of the shade. "I'll be right behind you, Princess."

"I told you not to call me that." She jerked on the laces to tighten the leather around her ankle.

Librettowit watched her. "Make it good and firm to protect your ankle from a sprain."

She tried to keep the exasperation out of her voice but didn't quite succeed. "I am!"

"This is steeper than the previous inclines we've faced," Bealomondore explained.

"I can see that." She started working on the other boot's stiff cords that stood for shoelaces.

Taeda Bel and Maxon skidded into their presence. They'd already been up the slope and catapulted down with no trouble.

"Once we get to the top," said Maxon, "it won't be so difficult. A wide meadow stretches out to the River Hannit. We'll be able to get a boat and travel with ease."

Tipper stood and stamped her feet. The boots felt heavy and stiff, but Librettowit insisted she protect her feet. And so far, all his advice for traveling had been correct.

She resented being bossed around. No one had ever been in authority over her during her father's absence. Sir Beccaroon had offered advice but never demanded she do things his way. She had enough good sense to know that Librettowit was the most experienced in trekking across an uncivilized section of land, but that didn't make taking orders any easier.

Begrudgingly, she acknowledged that Bealomondore did a much better job of not complaining. Since the horrible realization that *she* was the whiner, she'd clamped her lips shut. Still, a steady stream of acerbic remarks threatened to flow from her with every aggravation. She admitted to herself that worry for her father caused her short temper.

"All right!" Librettowit rubbed his palms together. "I'll lead, with Maxon and Taeda Bel flanking Tipper, then Bealomondore can bring up the rear."

"Wait a minute," objected Tipper. "I need to check on Rayn."

Taeda Bel and Maxon crowded her sides. The minor dragon fascinated both kimens. Tipper opened a bag that hung loosely from her belt. Rayn's head poked out. At the moment, his scales shone bluish gray in the sun. Without waiting for an invitation, he shot out and climbed Tipper's arm to her shoulder.

She grinned. "He wants to ride outside."

Librettowit nodded and turned to begin the trudge up the steep hill.

Tipper followed, and the constant encouragement from Rayn helped erase her gloomy mood. She used the mindspeaking between them to keep her thoughts off the hot sun on her back, the physical discomfort of hauling herself up the awkward terrain, and the general despair she felt over the unsettling situation in Chiril. She missed her parents, and more perturbing was the constant longing to see Paladin again.

But if the rumors of invasion were true, real trouble might keep her away from the ones she loved. She'd heard nothing of that possibility while in the kimen village. Now her comrades discussed little else.

Maxon and Taeda Bel issued warnings about avoiding strangers and not talking to those they met at taverns and inns.

The dust kicked up by Librettowit landed in her face, and Tipper sneezed. She took a moment to rub her tickling nose.

Bealomondore rested his hand on her back. "Are you all right?"

"Yes."

"I tied on a handkerchief."

She turned to see what he meant. A bandana covered the bottom of his face, and his kind brown eyes peered out at her.

He pulled out another large, soft linen square and folded it into a triangle. "Turn around. I'll tie it on."

"Thank you."

"Are you coming?" Librettowit called.

"Just a minute," answered the other tumanhofer. He tightened the cloth before tying a knot at the back of her head. "You worry too much, Tipper. Relax and allow someone else to bear the responsibility."

In her mind, she heard Rayn laughing. She brushed aside the little dragon's obvious reaction to Bealomondore's advice and spoke to the artist. "That's hard."

"True, considering the burden you bore while your father was gone."

They continued their struggle to conquer the slope. Bealomondore stayed beside her and huffed a bit as he spoke. "Librettowit said something the other day regarding Wulder that really stuck in my mind."

"Hmm." Tipper didn't care to encourage this topic of conversation.

"Librettowit said that every person uses something as a plausible reason not to hand over his life to Wulder. Everyone has a core of willfulness that he doesn't want to give up. These reasons, or excuses, are vastly different in nature for each individual but very similar in purpose." He changed his voice to sound like he quoted someone. " 'No one else will love me as much as I love myself. I will do a better job of looking out for me.'" Bealomondore put his hand on her elbow to steady her over some loose gravel. "And that's a lie. Wulder cares more."

"Are you saying you're beginning to believe all this about their Wulder?"

"Not exactly."

"Then what?"

"Not beginning. I've already decided to believe." He paused, then went on in a tone that sounded like he wanted to justify his choice. "I've been puzzling over it for a long time, since I met your father in fact. And Librettowit's assurance seemed to be the binding element."

He paused to untangle his pant leg from a thorny twig. "I find it fascinating. That Someone, who made the sky and the sea, the land and everything we see, would take time off from His daily concerns to take an interest in me."

"Oh, now *that* is impossible. I know for a fact that one cannot watch the cooks in the kitchen and the workers in the field, the well digger, and the laundry maids all at the same time."

Bealomondore didn't seem to have an answer for that, and Tipper felt a strange sense of satisfaction in having silenced him...and a peculiar disappointment.

They reached the highest ridge of their climb and stood. Tipper rubbed the small of her back and surveyed the wide expanse of waving grass.

"Do you see the sky, Tipper?" asked Bealomondore.

She pulled the cloth down before she spoke. "Of course I do."

"Do you suppose the creator of the sky is bigger than the sky? Wouldn't that be logical?"

Tipper rested her fists on her hips. "Provided you believe that someone *made* our world."

"As an artist," Bealomondore countered, with a sweeping gesture that included the vista around them, "I have no doubt that someone created all you see. There is no picture without an artist."

Rayn turned bright purple and opened his mouth. A song of joy poured forth. In the way of minor dragons, no words formed within the melody, but Tipper heard exclamations of praise and gratitude that she had heard on the lips of the kimens and Librettowit when they sang. Sadly, Tipper realized her own voice would not harmonize smoothly with her favorite dragon's.

She chose to coldly ignore the prompting to join in his song and sat down to change her boots to more comfortable shoes.

17

Swordplay

Tipper welcomed the gentle breeze as they walked through the tall grass. She couldn't see the river, but Maxon said it was there just beyond the horizon. He also said that a boat stop supplied those using the River Hannit for transport with a myriad of services—showers, meals, supplies, and a few hours of rest from the rigors of moving their cargo vessels up or down the river. Once Tipper's comrades were on the banks, the small establishment would be only a mile or so downstream.

The group walked side by side. The two tumanhofers flanked Tipper, and the kimens took the outside positions, Maxon next to the artist and Taeda Bel next to the librarian. Rayn sat on Tipper's head. She tried to persuade him to sit on her shoulder, but he preferred the higher perch.

"Stop!" The word came out of Tipper's mouth before she heard it in her mind.

Everyone froze.

"What?" asked Bealomondore.

"Snake," said Taeda Bel.

Librettowit's head whipped back and forth. "Where?"

Maxon pointed, but Tipper didn't see anything. Rayn hissed from his post, and she realized he had been the one to put the warning on her lips.

"Bealomondore," said Maxon in a hushed and urgent voice, "where is the sword Wizard Fenworth gave you?"

"In a hollow."

"I think it would serve us well in your hand."

"I'm not a swordsman. I've no skill."

Librettowit gave a choked chortle. "Get it out, son. Move with care. Don't attract the snake's attention."

Tipper held her breath as Bealomondore carefully moved the cloak aside and reached into one of the inside hollows. He seemed to put his hand on the right object immediately. She heard him sigh and watched out of the corner of her eye.

As he pulled out the sword, a large snake raised its head above the two-foot-high grass. Black with a pattern of red and blue stripes, the reptile swayed as its eyes appeared to measure their group. With a hiss, the snake sunk to the ground.

Tipper stepped back at Rayn's urging. Again she realized it was he who pointed out the slight disturbance across the top of the grass that displayed the snake's movement.

"H-how long do you think that snake is?" she asked.

Librettowit pursed his mouth. "Nine feet? Ten?"

Rayn dashed down from his lookout point and dived inside her cape.

Tipper would have liked to have wings to fly or be small enough to fit in her own pockets.

Bealomondore stepped forward, but it looked like the sword pulled him. The snake's head bolted into the air right in front of the tuman-hofer. With one swing of the blade, the artist decapitated the snake.

Maxon jumped up and down. "Well done! Well done!"

Bealomondore gasped, and the hand holding the sword dropped to his side. He pulled a handkerchief from his pocket and wiped his brow.

Tipper couldn't help beaming at him. "I didn't know you could wield a sword like that."

"I can't." Bealomondore pointed at his shaking hand holding the weapon. "I can't even hold it still. The sword killed the snake. I didn't."

Librettowit nodded sagely. "A weapon bestowed upon you by Wizard Fenworth is likely to have unusual properties."

The younger tumanhofer thrust the sword hilt toward the librarian. "You take it."

Librettowit raised his hands in front of him, palms forward. "No, the sword will work for you, not me. Do you have a sword belt in that cape?"

"Yes, I think so."

"Put it on."

Rayn came out of hiding. He, Maxon, and Taeda Bel expressed enthusiasm by jigging around. Rayn danced on one of Tipper's shoulders, prancing over her head to bounce on the other.

"He's going to be a warrior," said Maxon.

"No," said Taeda Bel, "one of those fancy fencers."

"No, no, no." Bealomondore held the belt in a fist and shook it in the air above his head. "I am a painter, an artist. I have no intention of becoming a swordsman."

Interrupting his wild shindig, Tipper caught Rayn and restrained him against her chest. "Are there more snakes?"

Taeda Bel and Maxon stood still, paying attention to their surroundings. Taeda Bel's face took on an expression of wariness, and she scooted closer to her emerlindian.

"Dozens," said Maxon. "Seems they're having a get-together."

Tipper frowned. "Snakes have get-togethers?"

"Mating season."

"Really?" Tipper doubted him, wondering if he was taking advantage of her ignorance.

He tossed her a cheeky grin. "Let's get moving."

"You're going to watch for snakes, aren't you?" Tipper cringed. "I don't want to step on one."

"We won't let you," said Taeda Bel, "and Bealomondore can practice by dispatching the ones that are aggressive."

Bealomondore deliberately sheathed the sword, then put the belt around his waist. Squaring his shoulders, he scowled and marched forward. Tipper placed Rayn on her shoulder and followed.

They hadn't taken ten steps before another snake raised its head and threatened the tumanhofer in front. Bealomondore jerked on the sword hilt and brought his weapon out. Again the blade directed his arm. Tipper gasped as the snake lunged, but Bealomondore managed to lop off its head.

Librettowit came up beside him. "You might as well keep your weapon drawn. These snakes are mongers. At least they look and act like the snakes back home that populate our southern regions. Mongers will challenge any man or beast that crosses their territory."

Tipper joined the two tumanhofers. "Are they poisonous?"

"Slightly venomous most of the year, but deadly during mating season." Librettowit sighed. "I don't suppose there is a way to go around this little patch of land they seem to claim as their own."

Maxon and Taeda Bel looked behind them, paused for a moment, then shook their heads.

The male kimen indicated the land they had just crossed with a sweep of his hand. "They've closed in. We're surrounded."

Tipper glared his way. "Who was it who said that this would be easy? That once we got to the top of that horrible hill, the next part would be easy? I think the word you used was 'easy,' wasn't it?"

Taeda Bel shook her head. "No, he said, 'We'll be able to get a boat and travel with ease.' I don't think he said crossing the meadow would be easy."

"Keep together," said Maxon. "I think the snakes are tightening their circle around us. Let's move."

Tipper gave Bealomondore credit. He went ahead of the others, ready to protect them. The next snake gave him less than a second to react, yet the tumanhofer managed to behead it. She thought he handled the sword with a little more finesse.

By the time they finally reached the far edge of the field, where the land dropped to the riverbed, he looked much more comfortable in the role of champion. She'd lost count of how many mongers had challenged him and lost their lives.

The steep cliff would be difficult to descend, but enough rocks jutted from the face to provide steps, and astain bushes dotted the surface. These stubby plants thrust deep roots into the ground, and scrappy branches grew from a short, thick trunk. Tipper worried more about the snakes in the field than the climb they would have to make.

She couldn't help hoping that the snakes had been dispatched before they'd had a chance to make babies. As far as she was concerned, the world didn't need more poisonous, feisty snakes. Her mother used to fuss about the snakes Tipper might run into in the jungle next to their estate. Counting all she had seen throughout her life, the number was just a small fraction of the populace of this one field.

Librettowit clapped Bealomondore on the shoulder. "Good work. You'll be able to face down any foe by the time the sword is finished training you."

The artist's shoulders drooped. "I have no desire to be a warrior."

"A swordsman is quite a different prospect from your run-of-the-mill soldier fighting on a battlefield."

Bealomondore grunted.

"Fencing is an art form akin to the dance. The intricacies of a sword fight display grace and fluidity of motion like a ballet."

The tumanhofer artist cast the older man a look of interest. "Really? I'm a pretty accomplished dancer, quite in demand when hostesses need males to round out the numbers for a successful soiree."

Maxon snatched a stick to represent a sword and proceeded to do a rather elaborate display of swashbuckling swipes at the empty air. "I can help. Taeda Bel too. We've seen the Miskeen Minstrels."

Librettowit harrumphed. "What do singers have to do with Bealomondore and his sword?"

"Oh, they're jugglers and acrobats and players of scenes of history." He turned to call to Taeda Bel, who had already descended to the wide bank beside the River Hannit. "Taeda Bel, come show how the Miskeen Minstrels enacted the play *Noble Nonsense.*"

"You come down," she answered. "I don't want another snake sneaking up on us. I don't think there are any down here."

"That sounds like a sensible plan to me." Tipper started down the cliff, using rock ledges and the astain bushes as handholds and footholds.

Librettowit peered over the edge. "You should be wearing your boots."

"I'm all right."

She placed her foot at the base of one of the bush stubs and grabbed hold of another. Her hand closed on a broken branch that jabbed into her palm.

"Ouch!"

She let go. In the next moment, she slid down the last eight feet and landed hard on her right foot. She crumpled, and before she could cry out in pain, both kimens and Rayn clustered around her foot, examining the ankle.

"Sprained," said Maxon.

"My foot's on fire." She rocked back and forth with her hands cradling her ankle.

"Better take your shoe off," said Taeda Bel.

Rayn turned green and sat on her leg, very much in the way as Taeda Bel untied the laces and Maxon eased the soft leather from around her foot. Tipper cringed with every movement.

"Broken," said Maxon.

Tipper heard the tumanhofers scrambling down the hill, but she'd shut her eyes against the pain. She willed herself not to whine and make a big to-do. Her jaw trembled, and she clenched her teeth.

A hand rested on her shoulder. "We'll take care of you."

At least Bealomondore was optimistic.

Librettowit didn't sound as cheerful. "Where's a wizard when you need one?"

At least he hadn't reminded her she had changed out of her sturdy boots.

Rayn slipped closer to the break. His cool body, draped over the bone pressing against her skin, felt wonderful.

"Just take the pain away, Rayn," said Maxon. "We'll have to set the bone before you do your healing."

Tipper let the tears fall. She leaned back and found Bealomondore sitting behind to support her. His arms slipped around her, and he leaned his cheek against her hair.

"There, there, Princess. It's going to be all right."

A sobby giggle escaped her lips. "Don't call me Princess."

"Whatever you say." He paused. "Your Highness."

18

A Song of Peace

Tipper held Bealomondore's hand as Librettowit and Maxon prepared to set the bone that arched across the top of her foot. Due to Rayn's ministrations, her foot had lost the agonizing pulse of pain. The dragon, in his role of healer, had numbed the area. Still, the thought of Librettowit and Maxon pulling her foot like the rope in tug of war made Tipper want to escape into oblivion.

Bealomondore didn't complain even though she knew she squeezed hard enough to break *his* bones. She heard hers snap into place, and then Rayn sat on the swollen purple hump, pronouncing through mindspeaking that the two ends were where they should be. He cooed and hummed as he nestled down to provide his healing touch.

"I suppose," said Taeda Bel, "that we should set up camp. Surely our princess shouldn't walk until tomorrow."

Tipper cast her a disparaging look. "Walk?" She deepened her scowl. "And you are not to call me princess either."

Taeda Bel's face lit up with mischief.

"Don't," ordered Tipper.

"Your—,"

"Don't!"

"You're"—a big grin stretched across Taeda Bel's delicate features— "no fun."

Tipper relaxed against the sturdy tumanhofer. He'd held her ever since she'd fallen, and she'd gotten quite used to his solid chest behind her back.

He removed his hand from her grip and flexed his fingers. "I *think* I can still hold a paintbrush."

Librettowit ran his fingers over her arch, top and bottom. Satisfied with their work, he sat back on the ground and crossed his legs. He looked at Bealomondore massaging his hand. "I think at this point in our venture, holding that sword is more important."

Maxon and Taeda Bel both grabbed semistraight sticks and began a fencing match of sorts. Tipper and the two tumanhofers enjoyed the showy antics of the kimens. Their performance combined elements of dance and acrobatics.

They all laughed, but Tipper noticed that Bealomondore gradually grew quiet. She peeked over her shoulder to find his face serious and his eyes glued to the swordplay.

He became aware of her scrutiny and gave her a nod. "I think I can do that, Tipper."

Librettowit turned toward them. "I know a little about keeping myself alive in the middle of a fray. I'll help."

He focused more sharply on Tipper and Bealomondore. His eyes settled on the younger tumanhofer's arms wrapped around her waist. Bealomondore loosened his hold. Then the stalwart friend of Tipper's father glared at the spot where her head rested against Bealomondore's chin. She sat up a bit straighter.

Librettowit cleared his throat. "In my role of chaperone, I think it's time Bealomondore and I make camp."

Taeda Bel and Maxon burst into laughter, dropped their stick weapons, and did somersaults until they landed in front of their audience.

"Yes, let's," said Maxon. "Then we'll have food, song, dance, and lessons in swordsmanship and tomfoolery."

"Tomfoolery?" Bealomondore said as he struggled to rise without disturbing Tipper.

Taeda Bel rubbed her hands together in glee. "Right! That's when you dazzle and befuddle your opponent to his confusion and your advantage."

First on Tipper's comrades' agenda was to make their injured princess as comfortable as possible. They succeeded to the point that she curled up against the cushions and blankets and fell asleep.

The smell of frying fish woke her. She sat up and surveyed the neatly erected campsite. Both tumanhofers worked over the dinner. The kimens were nowhere to be seen. Rayn raced from his perch on her leg to sit on her shoulder, snuggling against her neck.

She giggled and petted his smooth scales. "You're the most affectionate minor dragon I've ever met. And the most interesting."

She felt his pleasure wash through her own body. She breathed deeply, enjoying peace and contentment. Paladin had given her the chance to really bond with someone. The someone was a dragon. Was she not ready to bond with a person?

Where did that thought come from?

She picked Rayn up and held him in front of her so they stared eye to eye. His intelligent expression filled with humor. His skin had mottled with blue and green splotches.

"What talent does a dragon of this color have?"

He chirruped as he did when he found something funny.

"How's your foot?" asked Taeda Bel at her elbow.

Rayn dove below her covers and disappeared.

Tipper jumped. "My foot?"

Taeda Bel's natural surprised look doubled in intensity. "You broke your foot. You forgot?"

Tipper's eyes shifted to the blanket lying over her. One bulge at the bottom of the pallet was twice as big as the other. "It doesn't hurt at all. Rayn's work. But look at it. It must be swollen to the size of a melon. Oh my!"

Taeda Bel snatched the blanket away, revealing a grinning Rayn.

The green dragon partially hid a slightly swollen, slightly green and yellow appendage. Rayn stood and stretched, circled the foot as if doing an inspection, then raced up to cuddle under Tipper's chin.

Tipper flexed her ankle and cringed. "Ow! It's not good as new, but it sure looks like an old injury. Was I asleep for a couple of weeks?"

Taeda Bel shook her head. "Two hours."

Tipper stroked her dragon friend. "Thank you, Rayn." She breathed deeply. "He says that he's done all he can do for now. I'm not to walk on it."

Bealomondore brought over a bowl of soup. Tipper took it and closed her eyes as she smelled the appetizing spicy fragrance.

Grinning as she looked up at her tumanhofer friend, Tipper gave him an exaggerated wink. "If you ever decide to leave your paints and brushes for the culinary arts, you're going to be rich."

"Tonight I will be exploring the art of the swordsman. Enjoy your meal. There will be an after-dinner show. I'll get your second course ready—fried fish and creamed greens."

Tipper surprised herself by speaking to Wulder before she dipped her spoon in the aromatic dish. As Bealomondore walked away, she thanked her father's God for the tumanhofer's friendship. The simple thought brought up a slew of questions. Did she believe what her father had said about Wulder? Was she following in Bealomondore's footsteps? He believed in Wulder now. Did she believe in Wulder? If she spoke to Wulder but didn't really believe, did He hear her? She laughed to herself. If He heard her, then He existed, so she should believe. Since she talked to Him, she must already believe in Him. Had this acceptance sneaked up on her?

"So He exists," she muttered, "but what is He like?"

Rayn burst into a wild chittering that flooded her mind with one-word descriptions.

Creator. Wise. Mighty. Strong. Preserver. Perfect. Sufficient. Holy.

The words kept bombarding her, and with each word came an advance of surety.

Healer. Provider. Just. Redeemer. Shield. Judge. Father. Everlasting. Righteous. Deliverer. Patient. All-seeing, all-knowing, ever-present. Counselor. Prince. King.

One word rushed out of Tipper's mouth in an awed whisper. "Wonderful."

Rayn landed on her knee, and she noted the rich purple of his skin. He sang. All the beauty of the kimens' voices poured out. And again his vocalization contained no words, but lyrics formed in Tipper's thoughts. She pulled in a deep breath, opened her mouth, and sang with him. A song of praise, then a song of adoration. Her voice blended with his. Soon Librettowit's baritone joined in with the higher ranges of Bealomondore's tenor and Taeda Bel's soprano. Tears tracked down Tipper's cheeks as she sang a song of her own, a song of devotion, promising her own dedication, allegiance, and faithfulness.

Sometime later, she heard Bealomondore speak. She looked up from where her hands still cradled the bowl he'd given her.

"Princess, your soup is cold. Let me replace it."

Coming out of a daze, she handed him the bowl. "Did we just sing?"

He smiled. "That was an hour ago."

"I'm not hungry."

"I know. You're full. But you need physical sustenance as well as spiritual. I'll bring you hot soup."

He left and Librettowit came to sit across from her on a boulder half-exposed in the bank of the river.

She studied his face for a moment. She used to think he was ugly and a bit scary. Now she thought he was a kind but gruff friend.

"What happened?" she asked.

He grinned, showing his two rows of huge teeth. "You met Wulder."

19

Boat Stop

Tipper gasped as pain shot from her foot up her shin and beyond her knee. She braced herself on Bealomondore's shoulder on her first attempt to stand. Rayn sat on his favorite perch, her head. He ranted in a series of harsh chirps, the words of the diatribe delivered straight to her mind. He'd been protesting her need to rest since early morning, when the questers decided to break camp and head for the boat stop downstream.

Tipper eased herself down to sit once more on the rock that had been her throne all morning. "Rayn says it's too soon to attempt to walk. Not only was the bone broken, but I also strained numerous muscles in my leg all the way up to my hip."

The tirade from the little dragon continued as she spoke. His scaly skin turned various colors as he vented.

"He's saying a lot of other things," Tipper explained to those around her. "Mostly that we will undo the good he has done as a healer if we don't listen to his advice."

Bealomondore's face wore a mask of doubt. "He's only a few weeks old. Where does he get all this knowledge and the audacity to boss us around?"

Librettowit removed Rayn from Tipper's hair and held him close to his chest. He stroked the dragon and uttered a few soothing words. "Calm yourself. We'll listen." He glanced up at the other tumanhofer. "Minor dragons are extremely adept at mining the minds of those around them."

Taeda Bel and Maxon chortled over his pronouncement, but Librettowit ignored them.

"During the first few weeks of their lives, they harvest a library's worth of information from anyone within reach. Of course, most minor dragons have specialized talents. As a chameleon dragon, Rayn has a wider variety of expertise. The things he pulls from our minds are sometimes things we have forgotten on the conscious level but nonetheless remain stored in the recesses of our brains."

Tipper squirmed on the rock, trying to find a smoother spot. Adding to her discomfort, her backside objected to the ridges of hard stone. The River Hannit flowed peacefully close by, with hardly a ripple marring its pale green surface. An occasional fish flipped out of the water, causing the only disturbance in the wide river. No boats had passed. For this reason, she doubted they could catch a ride on some sort of transport going downstream.

"Is there anything stored in our brains that will suggest a way to get me to the boat stop?" she asked.

Librettowit held up a finger. "Not in my mind but in one of my hollows." He began rummaging through the many hollow pockets inside his long jacket. "I believe I have a boat. More like a raft actually."

After reaching as far as he could into one hollow, the librarian brought out a small pamphlet. He looked at it and grinned. "The instructions. The rest should be here."

He handed the booklet to Bealomondore, who opened it and started to scan the contents. The artist shook his head. "I don't know if I'm handy with a saw and nails."

Maxon looked up at him. "I believe that should be hammer and nails."

Bealomondore's only response was a quick nod. He continued to peruse the pages in his hands.

Librettowit exclaimed, "Aha!" and pulled out a board. Tipper and Taeda Bel both giggled as he pulled more and more planks from the depths of the hollow. He found other things as well.

"Clamping rods. There should be sixteen. Tipper, keep count." He handed her a metal contraption that had a hinge and two bolts. "Rudder. I'm not sure we'll need that. Let's put it to the side. The sail might be unnecessary as well. I'm thinking we'll handle the craft as a barge. I do believe we can do both poling and the ropes."

Taeda Bel looked into Tipper's eyes. "Do you know what he's talking about?"

"No, but I bet if we're patient, we'll find out."

Bealomondore and Librettowit helped Tipper get comfortable on the ground again before they put all the boards together to make a flat platform. Tipper and Taeda Bel watched with amazement as the two tumanhofers and Maxon accomplished their task so easily.

Rayn first sat on her foot in all his green glory. Slowly he took on a brownish hue, then hopped off Tipper to join in the efforts to assemble the raft. He deftly wove a cord through the maze of planks.

Bealomondore studied his movements and compared them to the illustration in the manual. "He's following the instructions precisely."

"I've done this a time or two with Fenworth," the librarian explained.

"Not you, the dragon."

Librettowit squinted at the brown minor dragon. "So he is. Handy to have a chameleon dragon. I'll have to talk to Fenworth about befriending one once we get back to Amara."

They worked quickly and finished before noonmeal. Boards crisscrossed into a large square, big enough for one person to stand and pole and Tipper to recline. Two ropes attached to opposite sides would aid the progress of the raft.

"Aren't we supposed to have kindia or mules or horses or goats or some kind of animal to pull the ropes?" asked Maxon.

Librettowit pinched his upper lip. "That would make our journey more pleasant. But I understand from you that the boat stop is only a mile or so."

"Yes, but who is going to pole, and who will pull?" Maxon winked at Taeda Bel. "We can handle one rope, but someone will have to take the rope on the opposite riverbank."

"And I have experience with the pole," said Librettowit.

"That leaves me on the other rope." Bealomondore looked at the river. "I'm not the best swimmer in the world. Someone else will have to swim across to the other side."

Taeda Bel jumped up from her place beside Tipper. She bounced toward Maxon. "We can. We can."

Bealomondore examined his hands.

"What's wrong?" asked Tipper.

"My hands are tender. I've a couple of splinters, and I'm wondering how I will hold a sword if the rope brings up blisters."

"Gloves," said Tipper. "There were gloves in that pile of gear Fenworth gave you. And Rayn can take care of the roughed-up places before you put them on."

The eager dragon changed from brown to green as he raced to help.

A few minutes later, Tipper lounged on a cushioned pallet, with Librettowit pushing his pole against the riverbed. She remembered the quest to find her father's statues. She'd enjoyed their trek through the mountains.

The present trip held similar attractions. At this moment, questing included a fair breeze, the scent of fresh water, the sound of birds in bentleaf trees, the feel of a warm sun, and the pleasant companionship of good friends.

Librettowit and Wizard Fenworth often bemoaned the rigors of questing, but the journey was not all bad. Tipper told herself that floating down the river with nothing to do but relax and recover was acceptable, not lazy. Rayn roamed up and down her injured leg, and the aching muscles loosened and the sharp pains faded away to nothing.

She smiled at Bealomondore, and he winked back. "I'm going to paint a picture of you, Tipper. I shall title it *Princess on Her Royal Barge*."

She gave him a scornful look but refused to reprimand him for referring to her royal heritage.

The current helped pull them along, and a little bit later, Tipper saw the dock of the boat stop jutting out on the south side of the river. They floated toward it too quickly and bumped into the wood pilings with a loud whack. The impact jarred Tipper's injuries. She gritted her teeth against a protest that sprang to her lips.

"We'll have to practice landing," said Librettowit.

He poled to help maneuver the raft closer to the shore as Bealomondore pulled on the ropes. They managed to come alongside the steps leading up to the dock.

Two mariones from the boat stop rushed to aid them. The younger of the two assisted Bealomondore in tying his rope to a horizontal beam under the wooden walkway. When he finished he tipped his hat to the passengers.

"Good afternoon." His smile reinforced his cheerful greeting. "Business has been rather slim these past few weeks. We're mighty glad you stopped. Come ashore and rest a bit. My mom makes the best travelers' stew on the river. We've clean, soft beds, bathtubs on every floor, and even a shower on the second. My mother owns the boat stop, and she knows her business."

Tipper couldn't get up immediately. Her stiff muscles complained as she followed Rayn's directions. Arms extended above her head didn't hurt, but rotating her feet without waiting for Rayn's signal to begin caused tears to roll down her face. With the green dragon's soothing touch, and by pushing only to the beginning of pain, she managed to reach a state where Bealomondore and Librettowit could help her stand.

They made a seat with their hands between them and carried her up the steps to the wooden porch of the boat stop.

Four weathered doors stood across the front. Labels on faded signs read Store, Wash, Sleep, Eat.

A woman stood at the door marked Sleep. Her long hair fell from a plethora of combs stuck around her crown. Once upon a time, her dress might have been a party gown.

"She can't walk?" The woman didn't wait for an answer but grimly motioned them to come in the door she held. "Bring her in here." She ignored Tipper but examined the two men carrying her with great interest.

Tipper looked over the dim interior of the front room. Disordered furniture appeared to be the leftovers of a parlor. A table with an open book served as the registration desk, and the stairs behind it probably led to beds. Four shabby chairs lined a low bar on the other side of the room. No wall hid the kitchen from view.

The most noticeable feature of the room sent a shiver skittering up Tipper's spine. Five mariones and three bisonbecks lounged on the scattered furniture.

She spoke to the lady proprietor in an undertone. "Your son said business is slow."

The proprietress sniffed. "Slow on the river. These farmers are hanging around, waiting for seed and other supplies to be delivered."

The tumanhofers carried Tipper over to an empty chair and helped her get settled.

Librettowit turned to the woman and bowed. "I am Trevithick Librettowit, librarian."

The woman preened under his courtly attention. Her face cracked with a miniscule smile, and she actually batted her eyelashes.

Tipper watched with fascination. She'd never thought of the wizard's librarian as a ladies' man. But the owner of the boat stop positively glowed at his attention. Librettowit showed no signs of being embarrassed by the woman's sudden coquettish stance. In fact, he looked like he didn't notice.

"My name's Edrina Posh."

Librettowit smiled, and Tipper decided that he did know the woman displayed an interest in a flirtation. His monstrous teeth did not show in this restrained smile, but definite approval shone from his eyes. He nodded slightly. Tipper wondered if she could reach him with her good foot and give him a kick.

"You'll be staying the night, won't you?" asked the predatory female.

Tipper didn't like her, and the men sitting so casually around the room seemed to be listening while trying to look like they were not.

"Of course," said Librettowit. "We will require two rooms."

"Right," said Edrina Posh. "I'll have the boys carry up your luggage."

Librettowit shook his head, looking sorry to disappoint her. "We have none."

Mistress Posh's eyebrows drew together. "It's not safe to leave valuables on your river craft. There are thieves in the vicinity."

"We have nothing of value to steal."

Her eyes narrowed for a fraction of a second, and then the smiling welcome returned to her face. "I assume you can pay."

Librettowit nodded.

She took his arm and guided him toward the desk. "Just sign your names in the book." She patted his thick arm. "We'll make you comfortable. It's our specialty."

20

In the Night

Bealomondore shifted the tray to one hand and tapped on the door to Tipper's room with the other. Taeda Bel opened the door.

"Is she awake?" he asked.

Taeda Bel nodded and opened the door wider. Tipper sat in a cushioned chair beside a large open window. Beyond, the river flowed quietly by. The setting sun reflected off the smooth surface, tingeing the water an unreasonable pink. Tree frogs chorused, welcoming the evening.

Bealomondore stood for a moment, capturing the vision in his mind. Tipper, framed by the window, composed an almost perfect painting. She stroked the small green dragon, who had curled himself comfortably in her lap. The contrasting colors made his fingers itch to pick up a brush. Wistfully, he gave up the longing to capture this moment on canvas.

He sighed. "I brought dinner for you and Taeda Bel."

Taeda Bel wrinkled her nose. "It smells like travelers' stew."

"It *is* travelers' stew."

"Will you keep Princess Tipper company?" Taeda Bel opened the door to leave. "I think Maxon and I will go out to eat."

Bealomondore nearly laughed out loud at the wide-eyed stare Tipper cast upon the little kimen.

"Out? Out where?" she asked.

"The fields." Taeda Bel spun in the doorway to face them. "There are enough vegetables in the wild foliage behind the boat stop to feed a whole kimen village. Want to come with us?"

"Not me," said Bealomondore. "I like travelers' stew."

"I like it too." Tipper wagged a finger at her kimen guard. "You be careful out there. Remember all those hideous snakes."

Rayn raised his head, stretched his neck toward the offering Bealomondore had brought, took a deep sniff, and sneezed. He flew to the kimen about to leave and landed by her feet. Taeda Bel tossed Tipper a cheeky grin and shut the door. Rayn had deserted her.

The tumanhofer put the tray on a round table and scooted it close to Tipper's hand. He then reopened the door for propriety's sake.

"Will you sit with me and eat?" asked Tipper.

"Yes, but I must confess this will be my second helping. The young man on the dock was correct in his assessment of his mother's skill in the kitchen."

Tipper took the bowl he handed her. "What did you do all afternoon while I slept?"

The tumanhofer glanced toward the hall and answered in hushed tones. "Tried to pry information out of those so-called farmers downstairs." He pulled up a wooden chair. "Librettowit didn't have any more success than I did, but we both agree those men aren't farmers waiting for seed."

"Did they refuse to talk to you?"

"No, they talked a great deal, but it was all stories, tall tales of life on a farm. Mice in the corn crib, raccoons raiding their crops, and weevils infesting their fields."

Tipper scrunched her brow and tilted her head. "What's wrong with that?"

"Well, first they monopolized the conversation, making sure we didn't get a chance to ask questions. And second, we haven't seen any corn crops. Librettowit says this isn't the right climate or the right terrain to grow corn."

"Did you get to ask any questions at all?"

"Librettowit did. I think he's better at ferreting out information than I am."

"What did he ask? What did they say?"

"He asked them if they'd seen any strangers lately."

"And?"

"One man, who came in to inquire about deliveries, said Edrina Posh and her son, Danto, were the only strangers around. Seems they just bought the boat stop from the previous owners a couple of weeks ago."

Tipper chewed and swallowed before asking another question. "That could be legitimate. But if they're new, then they wouldn't know if these men are truly farmers from the area. Did you ask them questions?"

Bealomondore nodded. "They were excessively busy, and that made an excellent excuse not to talk to us."

The whole situation at this boat stop didn't feel right to him. The men made him uneasy, but then the quest already had his teeth on edge.

Librettowit declared they were not on a quest, but their activities came together in the artist's head as a quest. What else would you call carrying statues to safety, searching for clues about the enemy, and trying to locate Verrin Schope?

Bealomondore wanted to abandon the whole adventure and go paint somewhere. But first he would deliver this beautiful emerlindian into her father's protective hands.

"Do you think you can travel tomorrow?" he asked.

"Yes, most definitely." Tipper reached for the glass on the tray. "Rayn said I needed sleep. A person healing fast tires like a person pulling weeds. I know a lot about pulling weeds. That was about the only thing Gladyme would let me do in her kitchen garden."

"It's hard to picture you working."

She harrumphed. "I washed clothes, changed beds, swept, and polished furniture. Do you remember the manor you found me in?"

"I was so excited about my chance to meet your father that it took a while for me to realize how shabby—" He felt his face burn. "I beg your pardon, Tipper."

She laughed, and he sighed in relief.

Tipper reached across the table and touched his hand. "You didn't worry much about offending me on our last quest."

He carefully removed his hand from under hers. "Well, you were a bit of a pest back then, weren't you?" He grinned at her, hoping she would take his comment in the context of a teasing brother. Her gasp turned into a ripple of laughter.

There. He'd cheered her up. Now he'd best leave before he said something tactless again. She befuddled his polished courtly air.

He stood. "Mistress Posh will probably come fetch your tray. Sleep well tonight. Tomorrow we'll go on down the river."

"You're going to pull the raft again?"

"No, Librettowit found someone who will bring us two donkeys. This so-called farmer was willing to part with them for some hard cash."

"If he's not a farmer, how can he get donkeys?"

Bealomondore shrugged.

"Why are we going downstream?"

"Toward the village of Selkskin. Librettowit suspects a painter there is your father."

"Isn't that too close to Ragar? I'd think it would be unwise to take the statues right back to where we began."

He chortled. "No, we are closer now than we will be in Selkskin. Didn't study maps growing up, did you?"

She shook her head.

"Well, no one knows we have the statues. The rumor is that the king has moved them to a safer location."

Bealomondore backed toward the open door. Tipper looked woebegone. He would have liked to comfort her, but he was alone with her in her bedroom, and his sympathy might be looked upon as an attempt to woo her.

"Don't worry, Princess. The kimens sent out scouts, and they know which route we are planning to take. It is not quite like searching for a boat in Librettowit's hollow. We'll find your parents."

He beat a hasty retreat. Not only did he not want to go on a dangerous quest, he did not want to become enamored with an emerlindian lady who had set her heart on another man.

A hand pressed against his chest. Thick, fetid breath assaulted his nostrils. A sharp, jabbing pain poked at his neck. Bealomondore awoke to find the ugly, snarling face of a bisonbeck two inches from his own.

"Silence," the rough man hissed, "or I'll put this dagger through your throat."

He grabbed the front of Bealomondore's nightshirt and lifted him out of his bed. The covers fell to the floor. Bealomondore tried to relax, relieved that the sharp blade no longer pressed against his neck.

Bealomondore whispered, "I've very little money, but you may have it all."

"Ha! We don't want your money. We heard you call that girl Princess. We'll get more money in ransom than you have in your pockets."

"Princess? That's a joke. What would a princess be doing away from the palace in Ragar, traveling on a puny raft? Why would she be staying here instead of in a fancy hotel? If she's a real princess, where are her ladies-in-waiting?"

"Shut up! The boss says we nab her and kill the rest of you. We do what the boss says."

"Your accent tells me you are not from around here. Your boss is mistaken about the girl, and you're going to go to a lot of trouble for nothing."

The bisonbeck returned his knife to the tumanhofer's neck. "I think your squawker box is right about here. If I don't carve it out the first time, I'll try again."

Bealomondore clamped his lips together. The bisonbeck nodded his approval. He carried his prize out the door, down the hallway, and up a flight of stairs and dumped him on the floor of a storage room. Two other bisonbecks grabbed him and tied him up. They propped him against a wall.

The bisonbeck who had captured Bealomondore left and came back in a few minutes with Librettowit. The librarian was trussed up and planted next to the younger tumanhofer. The three bisonbecks departed. A key scraped. The click of the lock punctuated their loss of freedom.

Librettowit leaned closer to Bealomondore. "There's still one outside the door."

"How do you know?"

"Listened to the footsteps. Only two went down the stairs."

"Do you think the son and Mistress Posh are in on this?"

"Of course."

"Why?" asked Bealomondore.

"I'm fairly sure these men were planted here by Odidoddex. They have an accent that Maxon says hints of their being from Baardack."

"Where are Maxon and Taeda Bel?"

Librettowit squirmed as he answered. "I saw them go out together. Rayn was with them."

"That was hours ago. They went to find food more to their liking."

Librettowit grunted, then pulled his hands out from behind him. He began untying his feet.

Bealomondore watched with amazement. "How'd you do that?"

"When you are a wizard's librarian for a century or two or three, you pick up some useful tricks." He finished freeing his feet. "Lean forward, and I'll untie your hands."

In another minute, they both stood, rubbing their wrists where the ropes had left chafed skin.

Bealomondore tilted his head toward the door and whispered, "That oaf said they were going to kill us."

"They would have killed us by now if they were going to."

"Not that I object, but why didn't they?"

"Probably wanted to use one of us as a messenger. Or they are hoping they could get a ransom for us as well."

"I distinctly heard him say 'kill you.'"

"Probably just wishful thinking on the thug's part."

"What do we do now?" asked Bealomondore.

"Do you have your sword?"

The artist looked down at his nightshirt and shook his head. "Not at the moment."

"Harrumph! What good is a sword if you don't take it with you?"

Bealomondore started to protest, but a noise from the hallway silenced him. A thud on the landing followed a grunt from their guard. He tensed as unnatural quiet conjured up all sorts of dire images in his mind.

Librettowit signaled for him to step aside. Bealomondore mimicked the older tumanhofer's actions. Picking up a leg from a broken chair, he stood with his back to the wall beside the door. It would seem he and the librarian were ready to bash the head of anyone who came in the room.

21

Sword of Valor

Bealomondore raised his table-leg club and then stretched to raise it higher. He didn't think he had the height to whack a bisonbeck on the head. The dark room added to his apprehension. His eyes had adjusted to the light, but he saw only a shadow where he thought his friend now stood.

He didn't want to accidentally clobber Librettowit or Edrina Posh should she be the one to come through the door. He and the librarian would both swing their meager weapons in the same direction. Would the clubs collide, bounce off each other, and do no harm to the villain? Would he miss and knock out Librettowit? Would Librettowit miss and knock him out? They should have thought of a better plan.

A key rattled the lock. The doorknob turned. The door eased open and stopped.

The light in the hall must have gone out. The shadows deepened. A cloud over the crescent moon? Or was the evil lurking outside the door overcoming shades of gray to bring a black triumph?

Bealomondore readied his weapon to strike.

"Down here," Maxon whispered from beside his ankle.

Bealomondore jumped, dropped his club to his side, and put his other hand on his heart. "You scared ten years off my life."

Librettowit leaned through the open entry. "The guard is out."

Bealomondore pulled the door all the way open. The oversize bulging mass on the floor could easily be the crumpled figure of a bisonbeck.

He looked from the fallen guard to the tiny man. "You did that?"

Maxon nodded. "It's an old kimen trick. I'll tell you about it later. Go get dressed and ready to move. Rayn, Taeda Bel, and I are going to free Tipper."

"I'll go with you."

"No, you're too big. Meet us at the raft."

Librettowit put his hand on Bealomondore's arm and propelled him around the unconscious guard.

Bealomondore wrinkled his nose at the odor that arose from the body. "Is he dead?"

Librettowit spoke hurriedly. "No, knocked out. And he won't see very well when he comes to."

"Why?"

"The kimens have the ability to produce a flash of light. I presume they did this to the guard. He stumbled and probably hit his head. The light by itself wouldn't render him unconscious."

Bealomondore didn't think that was a good explanation. "They wouldn't clobber him?"

Librettowit let out an exasperated sigh. "Or they could have clobbered him."

"Librettowit, I don't like bringing this up again, but the man who captured me said he was ordered to kill us. Ordered! I'm a bit nervous about wandering around this inn. At any turn we might run into one of them, and this time they might not imprison us."

The librarian sighed and turned to look directly in the artist's eyes. "He said that with the purpose of intimidating you. He wants you to be afraid."

Bealomondore thought about this as they crept down the stairs. The bisonbeck's threat had indeed intimidated him.

"Come on," said the older tumanhofer. They reached the second floor. Librettowit leaned closer. "We're almost out."

Bealomondore took a deep, steadying breath. "I should go help rescue Tipper."

"Let Rayn and the kimens handle it. They won't make any noise, and they can be practically invisible."

Bealomondore grumbled. "Tumanhofers are next to the smallest of the high races and yet we're too big?"

"Don't be affronted. They know what they're doing. Go get dressed, and this time remember to strap on that sword. Don't talk yourself into doing something noble like rescuing Tipper. And don't scare yourself silly by thinking there is an enemy hiding in every shadow."

The sound of footsteps below separated the two tumanhofers, each bolting for his own room.

Once in his quarters, Bealomondore made sure his curtains were closed before he lit a candle. The soft light almost took away the dread that filled him. Unfortunately, it exposed the mess he'd made before turning in. He began to gather his things.

He picked up a sketch of Tipper, framed by the window, rolled it, secured it with a ribbon tie, and thrust it into a hollow in his cape. He pulled out the sword and belt, threw them on the bed he'd been snatched from, and began searching for clothes suitable for a nighttime escape.

Dressed in appropriate dark but stylish attire, Bealomondore finished off his ensemble by fastening the sword belt around his waist. He pulled the sword from its sheath and gave it a close inspection, squinting at the hilt. Along the silver cross guard, an etching looked like words. He moved closer to the candle and let the light shine on the delicate lines.

He whispered the words, "The Sword of Valor slays only the wicked."

Standing erect, Bealomondore made several passes through the air. He liked the swishing sound. He sheathed the sword. " '...slays only the wicked.' I hope that means I won't accidentally slice myself into bits."

Maxon came to retrieve him just as he reached for the door. Startled, Bealomondore jerked his hand away, allowing the kimen to swing it wide. The kimen's clothing barely showed. He'd darkened it for sneaking around the boat stop.

"What is taking you so long?" the kimen fussed. "Everyone else is at the raft and ready to depart."

"Donkeys?"

"No donkeys."

Bealomondore followed Maxon. They passed the stairway that led to the registration desk and the common room of the boat stop. The voices from below reminded the artist to be extra quiet. At the end of the hall, they came to a second stairwell, narrow and dark. The kimen brightened his clothing and went first, giving off enough light for Bealomondore to safely follow.

When only three more steps remained before them, Maxon extinguished his light. Bealomondore froze. He listened and heard someone moving around in the room directly ahead.

Someone else walked in, and his voice gave him away. "Edrina, Bosk and Drowder want more food."

Bealomondore muffled his sigh of disappointment. He'd liked the young man on the dock, but Danto's friendly tone had changed as he addressed the other person in the back room. And what civilized son called his mother by her first name?

"Tell them they can wait until morning," said Edrina. "I'm not their servant."

The tone of Danto's voice changed again. He sounded fearful. "Do you think…"

Bealomondore cocked his head, trying to determine what could cripple this healthy young man's confidence.

"Do you think The Grawl will be with the others when they get here tomorrow?"

"Groddenmitersay didn't indicate he would be bringing Kulson's unit to this location. And even if he did, it is said The Grawl can't abide being in a building for more than a few minutes. He won't bother us. That is, unless someone has put your name on his list to exterminate."

"I would have preferred to kill these travelers rather than keep them for Groddenmitersay to interrogate."

"Bosk said wait, so we wait. Help me move this crate to the kitchen."

Bealomondore listened. Edrina and the young man grunted as they shoved a heavy object across the floor. The noises moved away from the stairwell, probably toward the door leading to the common room.

Danto groaned, and the scraping of wood against the stone floor ceased. "One of the bisonbecks could pick this up and haul it with no trouble. Let me go get one."

"They're busy," Edrina snapped. "And I don't like them anywhere near me."

"Why do you think Bosk wants to give these travelers over to Groddenmitersay? I didn't think there was anything special about them."

"Ha! And you think you're so smart. You need to learn to have sharp eyes."

Bealomondore fought down the urge to move closer and perhaps peek out of the stairwell. He wanted to see these two as they talked so calmly about turning them over. He wished he could mindspeak. He could hear what they said well enough, but what were they thinking?

Danto snorted. "What have you seen that I haven't?"

"I've seen them guard that emerlindian girl. And all of them wear clothes finer than any ordinary traveler. The librarian speaks with an accent. He's not from Chiril. And when I reached my hand into a pocket of one of their cloaks, my hand burned. Burned! I jerked it out fast enough, but I had to coat it with butter to ease the pain."

"But—"

"Enough of your stalling. Put your shoulder to this crate."

In a few moments, the sounds indicated they'd reached the other room. Maxon signaled, and Bealomondore followed him out the back door into an inky night.

22

Difficulties

Librettowit and Tipper had already boarded the raft. The princess sat on a box. Librettowit held his pole, ready to push away from the dock. Taeda Bel gripped her rope, holding it taut where she stood on the opposite bank. Maxon ran across this rope bridge from the raft to the shore in order to help her pull the bargelike craft.

Bealomondore snapped his mouth shut after witnessing this acrobatic feat and answered Librettowit's urging to grab the line he would use.

To get the flatboat around the end of the dock, Bealomondore would have to walk to the end and reach out over the river. The dark water did not look inviting to the land-loving tumanhofer. The thought of falling in and drowning quickened his movements. The sooner this task was done, the better.

He and the librarian did their best to minimize the thuds. Each tap against a piling sounded like a loud knock on a nearby door. Bealomondore dropped the rope and picked up an oar. He used that to keep the raft away from the dock as they maneuvered it to the end and around to open water.

He quietly put the oar back where he'd found it, then picked up his end of the rope. He had to scurry to get to the bank and the trodden path. The smooth surface of the bank testified that many shippers used barges to transport their goods. This further compounded the mystery as to why there had been no traffic other than their small party.

An owl hooted. Bealomondore jumped and glanced back toward the boat stop, thinking it a miracle that no one inside heard their departure.

Without speaking, the men and Taeda Bel guided the raft down the gently flowing river. The sliver of moon gave just enough light to keep him from stumbling.

The rough rope scratched his palms. He paused to dig out the gloves from his hollow and put them on. They came to a bend in the river, and both water and land sloped downward. Now rather than coaxing the raft along with tugs, he had to hold it back. He needed the gloves more than ever.

"Watch out!" Tipper exclaimed.

Bealomondore looked at the path in front of him. Nothing obstructed his way.

"Behind you," she shouted.

He wheeled around and saw a bisonbeck bearing down on him. He dropped the rope, threw back his cape, and pulled out his sword.

Having practiced with the kimens and Librettowit, Bealomondore knew a little more about how to stand and position the weapon. He braced himself to counter the assault, but the Sword of Valor still did most of the work. For the moment, the exertion to keep alive drove away any marvel he felt over how the sword slashed and parried.

Rayn flew from Tipper to give him aid. He appeared as a black shadow and spit caustic saliva into the bisonbeck's face. Bealomondore managed to make a few scores with his sword. His opponent folded over a wounded arm with a gasp.

"More coming," screeched Tipper.

Bealomondore knocked the wounded man into the river and backed away. The raft bumped over the choppy water, taking Librettowit and the princess farther downstream. Bealomondore ran to close the distance, then turned to confront those barreling toward him.

A bisonbeck reached him first, and by sheer luck, he managed to trip the brute into the river. The three mariones coming were shoulder to shoulder. How could he deal with three at once? He raised his sword and hoped his face looked resolute instead of petrified. He sliced his weapon sideways but only ripped one man's sleeve. Bealomondore danced backward and swung again. Out of the corner of his eye, he glimpsed a globe of light skimming across the water.

In another second, Maxon, quick and definitely wet, buzzed around the attackers' feet. It took Bealomondore a moment to realize the kimen had a ball of twine. Maxon tangled the mariones' legs together, severely restricting their footwork. They fell to the ground in a heap. One marione pulled out a knife and sliced through his bonds.

A squeal from Tipper caused Bealomondore to run down the bank to where the raft dipped and swayed in the water. The flow of the River Hannit ran faster as the land slanted more steeply. Librettowit desperately tried to use the pole to steady them, but the rushing water defied him. Taeda Bel held on to her rope. As Bealomondore watched, she fell on her face. The raft dragged her along the path.

"Let go," Bealomondore yelled as he searched for the rope he'd dropped. He spotted it thrashing in the water, out of his reach.

Taeda Bel now lay in the dirt. Her rope trailed in the water as well. Librettowit shoved his pole against a rock and kept them from crashing. Tipper clung to the raft. The box she had used as a seat was nowhere in sight. Bealomondore ran to catch up.

A great weight hit his back, and he fell forward. His sword flew from his grasp. Bealomondore rolled, pushing the marione off. He scrambled on all fours toward his weapon, but the man tackled him again. This time the tumanhofer used his feet and fists, kicking and hitting at the bigger marione. His assailant easily held him down.

Realizing he'd never defeat this stronger opponent in hand-to-hand combat, he grasped for memories of boys he'd seen scrapping in the streets. *Think,* he demanded of himself.

He grabbed one of the marione's ears, twisting and pulling. The marione yelled with pain. The tumanhofer got his other arm free and poked his finger in the howling man's eye. Bealomondore squirmed loose and dove for the sword.

He grabbed the hilt, rolled on to his back, and sliced at the marione as the creature leaned over to grab Bealomondore. He gained his feet before the surprised marione came at him again, this time with a long, curved knife. Rayn swooped in and spit on the man's face. The marione growled and wiped at his forehead with his empty hand.

Bealomondore hopped backward. The curved blade bothered him. *That looks wicked. It looks sturdier than my blade. It looks like I'd better run.*

But running was not an option at the moment. The marione would just as soon stab him in the back as in the front.

Rayn bombarded the stout enemy once more. The saliva landed on his jacket. For a moment the man's attention wavered. Bealomondore managed a thrust that pierced his clothing but apparently did not hit flesh.

The marione swung his arm at a height that would decapitate his adversary, but Bealomondore tucked himself into a somersault position and bowled into the man's legs. He sprang to his feet and saw his foe rising. While the marione was off balance, Bealomondore kicked him in the face, sending him careening into the river.

"Maxon!" he called.

"Here." The kimen approached, allowing his clothes to resume a soft glow.

"Weren't there two more?"

"I secured the twine that holds them."

Bealomondore bent at the waist, his hands on his knees, and panted. At the moment he didn't have the strength or the breath to tackle another foe.

The light from Maxon shone on the hilt of his sword, which he still held in his right hand.

The kimen squinted and peered at the cross guard. "You've scratched your fine sword."

"No, it's words." Bealomondore bent over to point out the inscription but paused. "That's odd."

"What?" Maxon leaned closer, and his light flickered over the shiny silver.

"It changed. It says, 'Grip the Sword of Valor to protect the innocent.' Before it said, 'The Sword of Valor slays only the wicked.'"

Maxon leaned back to tilt his head up and look into Bealomondore's eyes. "That wizard gave you the sword?"

"Yes."

"Well, it's teaching you how to fight, and I suppose it's teaching you words about being a knight."

"Knight?" Bealomondore's voice cracked. He stared at the kimen. What kind of craziness was this? "I don't want to be a knight. I've already got a perfectly satisfactory occupation."

Maxon said nothing.

Bealomondore managed to stand erect, but he still hauled air in and out of his starving lungs. It was hard to talk, but his anger pushed the words out. "I dropped the sword when that marione plowed into me. The inscription must mean hold on to the sword."

"And if you were training to be a knight, you would be admonished to hold tight to valor."

"I dropped the sword. That's all."

Maxon smiled, looking wise and self-assured.

Annoyed by the patience also exhibited on Maxon's face, the artist averted his gaze and peered into the gloomy night. "We must catch up to Librettowit and Tipper. Will you go check on Taeda Bel? The last time I saw her, she'd fallen."

"I'm coming." She approached them from downstream, a sodden librarian at her side.

"What happened? Where's Tipper?"

Librettowit shook his arms, and water showered from his coat sleeves. "My pole broke. I fell in the river. Rayn returned to Tipper. We best send Taeda Bel and Maxon ahead to keep an eye on her."

The two kimens raced off.

Bealomondore took a minute to look at his tumanhofer friend. He couldn't see much more than his outline. "Are you all right?"

"Yes." Librettowit turned downstream. "We better get going. Hurry, please. I'm nervous about the girl."

Tipper watched the attack from her perch on the box. She could only yell a warning to Bealomondore. A dip of the raft threw Tipper down on her knees. Then she couldn't see Bealomondore anymore. The water carried them too quickly away from the fight.

"Rayn, go find out what's happening."

The minor dragon objected.

"Go!" Tipper peeled him off her shoulder. "He needs help. I'm safe for now."

The dragon flew off, and Tipper flattened herself against the rough boards. Water splashed in her face.

The tumanhofer librarian stumbled and climbed back to his feet. He poled against a rock.

"Librettowit, can I help?"

"You can stay out of my way."

Tipper scanned the opposite bank and finally caught sight of Taeda Bel. "Taeda Bel's going to be hurt."

"Not much I can do about that right now."

"Here comes Rayn and Bealomondore."

"Good." Librettowit puffed between each word. "I can use some help."

"Taeda Bel's fallen."

"For the love of tangonut crème pie, I don't need an update on everyone's doings."

"Bealomondore's been attacked again."

She heard a snap and a splash. The raft twirled, and she saw Librettowit's head bob to the surface in the water. Scrambling to the side, she tried to reach him. The current carried her away.

"Stay with the raft, Princess," the tumanhofer called. "We'll join you downstream." He swam toward the bank but turned to yell at her once more. "And stay out of trouble."

Tipper clung to the boards with her hands clamped to the edge. Her long legs allowed her to tuck her toes over the opposite side, and she curled her feet under as best she could. Without Librettowit and his pole, the raft spun slowly around and around, dipping with the rapid water and bumping into rocks along the banks.

Tipper's injured foot and leg cramped, and she had to shift to allow the muscles to relax. Queasiness warned her that her body did not take well to the combination of a dizzying ride and the pain in her leg.

Rayn called to her from upriver. She heard him in her mind first, but as he came closer she also heard his concerned chirps. He landed on her back.

"I'm okay," she told him. "Are the others all right?"

His answer reassured her, and his healing touch calmed her stomach within minutes. The flow of the River Hannit slowed. She rolled over on her back and watched the stars for some time while her racing heart calmed down. The chill of the night seeped through her damp clothes. Shivering, she dug in the hollows of her cape and found several blankets. She made a nest and buried herself within the dry folds. Rayn turned from green to purple and cuddled under her chin.

"The others should catch up soon," she whispered to her crooning dragon. She wasn't all that confident they'd find her, but she was too tired to fret. "Wake me when you see them. I don't like being alone." She closed her eyes. They popped open again when Rayn objected. "Of course I'm not really alone when I have you. I beg your pardon. Good night."

A niggling worry poked at her drowsy thoughts. She stroked Rayn. "I do hope there is no more rough water. We'd hear it, wouldn't we? I can't stay awake, but what if—"

A sound rumbled in the wee dragon's chest. She felt the vibration against her neck. "Oh, thank you, Rayn. I trust you to keep an eye on things. Good night."

23

Tangonut Crème Pie

Hollee skipped up the bank and slid down. Exposed roots sticking out of the steep slope showed how far the river could rise. She glanced at Wizard Fenworth. He still slept. She'd gotten very good at recognizing him, even when he was in his woodiest state. At the moment he looked like a log that had tumbled downriver and lodged against another spinet tree. A bossvetch vine grew over both the log and the real tree.

She stopped midway up the incline as voices reached her ears. She jumped down, poked Fenworth, and said, "Someone's coming."

The wizard snorted but did not wake up. Hollee zipped along the path beside the river and spotted two tumanhofers and two kimens. She raced back and bounced on the log that was Fenworth.

"Tipper's not with them. You said Tipper would need our help, but she's not with them."

A bit of crackling and popping accompanied the emergence of the wizard from his arboreal state. He shook the vine loose from his arms and stretched.

"Confound it, Hollee." He frowned at the kimen and removed her from where she clung to his robes. "I was having a good dream."

"You told me to wake you when they came."

"So I did. Should have thought that one out more before issuing such a silly request." He watched as the small party rounded the corner and came into view. "There you are, Librettowit. I've got something for you."

Fenworth stood, pulled out the brownish fabric of his wizard mantle, and plunged his arm into one of the hollows. He carefully removed an object.

"Tangonut crème pie, my friend. I sensed you were in need of its supportive qualities." He handed the dessert to Librettowit, whose face showed appreciation for the offering.

"No need to share," continued the wizard as he produced two more pies from his clothing. He handed one to Bealomondore and the other to the kimens. "For myself, I have grasshopper pie. Hollee and I have had our fill of tangonut crème pie for now."

"Where've you been?" asked Librettowit.

"On a beach in the land of Baardack. We taught the natives to bake pies and learned a great deal about this King Odidoddex and The Grawl."

"That should be helpful." Librettowit sat on a rock, licking his lips and barely acknowledging Fenworth's presence.

Bealomondore looked at his pie, then studied the terrain downstream. "We've misplaced Princess Tipper. Even the kimens could not find her last night. I think we should keep walking."

Maxon and Taeda Bel sat on the ground, cross-legged, with the pie between them. Taeda Bel glanced at Bealomondore. "We haven't had breakfast."

"Bad idea," said Fenworth. "Can't go questing with no sleep *and* no food. Maybe no food, if you've had a full night's rest. Maybe no sleep, if you've eaten your pie. But definitely not both. And besides, Tipper didn't float down this branch of the River Hannit."

Bealomondore stared at the wizard. "She had to. We tossed a stick in the river where it split in two. In fact, we tried three times. All the sticks followed the current of this branch. This one is the stronger, wider, most logical choice."

Even though Bealomondore had not seen the wizard cut the pie he held, Fenworth lifted a piece and handed it to Hollee, shaking his head. "Logic. Logic is a funny thing. Works when things are progressing logically and is totally undependable when variances poke their long noses into the regular way of things."

Librettowit spoke around a mouthful of gooey pie. "Don't think you can say that variances possess noses with which they poke."

"Ah!" Fenworth looked fondly at his librarian, then winked at Bealomondore. "I've missed him, you know. Did you note how he did not end the sentence with a preposition? It's a good trait in a learned man, the ability to speak a sentence properly arranged. But the variance with a nose is a figure of speech, not meant to be taken literally."

Bealomondore tensed, trying to control his frustration. "How do you know she's gone down that other branch?"

"I wouldn't be a very good wizard if I couldn't pinpoint the location of a damsel in distress."

The younger tumanhofer nearly dropped his pie. "Distress? Tipper's in distress?"

Fenworth shook his head again and settled himself on a thick root extending from the spinet tree. "Figure of speech. Damsel? Yes. Distress? Only moderately so. We'll have plenty of time to backtrack and take the correct path." He raised a big slice of pie to his mouth, but before he bit into it, he gave Bealomondore a scowl. "Eat your breakfast."

Tipper shifted in her nest of blankets, trying to find a more comfortable position. She breathed in deeply, enjoying the serenity of her surroundings, before opening her eyes. Water sloshed against the sides of the raft, and the air smelled of wet riverbank, the dirt sodden and somehow fresh. Birds and insects overindulged in chattering their early morning messages. The warmth of the sun bathed her face, and her dark blankets had absorbed the first rays. The chill of the night vanished, her covers felt toasty and comforting, and the idea of being lazy enticed her to stay cocooned and not bother with questing today. The only sensation that disturbed her was pressed against her elbow. The raft was not a downy mattress.

Rayn! Her eyes flew open, and she sat up. She searched the blankets and then the shore. Where was the little dragon?

Roots from a tree entangled the front of her flatboat. One corner wedged into a thick mud bank. She stood. Since Paladin had first given the sad and puny dragon into her care, Rayn had always been on her or beside her when she first woke.

"Rayn! Rayn!"

"Is this what you are looking for?"

She whipped her head toward the sound, trying to find the person who spoke. If he hadn't moved, she doubted she would have seen him. Just six feet away, half hidden in a bush, a creature rested. His size and ugly features alarmed her. But more frightening than his wild animal appearance, he held Rayn. The unknown man-animal pinched the dragon's tail between his thumb and forefinger. Rayn's drooping gray body hung from his meaty hand.

Tipper gasped. She looked from the tiny dragon to the beast. His large face had some of the characteristics of a grawlig. He was bigger and dressed better, and his eyes, though cold, glimmered with intelligence. His speech sounded much more like one of the high races.

"I decided not to eat him."

Tipper stuck out her chin. "Give him to me."

Promptly, the beast flipped the little dragon toward her. Tipper snatched Rayn from the air. She held him close under her chin, then lowered her hands to study his limp form.

As she stroked his belly with her finger, Rayn twitched. "He's alive."

"Of course," said the creature. "I didn't mean to kill him. If I had, he would be dead."

"What did you do to him?"

"Nothing but catch him as he flew by."

"He's hurt."

"Perhaps I squeezed too hard."

The beast's steady breathing and his unwavering gaze teased the fine hair on her neck. She turned away from his staring eyes, then whisked back. Better to face the abomination.

Tipper almost asked what he was but caught herself in time to say, "Who are you?"

"I'm called The Grawl."

"Where do you come from?"

"North." An unpleasant smile twisted his lips. His eyes remained distant. "And who are you?"

"My name is Tipper Schope."

"And where do you come from?"

"Upriver."

He laughed at that. The hard, loud noise did nothing to calm Tipper's trepidation.

He stood, and Tipper realized he must be over seven feet tall. He didn't have the bulk of a bisonbeck. He wasn't flabby, as grawligs tended to be.

"Trying to figure out my heritage, aren't you?"

"I'm sorry. I didn't mean to be impolite."

He laughed again, rattling her this time as much as he had the first. How could a sound produced by humor be so unsettling?

The Grawl narrowed his eyes. "Few people bother to concern themselves with manners around The Grawl."

"That isn't as it should be."

"But it is so, and I find no reason to dwell on it."

He reached his hand toward her. "May I steady you as you come ashore?"

"No, I was told to stay on the raft. Someone is coming for me."

He withdrew his hand. "Then I shall keep you company. I am curious to meet your companions."

Tipper sat down on the pile of blankets, cradling the unconscious Rayn. She preferred to not have company but didn't think it safe to say so.

24

Bridge

With her stomach full of grasshopper pie, Hollee skimmed over the ground at the speed she loved. Taeda Bel and Maxon easily kept up with her. Some people believed that kimens actually flew. The kimens, by agreement, neither confirmed nor denied the assumption. Hollee delighted in withholding the secret from the other races. While zipping ahead, the kimens visited, catching up on all that had happened during the time they'd been apart.

The tumanhofers and the wizard trudged up the trail at a sedate pace. With the others far behind, the kimens talked with expressive and rapid gestures. After covering the less heady subjects of conversation, they slowed their speech if not their gait. A more serious topic deserved attention.

"What did you learn about Odidoddex?" asked Taeda Bel.

Reluctant to delve into the problem, Hollee sighed. "Not many country-folk like him. He has a larger following among city dwellers."

"Why?"

"He deliberately curried the favor of the city population to strengthen his power."

"How?"

"He forced the farmers to overproduce and drained the land of what is needed to keep the soil rich. Now their farms grow lots of weeds, and they only get a puny harvest."

Maxon shook his head. "Now that would make wise farmers mad. Very mad indeed."

"It makes *all* the farmers angry. And Odidoddex sent his army to confiscate all the best animals. That left the people with no breeding stock.

Now the cities are demanding he keep up the largesse, and he has decided to plunder Chiril. It is uncertain whether he plans to overthrow our king or take the goods and run."

Taeda Bel tugged on Hollee's arm. "What about The Grawl?"

She shuddered. "I've seen him up close. He's horrible."

"But what is he?"

Hollee hesitated. She'd heard rumors, but she didn't like to repeat things she didn't know for sure. "I don't think anyone really knows. Some say he was birthed by a woman of the urohm race, but the father was a grawlig from a marauding band. The woman was captured and ill-used. She died giving birth, and the raiders abandoned him in a village in Baardack."

"They raised him?" asked Taeda Bel.

"Not exactly." Sadness for a small, ugly child filled Hollee's heart. "The legend says that the men of the village used him like a hunting dog. It was there that he became known as The Grawl.

"He was slow to talk, and they thought he was little more than an animal. When he grew older, his intellect blossomed, and he outshone them all. They turned on The Grawl and threw him out."

"That's distressing." Maxon slowed their pace. "I wonder if they would have treated a hunting dog as badly. Fear often overwhelms compassion."

Taeda Bel brushed a tear from her cheek. "Where did he go from there?"

"That's the point where folktales take over." Hollee spread her hands out in front of her in a questioning gesture. "There's no telling which ones are true and which aren't. The common theme is that he hunts people down for money. That if one could find his hoard, one would behold a fortune greater than any other."

"That sounds like the typical exaggeration of a legend." Maxon pointed ahead. "We've come to the fork in the river."

Hollee looked over her shoulder. "Wizard Fenworth does not like to get his feet wet."

"But he's a bog wizard, isn't he?" Maxon asked. "He should be accustomed to damp."

"He says that's exactly why he doesn't like to be soaking wet."

A wide grin spread across Maxon's face. "His librarian is rather fond of the water. But Bealomondore can't swim."

Taeda Bel frowned. "I hope they don't take forever getting across. I'm worried about Tipper."

"Why don't you go ahead?" Hollee gave her friend's arm a pat. "We'll catch up to you."

Taeda Bel jumped and did a somersault. "Come as quick as you can." She charged into the water and was on the other bank, waving good-bye, before the wind could catch up. With a hop and a twirl, she darted off.

Soon the wizard and the tumanhofers approached the spot where the two kimens waited to make the crossing. Wizard Fenworth leaned on his walking staff as he tramped up the hill and sat down as soon as he got to a sizable boulder. He took off his wizard's hat and fanned himself.

After a moment, he jammed the hat back on his head and frowned at the water. The flow here was more sedate than upstream. "How do you think we should ford the river, Wit?"

"Swim," said the librarian as he took a seat next to Fenworth.

"You can, but I don't care to get my feet wet. Swimming would definitely get my feet wet and other parts of my anatomy as well."

Librettowit shrugged and pulled a flagon of water from one of his hollows. He took a deep draw from the flask.

"A bridge?" Fenworth pulled on his beard. A caterpillar crawled out and away from his fingers.

Librettowit shook his head. "It would take too long. We really ought to see what that princess is up to."

"A simple gateway then?"

Hollee clapped her hands and nodded. "I like that idea. I like the sticky feel of going through a gateway. And I like the lights."

Again Librettowit shook his head. "Are you just going to leave gateways dotting the land? You'd have to dismantle it. Doesn't take long to make one, especially if you have helpers, but you must admit that taking one apart can be tricky."

Fenworth laid his staff across his knees and glared at the River Hannit. "I could whirl us across. Do it all the time. Hollee used to get motion sickness, but now she likes whirling almost as much as gateways."

The little kimen nodded so hard she bounced on the spot where she stood.

"And how much whirling have you been doing?" Librettowit examined his wizard. "You look a little worse for wear. Whirling requires a great deal of kinesthetic energy and more brainpower. You'll wear yourself out, and then where would we be?"

Fenworth looked away. Hollee had been with the wizard long enough to recognize the look on his face. Something astonishing was about to happen. She followed the line of his gaze and promptly saw something that only the wizard could do.

The roots of a nearby tree stretched toward the water. New growth pushed out of the old, and pale green tendrils snaked across the bank. Soon a mass of tangled roots stretched halfway over the river.

Maxon ran to the edge of the bank and placed a foot on the half-assembled bridge.

Hollee shrieked. "Don't!"

Maxon jerked back as Fenworth's head whipped around to see why Hollee had interrupted him.

"Silly kimen," said the wizard. "Wait until it has finished growing. Your feet might be caught in the twisting new roots, and we'd have to cut you out. We are trying to make time, not waste it." He turned back to his project. "Now where was I?"

It took a minute or two for the growth to pick up speed. Hollee waited as patiently as she could. She twitched a bit and explained to the others that Wizard Fenworth worked better without interruptions.

"I know that, child," said the librarian with an even tone. "Best to play a game of solitaire or read a book while you wait."

Maxon and Bealomondore dealt out cards for a game of Rat Tail while Hollee flitted from bush to bush looking for a butterfly she'd seen earlier. She found it and danced with the green, orange, and blue insect until it flew away. Disgusted at her pretty playmate's departure, she stretched out on the ground and caught minnows in her quick hands. She released them and caught them again.

"A brainy fish," she whispered, "would not swim back here to get recaptured time and time again. You lot lose the cunning and crafty ribbon of honor."

A half hour later, a massive tangle of roots bridged the river. Fenworth stood, tapped his walking stick on the ground, and said, "Let's go."

He marched forward, leading a parade of two kimens and two tumanhofers across the root bridge.

On the other side, Librettowit took hold of Fenworth's sleeve, stopping him from continuing down the bank of the other river branch.

"Haven't you forgotten something, Wizard Fenworth?"

The old man tilted his head, scratched his beard, dislodging a clutch of ladybugs, leaned on his staff, and finally answered, "No, I don't believe I have."

He would have started downriver, but the librarian still held on to his sleeve. When Fenworth gave him an impatient stare, Librettowit cleared his throat and nodded toward the root bridge.

"Oh," said Fenworth. His eyebrows arched, his eyes widened, and he muttered, "Tut, tut. I don't believe I've ever seen such a thing growing across a river."

He took a long, studying look downstream and then paid just as much attention to the water flowing above the fork. His gaze fell back on the root structure he had provided.

"Well, someone must do something about that. The water is already backing up. This"—he waved his hand toward the bridge—"would soon make this second little river"—he waved his hand the other direction—"the main water route and reduce the first to a mere trickle. Tut, tut. Oh dear, oh dear. What do you suggest we do, Wit? Some kind of explosive? A fireball? I do love fireballs when they work properly. How about a small tornado or a herd of beavers? No, beavers wouldn't do. Confound it, man. You're the librarian. Can't you remember something you've read in a book that would do here?"

Librettowit raised his eyebrows and said nothing.

"What eats tender roots?" asked Fenworth. He put his hand on his chin and pondered the question.

Bealomondore stomped over to the bridge and kicked it. Nothing moved. He put his hands on his hips. "We can't stay here all day. Tipper is alone."

"Rayn is with her," said Maxon.

"And Taeda Bel has probably caught up with her as well," said Hollee.

Fenworth seemed not to hear them. "Who would profit from the unexpected boon of a root bridge?"

He continued to ponder.

"Aha!" Wizard Fenworth strode forward, tapped his staff on the roots closest to him, and pointed to the other side.

The roots retreated, pulling back into the tree, disassembling the bridge much faster than they had formed it.

Fenworth crossed his arms over his chest and observed the process with pleasure. "The backward spell. Plain and simple. Nothing to it."

He turned on his heel and hiked along the faint trail beside the smaller river. "Very good, very good. Let's get moving now. Princess Tipper is getting impatient with us, I'm sure."

25

Confrontation

The Grawl sat a little higher on the bank of the river than before. He'd moved away from the emerlindian girl. Her smell unsettled him. He found the sweetness of her base odor unpleasant, and the thin overlay of acrid fear irritated him further. Ironic, since his main purpose in staying was to watch her squirm.

He'd left Kulson and his crew to do this work on the River Hannit. Groddenmitersay had given him another assignment, one that suited his solitary nature. Fourteen days ago, he'd helped a unit headed by Bosk overtake the boat stop. Since then, he'd removed freighters from their vessels on the river, dispatching the men and allowing their boats to float away.

He chortled when he thought of the consternation developing as more and more barges arrived at the town of Flat Morgan with no people on board. Expressions of puzzlement and unease on the faces of the high races amused him. He knew they conjured up all sorts of scenarios to explain what they saw.

Most of the outrageous speculation outdid the truth in every way. No quiss swam the River Hannit. No bands of wild grawligs raided travelers. Just him. One Grawl, perfectly capable of creating chaos without the help of any of the low races. He didn't need assistance from Kulson and his boorish soldiers either.

And he didn't covet any position of power among the high races. Totally self-sufficient he was. His indifference to both high and low races gave him the kind of power no one but The Grawl could acquire. He paused a moment to contemplate how perfectly in control he was at this moment. The feeling gave him much pleasure.

Two tumanhofers and two kimens traveled with the girl. He'd watched during the night as the bumbling swordsman and the nimble kimen foiled the efforts of three mariones and two bisonbecks. Where five men failed, one Grawl would succeed.

The sword interested The Grawl. He would wait until the emerlindian's company arrived. Then he would take the measure of these strange companions and perhaps take the sword.

Tipper held Rayn close to her heart and prayed for him to wake up. She glanced up at The Grawl. He didn't seem to be watching her at the moment.

His presence unnerved her. He just sat, but even that was unnatural. He'd only moved once in the hours since she'd opened her eyes. She'd had to get up, stretch, pace a bit, then sit down again. Her foot hurt, but not as much as her aching heart. Rayn might die.

She'd rearranged the blankets, washed her hands and face, combed her hair, and a hundred other things to make the time pass. Or at least it seemed so. Perhaps she'd done only a half a dozen things and only minutes had passed. No, the sun was almost straight overhead. Most of the morning had been spent under the eye of The Grawl.

She tucked Rayn into her pocket, then took him out again. She smoothed a piece of cloth in the sunshine and put him there to rest when she thought he felt cold. She wiped him with a damp rag when she thought he felt hot. His little chest rose and fell. Occasionally his tail twitched. She wondered if Wulder cared as much as she did about the life of a minor dragon. Would He do something to help?

Her anxiety over Rayn compounded her lack of patience. She wanted Wizard Fenworth and Librettowit here because they had helped so much when her father was ill and when Beccaroon was injured. She wanted Paladin because she always wanted Paladin. She even wanted the two men from the Insect Emporium because they knew so much about healing.

All she had was a beastly man called The Grawl.

Bealomondore trudged in front of the others. He'd taken the lead to set the pace. The others weren't exactly eager to keep up, but he felt an urgency to find Tipper. Surely they would catch up with the raft soon. This lower part of the River Hannit narrowed progressively. Soon the banks would be too close together for a craft to squeeze through. The shores had never been leveled for traffic, and rich vegetation made it hard to proceed.

With his eyes always searching through the leaves ahead, he finally caught glimpses of color that did not match the foliage. He quickened his step and called, "Tipper!"

The streak of grayish blue material shifted, and he heard her voice. "Bealomondore! Here! I'm here."

Tipper stood, hopped to the ground, and tramped through the underbrush. She held Rayn to her shoulder, his ghastly gray color like old porridge.

Tipper waved with her other hand. "Are the others with you?"

"Behind me. Taeda Bel is supposed to be here with you."

"I am!" The kimen dropped out of branches overhanging the bank.

Bealomondore stopped and stared at her. "What were you doing up in a tree?"

She pointed ahead, close to where the raft had run aground. "Because I didn't want him to know I was here until more of us arrived to deal with him."

Bealomondore squinted, trying to see the person who'd scared Taeda Bel. He spotted the outline of the creature and heard the swish of metal leaving leather at the same time. The weapon in his hand surprised him. The Sword of Valor pulled him beyond Tipper so that he stood between the two ladies and the beast rising from the shade.

Bealomondore heartily wished that Fenworth, Maxon, and Librettowit would appear behind him. But he'd outdistanced them. He'd stand his ground until reinforcements came. Hopefully they wouldn't stop for another slice of tangonut crème pie.

He lifted his sword to salute the brute that stood before him. "The Grawl, I presume."

He nodded. "I am The Grawl."

"I'm Graddapotmorphit Bealomondore of Greeston."

The Grawl bent his head in acknowledgment, as smoothly as any nobleman of the king's court. Bealomondore shook off the feeling of being boorish in comparison to the huntsman. The cultured tumanhofer rarely greeted gentlemen by brandishing a sword. In fact, he'd never before worn a sword to brandish. If he had to defend his lack of etiquette in this situation, he'd claim the sword took the initiative and brandished itself.

My mind is babbling. Where are the others? If I could mindspeak, I'd holler for help.

"I'm interested in your sword," said The Grawl. "I have a fine collection of unique weapons."

"It was given to me by a friend."

The Grawl took a step closer. "Then you wouldn't be willing to sell it?"

"Stay where you are." Bealomondore heard Tipper move behind

him. "Tipper, you go on upstream. Our friends are only a little behind me."

One moment The Grawl stood next to the raft. The next he loomed in front of Bealomondore. The girls behind him squealed. The Grawl's long arm reached the remaining distance, and his large hand grasped the top of Bealomondore's head, lifting him off his feet. The sword swung once, slashing through the underside of The Grawl's sleeve. The beast jerked from the pain but held on. His other hand captured Bealomondore's sword arm above the elbow.

The fingers squeezing his arm felt like they would meet around the bone. Bealomondore couldn't feel his own hand, but he heard the sword drop to the ground. The Grawl released his arm and lifted him higher by the grip on his head. Bealomondore heard a crack, and the intense pain in his head convinced him his skull would collapse. He ground his teeth. He couldn't stand much more. With a flick of his wrist, The Grawl sent him flying through the air. He sailed into darkness, knowing he'd land in the river.

The splash of her friend's body hitting the water galvanized Tipper. She rushed to pick up Bealomondore's sword, but The Grawl snatched it first. Seeing the rage on his face, she halted and scrambled back. The beast dropped the sword and roared. Clasping the hand that had gripped the hilt with the other, he dropped to his knees beside the river. Plunging his hand into the water, The Grawl let out a sigh of relief. Then he stood, towering over Tipper, his eyes bulging.

"The sword burned me." Fury boomed in his voice. "What type of metal is this?"

"I don't know." She scanned the river. She couldn't see the tumanhofer. Her voice quivered. "It's never hurt Bealomondore."

"There he is, Tipper." Taeda Bel jumped in the water and looked like a skipping stone as she sped to his side.

Tipper clutched Rayn's limp form against her shoulder. She had to follow. Stepping into the shallow water, she kept her eye on Bealomondore. She had to follow, had to reach him in time.

Her long skirt clung to her legs, constraining her stride, tripping her with every other step. Anger brought tears to her eyes but gave her the strength to forge on.

He needed help. She would get there.

Taeda Bel struggled to turn Bealomondore over where he floated facedown. Tipper arrived at last. Tucking Rayn in a pocket, she managed to flip her friend's body.

She jerked around at the sound of splashing. It wasn't The Grawl but Librettowit and Maxon. And Hollee!

"He's hurt," she called. "The Grawl threw him."

Librettowit, Hollee, and Maxon passed her. They surrounded Bealomondore and helped her support his body with their hands.

Tipper looked to the shore and saw The Grawl standing erect and glaring at Wizard Fenworth. As she watched, Fenworth grew taller, until his height matched the huntsman's. The Grawl withdrew a step, not as if he would flee but as if readying himself to spring.

The sword left the ground and landed solidly in the old wizard's hand.

"Go," said Fenworth, pointing the Sword of Valor. "I don't have the time to deal with you now. Go!"

The Grawl sprang sideways, landing among the foliage above the embankment. Tipper heard a crash of splintering branches and tearing limbs, then nothing. She knew he had gone, but she heard no further noise announcing his retreat. Still, the heavy presence that had terrified her all morning no longer permeated the forest.

Librettowit and the kimens pulled Bealomondore's body across the river, toward the raft. Fenworth strode through the underbrush to reach the flatboat. His size diminished with each step. Tipper put Rayn on the pile of blankets and helped hoist Bealomondore onto the wooden barge. Fenworth knelt behind him and touched his neck.

The wizard leaned back, sighed, and shook his head. "This is no way for an artist to die."

26

Life or Death?

Tipper wailed, "No-oo!"

Reaching for the wizard's arm, she searched the tumanhofer for some sign of life. Bealomondore couldn't be dead. She clutched Fenworth's sleeve and shook it. "Isn't he alive? Fenworth? Fenworth, do something."

"He's not breathing, but he's still alive. Don't have one of your excitable fits, Tipper. You've been doing so well." The wizard went back to wagging his head. "Tut, tut. Oh dear, oh dear."

Fenworth carefully straightened Bealomondore's arms and legs. "The Grawl has not treated our friend as a decent tumanhofer should be treated." He sat down, cross-legged, at the unconscious man's head. "Could use some help from that dragon of yours, Tipper."

"He can't." Tipper bent over, dripping water onto the blankets and splashing the minor dragon as well. "He's unconscious. That Grawl grabbed him."

Fenworth looked sharply where Tipper pointed. "Oh my! I don't like that color. Hold him, Tipper. He'll recover more quickly in your hands."

She hoisted herself onto the raft and cradled Rayn in her arms.

The wizard pointed at Hollee. "I'm going to need preparations from my hollows."

He stood and took off his robe. Stepping onto the shore, he spread his cloak inside out over some bushes. "Librettowit, she's going to need your help identifying the objects I call for."

Librettowit waded to the shore with Hollee. Fenworth came back to his patient and took up his position at Bealomondore's head. He turned the tumanhofer's neck so that his mouth pointed to the side of the raft. "Wit, I need that thingamajig for air in, water out."

The librarian nodded and murmured something to Hollee. She dove into one hollow as he reached in another.

"Tipper, I need you to hold his chin this way. But stay clear of his mouth. Our friend has swallowed some of the river." Fenworth tapped his patient's stomach. "Maxon, jump and land with both feet right here."

The kimen did as he was told.

"Once more," said Fenworth.

The second pounce produced the contents of Bealomondore's stomach. With a glare from Fenworth, the mess congealed and wiggled off the boards of the raft.

"Good, good. Now to get the water out of his lungs and some air in." He gestured to Librettowit.

The librarian pulled his hand out of a hollow with a contraption of two oval bulbs with four dangling tubes.

"Right on top, Fen. You haven't used it lately, have you?"

"No, not at all. Maxon, would you be good enough to carry things to and fro?"

Maxon raced to Librettowit and back.

Tipper sat on her heels and watched the wizard. Soon he had two tubes thrust into Bealomondore's mouth and one hanging over the edge of the raft. The two bulbs he held in his hands. He pumped the flexible orbs with his fingers. Water dripped into the river through one of the small hoses from his patient's mouth. Bealomondore's chest rose and sank.

"Very satisfactory," muttered the wizard. "Now a good cough or two, young man. That would help."

Maxon coughed.

Fenworth laughed. "Not you. Our patient."

The unconscious tumanhofer coughed.

"Very obliging," said Fenworth and pulled his equipment out, handing it to Maxon. "Take that back to Librettowit. He'll know how to clean it." He hollered over the departing kimen. "Wit, I need some admitriol ointment."

Fenworth pointed to a bluish smudge on Bealomondore's temple. "The thumb here and four more bruises coming up along the back of his head, under his hair. The Grawl has a powerful grip. Tut, tut. Could use it in more constructive endeavors. Oh dear, the folly of men."

With gentle movements, he felt the scalp and then ran fingers down Bealomondore's neck. "He's going to have quite a headache. He's got these five indentations around his noggin. The bone is shattered but not pushed in too deeply. His brain is all right, no damage to his thinking. Nasty headache, very nasty I should think. And The Grawl jarred his neck muscles in quite a beastly manner."

Tipper relaxed. Fenworth had called Bealomondore's head a noggin. No nonsense had come out of the old man's mouth since he first started working on their friend. *Noggin* meant the wizard was hopeful. *Muscles jarred in a beastly manner* referred to that creature, The Grawl. A pun of sorts. Obviously the seriousness of the injury was no longer an issue that quelled Fenworth's fantastic flamboyance. Bealomondore would be all right.

"Tipper, rub this ointment very gently on the bluish spots." He handed her the glass jar Maxon had brought from Librettowit. "And give me your dragon. I can't stand that awful color for another moment."

The wizard got up and traded places with Tipper. She knelt beside Bealomondore's head and unscrewed the jar lid.

"Phew! Are you sure this goo is still good, Wizard Fenworth? It smells like it turned."

"Turned? Confound it, girl, it smells like the admit root it comes from. Admitriol is supposed to stink, or it wouldn't do any good. The ointment will foster the healing of all those shattered vessels carrying blood, and the smell should bring our patient around. When he starts complaining that he can't breathe through the stench, we'll know he's out of the woods."

Fenworth stroked Rayn's back. Tipper divided her attention between smoothing the smelly medicine onto Bealomondore's battered head and watching the wizard work with her dragon.

"Librettowit, Hollee," he called, "look for tincture of trussell. I shall need two types of torleo, the red and the blue. Of course there is the yellow, but that is for aching feet, and our patient isn't awake to tell us the state of his feet. And Librettowit, didn't we pack croomulite? Yes, yes, I'm sure we did. See if you can't find that as well."

The Grawl advanced through the forest with as much stealth as usual, but he had tuned out his awareness of his surroundings. Images of the old man plagued him. The sword had sprung from the ground of its own accord. No, the wizard had seized the sword with his magic.

Where had he come from? He hadn't been with the others when The Grawl watched their clumsy escape from the boat stop. He hadn't shown up to aid in the fight against the attackers. This morning The Grawl had not bothered to check on the progress of the emerlindian's lost comrades.

To be taken by surprise was humiliating. To be vanquished by mere words was unthinkable.

Something about the authority in the old man's voice had sent a tremor of terror coursing through his veins. Now that he was out of the o'rant wizard's sight, it seemed implausible that he, The Grawl, had reacted so.

There hadn't really been fire in the wizard's eyes. The air around them had not turned frigid. The Grawl had not felt panic, no sensation of being trapped, no quailing before a person of greater force than himself. It was all nonsense.

Before, he'd been content to allow the old man to exist.

Now, The Grawl would subdue this wizard.

But first he would go home. His arsenal would provide him with the edge he needed.

He stopped in a clearing no more than six feet across. From a state of complete stillness, he tested his surroundings. What animals hid in the vicinity? What animals had passed this way recently? What could threaten his secret? Nothing.

The Grawl used a thumb and forefinger to pull an object from his inside pocket and then placed the flat box of silver in the palm of his hand. He stroked it, smiling at its beauty, at the secret.

He banished every movement, every thought, even the pleasure he enjoyed as the device beckoned him to use it. He once more took stock of his surroundings, checked for intruders, and derived satisfaction from knowing he was alone except for the base animals of the woods.

He opened the silver box like a book. From its center, a flood of lights in strings poured over the edges, pooled on the leaf-covered ground, then began to grow upward. A framework became visible, a large archway. The lights played around the exterior while the image of the other side of the small clearing shimmered as if The Grawl looked through pebbled glass.

When the structure stabilized, no longer stretching and no longer swaying, The Grawl closed the box and tossed it through the center. It did not land on the other side among the leaves. Without hesitation, The Grawl walked forward, straight through his gateway.

On the other side, he stood in an enclosed garden, one barricaded with an eight-foot wall all around. He leaned over and picked up the silver box, opened it, and waited for the structure he'd just unleashed to dissipate. The same strings of light that had poured out of the device now flowed in. When the silver enclosed the last vestige of his secret, he shut the lid, savoring the sound of the click that secured his special prize.

Nighttime, always nighttime, when he arrived home. He strode to the locked entry to this secluded area of his estate. Again he listened, and again he heard nothing to interfere with his progress. He didn't go through the wooden door but leaped with a single action to the top of the brick wall. He dropped soundlessly to the other side, then strolled through the formal paths of a manicured garden to a two-story mansion. He slipped behind a hedge to a corner where a tower rose another story over the rest of the building. Scaling the network of oubotis ivy, he entered a window at the top.

He immediately pulled on the servants' bell.

A tinny voice responded. "Yes sir?"

"A bath in my bedroom and a meal."

"Yes sir."

The Grawl trod the circular stairs without a sound. He entered his chambers and removed his soiled clothes in a dressing room lined with elegant clothing of silks and brocades. He heard the servants deliver the tub, then fill it with hot water. When they had retreated, he walked into the room and lowered his body into water too hot for any other creature to tolerate. He leaned his massive back against the side of the tub and allowed himself to relax.

He would look at his beautiful things, wear the fancy clothes, deposit his ill-gotten gains in the vault in the cellar, and perhaps spend some time stacking coins of gold. He would contemplate the control he had over this domain. He'd allow the pleasure of knowing that his strength grew greater with every gold coin he acquired, with every piece of art. He ruled here as well as in the woods. Two distinct worlds. One Grawl.

Then he would return to the forest in Chiril and kill a wizard.

27

Searching out the Truth

Groddenmitersay sat across the room from Verrin Schope and his lovely wife, Lady Peg. A merchant couple had joined them for dinner that night, and the tumanhofer commander of Odidoddex's tactical force wanted to hear the conversation. Unfortunately, no empty spaces existed at a table nearby.

Kulson entered the room, and most people glanced up to watch the bisonbeck stroll over to the bar. He ordered food, and when the tender served him, he picked up his plate and brought it to Groddenmitersay's table. He hesitated.

"Go ahead and sit," Groddenmitersay said. "Everyone has figured out that we do business together. Let's hope none have figured out what that business is."

Kulson sat and shoveled a large spoonful of stew into his mouth before he spoke. "Now that The Grawl isn't with us, they don't pay as much attention to what we're doing."

"I wouldn't be so sure about that."

Kulson paused for a moment to look up at his superior. Groddenmitersay knew exactly what he was thinking. The bisonbeck wondered if the statement indicated that he and his men had neglected some duty.

They hadn't, but they failed to see what was right before their eyes. Groddenmitersay glanced over at Verrin Schope's table and then to the grand parrot, who sat on a perch the innkeeper kept at the bar just for his distinguished guest.

The captain followed his gaze, obviously unaware of the significance of these people. He went back to eating, perhaps chewing on a new idea as he ground beef and cabbage into pulp with his overlarge teeth.

The commander sighed. "Lady Peg's father is King Yellat. Her husband is a genius, both artistically and in the sciences. Sir Beccaroon is a magistrate from the Indigo Forest. He is also a friend of Verrin Schope, even though they pretend not to be acquainted. If you would *read* the reports we send you, you would be more aware of the societal structure in Chiril."

Frustration crossed the soldier's face. He masked it fairly well, but Groddenmitersay knew the man did not enjoy dry reading. And he had no one in his unit who could intelligently read and summarize the reports.

Kulson despised The Grawl. Therefore, Kulson had been relieved when Groddenmitersay sent The Grawl away. The speatus had no idea that the beast was perhaps the most intelligent of all of Odidoddex's agents. Groddenmitersay appreciated his intelligence and regarded this tool of war as a volatile entity. Few knew enough about the beast to realize his complexity. No one felt comfortable, not even the commander, in his presence.

"Schope and the bird talk to each other," Kulson said around a mouthful of food, "but they made it look like they met for the first time here."

"Yes, yes, I'm sure they did. But that is what alerts us to the fact that they are not… Rather, what they appear to be doing is merely a cover for what they are really doing."

Kulson stopped chewing for a moment, then resumed. Groddenmitersay fought the urge to sigh again. Loudly. Pointedly. The man wouldn't pick up the cues in any way.

"What does Verrin Schope do?" he asked, hoping to lead his captain carefully to a logical conclusion.

"He paints pictures."

Before the bisonbeck could load his spoon again, Groddenmiter-say fired off another question. "What does he do with the pictures?"

"He sends them to a shop in Ragar."

"In Ragar? The capital? Where the Amber Palace is?"

Kulson hesitated, then nodded.

"And the king lives in the castle, and the king is his father-in-law, and the king is interested in what we are doing in his country."

Kulson shook his head and used his spoon to gesture as he made his point. "The king doesn't know about us. We've been very stealthy in our work. My men do a good job. And now that The Grawl isn't around to stir up curiosity, we don't attract much notice."

The commander surveyed the room. Every so often one of the villagers stole a glance at the bisonbeck sitting among the collection of high races. They wouldn't ban him from eating there, but they didn't trust him.

Groddenmitersay sent The Grawl "away" because the beast would be more efficient without Kulson and his men. But The Grawl was also unpredictable. He only stayed on a job as long as it satisfied him. Having Kulson reporting on his performance had been necessary as long as the commander had stayed in Baardack.

"During the time I've been here," said Groddenmitersay, "I've become suspicious of these three *innocent* people. I want you to rob the next transport to Ragar and steal the drawings. You will, of course, take other things of value so no one will suspect that it is Schope's pictures we are after."

"They'll know it's us. We can't disguise the fact that we're bison-becks, and we're the only bisonbecks in the area."

Groddenmitersay almost smiled. The speatus had actually thought of a reasonable problem that might arise. But he had not come across a solution. Given the time to think about it, he would undoubtedly work out a way around the dilemma.

The commander decided not to wait. "First, don't do it right outside of town. Second, don't leave any witnesses."

Kulson nodded and continued with his meal. Groddenmitersay lifted his tankard as a server went by. He needed a drink.

<hr />

The pretty day would lure the lady from the inn. Odidoddex's chief of tactics sat on a bench in front of the barbershop. He clutched a newspaper but didn't read. The front of the inn held his interest. He waited for Lady Peg.

She often walked, sometimes with her husband and sometimes with the parrot. And sometimes alone.

Groddenmitersay hoped today she would happen to be alone. He wanted to talk to her. Typically it was the female in a group who could be easily confused and maneuvered. A little conversation, and he would have information concerning the real purpose of the threesome's long stay in this obscure village.

He watched the open door at the inn. A flash of color signaled that the lady in question stood in the doorway. He recognized a dress he'd seen before. She had turned, possibly to speak to someone.

"Come on, Lady Peg," whispered Groddenmitersay. "Take a stroll, but leave the others behind."

In another moment, she stepped into the sunshine. The tumanhofer held his breath. Lady Peg pulled on her gloves and adjusted her hat, then proceeded down the street toward the village garden.

Groddenmitersay left his bench and took a path that would intersect Lady Peg's. He pulled a dainty lace-edged handkerchief from his pocket. Allowing her to get a bit ahead of him, he then scurried to catch up.

"Madam?" he called. "Madam?"

Lady Peg stopped and turned, giving him a quizzical look.

He held out the handkerchief. "Did you drop this yesterday, Madam?"

She took it to examine. "What a fine piece of workmanship! My cousin does exquisite needlework like this." She thrust the handkerchief into Groddenmitersay's hand, turned, and walked away.

"But, Madam—"

Lady Peg faced him and raised one eyebrow.

"Forgive me," said the tumanhofer. "I should introduce myself. I am Doremattris Groddenmitersay from Baardack."

She nodded but did not give her name.

"I know I presume, but are you not the wife of the fascinating artist Verrin Schope?"

"Yes, I am, but I don't know that I would call my husband fascinating. His art is fascinating, but he is more intriguing. The difference being that fascinating people fascinate one and intriguing people are more likely to intrigue. I daresay I find blooms fascinating because out of that tiny bud of color so many individual petals unfold. You know it is going to happen because it always does, but it is fascinating to watch all the same. However, my husband is intriguing because very often you don't know what he is going to do next and you definitely don't know why, even after he has done it and explained why."

Groddenmitersay blinked as he tried to make sense of what she said. He had to engage her in conversation. A little flattery perhaps?

"Quite so, Lady Schope, quite so. How astute of you to define the ever-so-slight distinction between the two terms." He held out the handkerchief once more. "May I return this to you? Since it is evidently your cousin's work, I'm sure you don't want to have mislaid it."

"Oh, but I don't own any of my cousin's needlework. Whenever she sends me a piece, I straightaway give it to the mayor's wife. She works with the poor, you know."

Lady Peg turned to leave.

He determined not to let her get away. She obviously sought to confuse him, but he would bring her to the point of disclosing pertinent information.

Groddenmitersay hurried to catch up to her longer stride. "May I walk with you? I am interested in words, and you have an astonishing command of language."

She raised her chin. "Normally a formal introduction would be called for, but I am merely going to walk through the village garden three-point-six times, and that is a very public place."

Groddenmitersay bit his lower lip. Was this a code? Perhaps she thought he was one of the king's men. "Three-point-six?"

"Yes, my intriguing husband informed me the other day that we did not actually complete the fourth turn and had only managed three-point-six rotations. This is because we left at a different gate and visited the pastry shop. He's mathematical as well as intriguing."

"Yes, I see. I've heard that you are King Yellat's daughter. May I ask why the villagers refer to you as Lady Peg instead of Princess Peg?"

"You may."

Groddenmitersay waited. She was toying with him, laughing as she played these word games.

He cleared his throat. "Lady Peg, why are you addressed thusly instead of with your title, Princess Peg?"

"Well, one reason would be that my mother and father don't approve of me and so I am not Princess to them. My sister is also out of favor because she always said our parents were unreasonable in expecting me to conform."

The tumanhofer congratulated himself. He had directed the conversation toward his goal.

"So you are unconventional?"

"Yes." With a contented smile on her face, she bobbed her head.

"Perhaps you like danger and intrigue?"

"Oh, intrigue most definitely. Remember my husband. I do like him a lot. But danger I prefer to leave in my daughter's hands. She's more suited to it, though Wizard Fenworth says she's excitable."

Groddenmitersay resisted rubbing his hands together in glee. Aha! A wizard. An interesting component complicating the scheme.

He needed to worm out a few more details. "So your daughter is involved in your escapades? How proud you must be of her."

Lady Peg tilted her head and gave him a sideways glance. "Are you thinking of accolades, promenades, or balustrades? Because escapades are not exactly proper, and the royal family does not indulge in things that are not strictly correct. Even those in the family who have been cast out of the family but then returned. Accolades are common among royal circles. And I do enjoy a brisk promenade. And there are balustrades galore in the Amber Palace. But escapades are few and far between. I suppose you could say that escapades are questly by nature, and I do know family members who have participated in quests."

The tumanhofer panted as they went through the gate to the square village garden. He had to walk quickly to keep up with her longer stride, and spewing all those words while practically racing down the street added to his breathless state. He'd barely made sense of what she'd said.

In truth, much of it hadn't made sense. She was onto his game, most certainly. And the clever woman hoped to disarm him with chatter. Fortunately she slowed her pace once on the garden path.

The tumanhofer waited until his words would not be interspersed with gasps for air and then endeavored to restart the conversation with a new goal. "I imagine your house is a museum of fine art. I've noticed that your husband ships his paintings away. Do they go to your home to be hung?"

"Oh goodness, no! Who would want to live in a museum? I don't even go into Verrin Schope's library. That many books wanting you to take them down and read is discouraging. Even if you read one a day, it would take too long to read them all. Rather than disappoint those I wouldn't get to, I don't read any of them. That way none could feel slighted."

"You believe the books have feelings?"

"Of course not. What a peculiar thing to say."

"But you said—"

"Well, I guess I was a little sharp with you, but I can't abide nonsense, you know. And trying to see things through your eyes, I can see that one could say that books have feelings. One feels heavy and another feels light. One is bound with leather, which feels different from one bound with cloth pressed on board."

Groddenmitersay realized she had not answered the question of where the paintings were shipped. She was, indeed, a clever adversary.

His head hurt. He squinted at the sun. They would soon pass a bench in the shade.

"Would you care to rest, Lady Schope?"

"Not at all. I find this extremely invigorating."

The tumanhofer scowled. She'd evaded his every attempt to elicit information as to the purpose of their stay. He felt sure the paintings hid something of value. Did they transport messages or reports with the pictures?

So she found this little exercise of wits invigorating? The woman strived to appear foolish, but he was too seasoned to fall for such a trick. She overplayed her hand and thus gave herself away.

He'd walk with her until she returned to the inn. The pretense would trip her up. The hoax was too elaborate to maintain. He need only be patient.

28

Scoundrels

At the knock on the door, Groddenmitersay jumped to answer. Kulson stood in the upstairs hall of the inn, a flat, oversized bundle under his arm. The tumanhofer waved him in.

"You were careful?"

Kulson grunted. "No one saw me."

"Put the package on the bed, and light more lanterns. Bring them close so we can see."

The tumanhofer took care in removing the cloth covering that protected Verrin Schope's art. Six pictures. He took out the sheets of heavy vellum and lined them up across the bedspread.

"Still life," he said.

Kulson placed another lantern on the bedside stand. "What?"

"The picture is of a collection of objects on a table. This subject matter is called a still life."

Kulson studied the various poses of fruit, vegetables, and a lone candle as Groddenmitersay picked up one picture after another to study in the bright light from three lanterns.

"I get it," said the bisonbeck. "A horse moves, people move, even trees move in the wind, so things that don't move are still."

Groddenmitersay cast his captain a resigned expression. The man couldn't help being built for battle and not for intellectual pursuits. Kulson came in handy as long as one remembered to think for him.

"Yes, you're correct." Groddenmitersay went back to his inspection of Verrin Schope's pictures.

The items in each of the six pictures were identical but arranged differently. Verrin Schope had executed one in black and white. Each of the others blushed with colors of varying vibrancy. Brilliant hues embellished only one painting.

Groddenmitersay saw no obvious message in the pictures. He turned over the one in his hand. In the lower right-hand corner, he spotted a scribble. Holding it closer to the light he made out the handwritten notation, "three."

"Aha!"

"What?" asked Kulson.

The tumanhofer picked up another picture and checked the back. "Five. They're numbered."

He sorted the artwork according to the numbers. The first was the black and white. A slight wash of color appeared in the second. Each progressive picture carried a darker shade, until bright colors enlivened the last sketch.

The tumanhofer stood back, cradling his chin in his hand and contemplating the designs. "The first picture looks like it might be a letter. The letter *L*."

Kulson grunted.

Groddenmitersay pointed to the fourth picture. "That could be a *D*."

Kulson leaned forward, squinting at the paintings. "I don't see any letters."

The tumanhofer didn't respond. He studied Verrin Schope's art. He turned them so they were upside down. Then he left the top three upside down and returned the second row to the original position. Then he arranged them so every other one was turned topsy-turvy. He laid them end to end on the floor. Between every arrangement, he considered what hidden message could be in the line placement of the fruit, vegetables, and candle.

"The key could be the placement of the candle in relationship to the other items." He sighed. "And there are extraneous lines all over the place." He reached for two of the papers. "I might be able to match that random mark at the ends of the paper. I doubt these background marks are really haphazard."

Groddenmitersay placed the paintings on the bed again and spent a few minutes testing his new theory. With the pictures in numerical order, he lined up the background contours so that one mark flowed off one paper and onto the next. Because he had arranged the pictures in two rows of three, the line made a circle. Almost. In just a few places, the lines did not connect.

He snapped his fingers. "I've got it. Three-point-six rotations."

He picked up the fourth and sixth papers and exchanged their places in the order. With a little more finagling, all the lines met at the edges. The oblong loop ran an irregular pattern through the six pictures, going from one painting to the next.

"Do you see, Kulson? The wavy line completely encompasses the papers. That's probably the outline of a territory, and the fruits and vegetables will denote civilians and military. The position of the food items may signify numbers." He pointed to the second picture in the bottom row. "See, the pear is pointed toward three o'clock, and that would indicate one number, while it points to seven o'clock in this next one. That would be a different number."

The smile on Groddenmitersay's face faded when he looked at his henchman. The elaborate message completely baffled the first speatus.

Kulson grunted. "Can you tell what it says?"

"Not yet, but I've already solved one element of the puzzle."

"You still think there's a message hidden there?"

"Of course. He's sending reports to King Yellat."

"How does he get information to send on? He doesn't do anything but paint all day."

Groddenmitersay sighed his frustration. "Haven't you noticed how many people come to see him?"

"Well, yes, but he is interesting. A famous artist. Kind of royalty because of his wife. He wears different clothes too. He puts on a show, you might say. And he's got those dragons. Lots of people come to see the dragons."

"Curiosity would explain some of the visits, but there is a steady stream of coming and going. Some of those people are relaying information gathered to inform the king of our doings."

Kulson looked so uncertain that the tumanhofer wanted to slap some sense into him.

He held his temper. "Don't try to figure it out. Just take my word for it."

The tumanhofer picked up the heavy papers off the bed and stacked them on the table. "It might be worth our while to capture one of these three pawns of King Yellat. Lady Peg, Verrin Schope, and Sir Beccaroon are high-class informants. We will force the code out of one of them." Groddenmitersay waved a dismissing hand at the first speatus. "You can go now. I'll continue to scrutinize this work, and quite probably I will uncover the key."

Kulson had already bolted for the door, but he stopped with his hand on the doorknob. "Do you want us to kidnap the lady?"

"No, she's too clever to give anything away. The artist is probably too noble." He huffed in disgust. "One of those who would die with a secret rather than face the shame of a traitorous act."

The bisonbeck's eyes grew large. "The bird?"

"The bird will have to do."

"We can't catch him and bring him here. It's too risky."

"I know that, Kulson. Have your men search the countryside for a deserted barn or something."

"Yes sir." He opened the door but quickly closed it again as Groddenmitersay continued.

"It can't be too far from here as I'll have to be able to get to it and back in a day."

"Yes sir." He twisted the knob and pulled.

"Shut that door. And don't do anything until I give the order. I may be able to break the code on my own. I wouldn't want to cause an unnecessary disturbance."

First Speatus Kulson nodded and waited, his hand twitching on the door's handle.

Groddenmitersay glared at his subordinate. "Dismissed."

The soldier fled. The chief commander had frequently met bisonbecks with more intelligence than this one. At least Kulson wasn't as blustery as some.

The tumanhofer sat in the only chair in the room and systematically inspected the wrapping that had protected the art. He saw nothing unusual. He returned to the pictures, and after an hour of speculation on the front side, he carefully put the pieces together upside down so that he could scrutinize the odd smudges and scratches across the back.

In the end, he had to admit the code mystified him. He felt sure the grapes represented his forces, or rather the king's infiltrating units.

King Odidoddex would not appreciate Groddenmitersay's personal claim to this venture, but the tumanhofer gave himself credit for the success they had encountered so far. He had masterminded the strategy. The king only provided men and a full purse.

Groddenmitersay had been the one to enlist the aid of The Grawl. That stroke of genius no doubt accounted for the amount of secrecy they had been able to maintain. The Grawl worked silently.

He put the pictures away and got out the maps of Chiril he used to plot the demise of the country. Pleasure warmed him as he went through a packet of reports from each of his first speatuses. Small forces surrounded the capital of Ragar, no more than six highly trained men in each unit. Four major trade routes had been disrupted. At his word, the king's city would be completely cut off, under siege.

An army encamped in the foothills, having crossed through dangerous territory undetected. If anything, the encounters with the wild beasts of the mountains had honed their fighting skills. The weak or ill-trained had died in the frays. That was as it should be.

Next he marked each of the cities where spies maintained ordinary jobs, waiting for his command. It would be his command that brought victory. King Odidoddex would claim the honors, but the real power lay in Groddenmitersay's hands. Those whose opinions he valued knew the truth.

The tumanhofer enjoyed his position. And to be quite frank, sitting on a throne and currying favor among a court full of idiots did not suit his taste. Ordering strong, fierce, and barbaric men to do his will gave him great satisfaction. He had squelched rebellions for the king. Now he would conquer another country. And the monetary gains he made from his occupation richly rewarded his efforts. Yes, he was a happy man. He folded the maps and prepared for bed. Tomorrow would be a busy day.

29

Pulling It Off

"Awk!" His startled cry reverberated against the wooden walls of his room at the inn.

"Oh, I'm sorry, Bec." Lady Peg patted his feathered back. "Did that hurt?"

"A twinge," said Sir Beccaroon, squinting and refusing to utter unkind words to Tipper's mother.

The glue they used to fasten his prosthesis showed its age by getting more and more difficult to dissolve. The ordeal of removing the artificial tail so that a skin treatment could be applied caused Beccaroon to fall into a foul mood. He preferred Lady Peg's gentle cleansing of his stump over Verrin Schope's quicker methods. But right now he wanted to talk to the wizard sculptor.

"When did you say Verrin Schope would be with us?"

Lady Peg wrung water out of a cloth and draped it over the stubborn glue. "In just a little bit. He's shipping more paintings to Ragar. He's been very productive of late. He told me this collection will pay for new drapes and rugs at Byrdschopen."

A knock on the door and a call from the other side indicated Verrin Schope had arrived. He entered the room with Hue and Grandur perched on his shoulders. They flew to Beccaroon, intent on aiding the glue removal procedure.

The wizard took off his coat and rolled up his sleeves. "I sent a letter off to the Insect Emporium for the ingredients to make fresh adhesive."

Lady Peg looked up at her husband. "But you sent the letter last week."

"We should have heard from them by now. Perhaps my letter followed the route of my paintings."

"Now why would a letter do that?" She shook her head. "Many of the problems of our world would be solved if people, and in this case, things, retained an awareness of purpose. Acquiring a list of ingredients is the purpose of the letter. Acquiring funds for the upkeep of Byrdschopen is the purpose of Verrin Schope's art."

Her husband lifted the soaking rag, his face a model of control. Beccaroon suspected her last remark had irked him. Verrin Schope and the dragons took over picking the pieces of glue off the parrot's skin. Hue provided cheerful humming as they worked.

"Peg, my lady love, my art has a broader purpose than just to provide us with money."

Her eyebrows rose, and she gave him an incredulous look. "Really?"

He frowned at her, and she became flustered.

"Well, of course." She waved a hand above her head.

Beccaroon wondered if she were trying to collect scattered thoughts with the fluttering gesture or disperse them even more.

Her hands came to rest on her husband's arm, and she looked into his face with sincere love. "I know you do things to please me, Verrin, but I hope you know you don't have to. I am delighted with your paintings and little carvings. But if you only held my hand and walked with me, it would be enough."

He placed a gentle kiss on her lips. "You know what you have just said to me is exactly what I have said to Wulder."

Lady Peg startled out of the calm of contentment and frowned. "He gives you pictures and statues?"

Verrin Schope nodded with his mouth twisted in a lopsided grin.

"In a way. But all He wants from me is that I hold his hand and walk with him."

"That sounds very reasonable," said Lady Peg, "as long as He loves you."

"His love is never-ending."

She picked up the cloth to dip in the warm water. "Oh, I'm so glad He's not fickle. I just can't stand it when a person starts down a road and then makes a lot of detours. It's hard to keep track of a person who does that."

"I have a problem," Bec announced. He didn't want to hear about Wulder. The way Verrin Schope talked as if he could actually communicate with this Wulder made the parrot uncomfortable. Beccaroon had important matters to discuss.

"Are you cold?" asked Lady Peg as she draped the soaking rag on his exposed rump. "We'll pay attention now, Bec. I promise."

"No, I have something of importance to tell Verrin Schope. I've been waiting for him."

Lady Peg tugged on her husband's shirt sleeve. When he looked at her, she jerked her head toward the grand parrot. He gave her a puzzled look, even though Beccaroon was sure he knew what she wanted. She jerked her head twice more with added vigor.

Her husband pantomimed, "What?"

"Oh goodness, Verrin Schope! Sir Beccaroon wants to tell you something. He's waiting for you."

"Bec, are you waiting for me?"

"Not anymore."

The wizard turned back to his wife. "He isn't."

Her face transformed from impatient to confused. "Isn't what?"

"Waiting for me."

"Well, of course he isn't. You're here now, but he wants you to ask him to tell you, so ask him."

Verrin Schope removed the soaking cloth as he spoke. "Bec, do you have something to tell me?"

Beccaroon had grown tired of the game and forestalled another round of confusing Lady Peg by answering directly.

"Those bisonbeck buffoons have been trying to capture me."

Lady Peg gasped. "Oh dear, do you think they want to roast you?"

The comment startled Beccaroon. It had never occurred to him that he might end up as their dinner.

"No, no, Peg," said her husband. "Remember all we've learned about these ruffians. They were sent by Odidoddex to disrupt communication and supplies and to eliminate people in authority so that when it comes to war, our citizens will be hampered by a lack of leadership."

"Oh yes." Lady Peg looked devastated. "You did put an end to that, didn't you, dear?"

"We've been able to thwart most of their attempts in the last week or so." He gave her shoulder a squeeze. "We know that First Speatus Kulson is in charge of two men. And we have learned that Grodden-mitersay is the mastermind behind this invasion scheme. They are stealing my pictures—"

Lady Peg scowled. "Now that is not nice."

"Correct, not nice at all. And they are trying to decipher the code within the pictures that informs the king of their movements."

Lady Peg grinned at him. "I do remember that part. There are no hidden messages, so Master Groddenmitersay is pulling his hair out trying to find something that is not there. But how are we going to buy new drapes and rugs if he steals all your work?"

"I send the pictures I really want delivered with a special courier. I only send the pictures I want him to puzzle over by mail. And in those, I put various stray marks to confound the man."

Grandur chirruped, reminding the wizard and his wife that it was time to put on the soothing ointment.

Sir Beccaroon talked as they worked. "At first I thought the three bisonbecks were just following me. But it has become more obvious, as they have become more desperate, that their goal is to entrap me in some way. On several occasions they have very nearly pulled it off."

Lady Peg paused. "Now that would be embarrassing."

Verrin Schope whispered, "Not Bec's tail, my lady love. The bisonbecks nearly pulled off the kidnapping of our grand parrot friend."

She went back to spreading the ointment. "I suppose that could be embarrassing too."

Beccaroon continued. "I've received a message today. Unfortunately, a great many of Odidoddex's soldiers have made it through the mountains of Mordack and are now camped within our borders. And from all accounts, these soldiers are not as incompetent as the ones we've been observing."

Verrin Schope wiped his hands on the soaking cloth as he considered the news. Bec waited for his thoughts on the matter. Lady Peg tidied up, putting things away.

"I think," said the wizard, "that it is time we uprooted our cozy little information station at the Round Baker Inn."

"Wonderful!" Lady Peg clapped. "Are we going home or to find Tipper?"

"Which would you prefer, dear lady of mine?"

"Tipper."

"Then finding Tipper it shall be."

30

The Calm Before

Tipper's foot hurt, but she had been doing an admirable job of not complaining. However, her not complaining caused a problem. No one knew how much her foot hurt.

Except Rayn. He rode on her head and sang encouraging marching songs. He'd come out of his unconscious state cheerful and ready to carry on. She couldn't see him but knew he would be a shade of purple. He couldn't use his healing ability as long as she kept moving. She longed to lie down under a tree and relax.

When they could ride on the raft, her foot gave her no trouble, but the turbulent water of this part of the river had forced the passengers to walk while Librettowit, Bealomondore, and the kimens manned the barge ropes to keep the craft from breaking away and disappearing downstream. Bealomondore had fully recovered from his near drowning and even from the five indentations in his skull. She was the only weakling.

Wizard Fenworth marched beside her. But he was deep in thought about something and provided no diversion from the pain that shot from her ankle to her hip every time her foot hit the hard dirt.

Finally she spotted the island Taeda Bel and Maxon had reported after a scouting trip. The river pooled around a small mound of earth and spread out to become a large pond. One tree dominated the landmass at the center. Grass and shrubs grew green and lush on the banks of the river. Purple wildflowers covered one side of the island, and the same color scattered over the slopes around the pool.

Librettowit declared a time of rest and refreshment. Tipper sank down under the bentleaf tree while the others tied up the raft and Wizard Fenworth collected windfall from a fruit tree.

Rayn settled on her foot, his insistent chirring captured her attention.

"All right. I'll take off the boot, but my ankle will swell up, and I'll not be able to get it back on."

Taeda Bel helped unlace the boot and ease it off Tipper's sore foot. She also removed the stocking.

"Oh, Princess, it's such an angry red!"

Rayn chirred softly and draped his body over the sorest part.

"It will be better in a bit," said Tipper. "And really, Taeda Bel, please don't call me Princess."

Tears surprised Tipper, running down her cheeks. She swiped at her face, but not before her kimen guide saw them.

"You're tired and hungry. I'll bring you a cloth to wash your face, and then you're to lie down until we have noonmeal ready."

Tipper smiled as the bossy kimen raced to the stream and came back just as quickly with a cool, damp rag. Fenworth sat beside her and gave her a handful of plump doppers. The juicy orange fruit were no bigger than her thumb and had a solitary pit in the center. She pulled the dopper off its stem with her teeth, chewed, and then spit out the pit.

"Thank you, Wizard Fenworth. They're the best I've ever had."

He chortled. "One principle from Wulder's Tomes is 'An empty stomach gives the tongue an appreciative disposition.'"

Tipper didn't reply but ate the rest of the little doppers. Taeda Bel brought her more, this time in a silver bowl.

"We're going to have a fire and fried fish. Librettowit is catching the fish, and Bealomondore is building the fire." The wizard stirred as if to get up, but Taeda Bel bowed to him. "The artist told me to tell you not to put yourself out. He'll start the fire without one of your spells."

Fenworth harrumphed and settled back in his comfortable position. "Tell him one tiny fireball wouldn't put me out even a miniscule iota. But if he insists on doing it his way, he can. Tipper and I will rest."

Taeda Bel skipped away, and Fenworth shifted his attention to Tipper's red and puffy foot. In the few minutes since she had removed her boot, swelling had rounded the flesh from toes to ankle.

"Oh dear, oh dear. Tut, tut, tut. Something has gone amiss."

He scooted to sit next to Rayn and cupped one hand under Tipper's foot and the other next to the green dragon. "You could use a little help with that, could you not, young fellow?"

A pleasant tingle replaced the throbbing ache, and Tipper sighed with relief as she leaned back to rest against the trunk of the bentleaf tree. Her heavy eyelids drooped, but just over the horizon she saw three shapes in the sky. She sat up abruptly.

"Look!" She pointed. "Dragons!"

Bealomondore shaded his eyes with his hand. "That's a sight not seen often in Chiril."

As they watched, the flying dragons banked and came their way. Rayn ran from Tipper's foot to her shoulder. He chittered excitedly.

"Paladin is with them," she said.

Wizard Fenworth patted her foot. "There's infection in your foot from one of the scrapes. We'll clean that out and have you dancing in the moonlight with the prince in no time."

Bealomondore scowled at the wizard. "I doubt that he knows how to dance. Remember, he's lived alone in his one-towered castle since his youth."

Librettowit and Maxon approached. The librarian carried several freshly caught fish threaded on a slender bentleaf branch.

"Then the ideal thing to do," said the librarian tumanhofer, "is for you to give Paladin lessons on ballroom comportment, and he should give you lessons in battlefield swordplay."

Fenworth stood and shook out his robes. Tipper grinned at Hollee's delight. She danced on her toes as tiny fish fell to the ground and flip-flopped their way to the river.

The wizard frowned. "Don't know where those came from. Couldn't have been with me for long. They're still wet." His face brightened. "You were talking about swordplay. Bealomondore, didn't that sword I left teach you anything?"

"Quite a bit actually. Enough to keep us alive, but not so much that I now feel comfortable with the thing in my hand."

Fenworth squinted in the direction of the three dragons. "Paladin will be here before long. Librettowit, allow me to assist you in the frying of those fish. Do you have a lemon with you, an egg, some meal to provide the crunch?"

The librarian shook his head.

The wizard sighed deeply. "Up to me. Always up to me. Glad to help though. That's my call, servant to many, leader of all." He headed for the fire that Bealomondore had built. "You've cleaned the fish already, haven't you, Wit? Good, good. I'll just pull out a frying pan, a bit of bacon grease, and more, much more. We'll have a feast while the sun is high and hot, then proceed in the cooler part of the day."

Tipper found she could not relax. But Taeda Bel would not let her get up.

"You'll pace, mistress, and ruin all the good Rayn and the wizard did with your foot."

Tipper leaned forward and wrapped her arms around her knees. She rested her chin on her arms and gazed at the dragons drawing nearer. With her mind, she reached out to Prince Jayrus, Paladin of Chiril. She jerked in surprise when she actually heard his voice.

"Mindspeaking?" he said. *"I didn't know you could mindspeak."*

Taeda Bel has been helping me, and she says that communicating with Rayn has increased my ability.

"Very good. Has she also taught you how to protect your mind from unwanted intrusion by the enemy?"

Yes, but I hope never to have to use those techniques.

"I sense a peace in you, Tipper."

I…I understand now who Wulder is.

"Good indeed, for the techniques of protection do not work for those who reject Him."

Tipper felt a buzz in her head as if bees swarmed around her.

"Sorry," said Paladin. *"I was thinking several things at once."*

I didn't know that was possible.

She heard him laugh and felt it too, as if her body responded to a laugh of her own.

"Tipper, I have learned so much since I left the Valley of Dragons with you and your questers. I am so much more aware of what responsibilities I will have to carry. I know there are many obstacles in my way. The part of me that is Prince Jayrus trembles at the responsibility. But the paladin in me joins his heart with Wulder and knows the outcome will be good."

Tipper closed her eyes and concentrated. Some thought she could not catch whirled around with others in his mind.

She felt anxiety tremor in her breathing. Nothing disturbed her at the moment. The feeling must come from him.

You're worried?

"Troubled. I bring you news that will burden your heart."

Before she could completely form the thought, he answered, *"No, not your parents. They are well, and so is Sir Beccaroon."*

The buzz crescendoed until she put her hands over her ears. That didn't block any of the irritating drone. She retreated with her mind and broke contact. Breathing heavily, she opened her eyes to see the dragons descending. She heard the rush of air beaten by strong, leathery wings.

Rayn jumped up and down, sprang into the air to do somersaults, and jigged like a street dancer on her shoulder. She gathered from his celebration that he was overjoyed to see the riding dragons.

She laughed, infected by his exuberance, but felt it necessary to point out a pertinent fact. "You've ridden on one when Paladin brought you to the kimen village."

He gave her an image of his sorry state at the time. Paladin had doubted he was strong enough to survive and hadn't handed him over to Tipper until he was sure the young dragon would live.

The image of the puny minor dragon caught on another thought. She winced as a word covered the visual impression. Heavy, oppressive, inevitable. Death, slaughter, pain, tears.

She shook her head, trying to rid her mind of the fearful prospect. A strong, gentle hand came through the wavering vision, larger than an ordinary hand. She held out her own and felt her fingers clasped in a tender embrace. She looked at her empty hand but felt the presence nonetheless.

Fear banished, she once more looked at the terrifying revelation with calm. The prediction remained. *War.*

31

Bad News

The dragons landed in the field above the river. They trumpeted a greeting to those watching, then wandered away, evidently not interested in the plans of their two-legged friends. Paladin strode through the tall grass, his face reflecting the somber images Tipper had viewed in his mind.

With one look at their guest's expression, the group waiting to greet him ceased waving. Tipper felt the air still around them. As if she or Paladin shared the essence of the news he brought, dread squashed the traveling troop's enthusiasm for their visitor.

Fenworth stared at the fish frying in the skillet. One flipped over to cook on the other side. The action distracted Tipper for a moment. Of course, the wizard had turned the meat, but for an instant she thought the fish had jumped in the same manner the minnows had rolled and twisted away from Wizard Fenworth toward the river. Common sense said a gutted, filleted, and battered fish could not rise up and turn over on its own.

Librettowit stepped forward. "Tell us straight out, son."

Paladin halted, drew in a deep breath, and expelled it. His jaw shifted back and forth twice before he managed to bring himself to speak. "Odidoddex has launched an invasion force. And Chiril's first defensive action met with defeat—a disaster. Our people had no hope of standing against them."

Bealomondore collapsed on a large boulder near Tipper. "Our country is not prepared for war. We have very few military institutions, a skeleton army trained to keep civil peace, and a navy that rescues stranded fishermen more than anything else. I think occasionally they intercept ships carrying off slaves."

Librettowit pinched his upper lip and tugged at his mustache. "You have magistrates and a justice system."

"Lightly used," said the tumanhofer native of Chiril. "Our populace, for the most part, are good neighbors. Thievery brings down shame on the entire clan. It's disgraceful to cheat. Until now, the disappearance of young men and women along the coasts has been the most distressing problem for those in authority to deal with."

"And what measures are taken against this foul business?" asked Librettowit.

"Slave trading comes from outside our borders and is an atrocious abomination claiming everyone's attention. But for all the talk, nothing much is done. Young people are urged to be alert and cautious."

Tipper watched Paladin's face during the exchange. The sorrow there caused her heart to weep.

"What can you do?" she asked the young leader.

Paladin pounded his fist upon his thigh. "Nothing. King Yellat does not appreciate my interference. I hope to be of help behind the scenes."

Wizard Fenworth spread his arms wide. "The panoramic view. What do we see when we envision the entire country as a whole?"

Librettowit nodded. "Quite. A country attacked from within and without. The statues being separated caused a rift in nature. Abnormalities sprang up as they did the first time. They have not had time to heal since Fenworth joined us."

Tipper turned to be included in the conversation. "It seems to me that the deterioration happened at a faster rate."

"Decidedly," agreed Librettowit. "And the deterioration went deeper. The citizens of Chiril suffer from a malaise. Those not sitting around in a stupor grumble and quarrel with one another. The geographical disturbances were well noted in the first onslaught before the statues were rejoined. The mental aberrations were not. That does not mean they did not exist, only that the condition was not of such an extent to cause alarm."

Paladin scowled. "And this emotional turmoil of the populace compounds our problems."

Bealomondore rubbed his palms over his knees. "We have a weak army, backed by a disheartened people, and complicated by short tempers and bickering."

"Hopefully we can get the statues set up in a safe place and eliminate the dismal mental state of our people. Unfortunately there is more," said Paladin.

"Well," Librettowit growled, "let's have it."

"Chiril can't transport goods from one area to another. Some parts of the country are without staples that are usually brought in from neighboring provinces. Those who should be sitting in seats of authority, helping to minimize the problems arising from shortages, are missing... gone."

Wizard Fenworth clapped his hands together and then spread his arms wide again. "Panoramic?"

Tipper had no idea what he meant, but Librettowit spoke up. "Put the statues together now. That will ease the disruptive influence of those who do not care to stir themselves and of those who would rather quarrel than work toward solutions."

Fenworth clapped his hands together again, but this time kept them clasped. Bees buzzed around his head for a moment before forming a swarm and leaving the campsite.

"Someone, fry these fish. Librettowit, see if you have some books with you on architecture. Paladin, you shall be useful. Of this I'm sure. But for now, entertain Tipper. She's broken her foot, you see, and can't do for herself." He turned away. "See if you can do for her. Perhaps add your healing touch to Rayn's?"

Librettowit and Hollee followed the wizard. Bealomondore, Taeda Bel, and Maxon headed to the fire. Paladin came to sit beside Tipper.

She reached out a hand, and he took it. His large hand completely enveloped hers, and the anxiety in her heart eased.

"How did you hurt your foot?" he asked.

Tipper smiled at him, unwilling to begin the conversation. Having him sitting beside her, holding her hand, their eyes meeting without any embarrassment, all of this warmed her and wrapped her in a cocoon of comfort. She didn't want to interrupt the moment.

His grin grew, and she knew she had to answer.

"I went from the top to the bottom of an incline a bit more speed-ily than I anticipated."

"Let me see."

He let go of her hand and moved to examine her ankle and foot. Her dragon inched aside so he could see. "Ah! Rayn and Wizard Fen-worth have helped tremendously." He rested his hand on the swelling. "Suppose I use a little of Wulder's gift while we talk." Rayn wiggled closer and put his chin on the back of Paladin's fingers.

Tipper's contentment multiplied with the increased pleasure ema-nating from the green healer. She leaned back and closed her eyes, rest-ing her mind, her body, and her spirit. A sheltering warmth surrounded her like a cozy blanket. The closest image she could relate to the sensa-tion involved her father, a large cushioned rocking chair, and a stuffed doll she'd had as a very small child.

Paladin had said they'd talk, but they didn't utter a word. A com-munion passed through the three, Paladin, Tipper, and Rayn. With a gasp, Tipper realized another entity joined the circle. Wulder. She opened her eyes to find Paladin and Rayn peaceful.

Their eyes remained shut, their faces relaxed in pleasant smiles, and the thrum of union circled. She felt the energy leave her body at the point where Rayn's soft stomach touched the arch of her foot. The steady flow reentered where Paladin's hand rested.

A tip of the vision of war surfaced and sank in her mind. She knew the terror remained but also knew it was important to stay in this place, absorb this strength, and connect for a few more minutes with the power that created beauty.

Later she might be called upon to deal with the evil advancing upon her country. Whether she stood against that malevolent entity depended on what she gleaned from these brushes with Wulder. Deep in her soul, she knew the beauty and power of Wulder would sustain her if she had to enter into those images of devastation she'd seen in Paladin's mind. Those visions of destruction could not coexist with the present joy of communion with Him and His servants.

32

The Wizard's Plan

Fenworth did not take the plate Bealomondore offered. Instead he waved the tumanhofer away. Hollee ate her portion in silence. Her wizard worried her. He'd been thoughtful before, and she knew he pondered many weighty matters. His long stretches of stillness, which ended in a treelike state, she'd come to appreciate. But now a frenzy bubbled beneath his atypical commotion.

He drew on a sketch pad of thin paper and muttered. His pencil flew furiously over a clean page and then lost the energy that drove it. As his hand slowed, his muttering increased, until he tore the page out, crumpled it into a ball, and threw it down. At least two dozen wads clustered around his feet.

Librettowit had walked away once Fenworth became noncommunicative. Hollee couldn't walk away. Whatever the wizard had on his mind, she wanted to be a part of it. She wouldn't risk wandering away and missing the action. Her mind churned with possibilities.

Would they go to war, face the invading army at the base of the Mordack Mountains? Her wizard liked his comforts, and he tired easily. Should an old man go into battle?

Her eyes narrowed as she watched him. She believed he had strength and power that didn't surface until he needed them. Her eyes opened wide. He might stride onto the battleground, wave his walking stick, and *poof,* the enemy would go up in smoke. Or he might be killed while he tried to remember a particular spell.

Would they enter the cities and proclaim the truth? She loved to listen to Wizard Fenworth talk. If she concentrated, she could follow one thread that went through his discourse. She considered this a talent she had cultivated.

Paying close attention gleaned the most marvelous truths about Wulder and life. Fenworth even revealed how He manipulated elements of the natural world to change. Like a cup of ocean water becoming a handful of salt. That was one of the lessons she'd learned while sifting through a muddled monologue on the ocean's being a salt mine but fish drawn from the ocean still needing to be salted when cooked.

Though most people would grow impatient as bits of recipes, news of oddities he'd seen, and crumbs of history littered Fenworth's instruction, Hollee thought it the most stimulating mind game she had ever played.

Would the wizard lead her on a quest to acquire necessary equipment for defeating the enemy? Would they whirl to destinations, gather weapons, and then deliver them to King Yellat's men-at-arms? She thought not. Her wizard didn't seem the type to go on an errand.

What was he drawing, and what would be her part in whatever grand scheme developed? How long before fruition came from this frantic plotting? Surely he'd dropped a hint when he did that broad gesture and declared they must think in panoramic terms.

She puzzled over the conversation between her wizard and his librarian at that time.

The statues. Librettowit had said the statues must be reunited. Assurance washed through Hollee. She and the wizard would protect the statues. Perhaps Librettowit as well. She studied Wizard Fenworth's frenzied drawing and cyclic muttering with confidence. The importance of the statues drove this manic planning. When the wizard came to his conclusions, the project would be elaborate, magnificent, so far beyond exceptional that ordinary people would be stunned.

A shiver of anticipation trembled the soft material of light Hollee wore. She picked up a bite of fish and popped it in her mouth. She grinned as she chewed.

Bealomondore eyed first Paladin sitting with Princess Tipper, then Hollee as she watched the wizard. Librettowit sat under one of the many trees with his nose in a book. He went back and forth between two books of architecture—one on chapels, the other on fortresses. Maxon and Taeda Bel helped Bealomondore clean up after their noonmeal.

He shrugged guilt off his shoulders. He was not much help to the two kimens. He picked up the bowl he'd used to mix batter and handed it to Maxon, the designated dishwasher. Bealomondore glanced at the collection of ingredients left from coating the fish and looked over at Fenworth. Most everything needed to be put back in the wizard's hollows, but the old man was busy.

With a huge sigh, Bealomondore gave up the pretense of being useful. He strolled to the river, where the water had slowed to a steady pace, almost still. It looked brown, but he knew better. He cupped his hand and dipped it in the river. The liquid was mostly clear with a tinge of green, like a mint wine. Small particles of dark material floated aimlessly about, disparaging the clean feel of it on his fingers. The silt on the bottom gave the river the illusion of a dark color.

He let the water dribble out of his hand and sat down on a log just inches from the edge of the river. He gazed for a while at the flow beside him. Several yards back, the river tumbled over rocks. He could hear the rush of foamy, tumultuous water. There the collection of rubble in the riverbed came to an end, and the water calmed and spilled into this placid pond. The splash and burble contrasted with birds twittering, leaves rustling, and high grasses rubbing with a swishing sound against each other.

The river went on, and Bealomondore believed that his life would go on as well. This place would remain, but its substance changed even as he sat there. Everything living, and even the river that could not actually claim life, would leave.

He picked up a dried leaf from a platter tree that stood nearby. When it first fell from the tree, the leaf had been huge and round, bigger than both Bealomondore's hands laid side by side. But in drying, the edges had curled inward so that its bowl-like shape covered only one of his palms.

He placed the brown leaf in the water and watched as it edged away from him. A slight current caught the miniature vessel. Its speed increased slightly as it ventured farther from shore. Bealomondore recognized beauty in the way it dipped, swayed, and occasionally twirled as if performing a ballet on the watery stage.

In his youth, he'd chosen to see beauty. His family owned a mine. They personally managed the work done there and grew wealthy from extracting precious ore from the ground. He felt the disdain of his father keenly, but he pursued the desire of his heart. To look up instead of down, to seek splendor instead of money.

The leaf passed beyond his view, disappearing around the swell of land at the center of the river.

Bealomondore surveyed his companions once again. The other tumanhofer still read. Maxon and Taeda Bel had joined Hollee in a kind of vigilance over the wizard. Fenworth had ceased moving. He stared off into the distance with his pencil still poised over the sketch pad. Paladin, Rayn, and Tipper looked content.

Any one of the groups would have made a good composition for a painting. Even Librettowit, with his nose in the book and only his forehead showing over the top, would have been an interesting study.

Bealomondore's heart squeezed in his chest. Looming beyond this idyllic scene, an army advanced on the life he loved. He shivered as a slight breeze lifted the hair on his arms. Did the air carry despair? Did he smell the blood soaking into the ground where brave men died? Did he hear the moans of those who would never stand again?

He picked up a handful of dirt and let the excess pour off the sides of his palm as he unclenched his fingers. Grains of sand in various colors mixed with richer soil. One clump contained a sprig that once was a stem and petal of a tiny flower. If he rubbed it between his finger and thumb, the transformation would be complete. A thing of beauty decayed and disseminated to nourish another thing of beauty as it grew.

As an artist, he'd trained himself to notice small things, to see detail, honor beauty, and grasp it in his hand, allowing the structure to flow through his fingertips into the implement of his art. The pen, the pencil, or the brush carried the image to paper or canvas. He recorded symmetry, oblique lines, light, shadow, form. Now that he knew of Wulder, all his art expressed what he learned about the Creator.

He scooped up another fistful of soil, tilted his hand, and watched the dirt cascade to the ground. Nothing was as simple as it first appeared. Nothing remained unchanged, unmoved.

Bealomondore studied the wizard. Leaves, bark, and stems now formed an integral part of the man's image. A plan was developing under that absurd hat that now sprouted a flowering vine. From the things the old man had said, Bealomondore felt sure the wizard would take charge of the three statues.

He would be relieved of the responsibility of keeping *Day's Deed* out of harm's way. He glanced around at his companions. Because he'd been in the company of these people, because he'd met Wulder, he could not turn from this awful duty and go back to the life of an aspiring artist.

He looked downriver, but the leaf had passed beyond his sight. He feared he would travel to places where beauty perished.

33

What to Do? What to Do?

Yelling like shrieking losibirds, intruders crashed through the bushes. The noise sent blood rushing to Bealomondore's head. He pulled his sword and twisted to face the attackers. He had time to recognize the crew from the boat stop.

So they hadn't given up and returned to the way station. *I would have,* he thought just before one of the mariones targeted him.

The Sword of Valor slashed forward and interrupted a downward swing meant to do him bodily harm. He pushed with all his might and turned the blade away. Jumping aside as Maxon and Taeda Bel had taught him, he managed a backward swing. His sword sliced the attacker's midriff. The man fell, and Bealomondore turned his attention to a bisonbeck roaring toward him.

Paladin rushed into the fray. He cut off the second renegade bearing down on the artist. Rayn dived from above and spit in the eyes of the enemy. Librettowit charged down the hill, bellowing a tumanhofer war cry, "About, you fiends!"

Bealomondore saw Tipper frantically scooting backward. She used her booted foot to propel her. Taeda Bel stood between her mistress and a charging foe. The tumanhofer artist raced to intercept the villain.

Tipper yelled, "Be careful!"

Of course he aimed to be careful. He wanted to tell her to take cover but didn't have the time. He pinned his attention on the marione he opposed at the moment.

The young man, who had pretended to be the son of the owner, fought with vigor but not much skill. The tumanhofer worked to keep from stabbing the fellow with a fatal blow. Injuring Danto Posh so that he could no longer fight was Bealomondore's goal.

The chaos around him grew less frenzied as Librettowit and Paladin downed their opponents.

"Give it up," said Bealomondore to Danto. "I've no wish to kill you."

With a panicked look around him, the young marione saw that he alone still stood from his party. He cast a glance behind him, where Librettowit now blocked a retreat.

"Don't run," commanded Paladin. "Talk to me."

Danto lowered his weapon.

"Drop it," said Paladin.

The marione's knuckles turned white before he loosened his grip and let his sword fall.

Bealomondore heard a rustling behind him and jumped to defend himself. Wizard Fenworth stood a few feet away on the bank of the river. Leaves and vines still clung to his garments. The wizard scowled.

"Pesky invaders. They disturbed my deliberations." He shook his head as if clearing something from his brain. The usual multitude of tiny bugs flew out of his hair and beard. "No matter. I have a plan completely formed and ready to implement."

"Really?" Librettowit snorted. "Completely? Ha!"

Bealomondore cleaned his sword and sheathed it. The bisonbeck lying at his feet groaned. Librettowit glared at him.

Fenworth stretched out a hand, pointing at the downed warrior. "So untidy, leaving bodies all around." He snapped the fingers of his other hand, and the man disappeared.

Bealomondore gulped. He looked at Danto and saw the marione's eyes widen as his face paled.

The wizard repeated his pointing and finger snapping until only

Danto Posh remained of the outfit from the boat stop. The captive's eyes darted from one of the wizard's companions to the next. Bealomondore thought he would jump out of his skin.

The tumanhofer artist took a firm grip of Danto's sleeve.

"Are you going to kill me? Am I a prisoner?" Danto Posh jabbed a finger at the spots where his comrades had fallen. "Where'd they go?" His body jittered, and his tongue kept spewing out questions. "Who are you? You're not regular citizens of Chiril. You don't look like an army unit. Who are you?"

Fenworth wagged his head. "Talks too much."

A long snake slid out from under the wizard's robe and shot across the grass toward the marione captive. The man screeched. Bealomondore lifted his sword, but the snake shot past him and disappeared into the pond.

Fenworth's scowl grew deeper, and he wagged his head again. "I can't abide the excitable people on this side of the globe, Librettowit. I think we should go home."

"In all fairness," said his librarian, "the people of Amara also tend to shriek and holler under snakish situations."

"Quite."

"And Wulder would not have us leave before our task is done."

The wizard patted his stomach. "Did we have refreshments?"

"We did," said Hollee. "I saved you some."

"What a good kimen you are." He smiled benevolently at them all. "I shall eat, then be on my way. Librettowit, I shall ask you to accompany me on this urgent venture."

The librarian closed his eyes, as if drawing on inner strength. "It's not a quest, is it?"

"No, a building project." Wizard Fenworth beamed and gave his tumanhofer friend a wink. "And the outside is already made."

Librettowit sighed. "I'll go."

"Me too," said Hollee.

"Of course," said the wizard.

Hollee frowned. "Where did you send those others?"

"An island. A pleasant sort of place. A few hungry predators, but other than that, a wonderful vacation spot. I deemed those fellows to be too intense, in need of hours and hours of peaceful meditation. I daresay they shan't bother us again."

He turned to address Paladin. "You wanted to question this man?"

"Yes."

"He's likely to tell you a lot of nonsense."

"I'm expecting that."

"Well, if you venture into his mind, try to avoid the self-righteous rigmarole. It's sticky stuff and can ruin your attitude."

"I will avoid all rigmarole, sir."

"Where's this leftover fish, Hollee? We've got whirling to do. But first I must eat."

Librettowit followed Hollee as she led the way to the campfire. The branches had settled into a bed of coals.

"Just right for warming buns. A bit of jam and nordy rolls." He searched his hollows and brought out a lumpy cloth bag.

"Yes," said Fenworth. "Hollee, you are going to like nordy rolls."

Bealomondore handed Danto Posh over to Paladin and sat on the boulder next to Tipper to watch the interrogation.

Paladin clamped a hand on the shorter man's shoulder and looked him in the eye. "You will tell me the truth."

Danto Posh nodded.

"Who sent you to the boat stop?"

"My mother"—at the second word he drooled an oily black substance with his speech—"bought the boat stop, and we came together."

Danto wiped the slime from his chin and looked at it in horror. "What is this?"

"Why don't you tell me the truth and see if it goes away?"

Danto gulped, then made a horrible face as if he had swallowed something foul. He rubbed his mouth on his sleeve.

Blinking his eyes rapidly, he began again. "Things are pretty bad back home—"

"Where is back home?"

"Baardack."

"Continue."

"And I got this opportunity for some work. So I took it."

Bealomondore watched carefully. So far nothing more oozed from Danto's mouth.

"A job?" asked Paladin.

Danto nodded.

"An honest job?"

He nodded again with his lips clamped together. He barely kept the black bile in his mouth for two seconds before he gagged and spit it out.

He glared at Paladin. "What are you doing to me?"

Paladin shrugged. "I'm not doing a thing. You're the one who controls what comes out of your mouth."

Danto sputtered. "This is impossible."

"Why don't you tell me about the job you were hired to do?"

Posh heaved in a deep breath and let it out slowly, taking the time to examine those watching. Bealomondore gave him a supportive nod when their eyes met.

The artist felt sympathy for the man's confusion. Dealing with Fenworth, Verrin Schope, and Paladin had often left the tumanhofer befuddled.

"It's better to accept," he said by way of encouragement, "that the ruler of these people is much more powerful than your King Odidoddex."

"King Yellat?" Danto sounded doubtful.

"No," said Paladin. "I serve Wulder, and He doesn't like deception."

Danto looked like he would ask another question but thought better of it.

Paladin guided him over to a fallen log. "Have a seat. Have you eaten lately? I know that bile leaves an awful taste in your mouth. Perhaps Taeda Bel and Tipper will fix you something to eat while we have a pleasant conversation."

Tipper rose to her feet and exclaimed, "The pain is gone! All gone." She tapped her foot on the ground. "I'll have to find my boot. Where is it, Taeda Bel?"

Taeda Bel jumped up and turned a somersault in the air. The kimen grabbed Tipper's high top shoe and helped her get it on and laced. They went off together toward the campfire.

Paladin sat down next to Danto.

"Now, young man, what was your objective in occupying the boat stop?"

Danto looked to Bealomondore once more. The tumanhofer nodded while wondering why the marione had chosen him as some sort of confidant.

Danto told only the truth as he answered Paladin's questions. He and his comrades had been sent to disrupt transportation, to cause shortages of goods, and to detain anyone who might have information that would benefit the commanders of the invading forces.

Tipper brought a plateful of fish and a bean casserole, a large chunk of bread, and cheese.

"Thank you," said Danto. "You people are different."

Tipper grinned. "Yes, we are."

"You're the princess?"

"Yes."

"Really the princess?"

"Yes, really the princess."

"What are you doing out here instead of living at your palace?"

"Well, I've never lived in the palace, and I'm not free to say why I'm here instead of in my grandfather's home."

Fenworth spoke up from where he sat by the fire, finishing his meal. "Doesn't matter. She's not going to be out here much longer doing what she is not going to tell you, as I am relieving her of the reason she is out here. Now where she goes next is an interesting puzzle." He tilted his head as he looked her over. "My dear, would you like to take a vacation? An island perhaps?"

"Decidedly not."

34

A Cavern

Hollee clamped her eyes shut as Fenworth started them on their journey. She focused on naming the numerous odors that drifted by in the rush of wind.

Her wizard had taken the two statues from Bealomondore and Tipper and put them in his hollows. He informed Hollee and Librettowit that they were going to build a suitable place for the *Trio* to be housed. Just before the commotion of whirling commenced, he told his two traveling companions they were going to a cave in the same valley in which Paladin had once lived.

Hollee could see flashes of light from behind her closed eyelids, but as the smells disappeared, the noises ceased, and the sense of air flowing erratically around her came to an end, she opened her eyes to total darkness. Hollee reached into the dark and grabbed Fenworth's robes.

"Are we in the cave?" she asked. "Should I brighten up?"

"Yes, no, not yet," said Wizard Fenworth.

"What? Give us a light, Fen," Librettowit grumbled. "Keeping us in the dark? No good in that. I'd like to see where I'm going to be spending my time."

"Coming, coming."

A light flickered above her head, and Hollee saw a sputtering ball grow in her wizard's outstretched palm. It grew until he had to hold it with two hands. The sight fascinated her so much that she forgot to look around. He placed it on the ground, and it continued to expand until it was as tall as Librettowit. The sphere emitted a series of popping noises and decreased in size.

"Here now," admonished Fenworth, "none of that."

A sizzle of complaint came from within the light, but the globe again began to expand.

When it was the same height as the wizard, including his pointy hat, Fenworth smiled. "That will do. Thank you."

Hollee danced around the light and spoke to it. "You're beautiful. Beautiful! Oh, you make my clothes feel tingly against my skin. I like you. I do!"

"Entirely suitable," said Librettowit.

The tiny kimen looked over her shoulder and caught a glimpse of the amazing chamber around them. Color exploded wherever the light hit the walls. She imagined that some collector of fine jewels had come into the plain cavern and embedded his best gems in glorious abandon on every surface. Floor, ceiling, and walls all sparkled as if they stood in a multicolored geode.

Hollee twirled around, trying to see all of the beauty in the crystal cave. Her whole kimen village would fit inside. And if it were possible to stack villages, then it would take ten, maybe fifteen, of her hamlet to reach the ceiling.

When she stopped twirling, she saw Librettowit helping Fenworth remove the statues from his robe.

"Right here in the center, don't you think, Wit?" Fenworth scooted one statue to face inward.

"Agreed," his librarian answered with enthusiasm. "Splendid idea, Fen. I can't think when I've been so pleased to be part of one of your schemes."

"I believe it must have been around four hundred years ago."

"Ah yes, the castle by the towering waterfall."

"Exactly. Move *Morning* a bit to the left, please."

"Lightrocks! I see what you're up to."

Hollee joined them so that she could see as well. "You're going to put them together around those lightrocks? They weren't here when we arrived."

Fenworth grunted as he pushed the farmer statue into place.

"They were here, just not on the surface."

Hollee put her back to the same statue and helped. "Do people come to this cave?"

"No," said Fenworth. "There is no way in or out. That shall be our project."

"You want people to come? What if they—"

"Steal the statues? We'll set up a watch of dragons to prevent that. But this gift of Wulder's must be seen. We can't hide the cornerstone now that we have a proper place to display it."

"Why not? I thought the idea was to hide them so they couldn't be taken."

"A temporary situation. In the end, these statues will cause thinkers to contemplate the completeness of Wulder's world. Feelers will experience the solidarity of His love. Doers will be forced to stop and recognize a power beyond themselves, a purpose underlying their many actions."

Librettowit gestured to the beautiful crystals surrounding them. "This will be a library of eternal truth, a museum of knowledge of Wulder, and a sanctuary for those who need His healing touch."

Hollee clenched her hands together, trying to contain her excitement. Fenworth called for her help, and she let the energy flow into their task.

With a few small adjustments, they had *Day's Deed* situated so that the farmer's extended hand touched the fingers of the female kimen in *Evening Yearns*. The o'rant in *Morning Glory* connected *Evening Yearns* and *Day's Deed*. Fenworth, Librettowit, and Hollee maneuvered the heavy statues until they brushed one another with the slightest of touch in exactly the right formation.

A hum rose from the statues as if their unity generated an energy force.

"This is different," said Fenworth. He looked at his librarian. "They have never hummed before, have they?"

Librettowit shook his head. "I don't believe so."

"Then we have finally arranged them in precisely the correct formation."

Hollee stood back and wondered at the sensation. Like the giant light globe Fenworth had produced, these statues made her clothing shimmy. But the feeling penetrated her body as well, and she began to feel in every ounce of her slim frame as if her nerves were coming awake.

"Oh," she said. "It feels like my foot was asleep and is waking up, only all over."

Fenworth nodded. "You'll get used to it. But I hope you never lose the marvel of Wulder that pulse represents."

Librettowit came around to where Hollee stood and put his hand down. She immediately took hold of a finger. His smooth skin seemed out of place on such a large hand. Hollee reminded herself that the tumanhofer turned more pages in a book than he built campfires.

She glanced up to see that he looked down, observing her. She smiled.

He winked. "It's a wonderful thing we do. Serving Wulder has taken me many astounding places. I've heard songs so beautiful that my heart almost stopped beating. I've smelled air more alive than the trees around me. I've tasted the foods of many a culture, and I've felt the extremes of hot and cold, smooth and rough, weak and strong. The books that I read are amazing, but the real world is incredible. I'm a lazy old fellow who is content in Fenworth's library. But Wulder knows my soul must be fed, and He brings me to places such as this."

Fenworth spoke to his light. "Put yourself out for a moment, if you please. But don't go far. I'll have need of you soon."

The globe blinked out. Only the lightrocks illuminated the three statues. The eerie blue glow reflected off the stone surfaces.

Hollee gasped. "They look like they will dance, talk. They look so real."

Fenworth pursed his lips as he looked them over. He strolled around them. Librettowit and Hollee followed, enjoying the artwork from every side.

The wizard cleared his throat. "If they move, I'm leaving. It will be proof that my old brain has overcooked from all the ideas I've been brewing in there. Verrin Schope has a rare talent, talent that can only be given by Wulder. But only Wulder can bring stone to life. These rocks start talking, and I'm going into retirement."

Hollee giggled. "On that island?"

"Maybe."

Fenworth restored the light globe and pulled off his traveling wizard mantle. "We're going to need to set up camp. We'll be here a long time. A comfortable night nourishes a busy day."

Hollee left Librettowit's side to watch the pile of things grow as her wizard unloaded his hollows. "Is that in Wulder's Tomes?"

Wizard Fenworth's attention snapped to her face. He held up the hammer he'd just pulled out. "This? This from Wulder's Tomes? Did you eat something unusual today? Poison berries? Had a drink of tainted water? Your mind's gone wandering. First you're expecting stones to dance and sing. Now you're thinking hammers come out of books. Librettowit, the child's cracked."

Librettowit shook his head slightly at Hollee. Only a bit of alarm had disturbed her at the wizard's words, but the librarian's expression told her not to worry.

He began sifting through his own hollows and pulling out things they might need. "She's hardly a child. A young kimen, yes, but a child, no. She said talk, not sing, and it was a comment of assessment not expectation. And the *that* she referred to was the comment you made. 'A comfortable night nourishes a busy day.' She wanted to know if that came from Wulder's Tomes."

"Well, then why didn't she say so?"

Librettowit didn't answer, and the two men concentrated on sorting the materials they needed to set up a suitable encampment.

Hollee waited as long as she could before asking a question that niggled at her insides. "What will we do first?"

Leaving behind the contretemps of their last discussion, Fenworth answered, "We'll eat. I'm always in favor of eating first."

"And then?" asked Hollee, squelching the eagerness to learn everything at once.

"We'll see what we've brought along to make ourselves at home here in this splendid cave."

"And then?"

"We'll set up temporary quarters, eat again, sleep. Maybe we'll have a bit of song and storytelling before we sleep."

Hollee scrunched up her face and let out a long sigh.

Librettowit turned her way. "We'll dig a tunnel out of here and find dragons to take over as guardians of Wulder's cornerstone."

Hollee squealed and did a hop, skip, twirl, and flip dance. "This is going to be so much fun."

Librettowit shook his head. "We didn't have much success the last time we tried to deal with the dragons of Chiril."

"Bealomondore told me that story. You'll need Paladin."

The tumanhofer frowned. "Paladin is busy elsewhere."

35

Reunion

Since her chaperone had gone off with the wizard, Tipper rode behind Paladin high above the countryside on his white and gold dragon, Caesannede. Tipper loved flying. She tightened her arms around Paladin's middle.

"Cold?" he asked.

"A little."

"It's not much farther. Tuck your moonbeam cape around you. The fabric rebuffs any unpleasant temperature."

Tipper did as she was told but kept her arms free to hold on to the man in front of her. Of course, the garments the kimens made would keep her warm, but that warmth was not as pleasant as that generated by the young man. Taeda Bel had tucked herself inside the cape, so Tipper used that as another excuse not to close the front completely.

Danto Posh rode on the second dragon. Tipper touched his mind with hers and found him sullen and not scared by his first flight. Paladin had persuaded Fenworth not to send Danto to the island with his comrades. Instead, the spiritual leader of Chiril decided to bring him along. The young marione vacillated between excitement over the chance to fly and resentment over the fact that the dragon would not heed his commands. The dragon obeyed Paladin. For the most part, the captured Baardackian wallowed in self-pity.

Maxon rode with Bealomondore. Tipper dragged her thoughts away from her riding companion and Danto long enough to check on the tumanhofer artist. His initial flying experience had been threatened by fear and nausea. He still had some of the medicine given to him by the proprietors of the Insect Emporium.

Wondering if her developing ability would let her speak to Bealomondore, she reached out to him with her mind. *Are you all right?*

He jumped. *"You startled me. I could have fallen off."*

You're not wearing the strap across your lap?

"Yes, I am, but I'm not comfortable up here."

Are you sick to your stomach?

"I'm not riddled with terror, but this is not my favorite mode of transportation."

You took the Rowser Remedy for Anxiety?

"I did."

She waited a moment to see if he would mindspeak something else. Instead she got impressions of falling, grasping the saddle horn in a hold that pulverized the leather, and a long, screeching sound she finally recognized as Bealomondore screaming. The artist's imagination worked overtime.

A group of men walking north on a wide country lane caught Tipper's attention. She mindspoke to Taeda Bel and all four men in her party.

Look, there's another dozen men going toward the Mordack Mountains.

"You want me to open my eyes? No, Tipper," said Bealomondore.

Paladin's responding laugh cut short. *"I assume they are volunteers to defend Chiril."*

The reaction from Danto Posh confused her, until she realized his agitation and disbelief linked to the fact that he had heard her voice in his head. He'd never experienced mindspeaking.

She focused on him. *Today has been rather mystifying for you, many unusual incidents.*

"Do I just talk and you hear me?"

You don't have to talk, just think.

"Do you listen to everything I think? Are you constantly eavesdropping?"

No, I have to intend to observe your thoughts. For the most part, your reflections are private.

"But you can listen any time you want to?"

Tipper hesitated before responding. *Well…I'm not as good at it as my father or Wizard Fenworth or Paladin.*

"Then you can't?"

I actually don't know what all I can and can't do yet. I'm still learning.

Paladin's voice interrupted her conversation with Danto. "Look below us. A fight has erupted among those travelers."

Tipper looked down and saw two of the men pushing at each other as the onlookers formed a ring to jeer them on.

Paladin made a growling noise. "That is how it has been since this awful business began. Cantankerous men volunteer and then fall into quarreling on the way."

Three more men joined the two fighting in the center of the ring. Tipper didn't know why they had gone forward, whether to break up the fight or to assist whichever one they chose, but the fracas grew. Within the span of time it took Caesannede to flap his wings twice, the dozen men participated in the brawl.

Tipper stretched up a bit to bring her mouth more directly behind Paladin's right ear. "If we could just put a few warriors from the enemy's army in front of them, they'd do a good job of milling them down."

"If Fenworth is successful in setting up the statues in a secure place, one of our obstacles will be eliminated."

"Father will know. He says he feels it in his being when Wulder's cornerstone is rightly aligned."

"I agree he'll know when they are set up properly, but a major concern is stability. If the *Trio* is in a fortress that can be breached, we will eventually have to deal with the problem again."

"Fenworth will do something. Probably different from what we expect, but it'll work."

"I agree."

Paladin looked over his shoulder, enough for Tipper to catch the wink he sent her.

"There's the village." Paladin pointed to a small town, and Caesannede began a descent. Villagers soon spotted the three dragons and gathered outside of town in an open field, the obvious place for the visitors to land.

Tipper watched with great interest. At last, she spotted Sir Beccaroon, his bright red feathers obvious among the common browns, blacks, tans, and blues of most of the townspeople.

She scanned the crowd around him and found her mother and father. Her mother wore a large hat the same color as her dress. Her father had on a conservative wizard's robe. She'd seen Wizard Fenworth's formal robes. The material shimmered and had elaborate embellishments, pictures depicting wonders of Wulder's creation. Her father's most distinguished robe had depictions as well, but he'd fashioned his with black on black so that the images changed with movement as the threads caught the light in different ways.

"I see them." She squeezed Paladin in her excitement. "Oh, I wish I'd taken time to change into something less grubby."

"Your parents won't mind what you're wearing. They are more concerned with your welfare. All the parents in Chiril are thinking more seriously about what may happen to their children. You know of the unusual effects the three statues had on the landscape and now the populace?"

"Yes."

"Well, men have been afflicted with malaise or a cantankerous attitude more than the women. And men who are ready to be independent and start their own families are the most often afflicted. That is why we saw a dozen men striding forth to protect the land and turning on each other instead."

"Oh, Paladin, are we ever going to conquer such debilitating circumstances? Will Baardack take over Chiril?"

"I don't know the answer to that. I thought Wulder wanted me to inform the citizens of Chiril of His willingness to accept them as His people. But perhaps He intends for me to be gathering in Baardackians as well."

Caesannede landed in the open field, followed by the other two dragons, Kelsi and Merry. Paladin yelled to Bealomondore before he dismounted.

"Watch Danto. We don't want him to escape."

Danto promptly slid off his dragon, Merry, and ran for the opposite edge of the meadow. The dragon reached out her long blue neck, snagged the back collar of the runaway's shirt in her teeth, and lifted him off the ground.

Some of the people in the crowd screamed.

Paladin announced, "The dragon won't hurt him." He turned to Merry. "Bring him here, Merry. I'll watch him."

She lumbered over to Paladin and set the man down carefully in front of him.

"Thank you," said Paladin. "Danto, do you remember what happened when you lied to me?"

The marione nodded.

"Would you like to experience what happens when you disobey me?"

He shook his head.

"Fine. Stay beside me."

Someone grabbed Tipper's shoulders and swung her around. Her father drew her into a crushing embrace. "My girl, my girl. Do you know you look even more mature, elegant, and like a princess?"

She laughed and pulled away, looking down at her tattered apparel and pushing locks of hair off her face. "This is not elegant, Papa."

Her mother beamed and gave her daughter a quick kiss on the cheek. "It's the way you carry yourself, my dear. All those years of balancing a book on your head did you some good. Of course, I always found you sitting and reading the book instead of balancing it, but that minor indiscretion didn't hurt your posture. I'm sure that in the end you may find it addled your eyes. We were just going to set off to find you."

Tipper hugged her mother. "Addled my brain, Mother."

"Now, Tipper, don't contradict. Eggs are scrambled, eyes are addled, and brains should never be eaten."

"Mother! Where did you ever come across *that* bit of wisdom?"

Lady Peg lifted her chin, looked down her nose, and employed her fan to demonstrate her disapproval. "Child, I did, upon occasion, open a book or two. You can see why I have chosen to forgo such endeavors. The things in books are quite shocking. I believe it was primitives who were touted as eating parts of animals that are best left undiscussed."

A smile wiped away Tipper's outraged expression. "Quite, Mother," she said around a giggle that threatened to escape. "Some things should not be discussed because they are disgusting."

Lady Peg turned to Verrin Schope with a triumphant look. "You see? I have done my part in raising her."

The wizard draped his arm around his wife's shoulders and pulled her close. "It is completely evident. But we must be about the business at hand."

"What business?" asked Tipper.

"We are going to war," said Lady Peg. "Not exactly we, which would mean all of us standing here. This *we* refers to our country. But not the entire country. The part of the country suited to defending us and banishing evil. And that *us*, in 'defending us,' doesn't mean all of us standing here either. It's very complicated, Tipper. I'm so glad you're back. You and I will go to Byrdschopen, and your father and your suitor"—she glanced over at Bealomondore, who leaned against Kelsi's side and fanned his face with his hat—"both your suitors will go stop that odious Odidoddex's army."

Even as her cheeks warmed, Tipper ignored the reference to her suitors. "Rayn and I prefer to go help with the wounded, Mother."

Sir Beccaroon pushed closer to Tipper. "Let us go back to the inn." He gestured with his wing to indicate the crowd of villagers. "Perhaps this isn't the place to discuss war."

Lady Peg frowned. "There isn't a good place to discuss war. There really isn't."

36

Decisions

Bealomondore followed Verrin Schope into the inn with the others. They passed through the small entryway with its registry desk and entered the tavern. A dozen men and a few women sat at the tables eating their noonmeal. Only three customers stood at the bar. Verrin Schope asked the innkeeper to join several tables so his party could sit together. Paladin, Tipper, Verrin Schope and Lady Peg, Taeda Bel, Maxon, Sir Beccaroon, and the artist took their seats. Danto had been left under Merry's watch. The wizard's four dragons and Rayn flew out the back window, probably in search of something palatable to their small appetites. Verrin Schope ordered beet, carrot, and onion stew for the table.

"It's called chukkajoop in Amara," he told the Chirilians surrounding him. "We've introduced it to the cooking staff here, and it has become a favorite among the villagers."

"It is very pretty." Lady Peg glanced around the table. "I'm sure you'll like it."

Bealomondore had seen pretty soups before. The chefs in some of the fancy houses he had visited drew pictures on the top of creamed bisque with a sauce that complemented the soup.

The wizard artist crossed his arms over his chest. "If you'll excuse me for a moment, I'll set up a sound shield so we may speak comfortably."

He closed his eyes. The conversations around them faded. Bealomondore looked around the room and realized people still chatted, laughed, and carried on with their activities, but no noise penetrated Verrin Schope's barrier.

The tumanhofer leaned toward the wizard. "Can they hear us?"

Verrin Schope relaxed his posture and opened his eyes. He smiled as he looked around the room. "Ah yes, they can hear us, but they will overhear our lengthy discussion of the peculiarities of weather. We are free to speak of anything we want, but they will only hear tales of various climates."

The serving girl came back with bowls and spoons to pass around. Behind her, a sturdy servant carried a large tureen of rich, red soup. Verrin Schope said a blessing, and Lady Peg ladled the chukkajoop into the bowls. The maid brought individual loaves of bread.

Bealomondore's stomach gurgled in response to the wonderful fragrance of their meal. With no competition from the noise outside the arena of their table, the rumble rolled through the silence. Tipper looked up from across the table and smiled at him. "Me too, Bealomondore. I think I shall starve."

Paladin nodded. "Flying always butters my appetite."

Lady Peg picked up a small dish of butter from the center of the table and passed it down to Paladin.

He leaned forward to see around Tipper and Verrin Schope. "Thank you, Lady Peg, but the comment was figurative."

Bealomondore saw Verrin Schope wink at the young ruler. From behind his napkin, the tumanhofer hid a smile. He waited for Lady Peg's response, speculating on how she would interpret the provoking statement.

"I agree wholeheartedly, Prince Jayrus," said the lady. She tasted the soup.

Bealomondore let out his breath. She'd missed a chance to insert a note of inanity. Was she ill? worried? distracted? That wouldn't make a difference. She was always distracted. He lifted his own spoon and relished the wonderful flavor of beets, carrots, and onions.

Lady Peg frowned. "I do wish one's figure did not reflect the love of good food. It's so annoying to butter your bread and find rolls around your middle."

As he tried to swallow the soup in his mouth, Bealomondore snorted and choked. Maxon jumped from his chair and stood on the back of Bealomondore's chair. With tiny hands, he pummeled him between his shoulder blades. When that didn't work, Verrin Schope rose and came around to his side of the table and placed a hand on his throat, lifted his chin, and pressed firmly. The muscles in the tumanhofer's throat loosened, and the spasm ended.

"Thank you," Bealomondore croaked.

The wizard patted him on the shoulder and mindspoke, *"I couldn't let my wife's comment murder a man we shall desperately need in the days to come."*

The words sent a chill down his spine. These people expected great things of him. If they expected a masterpiece on canvas, the pressure would be minimal. Why couldn't they understand he wasn't suitable for heroic deeds? He put his hand on the hilt of his weapon and felt warmth radiating from the Sword of Valor.

He noticed that Paladin had taken his glass and raised it. Verrin Schope returned to his seat and lifted his own. Reluctantly, Bealomondore did the same, without a clue as to what they would be toasting.

"To Wulder," said Paladin, "who gives us all we need even when we don't know what that could be. May He lead us to defeat His foes."

Glasses clinked. Bealomondore sipped, his mind on the unusual wording of the toast. Wulder's foes? Odidoddex was the enemy of Chiril. Did that make him an enemy of Wulder?

He still had a lot to learn about being a follower of the God of the Universe. So far he'd found a whole lot of things to delight in and some very prickly issues that he'd rather leave to someone else. He appreciated with new vigor the beauty he saw around him. He appreciated being accepted without having to prove himself. He'd never found that any-where else.

But now he was called to do things. He thought of his father. As a young man, Bealomondore had turned his back on the Bealomondore Mine and done what he wanted to do. Business didn't interest him. Dirty, money-grubbing business filled him with disgust.

He'd shunned his family's friends and moved himself up in society through his art. He loved his sisters and aunt. He ignored his brother and parents. Now he'd attached himself to Someone who wanted more of him. He'd gotten the message—Wulder expected him to shed his selfish ways. This truth was not as palatable as "Wulder loves lowly tumanhofers and provides good things."

The group ate and talked of minor issues until the maids cleared the table and brought huge slices of razterberry pie and steaming mugs of amaloot. Then the conversation turned to the serious business of strategy.

Bealomondore listened to the talk of war and felt his soul cringing, pulling back as a turtle might withdraw into its shell. Lady Peg said nothing. The tumanhofer joined her silence. Her eyes grew wide, and she clutched her husband's arm. Verrin Schope patted her hand. His touch smoothed some of the anxiety from her expression.

Bealomondore watched Tipper's face when she offered an opinion in the conversation. He brought a pencil out of his pocket and reached into a hollow to retrieve a sketch pad. He sought first to capture im-pressions of Tipper's mobile features. With a page full of her face from different angles and varying expressions, he moved on to a clean sheet and recorded the others at the table. His fear subsided as his hand worked. He took in the facts and ideas presented while he drew, but he did not engage his emotions, fearing they would overwhelm him.

Rayn reentered the room through the window and perched on Pal-adin's shoulder. He chittered.

"Ah," said Paladin.

The minor dragon trilled a note of pleasure, then hopped over to Tipper's shoulder, where he cooed and rubbed his head against her jaw.

Bealomondore looked to where the dragonkeeper pointed. Four kimens entered the tavern and came straight to the table.

Paladin greeted them, then explained to his friends. "I sent for minor dragons from the valley."

Bealomondore blinked, and in that short second, a dozen or so dragons leaped out of the folds of the kimens' clothing and onto the table. They raced among the leftover dishes, gathering up crumbs. One of the other patrons in the tavern shrieked. The dragons stopped, sat up, and looked around in puzzlement. Paladin and Verrin Schope laughed.

Lady Peg said, "Manners. They'll need etiquette instructions. I volunteer for that. I'm quite good at knowing when it is proper to run on your host's table and when it is not."

Rayn jumped from Tipper's shoulder to make the acquaintance of the new arrivals. He moved from one to the next as if he were a host circulating at a party. The scene lightened Bealomondore's mood, and he found himself grinning at the ritual greeting. The dragons first touched forepaws, then noses. Then they slid heads forward, rubbing cheeks. The pose was held for a moment before broken. Not quite a handshake but definitely the accepted formal salutation between minor dragons.

Paladin waited until Rayn had moved through the crowded table. Then with a glance, he communicated something to them that Bealomondore could not fathom. Each dragon circled the table, touched each person sitting there, then lined up in front of the dragonkeeper, prince, paladin.

"I asked some of the dragons from the valley to come to our assistance. This watch is the first to arrive. Our efforts to repel the invasion are greatly improved by their presence. They will willingly serve the needs of the army, carrying messages, scouting the enemy's entrenchment, healing wounds, soothing shattered minds, providing light, maintaining equipment, and encouraging our warriors in any way they can." He dipped his head as if acknowledging his appreciation of their willingness to help.

The line of minor dragons bowed in a similar gesture. Bealomondore resisted the urge to grab his pencil.

This historic moment would have to go unrecorded. Who would believe him anyway? Most Chirilians believed that the small dragons ranked with feral cats. A few of the elite kept them as house pets. His own attitude had been changed by his association with the people at this table.

"Bealomondore." Paladin's serious voice broke into his thoughts. "Laddin and Det have decided to travel with you."

Two dragons, a green mottled with blue and a plain green one, came to stand before the tumanhofer.

"Laddin is a healing dragon. Det will help you with directions. He has a head full of maps and geographical details. Tipper, Sheran, Pennek, Bevlo, and Trincum will accompany you and Rayn."

Tipper raised her eyebrows as four green dragons lined up before her.

"You did say you wanted to help the wounded at the battlegrounds?" She nodded.

A rather ugly fifth dragon, mottled gray and dirty white, scooted into the middle of the green crowd.

"This is Valo. He provides light."

Lady Peg pulled on her husband's sleeve. "I understand why this nice young man is not giving you more dragons, but I think I should like to have another dragon friend. One who talks to me. You know, Junkit and Zabeth do not."

"Lady Peg, I asked particularly for a minor dragon with a talent that will be of benefit to you," said Paladin. "I would like you to meet Bar Besta."

A pale blue dragon with thin purple stripes came to sit in front of the wizard's scatterbrained wife.

"Are you a he or a she dragon?" she asked.

She beamed and laid her hand on her husband's arm to give him a shake. "Bar Besta is male, and he spoke to me. I heard his voice in my head, but his lips didn't move. Isn't that clever? Is that his talent?"

"Partly," said her husband. "He's skilled at communication."

Lady Peg looked back and forth from her husband to her new dragon friend. "What else?"

Verrin Schope rubbed his chin. "I think we shall let you become acquainted with Bar Besta, and you will no doubt guess his talent."

Rather than being offended, Lady Peg looked pleased. "A guessing game. I shall try very hard, but I must warn you, Bar Besta, that I am not very good at guessing. Well, I am actually very good at guessing but not good at guessing the right thing. Only the wrong thing. But I am very proficient at guessing the wrong thing, and that should make up for not coming up with the right thing."

She cocked her head, then smiled. "Verrin Schope, he says that his secret talent will come in very handy. Do you suppose he guesses the right thing? That would be very helpful."

The wizard put his arm around his wife and gave her a hug. "My dear, you astound me. You have deduced his role in protecting you. Bar Besta's talent is, indeed, the art of guessing the right thing."

She reached out and touched the small dragon's shoulder with one lightly placed fingertip. "Oh, I see how that would be handy. Thank you, Bar Besta, for deciding to come with me. I didn't really want to go to war. But I suppose you already guessed that."

The dragon performed a slight bow.

"And he has manners," said Lady Peg. "I thoroughly approve of manners."

37

Research

The Grawl sat at the large table in his study with books open and spread out within easy reach. A stack of plain paper sat on one side, and papers filled with notes cluttered the other side. He'd shed his fine brocade longcoat and unbuttoned his vest. The lamp reflected off the white of his silk shirt.

A servant in livery entered with a tray. "Your dinner, sir?"

"Bring up the side table. There's no room where I'm working."

The man placed the tray on an ornate end table, went to a huge upholstered chair, and emptied the small table beside it. With effort, he lifted the sturdy piece of furniture and placed it at his master's elbow. He then retrieved the tray. He poured a drink from a carafe and removed a cover from a bowl of soup and a larger silver cover from a rack of lamb elegantly arranged as a crown with fresh fruit surrounding the base and paper tassels capping each bone.

"Do you require anything else, sir?"

The Grawl grunted.

The servant nodded and left.

With a big sigh, The Grawl leaned back in his chair, stretched his arms above his head, then lowered them slowly. He made a face as he picked up the food offered to him. The hot bowl warmed his hands, but the soup inside left him cold. He'd eat it, relishing the heat of temperature and spice, but he preferred the meals he foraged when out in the wild.

He tipped the bowl to his mouth rather than use the spoon. His eyes continued to scan the page before him. The word *schoergat* caught his attention. The name of the flying hunter had come up several times in his search for strategies in defeating wizards. His pursuit of information he could use against the wizard had led to an interesting find. The myth of schoergats might actually be more than stories told to frighten children into obeying.

The creatures resembled schoergs, one of the low races. Instead of being rail thin and covered with black fur, schoergats had thick bodies and calloused skin from head to foot. They also had wings.

The books said they blended into the rocky terrain they inhabited in high mountain ranges. Their skin felt like rough granite and provided a shell of protection from knives and arrows. Wings like those of an insect protruded from their shoulder blades. They flew in a darting fashion like certain swamp bugs or tiny, colorful fibbirds.

The Grawl drank from the tankard as he flipped through more pages. North of Baardack and miles to the west, a bridge of land connected two continents. High mountains rose out of the sea and stretched toward the sky. A few spots of population dotted the coasts, but the peaks were too steep to support normal life. The fables said that the schoergats congregated there. And they flew north to hunt dragons, having driven all the dragons in the southern continent into hiding. The Grawl continued to read, searching for what made the schoergats effective dragon hunters and if that skill would be helpful in defeating a wizard.

The Grawl's empty tankard clattered on the metal tray when he cast it aside. Since dragons no longer hid in the valley previously occupied by the man called Paladin, Chiril might have enough dragons to lure these schoergats south. If they engaged the animals favored by the old man, The Grawl might have the opportunity to slay a distracted wizard. He was no fool. The wizard would have to be distracted if he were to get the upper hand.

The journey to the mountains would take a week. What kind of reception would he get? A sly grin spread across his lips. The schoergats would be as wary of him as he was of them. But he'd done his research well. The creatures had three vulnerable spots—tender skin at each armpit and a spot an inch back from the underside of their pointed chins. The chin was the only part of their bodies that grew hair.

The Grawl doubted that the schoergats had reference books. And in any case, since he was the only grawl, no book recorded his traits.

He studied the one sketch he'd found in all of the books. What was the relationship of schoergats to schoergs, cave dwellers of limited intelligence and bloodthirsty ways? The schoergs lived in darkness, crawling in the bowels of the earth. The schoergats thrived in blaring sunshine, oppressive heat, and stark exposure. Their wings appeared too frail to support their bodies, yet they flew with incredible speed and abrupt twists and turns. Were they mutants? Or were they the result of crossbreeding, like himself?

He closed the volumes, one at a time, and leaned back in his chair. He'd travel to Icardia, where the mountains rose straight to the sky and dragon-slaying creatures dwelled. How long would it take to persuade them to join his cause? How long before they found the Valley of Dragons spoken of as the realm belonging to the Chiril Paladin?

He lifted the entire rack of lamb from the platter, tore it apart, and devoured the succulent meat. Grease dripped down his chin. He threw the bones, gnawed clean, into the fireplace.

It was good that he was a patient creature. Precision and cunning came naturally to him. He cultivated habits that supported his skills and shunned habits that undermined his ability. The schoergats would be found. The wizard would be killed.

Pulling a blank paper from the stack at his elbow, he drafted a note to his butler.

"I shall be traveling, Sanders."

That was as much information as he ever left his staff. He rose from the comfortable chair and went to his room. He shed all elegance and re-created himself as the ruthless hunter in rough, sturdy garb. He grinned. He'd found something interesting to do, and he had a goal of his own making. Enlist the schoergats and kill the old man wizard.

Hollee peeked around the corner and watched her wizard. She and Librettowit had been banished while he worked on the finishing touches of the great room. The librarian read from several big books while she basted a jimmin chicken in the oven the two men had constructed. Her curiosity dragged her to the archway for just one quick look.

Fenworth sat on a rock and contemplated a column he'd just sculpted from the salt-saturated sandstone. "Excellent." He jumped to his feet as if he were a young man and planted his fists on his waist. "Hollee, Librettowit! Come see! I am finished."

His two helpers emerged from a vestibule carved in one of the walls of the main chamber. Librettowit carried a thick volume, and Hollee's hand clasped a dripping spoon. She licked the sauce before more could soil the floor of the cathedral-like cave.

Even though she had seen every step of the transformation, the beauty of the underground tribute filled her with awe. Huge crystals made up the major part of the walls. Wizard Fenworth had fashioned lightrocks out of the raw material so that red lightrocks glowed from within red crystals. Blue lightrocks illuminated blue crystals. Since a myriad of colors naturally decorated the walls, the lighting projected rainbow hues on every surface.

He'd placed golden lightrocks in the circle of statues. Dark shadow silhouettes marched across the brilliant crystals. While Hollee skipped around the perimeter of the room, she watched the opposite wall. The statue shadows seemed to slide forward in a motion matching her own.

Parts of the cavern were not the spectacular crystals but plain salt-sandstone pillars. Hollee had suggested they remove them, but according to Librettowit's studies, it was imperative to the integrity of the structure to leave them. So Fenworth had decided to carve the columns with decorative ornaments and figures. By the time he finished, a story had emerged, depicted in the sculpted pillars. It told of Verrin Schope's accidental journey to Amara, his introduction to Wulder, and the quest that occurred after his return.

Hollee asked, "Are you going to do one about the invasion of Chiril by Baardack?"

"Tut, tut. Oh dear, oh dear. Perhaps when we can depict a victorious conclusion."

Hollee scrunched up her face. "Should we go back and help our side win?"

"Do you find it rather boring here, my little friend?"

She hung her head, not wanting to look into his kind eyes. "Sometimes."

"Then the next part of our venture will be more to your liking."

She raised her chin to see his face and widened her eyes in a question.

He grinned. "We are going to the Valley of Dragons above us. There we shall recruit fierce dragons to guard this memorial."

"It's a memorial?"

Librettowit joined them and put two fingers of his large hand on Hollee's shoulder. "Wulder has often told His followers to erect monuments to remind generations to come of His Providence. Just because our parents understand His Glory does not mean our children will see the same Truth. And it is not an arduous task. Keeping the Truth alive in the next generation is as simple as showing a child that a fire burns and a cloud holds rain. We demonstrate that some actions lead to destruction, some to further development."

Hollee tipped her chin back so she could look at the tumanhofer standing behind her. "Development?"

"New beginnings, like a dried seed is watered by the rain and becomes a stalk of wheat."

Fenworth grabbed his hat off his head and drew out an egg. "Or an egg is kept warm and out pops a dragon."

Within seconds, the shell cracked and a minor dragon baby rubbed his chin on the wizard's palm.

"Advancement," said Librettowit, "like building a staircase instead of climbing a rope."

"Improvement," said Fenworth, "like an oven instead of an open campfire."

"Progress," said the librarian, "like a flute instead of a reed pipe."

"Hollee," Fenworth said in his very serious and important voice.

Hollee leaned forward in anticipation. Sometimes the things Fenworth declared sent shivers of comprehension along her limbs. He opened doors of understanding with a few words.

"Hollee."

She leaned forward even more.

"Always test your intentions by this measure. Will your actions bring destruction or mark another step toward a positive end?"

She nodded, hoping he would continue and not veer off into some obscure thought.

He held up a finger.

She waited.

"For instance, feeding an old wizard should result in a positive outcome."

Librettowit laughed. "And starving your comrades might destroy the fellowship we are enjoying. I agree, Fen. Let's eat the jimmin chicken Hollee has prepared."

"I have another something to do first," she said.

The old men looked at her but did not speak.

"May I have the dragon you just hatched?"

"Ooh, I'm sorry, my dear," said Wizard Fenworth. "That was but an illusion."

Hollee sighed. "All right. We can eat."

Fenworth laid a finger on her slumped shoulder. "I shall ask the next real dragon I meet if he would like to be your companion."

Battleground

When Bealomondore returned to Ragar with the others, he was thrust into the organization of the army. He wasn't doing the organizing but fell into the hands of those who were. These men seemed to believe that because he was well-born, he must have been educated on military history and was therefore eligible to command. Bealomondore took this to mean that finding suitable officers for their fighting force had proven almost impossible. Why else would they choose him to lead? Perhaps the sword impressed them.

Before the men were trained or even fully equipped, the enemy army marched south, destroying farms and villages. The war had begun in earnest whether Chiril was ready or not. Bealomondore had been given a platoon to command. All he knew to do was to get between the enemy and unconquered territory and do their best to keep the invaders at bay. They had met with some success but more defeats.

Bealomondore sounded the retreat. His men had valiantly pushed back a surge of enemy soldiers, only to find fresh reinforcements beyond the last hill. He'd led his men into a trap, but fortunately Det had projected an aerial view into his thoughts before it was too late to withdraw. He and his men fell back in an orderly fashion, joining the main line of their forces.

He owed Laddin thanks for keeping his body able and his mind alert through hours of treacherous battle. The healing dragon rode inside his coat. He crawled out as they came closer to safety and wrapped his lithe green body around Bealomondore's neck.

The commander ordered Bealomondore's men to retire from the front and seek refuge in the camp. The tumanhofer helped one of his wounded soldiers navigate the uneven ground to the hospital tent.

Once he had the younger man on an empty cot, he sank to the floor and leaned against the canvas wall. He knew he should go to the kitchen tent and eat something, but exhaustion made the effort seem too arduous. Apparently Laddin's physical support had met its match. His two minor dragons sat beside him, their chins resting on his legs.

Tipper appeared with a cup of water. "Are you all right?"

He nodded and took the offered drink. "Just tired and probably hungry, though I don't feel hunger pangs sufficient to make me stand up again."

"I'll bring you something. Rest."

He slumped in a stupor, unable to bring a clear thought to his brain. He noticed two women attending the man he had brought in but couldn't recall the soldier's name when they asked. Several minutes later, he remembered and blurted it out. One of the ladies looked at him strangely, but the other refilled the cup and had him drink more water.

Tipper returned with dry bread and meat for him and a bowl of porridge for the dragons.

"I'm sorry there is not more for you. We are sorely in need of supplies."

"I thank you," said Bealomondore. "And my dragons say they will eat enough to recover a bit, then see if they can rid your tent of some of the bugs that have gathered."

"That would be wonderful. The healing dragons work until they can't tend another soldier. They're too tired to forage."

Bealomondore forced down the dry bread and meat, rinsed his mouth by swishing the last of the water through his teeth, and leaned back against a stack of rolled blankets. The day was hot and the humidity high. He'd be more comfortable if he removed his jacket, but he closed his eyes instead.

Tipper shook him awake some time later. "Paladin has come with supplies. He's in the strategy tent with King Yellat and the high command. My grandfather is muttering about your father and the family's mine. I think you should go."

She helped him to his feet, then handed him a drink. "Paladin brought water, food, and medical supplies. My grandfather chastised him for not bringing weapons."

Bealomondore sighed and handed back the empty mug. "I'll see what I can do."

Tipper leaned down to kiss his cheek.

"Don't," Bealomondore protested. "I am covered with battle muck." She straightened, and he regretted his harsh response. "I've been killing, Princess Tipper. I fear the stain on my soul is worse than the stain on my clothes."

She looked around the huge tent at beds occupied by wounded men. "It's hard, but King Odidoddex has proven he is a harsh ruler in his own land. To allow him to seize more power would not be right."

Bealomondore put his hand on his sword hilt and knew he was only alive because of the wizard's gift.

"I should clean up before I enter the strategy tent."

"I think it is more important for you to go while they are still plotting the next move our army will make."

Bealomondore left and crossed their encampment to the tent where the high command gathered around a table covered with maps. Two guards briefly stalled him at the door, but he was admitted at King Yellat's approval.

He stood back against the wall with the other low-ranking officers who would be required to take news to their commanders. In the center of the room, five men examined one huge map. Bealomondore saw it was the territory they now defended. Or were trying to defend. They had been pushed back three times in as many days. The opposing force, besides being stronger, outmaneuvered them.

King Yellat and his advisors discussed the advantages of pulling back to the south or to the east.

General Commert pointed to the eastern route. "If we remove to the Hanson Valley, the Perchant Crags will protect our flank."

"This invader came over the Mordack Mountains," said General Orchin. "What makes you think they can't handle the tangle of cliffs and crevices presented there?" He pointed to the thin strip of rocky terrain. "It's only a matter of a mile or so across."

"As the bird flies," said General Commert. "It's a two-day struggle for a man."

"But," said General Orchin, "we would be leading the enemy toward a populated area. If we go south, the battlefield will be pastures and cropland. East is crowded with villages and townships."

The king cast an angry glare at his commanders. "Perhaps if their homes are threatened, more men will volunteer to repel the intruders."

Paladin's jaw worked. Bealomondore wondered what words he chewed instead of spitting out. King Yellat had pointedly told the young emerlindian that his advice, based on extensive reading, was not appreciated. For weeks, Paladin had unobtrusively provided for the men at the front lines.

The third commander, General Fitz, held up a hand. "South we can see their approach, but we are also exposed. I say east is the best route." He gestured toward the cluster of populated areas. "We will be closer to supplies as well, and there are a multitude of roads to aid in our movements."

Paladin broke his silence. "I can provide supplies whichever direction you choose. I agree with General Orchin, there is no need to bring the war to the doorstep of civilian homes."

King Yellat squared his shoulders. "We could also make the argument that we are putting the army directly between Odidoddex's forces and the towns. We are thereby protecting our citizenry." He glared at Paladin. "We go east." He waved a hand of dismissal. "Bealomondore, I will speak with you. The rest of you come back in thirty minutes with strategies for tomorrow's campaign."

The room cleared quickly. Bealomondore waited. The king came straight to the point.

"I am sending you to speak to your father."

"My father doesn't listen to me, Your Majesty. It might be better to send someone he respects."

"You will be speaking for me. He'd better respect that!"

"Yes, Your Majesty."

"He must step up his production, and he must sell the raw ore to the Chiril Armory, and only to Chiril Armory. Tell him to keep an account, and the treasury will pay him after we've driven the Baardackians over the Mordack Mountains."

Bealomondore searched for words to explain that the message would be ill-received and that any messenger would most likely anger his father. Would he even be able to relay the king's command before he was thrown out?

The king continued, "I'll have Paladin deliver you to Greeston." The king fell into a chair, put an elbow on the table, and allowed his head to rest in his hand. "You may go."

Paladin waited for him outside the tent flap. The young man and Bealomondore walked back to the hospital tent.

"Has the king told you of his order for you to take me to Greeston?"

"Yes."

"I don't see that it will do much good if I am the one to propose that my father supply materials for arms."

"You need to know that King Yellat is giving your father one more chance to prove his loyalty to the king. There are rumors that he is making substantial profits selling to whoever offers the bigger purse. It is not the right time to be a businessman first and a Chirilian second."

"But that sounds like my father."

They walked on in silence. When the hospital tent came in view, the tumanhofer looked up to the tall emerlindian beside him.

"This war is going badly for us."

"The war is going badly for them as well."

"Really?" Bealomondore stroked his chin. "From my position this morning and yesterday and…" He looked around at the battered tents, the men sleeping on the ground in the middle of the day, and the women who washed and fed the army. They all looked ragged and incapable of enduring much more. "And from right here, right now, everything looks dismal and bleak. I see nothing brighter in the future. Another day of fighting. Another day of death. People dying, the land scorched. I hate this."

Paladin didn't answer, but Bealomondore's glance at his face told him how the young ruler felt. Prince Jayrus may have ruled over a peaceful principality of kimens and dragons, but he'd been tutored by a genius. Bealomondore suspected the man could offer advice that would shorten the days of conflict. King Yellat scorned the very man who could help him most.

Once inside the tent, Paladin went immediately to Tipper's side. Bealomondore checked on his men who were out of commission and then settled in the spot where he had slept.

He watched the quiet interchange between his princess and her prince. How did he know that Paladin had answers for this awful situation? He knew because Paladin relied on Wulder.

Darkness hid the marauders, but Sir Beccaroon had located four by their scent and breathing. Two mariones and two emerlindians.

He'd left Lady Peg and Verrin Schope in the Amber Palace in Ragar. He expected them to venture out of the city, on their way to aid the army, in a day or two. Staying another night indoors did not appeal to him. But he wished he had Verrin Schope with him now. The wizard could enter a man's mind and discern his objectives.

Beccaroon had no idea why the four men waited in the bushes while two men sat by a campfire. The four men hidden had eaten first, then taken blankets to their hiding spots. Blankets and weapons. And they didn't sleep. They guarded. The two men in the open talked, and their accents proved them to be Baardackians. The scenario spelled trouble of some sort.

A trill like a bellringer bird signaled a message of some kind. The two men nodded to one another and continued their charade of camaraderie.

"Yo, the camp." A voice came from the road nearby. "May I enter?"

"Certainly," said one of the men. He pulled a knife from his belt. "Show your face. Are you friend or foe?"

A well-dressed traveler stepped into the yellow light of the fire. His shambling walk revealed his age, and he led a horse by its reins. An instrument case hung across his back by a fancy strap that made a patterned red sash over the man's chest. "It isn't a good time to be camping alone, and I thought I might implore you to allow me to stay."

"We're Baardackians, but we're not part of this war," said the man who held his knife out of sight behind his thigh. "In fact, we're dodging their army as well. We don't want to be conscripted into fighting for our king. My name's Ephen, and this is my brother, Avid."

Avid nodded. He still sat and looked relaxed, but Beccaroon didn't trust him. Avid removed his cloth hat and scratched fingers through his thick blond hair.

"Yeah," said Avid, "King Odidoddex wants to rule the world, but he gives you no reason to love him. Taxes, commandeering, conscription, and mockery of justice. He's got no one to say, 'Long live the king,' where we come from." He reached for a pot. "Do you want some soup?"

"I don't mind if I do." The stranger came forward. "I was supposed to reach my destination in time for a banquet, but my horse is lame, and we've been walking for over an hour."

"You're heading to the capital?"

"No, the other way. I'm a minstrel, and I was to entertain at Sir Inger's mansion. My name is Thur the Third Bard of Themis."

Ephen laughed out loud. "Our treat. Some entertainment for providing your meal and safety through the night! Eat up."

"Boscamon favors us," said Avid. "It's just like the trickster to provide the stories we need to feel at home in this land. You'll sing us a tune or two of history. We don't know many of your Chiril ballads. Since we may end up living here to avoid our king, we could use some educating."

"Be glad to." Thur sat and took the offered bowl and spoon. "There's some old history in my songs, but the most interesting tune is of the new prince who showed up out of nowhere, the three magic statues, and two wizards—one from Chiril and one from Amara."

"Amara?" Ephen cast Avid an incredulous look. "You don't say? Isn't that clear on the other side of the world?"

"It's an interesting tale. Let this good soup warm my stomach, and I'll sing you the news of today as well as yesterday."

Beccaroon narrowed his eyes. Four men still in the bushes. Three men comfortable around the fire. The minstrel too willing to share information with men who were, more than probably, the enemy. He didn't like it. Not one bit.

39

Secret Revealed

Sir Beccaroon weighed his options. He'd already been perched when these ne'er-do-wells settled in. Any movement he made might attract the attention of the four thugs in the bushes.

They had bows and arrows at the ready, and he didn't feel like imitating a pincushion. He could probably fly at a sharp incline away from the camp and be out of range before they spotted him. If he flew to his right, his escape would be covered by tall trees. That would be favorable for him but not much help to the minstrel who'd walked into the trap.

What exactly did they figure to gain by ambushing the traveler? The road, as one of the major links to Ragar and Growder, carried significant traffic. Perhaps they expected to detain an important official or sneak into the capital by joining a group of innocent citizens.

The sound of a drummerbug came from below, then echoed from the other side of the clearing. It blended in nicely with other night calls from insects and birds, but Beccaroon knew it was man-made. He watched the men in the bushes. Three of them settled down as if to sleep. Around the campfire, the men ate.

Irked that he couldn't figure out their plan, the parrot decided to wait. He wouldn't leave before he determined their intent, and he wouldn't leave while he might have the chance to snatch this foolish old minstrel from some underhanded scheme.

He continued to puzzle over the situation. Could these men have hoped to waylay someone of more importance? Would the traveling musician inform these scoundrels about something of consequence with his songs?

After the meal and several drinks from a small keg, the minstrel took out his lute and strummed a few chords. The man had talent. The men pressed for the ballads relaying recent events, and the minstrel obliged. Sir Beccaroon would have preferred the older ballads, but whenever Thur moved to play an older tune, the men objected.

"It's not going to help us be a part of your citizenry if all we know is of long-ago battles and wooing between royal-type people," said Ephen. "Give us more of what the folks are talking about now."

"Aye," said Avid. "Tell me something I can brag about knowing and impress a lady or two with my great knowledge of the world."

They all laughed, and Thur began plucking a tune Sir Beccaroon did not know. The minstrel dived into the lyrics with enthusiasm, telling of three statues carved from one stone. The sculptor intended the figures to be placed in a circle. Great magic stirred from the center of the silent dance, and the world could come apart at their parting.

The second and third verses told that villains knew of the trick of turning each figure to dance in the opposite direction. This opened a door to evil lands. Then good men from afar came to rescue Chiril by foiling the two treacherous leaders of conquering armies. Now the stones were safe in the king's castle.

In the next song, the old minstrel sang of a man who reached into the mind of the immortal and told tales of gaining favor with the "Forever Ruler." This mortal man had been a prince with no kingdom, a dragonkeeper of a valley of dragons, and became the paladin, champion of the people and giver of truth.

When he finished, Avid asked, "This is like Boscamon, right? A god that controls things?"

"I don't think so, but I know only what I've been told. It seems Wulder is the god and the paladin is His worker of some sort."

"Then Paladin is real. You've seen him?"

"No, not me," answered the singer. "But I hear he was in the castle, and he travels with a foreign wizard and Verrin Schope, who carved the three statues."

"I'm more interested in those statues." Ephen struck a limb he was using as a poker against a burning log. A shower of sparks went up in the air. "Did that really happen? That army came pouring out of a hole in nothing and straight into the king's ballroom, right? That must have been something."

"Only those who were there that night know for sure," answered Thur. "There are lots of stories about many people being hurt in a brawl right in the ballroom of the Amber Palace. But if the evil men were there, they and their army disappeared as quick as they showed up."

"So these statues are in the Amber Palace?" asked Avid.

"No, they disappeared."

Avid slapped his hands on his knees. "Well then, that's simple. The evil men took the statues."

"No, first the wicked wizard and his henchmen disappeared, then later the statues were taken."

"So they came back for the statues." Avid's face, aglow from the firelight, looked stubborn.

Beccaroon thought the man too sure of himself when he had so few facts. The minstrel shook his head, but before he could say no to that idea, Avid jumped to his feet.

Ephen sprang up to stand between the minstrel and his brother. "Now you're making my brother angry. He likes to have things all figured out. Who's who. What's what. And where's a thing supposed to be. It bothers him some not to have a thing in its proper place." The sturdy man turned to his brother. "We'll not talk of this anymore tonight, Avid. You just think of this as a fairy tale, no truer than donkeys building houses or people being born inside a rosebud and never growing bigger than your big toe."

Avid remained tense, glaring at the man on the other side of his brother. Finally he relaxed, lazily picked up a couple of sticks, and laid them on the fire. Then he strolled off into the woods.

"Where's he going?" asked Thur in a voice so quiet Beccaroon had to strain to hear it.

"Nowhere in particular. Probably one last trip to answer the call of nature before we bed down. Don't worry about him. He gets riled quick, but then it's over."

Avid didn't return for some time. Thur unfolded a blanket given to him by the calmer brother, used his wadded-up coat for a pillow, and went to sleep. Ephen turned in next, and after a long while, Avid came back to lie on the third side of a triangle with the fire in the middle.

The night guard crouched behind a bush and watched. A drummerbug beat a rhythm in the dark. At the signal, the guard tiptoed to the nearest man. He touched the sleeping figure and repeated the drummerbug sound.

Soft words were exchanged, but Beccaroon could not hear. The first man settled down to sleep, and the second took over the watch. Beccaroon nodded. Nothing more was likely to happen that night. He allowed the calm sounds of real insects to lull him to sleep.

An oath, loud and foul but not of his language, rudely awoke him the next morning. He shook his feathers and peered through an early fog still clinging to the ground and bushes. Six men stood where the fire had warmed three the night before. One man, the minstrel, still lay in his blanket.

"Who did this?" barked Ephen. He glared at Avid. His gaze swept over the four other men. "Who slept through their watch and let this happen?"

No one answered.

"Let me see your knife, Avid."

The brother took his weapon from its sheath and handed it over. Ephen examined it briefly and handed it back.

"Why, brother? You didn't have to slice his throat. We could have just let him go on his way this morning."

The four men shuffled back a few steps.

Bile rose in Beccaroon's throat, but it was quickly doused with a healthy dose of anger. Why murder the man in his sleep? He waited to hear what Avid would say. When he didn't answer, the four men stepped back again.

"Oh, forget it," said Ephen. "What's done is done." He turned to address the men on the verge of flight. "Bury him, and do a good job of it. We don't want him found."

They jumped to obey. Avid still stood next to the body.

Ephen wiped his hand down his face as if to remove some horrid stain. "I'm going to find Groddenmitersay and give him the information we learned last night."

"Take him with you," said one of the men.

Ephen looked his brother over. "Yeah, you come with me, Avid."

After Ephen and Avid rode off and while the other four men took turns digging, Beccaroon flew off on an errand of his own. He intercepted the carriage bringing Verrin Schope and Lady Peg from Ragar. The coachman pulled up as soon as he saw the parrot beside the road.

The couple sat facing each other in the opulent coach. Verrin Schope stuck his head out one window, and Lady Peg peered through the other.

"You've news," said the wizard. He opened the door and stepped down to the road.

Sir Beccaroon nodded to Lady Peg. "Pardon me, Lady Peg, but I would like for your husband to sit on the roof with me for a while. We have some business to discuss."

"Oh, please, Verrin Schope," said the lady, "do go up instead of trying to talk with Bec here. I would try to understand, and that is something I really don't want to do. Instead, I'll sit here and compose a poem about our travels."

Sir Beccaroon tilted his head and peered up at the carriage where Tipper's mother could be seen through the window. "I've known you for many years, Lady Peg. How is it that I am unaware that you write poetry?"

"I don't write poetry, Bec."

"This is your first poem then?"

The look on her face told him he should have never responded to her first statement. A glance at her husband revealed the gentleman distracted by a fascinating tree growing next to the road. Fortunately, the good sculptor decided to take pity on his old friend.

Verrin Schope took his wife's hand through the window and placed a courtly kiss on the soft knuckles.

"Compose away, sweet, sweet lily of my heart."

Beccaroon flew to the top of the carriage, where Verrin Schope soon joined him. The driver gave the command to "Get on."

As soon as the horses had gathered enough speed to produce a clattering that covered their lack of conversation, Verrin Schope mindspoke to his old friend.

"You're upset about something."

I missed seeing a murder this morning. I slept. If I'd been more vigilant, I could have saved his life.

"Tell me."

Sir Beccaroon began with the first noises that came from below his perch, heralding the crew who would camp beneath him. The whole story took no more than ten minutes but changed the plan they were in the middle of executing.

"Going to Growder is no longer an option," said Verrin Schope.

"I agree."

"I'll send someone else to encourage the men to enlist. Have you noticed how much better the people have been these last weeks? Fenworth has the statues together, and the mental unrest among the people has all but ceased. The good citizens of Chiril are rising to the challenge of defending their homes."

Beccaroon tsked, shaking his beak. "King Yellat is still acting like he must punish someone for their original reluctance to rally 'round the cause."

"He took it as a personal rejection of his authority. I doubt that even a victory would erase the sting of their noncompliance with his orders." Verrin Schope stared at his hands folded together. White knuckles indicated his opinion of his father-in-law's pride.

Beccaroon prodded the conversation back to the problem. "But we can't do anything about that now."

"Correct." The wizard relaxed his grip and stretched his fingers. "We must endeavor to stop these people from informing their superiors of the statues and their value."

"At least they don't know where they are."

Verrin Schope remained silent. Beccaroon watched his clever friend's face. He knew exactly when a scheme was coming together in his mind by the pleasant smile that transformed his expression.

The wizard artist winked. "We shall need the talents of Lady Peg to pull this off."

"Poetry?" asked Beccaroon.

A loud bark of laughter escaped her husband. "No, we shall need her peculiar brand of logic."

"I pity the enemy," said Bec.

"As you should."

"Do we know where the statues are?"

"I do."

"With Fenworth?"

"Of course."

Sir Beccaroon squinted one eye at Verrin Schope. "And you know where Wizard Fenworth is?"

The sculptor looked offended, then winked. "Of course."

40

Confusion

Sir Beccaroon followed Verrin Schope and his wife as they strolled into the inn. "I'm not sure I understand what I am to do," complained Lady Peg. "Except what I am doing is for Wulder, my father, and the country."

The wizard patted his wife's hand as it rested on his sleeve. "Don't worry, Peg. What you do naturally is enough to confound the wisest of strategists."

Beccaroon admired her profile as she gazed adoringly at her husband. She had almost no wrinkles in her fair skin, and she radiated youth. Her stunning beauty turned heads everywhere. He loved to watch new acquaintances' expressions change when she spoke. He didn't quite understand what Verrin Schope hoped to accomplish but trusted his scheme would work.

Verrin Schope instructed the minor dragons to stay out of sight. Two flew to the roof of the Blue Moon, and two dived into his cape.

Inside the inn, Sir Beccaroon asked to be seated for noonmeal. Before his eyes could adjust to the dim light, he heard Lady Peg greet someone.

"I remember you," she said. "We met in the village of Selkskin. Do you remember we walked together one day?"

Groddenmitersay answered, "Yes, milady, I do remember."

"This is my husband, Verrin Schope, and our good friend, Sir Beccaroon of the Indigo Forest. It's more of a jungle than a forest. Huge flowers, snakes, and tiny fibbirds. We live on the edge, where we can see the beauty." She paused to take a breath and raise one finger. "But we do not have to deal with any unpleasantness, like rabbit-eating spiders."

She shook her head. "Sir Beccaroon is the magistrate and takes care of other unpleasantness. Not spiders, of course. I don't believe they would learn to eat cabbage instead of rabbits. The rabbits eat cabbage from our garden, and Bec has no jurisdiction over that either. But when our cow visited with some vagrants, Bec sent her home again. I don't think he reprimanded the cow, because she really didn't have much sense, so he must have talked to the scalawags. I suppose he spoke sternly, because they did mind him. You don't mind if he sits with us, do you? I'm sure he doesn't mind if you sit with us. Unless you are a vagrant or a scalawag. Of course, he doesn't mix business with pleasure and if you're—" She spotted the innkeeper. "We'd like a table now. We are very hungry."

Groddenmitersay gritted his teeth behind the false smile he'd pinned on his face. They'd followed him. She threatened him with the law. She considered him to be no better than a scalawag or a vagrant. And she might have implied he was lower than a cow. He wasn't sure about that.

Should he walk away or sit with them for noonmeal? What was her plan? It wouldn't surprise him if she gave the orders and the other two were merely her henchmen.

No matter how clever the woman was, he would not be bamboozled. He could match her cunning deceit.

"I would be pleased to dine with you, Lady Peg." Aha! He sounded just as ingenuous as she did. "Perhaps you or your comrades can tell me some news of this war." That should pique her curiosity. "I'm a long way from home and don't understand why my king would choose to invade Chiril. It seems we had an equitable trade agreement. Why cast that aside?"

Lady Peg made a face at the mention of war. Groddenmitersay cocked his head and waited. He'd caught her off guard with his pointed question. She would see he was more than a match for her subterfuge.

"War!" Lady Peg motioned toward the table where the innkeeper stood ready to serve them. "We don't approve of war."

She sat in the chair her husband pulled out for her.

Groddenmitersay sat on the opposite side of the table. "No civilized being approves of war."

The artist sat next to his wife. A male servant brought in a perch for Sir Beccaroon.

"We'll have our dessert first," said Lady Peg. "I would like anything hot with fruit in it and whipped cream."

The innkeeper suggested hot parnot layered between thin sheets of parted dough and cooked with seasonings from the east coast.

"Nothing," said Groddenmitersay.

The others ordered cake.

"Do you always eat dessert first?" asked Groddenmitersay.

"No," said Lady Peg. "But today is a day filled with good things, so it is only natural to begin with a sweet."

Groddenmitersay bit back his impatience. He would not let her taunt him into saying something he'd regret. This game would see him the winner. "And what is it about today that is so special?"

"We are celebrating Backward Day."

"I don't believe we celebrate Backward Day in Baardack."

"Well." Lady Peg pressed her hands together. "Some things are best done backward. For instance, when a woman washes her hair, you would expect her to wash it, comb it out, and put it on top in a do." She shook her finger at him and wagged her head back and forth.

His jaw ached from clenching his teeth. His cheeks ached from the false smile.

"But," said Lady Peg, "she must start at the other end of the process. She takes down her hair, combs out the tangles, and then washes it."

Groddenmitersay stared at her for a moment. She'd lost him. She looked so pleased with herself that the urge to strangle her rose violently in him. He wrapped his fingers around one of the inn's rough cloth napkins.

He glanced at the parrot and her husband. Neither showed any sign of being disturbed by the conversation. The parrot looked studious. Groddenmitersay decided the bird had two expressions, studious and interested. Studious for when he avoided being engaged in the conversation. Interested for when courtesy demanded he attend to the speaker.

The husband maintained a rather enigmatic but pleasant manner about him. He either entertained agreeable daydreams constantly or lacked brains to puzzle over a problem.

Groddenmitersay loosened his hold on the crumpled napkin. He deliberately relaxed his jaw and arranged his face in what he knew passed as the impression of polite questioning.

"I'm afraid I don't see the point, Lady Peg."

"Oh, you are so clever, Master Groddenmitersay. Of course you've pinpointed the bottom line in a backward day. The point is unfathomable. That means it is inexplicable. *Inexplicable* is a good word to say because of the way it sounds, but it is difficult to spell. My husband can spell it, but he does so many things well."

She patted him on the arm.

He smiled. "Thank you, my dear, but don't lose the point of your discussion on my account."

"The point?"

"Precisely."

She didn't speak.

Verrin Schope's voice did not indicate that her abstraction frustrated him. He merely reminded her of the topic under discussion. "The point of Backward Day."

"Oh yes, the point is unreliable." She turned her attention to the tumanhofer.

He thought her eyes might bore into his mind, seeing his confusion. She was getting away from him. He must concentrate, for there would be a clue. Something deep. Something profound.

She smiled. "It could be pointed this way or that but never as you would expect it. I love Backward Day because you can start at the core, rub through the nitty-gritty, travel past the heart, unless you are headed downward, and then you would pass the root. But in any case, after all your trouble, you finally get to the point, and it isn't where it should be, or it is still moving, or there are multiple points and no one bothered to tell you."

She took a deep breath and lowered her voice. "I'm never in favor of downward days. I did mention a downward path, but that is only in passing and one passes downward in order to turn upward, so downward is never really the purpose of the journey."

Groddenmitersay expelled a long breath, then pulled it back in. "What is the purpose of the journey, Lady Peg?"

She smiled graciously as the innkeeper delivered the desserts.

When they were all served and the man had walked away, Groddenmitersay cleared his throat. "The purpose, Lady Peg? The purpose of the journey?"

Her expression never altered. Her blue eyes swept the men around the table and settled on him. Again he had the uncomfortable feeling of being examined and found lacking.

He squared his shoulders. "The purpose?"

She dipped her chin, and her smile widened. "The same as the point." She leaned forward. Her voice came out in the barest whisper. "To come out on top."

<hr />

They left the inn after a filling noonmeal and continued their journey, not to Growder but to the Valley of Dragons in the Mercigon Mountains.

The grand parrot rested a shoulder against the side of the carriage, bracing himself. Jouncing over the rough road threatened to toss him off the slippery seat. He preferred to fly, but he needed information from his old friend. He longed for a perch, but he longed more to understand what had just happened.

"Verrin Schope," said Sir Beccaroon, "what was the purpose of Lady Peg's discourse on Backward Day?"

The wizard laughed out loud. "To thoroughly befuddle Grodden-mitersay. At this point he doesn't know up from down, backward from forward, or in from out. Any information he collects will be suspect. He won't know what is valid from what has been concocted to confound him."

"So the minstrel's tale of the three statues?"

The sculptor of those three statues shrugged. "Could be the vivid imagination of a man who is paid to entertain."

"Was paid. I should have gotten him out of there."

41

The Leader

The Grawl crouched behind a set of boulders, watching the kill. The schoergat swooped in with his lance tucked under his arm and pierced the side of his prey, a mountain goat. He shook the animal loose from the tip of his weapon. Swinging his legs forward and his wings into a horizontal slant, the schoergat stopped in midair and dropped to the ground. His feet landed next to the goat's head. Catching the struggling animal by one horn, he exposed its neck and sliced it with the sharp edge of his lance.

Patient, as always, The Grawl spent the day observing the creatures he hoped to enlist to battle the dragons. He noted their style of attack and determined when their vulnerable spots were exposed.

The lances they each carried would be no obstacle. He also used a lance and knew how to disarm a man quickly. But the schoergats' claws posed a problem. Long and sharp, the talons could pierce his skin and tear out parts of him that were better left inside. But their lack of height was in his favor. His arms and legs were longer, and once the lance was removed from a warrior's grip, The Grawl could kill without getting close to those bladelike fingernails.

He knew which of the schoergats held the position of leadership by the way the others deferred to him. This one he watched more carefully. If his plan worked, he would have to fight only the leader.

Telling the rest of the clan apart had been a challenge. By identifying small differences in their sparse clothing and variations in their movements, he named them and had them ordered as to importance. Torn Shirt had dominance over Right Limp. Itchy Back plagued the lowest of the males, Four Fingers.

The females amused him. They took great pleasure in stirring up strife. He pitied the males that had to keep them in line. One female reached behind her as she passed another, catching her in the act of stretching after a nap. She pinched the skin of the armpit hard enough to make the victim howl. It seemed part of their nature for the females to torment each other without reason.

When the sun coursed over the noonday sky, The Grawl had seen enough hunting by the schoergats to feel confident in his plan. He rose from his observation post and strode down a rough trail to the canyon floor. As he approached, the schoergats drew back, blending into their surroundings.

He stood exposed in a rock clearing. The area had been smoothed, and blood stained the dirt. The Grawl assumed this was the place where ceremonial feasting took place. The schoergats probably held judgment fights, combatants set against each other to settle a dispute. This would be the arena for that as well.

Soon the schoergats came forth, silently circling him. He counted sixteen, which meant two were still in hiding.

He stood tall and looked each in the eye before making his pronouncement. "I am The Grawl. I've come to lead you to a valley filled with dragons."

Leader stepped forward, his lance pointed at The Grawl. His beady black eyes had no whites around the pupil. He twisted his lips in distaste.

"We don't follow any creature other than the one appointed as head of the clan."

The Grawl found the raspy growl of the schoergat pleasant, a tone of voice he could get used to.

"I understand your people are the greatest killers of dragons among all creatures of the world. I also was told you eliminated the total population of dragons in the southern hemisphere."

Leader lifted his chin. "That's right."

"But it isn't. There are still dragons in Chiril."

He huffed. "Minor dragons, more like cats. We don't count one of them to make a single meal. The meat's stringy."

"No, not minor dragons."

The short schoergat tilted his head more to the side and looked up at The Grawl. "Why don't you kill them yourself?"

"I'm going after the wizard who tends them in the absence of the dragonkeeper. You slay the dragons. I slay the wizard."

"There isn't a dragonkeeper in Chiril."

"And you thought nothing but minor dragons lived in Chiril. You're wrong."

Leader growled. He cast a look at his clan. Nine men were ready to launch themselves on this intruder.

The Grawl read the eagerness to fight as easily as did their leader. He also knew of the two still hiding in reserve, to ambush him if necessary. He could probably take them all down, but that would defeat his purpose. And he didn't relish the hits he would take as he conquered this little band.

Grunts passed between the men and their leader. It irked him that he didn't know what had been communicated.

The leader pointed his lance toward The Grawl's throat.

"You tell us where this Valley of Dragons is, and I will lead my people there."

"No, I want your people to take orders from me."

The leader laughed, and those around him joined in. "I am head of clan. The people follow me."

"I challenge you for that position. You and I fight. If I win, your people hold me as leader. If you win, you remain the leader."

"What is your weapon?"

"My hands, my teeth, and my strength."

"I have the pultah." He held up his lance and shook it.

"You may carry your pultah into battle." He smiled, knowing that would unnerve his opponent. "But I will take your weapon away from you."

"A schoergat does not drop his pultah."

The Grawl merely raised his eyebrows. He could tell his arrogance vexed his small opponent. A warrior who entered combat in a riled state did not fight efficiently.

"If you drop your pultah, any of your clan is free to throw another for you to use."

Leader's eyes widened to expose a narrow band of red circling the black pupils. He swung around and grunted to the others. The look of anticipation fell from their faces, and each stepped away from the clearing.

Leader slowly pivoted to face his new enemy.

The Grawl nodded, squinting his eyes to disguise his pleasure in baiting the schoergat. "I won't fight you until you agree to the terms. I win, I rule. You win, you rule."

"Agreed." The drawn-out rumble in the word ended with the schoergat leaping into the air. His lance point turned down, and he plunged.

The Growl stepped aside, and his opponent had to avert a crash into the hard ground. He flew upward, circled, and came at The Grawl in another dive. The Grawl turned. The point missed him by inches, but The Grawl did not miss grabbing the end of the pultah. He followed the departing enemy with several running steps, and then he stopped their forward motion and swung the pole like he would hurl a sling around and around before he threw the projectile. When he let go, the pultah and schoergat slammed into one of the canyon walls.

While the schoergat gathered his wits, The Grawl marched over, took the pultah, and broke it over his knee. Leader pushed himself to his feet. Grunts from his clan encouraged him to straighten and glare at The Grawl. He gestured with his empty hand, and a pultah sailed down from Torn Shirt, one of the watchers.

Leader caught the weapon, hefted it as if to judge its balance, and charged. When he was within six feet of The Grawl, he leaped straight up, turned the pultah point down, and dropped out of the air to sink his weapon into The Grawl. Instead, the pultah struck dirt, and the point broke as the schoergat's weight forced the shaft to bend.

The Grawl stood several feet away, and the schoergats roared. Leader kicked the broken pultah out of his way and demanded another weapon from those watching. After a moment's hesitation, Itchy Back threw his pultah down. Leader had to move a few steps to pick up the weapon. He kept his eyes on his opponent.

The Grawl smiled. "I wouldn't attack you until you're armed. That wouldn't be fair."

The schoergat yelled, did a somersault, and came up with the pultah grasped in his hand. Leader's attack stance faced a huge boulder.

The Grawl had moved. Now he was behind Leader. He grabbed his wings, gripping them hard enough to shatter the delicate bones under the leathery skin. Leader screamed. The Grawl thrust him forward, pitching him face first into the boulder.

He held the schoergat pressed against the rock surface, twisting his wings with one hand and shoving his face into the boulder with a grinding motion.

"Acknowledge me as winner," he urged.

The creature dropped his weapon and brought a clawed hand up to tear The Grawl's grip off his head. But The Grawl had no intention of allowing those yellowed nails to dig at his flesh. As soon as Leader let go of the pultah, The Grawl whipped his body over his head and launched it at the other wall.

Bloodied and shaking, Leader heaved himself to a stand. "I'll kill you," he said.

"Too optimistic," replied The Grawl.

The schoergat curled his hands into weapons of ten razor-sharp blades. "I'll kill you."

He attacked in a straight-on run.

The Grawl picked up the abandoned pultah and held it firmly. Leader didn't recognize what defense his opponent had put up until it was too late. He impaled himself in a mad rush to slay The Grawl.

He choked on the blood filling his mouth. He glared at The Grawl, then shifted his gaze to the pole in his stomach. At last he slumped, and The Grawl carefully laid down the pultah.

He looked at the crowd that came closer. Seventeen schoergats circled him. The two who had hidden before had abandoned any idea of ambushing the stranger. The Grawl smiled at the acquiescence to his superior abilities.

"Who is your leader?" he asked.

They shuffled their feet and looked down.

Torn Shirt finally spoke. "We do not know your name."

"I have no name. I am The Grawl." He paused. "Who is your leader?"

A murmur went through the gathering. "The Grawl."

"I will lead you to the Valley of Dragons, once guarded by Paladin. Now two old men supervise the safety of dozens of dragons, all shapes, all sizes, all ages. You will have your fill of killing. The dragons are your reward for following me."

He waited. The idea penetrated their thinking. One female cackled, and soon the others joined in.

"We will follow you," said Torn Shirt. "The Grawl is our leader."

"So I am. So I am."

42

Seeking Sage

Hollee hummed a sprightly tune as she followed Wizard Fenworth through the long tunnel that took them from the statue site to the surface.

The old gentleman complained. "If we'd had a dozen tumanhofers to help us, we'd have three of these tunnels operational in the time it's taken to dig one."

"One's enough for now, isn't it? You've had to set up wards to keep villains from discovering our treasure. You wouldn't want to do that all over the valley."

"I would. I could. But botheration, I'm getting old."

Hollee did a cartwheel, and the wizard laughed.

"Tut, tut. Oh dear. I'm not that spry."

"Maybe your body doesn't jump and run like it used to, but your brain does."

"My brain jumps and runs?" He stopped and contemplated the idea. "Hollee, I believe you're right."

They continued up the incline, moving toward the spot of sunshine ahead of them.

"Are we going to talk to the dragons now?" Hollee asked.

"Just one, and Hollee, this will please you. Sage is the oldest living dragon. At least the oldest anyone knows about. He is older than I am."

Hollee's hushed and awestruck tone revealed her amazement. "No!" She did a somersault in the air and squeaked as she came down. "Really, really?"

Wizard Fenworth nodded seriously. "Really." He stopped only feet from the exit to the tunnel. "In fact, I believe some ceremony might be in order. Brighten your clothing, Hollee, and try to look a tad more groomed."

Fenworth stood perfectly still for a moment as his clothes changed from the working robes he had been wearing to his very best wizard attire. His outer robe sparkled with gemmed birds, glittering bushes dotted with colorful flowers, and an embroidered waterfall with shimmering aquamarine threads.

The water looked like it flowed. Hollee watched it pour over his shoulder, down one side of the dark robe, where it ended in a froth at the hem. She came closer to examine the way it rippled and discovered that a river streamed off from the base of the fall. She followed it around to where the water traveled up the wizard's back to fall again over his shoulder.

Fenworth remained still as his hat transformed to match the magnificence of his robe. Under the outer garment, his drab, light brown tunic changed to a glistening white. The walking stick that he almost always carried let out a brilliant light, and when it faded, her wizard held an intricately carved and polished staff.

"There, there now. I think we're ready." He looked down at his little kimen friend. "Tut, tut, Hollee. Is that the best you can do?"

He handed her a comb. She raked it through her flyaway locks, but the result did not please Fenworth.

"If anything, you're more disheveled than when you began." He tossed water on her head, and she squealed. She also sparked.

"Oh dear. I forgot about that. Are you hurt?"

She shook her head. Drips of water and sparkles showered around her. "No."

"Then pat down your hair."

She obeyed, carefully smoothing the wet tresses to lie flat around her head. With a smile, she peered up at her wizard. "Is that better?"

The fine hair dried in a moment. As each hair lost the weight of moisture, it popped up. In the end, her frizzle-do topknot crowned her head once more.

Fenworth gave her a wink. "Very much more like a distinguished kimen."

That sent Hollee off in a fit of giggles. When she could speak, she claimed that kimens didn't hold being distinguished as a very desirable state.

"True, true," said Fenworth. "And come to think of it, this valley is heavily populated with kimens as well as dragons. Sage will expect you to look like a kimen."

"Does he live in a cave or a palace?"

"Cave, under the lake. This valley is where Prince Jayrus lived. He told me about Sage. Sir Beccaroon visited the old dragon while he was here."

"Under the lake?"

"Yes."

"We have to go under the lake?"

"Yes."

"How will we breathe?"

Fenworth wrinkled his brow. "Through your nose or your mouth. I don't think it matters which means you choose to employ."

Hollee temporarily gave up her quest for details and skipped beside him as the tall o'rant wizard stretched his legs into a swift march.

The old man whistled a tune, then said, "My, my, it's good to be out in the sunshine."

"It is," agreed Hollee. She decided to have another go at pinning him down on how they would get to where they were going. "But, Wizard Fenworth, is the cave filled with water?"

"No, no, of course not. It is rather wet because that keeps the old dragon's skin in good condition."

"So we need to find the entrance to the cave and walk in a tunnel under the lake to find the cave in which Sage resides."

"Good work, Hollee."

The kimen grinned. After being with Wizard Fenworth for quite a while now, she knew how he appreciated not ending a sentence with a preposition. It gave her lots of opportunities to say "in which."

They crested a hill and saw the lake in the distance.

"Where's the entrance to the cave?" she asked.

"On an island."

She peered at the small lake and could see trees growing on the other side. "Where's the island?"

"In the lake, of course." Fenworth shook his head and looked at her with some concern. "Do you need a nap? Did you eat your breakfast?"

"No. Yes."

"Try not to ask questions that lead me to believe your brainbox is leaking and in need of restoration. And when we meet Sage, be especially careful not to offend him, because I may have already done so."

He took off with a swift stride down the grassy knoll.

"You offended him? How?"

"You must stand up straight, and don't fidget."

"How could he be mad at you?"

"Remember to say please and thank you and use your handkerchief. Don't sniff."

"What did you do?"

"Don't stare. I daresay, he is probably a sight. An old dragon, very old. Somewhat reddish because in his prime he was a magnificent fire dragon. But old now. Probably wrinkly."

"I won't stare. What did you do?"

"And if you get the hiccups, don't giggle. It's considered ill-mannered in most circles to laugh and hiccup at the same time."

"In most circles? I've never heard that. Are you sure?"

"Quite."

Hollee thought about that for a moment, then her mind returned to a possible quarrel between her wizard and the dragon Sage. "Wizard Fenworth?"

An exasperated sigh puffed out the wizard's cheeks before he let it expel between his lips. "I built our little project before consulting him, and this is his territory."

"Oh."

"Oh, indeed. Completely slipped my mind to take his leave, ask his indulgence, present the situation to him as the head of dragons in this valley. But I've thought of it now. Memory is a peculiar thing. Handy when it works. Inconvenient when it doesn't."

They waded through knee-high grass, knee-high to the o'rant. The field stretched from the base of the hill to the edge of the lake.

Hollee could no longer see the water. But she didn't mind pushing the towering blades aside and slipping between them. She wondered if they'd encounter some wild animal. She listened intently but only heard the *swish-swish* of Fenworth's robes in the grass.

Perhaps they'd come across lost treasure, something Paladin had dropped while doing his acrobatic stunts on the riding dragons high in the sky. An amulet would be nice. Or something magical. A stone, maybe, that when warmed in your hand would become clear and create a vision within of your loved ones.

The thought occurred to her that maybe Sage had treasure. "Do dragons really have heaps of gold and jewels? And do they sleep on them?"

"No." The wizard abruptly stopped. "Where are you?"

"Down here." She watched a small snake slither under the hem of Fenworth's robe.

"Come up here and ride on my shoulder."

Hollee skimmed up his garments and situated herself comfortably on his shoulder.

He began to walk again. "Why do you want to know about treasure?"

"I've never seen a treasure, and I thought it would be interesting."

"Well, our cavern cathedral is grander than any treasure I've ever seen."

Hollee grinned. "I'm sure it is. And I bet it is grander than any treasure I will ever see."

"Quite right."

Hollee bounced on his shoulder. "I see the island now."

Fenworth said nothing.

"How are we going to get across the water?"

"I don't like getting my feet wet."

"I know."

"By boat or by air."

"Do you have a boat?"

"Librettowit has the boat."

"Maybe we should have asked him along."

"Couldn't."

"Why not?"

"A true friend protects a friend from committing social gaffes."

"Librettowit doesn't know the proper formalities for conversation with a dragon? I thought he did. It seems like he knows a great deal of things."

Fenworth was silent.

"What social gaffe would Librettowit fall into?"

"Gloating."

Hollee thought about it for a while. She didn't think her wizard appreciated all her questions, and if she put her mind to the clues, she figured she could guess.

They reached the shore of the small lake, and Hollee hopped down. They quietly watched the water lap gently against the grassy bank.

Hollee figured that Wizard Fenworth was working on a plan to cross the water. She was working on the puzzle of Librettowit gloating.

He wouldn't gloat at something the dragon said, so he must be proud of himself for…what?

Something he said.

Hollee looked up at Fenworth. "Librettowit reminded you when we first got here to seek an audience with Sage, and you didn't do it."

He waved a hand in the air. "I had a lot on my mind."

She nodded. He did. He always did. If she'd known about it, she could have reminded him. Librettowit could have reminded him. Sometimes dealing with incredibly intelligent people took a lot of tact. That was probably why Winkel chose her to accompany the wizard.

She tilted her head back and let the sun warm her face. Even for a kimen, Hollee had untold skill in diplomacy. She decided to gloat and relish her fantastic expertise.

Gazing at a tiny cloud, she gathered words in her mind to define her cleverness. When she felt sufficiently armed, she closed her eyes and thought.

She handled problems with a great deal of sound judgment and discretion. With insight and discernment, she engaged acute perception in employing just the right methods for smoothing out a dispute.

She giggled. What she did was accept each player in the row and let it all blow over. Her job was to be of good cheer. And she excelled at amiability.

Opening her eyes, she saw that Fenworth was halfway to being a mullytawny tree. She grabbed his arm.

"Look, Wizard Fenworth." She pointed to where the cloud had been some time ago. "Here comes a dragon. Call him down from the sky. Ask him to take you to the island. I could swim."

The wizard shook off some leaves and glared at her.

"Do you know what you are, Hollee?"

"Amiable," she answered with a smile.

"I was thinking bossy."

43

Sage Advice

"Ah!" said Wizard Fenworth as he sighted the dragon flying toward them. "This is a dragon I know. It's Gus, and she'll be willing to give us a lift, no doubt."

Hollee watched the dragon land. She didn't admit it to her wizard, but the riding dragons made her a bit shy.

The dragon swung her huge head around to stare at the wizard.

"Oh dear, tut, tut." The wizard shook his head. "Maybe not."

"Maybe not what?"

"Gus seems a bit peeved with me." He sighed deeply. "She may not want to accommodate us by giving us a ride to the island."

"Oh dear," said Hollee. "Oh dear, oh dear."

"Perhaps you could speak to her."

Hollee took a deep breath and swallowed the lump in her throat. "Pardon me, Miss Gus. My name is Hollee, and I come from the Starling Forest." She waited for a response.

The dragon's face grew less fierce, and she tilted her head as she examined the small kimen.

Without taking her eyes off Gus, Hollee spoke to Fenworth. "I don't think I can hear her. I wonder if she can hear me."

"She can hear you. She hears through her ears. You have to hear through your mind, and it's her choice whether you hear her or not." The wizard took off his hat, bunched it into a ball, then shook it out to put it back on. "Well, try again."

Hollee just looked at him, wondering why he was so fidgety.

He raised his eyebrows and pointed to Gus. "Ask her, and ask politely."

"Miss Gus," Hollee began, "we need to seek the ad—"

The ground rumbled beneath her feet. The dragon shook. Hollee turned toward the wizard and found he was shaking too.

"What? What's happening?" she asked.

Wizard Fenworth's mouth turned down at the corners. "The confounded beast is laughing at you. You are the first to call her 'Miss Gus.'" Small creatures poured out of his clothing and made their escape, flying, crawling, and slithering away. A couple of lizards cantered off toward the high grass.

"I don't think you have any visitors left, Wizard Fenworth."

"Never mind that. Ask her while she's in a good mood."

"Miss Gus, we need to consult with the venerable Sage. Would you be so kind as to carry us across to the island?"

Fenworth spoke. "She's asking why we don't swim."

"What should I tell her?"

"The truth."

"I could swim, Miss Gus, but Wizard Fenworth doesn't like to get his feet wet."

Again the ground and everything else shook. Ripples danced across the lake.

Fenworth sighed and sat down right where he had stood on the grassy bank.

"She knows I'm a bog wizard and thinks it hilarious that I don't like damp feet. I think it's natural when one lives in a soggy place that one would be extra sensitive to the uncomfortable state of being damp. There's nothing absurd about that. Stands to reason if you've lived all your life a bit wet most of the time, you'd appreciate dryness more than the average person."

"Why is she mad at you, sir?"

"She thinks I am at fault for coming here and taking her Prince Jayrus away. Life isn't as much fun in the valley with him gone."

Hollee stepped closer to the huge dragon. Gus dipped her head, and Hollee jumped back.

"Miss Gus, Wizard Fenworth did indeed come to ask the dragonkeeper to provide transportation for a very important quest. Prince Jayrus decided to go on that quest, and it was a good thing he did. Do you know he helped save the world? Did you know that he battled dozens of villains? He slew the wicked, he championed the weak, he outsmarted the evil minions of a powerful and wicked slave trader. If he had not vanquished the fiendish foes, all of Chiril would have fallen under a depraved despot."

Fenworth muttered from where he sat. "He did have some help, you know."

"Even now, Paladin, your Prince Jayrus, battles an invasion by the iniquitous ruler of Baardack."

To Gus, Fenworth said, "*Iniquitous* means 'bad,' as in King Odidoddex does things that result in injustice. Like taking farmers' produce or unfairly taxing the citizens."

Gus's head swung around so that she stared off toward the island. Fenworth stood.

"She's agreed to take us, but she doesn't have a saddle. We'll be all right. Just don't say anything to make her laugh. We'd jiggle right off."

Fenworth strode over to Gus, stroked the side of her neck and flattered her with words expounding her beautiful colors. She lay down so that the wizard and Hollee could climb aboard. Gus stood, extended her wings, and with a few steps launched into the air.

Hollee leaned against Fenworth's back and held tight to his wizard robe. She did like to fly. Facing a dragon with its wise eyes and sharp teeth sent shivers down her spine. Standing on the scaly top of one with the wind fluffing up her wild hair did not even raise one goose bump.

They landed on the island in the only place large enough for Gus to set down. Hollee jumped off. Wizard Fenworth hefted one leg over to line up with the other and slid down.

"Thank you very much." He tipped his hat to Gus. "It was a delightful ride, and I will give your message to Prince Jayrus. I understand your irritation, and all is forgiven."

The dragon spread her wings and took off.

Hollee shouted, "Thank you, good-bye, good-bye!"

"This way," said Fenworth, and she followed him into the undergrowth of a small wood. Only a few paces into the stand of trees, Fenworth entered a dark cave. Warm air dampened Hollee's skin. Fenworth muttered about moisture, humidity, mold, mildew, mugginess, dankness, and clamminess.

As they traveled farther into the recesses of the island, the path sloped steeply. Someone had positioned lightrocks along the walls. The stone walk shimmered with a wet coating, but there were no slippery spots.

They turned a corner, and the floor leveled. Ahead, Hollee saw a different light from the blue glow of lightrocks.

"Do you suppose that's his cave?" she asked Fenworth.

A voice came from in front of them. "It is most certainly his, and you have awakened him."

"Sorry, Sir Sage," Hollee called out.

"Ah, the voice of a kimen. And one I don't know. Welcome, child."

"I am traveling with Wizard Fenworth, an ancient wizard from Amara, on the other side of the world."

"He is welcome as well. Perhaps he has Arbaneous Topicalee in one of his hollows?"

"I do," said the wizard. "Are you in need of a little pick-me-up?"

"I am in need of a larger pick-me-up than you are capable of supplying. It all comes from being old."

"I know the feeling."

They reached the entry to the cave. Hollee blinked rapidly at the brightness of many colored lightrocks covering the walls. "Ooh, this is beautiful."

"Thank you, child. It's home."

"I've never talked to a dragon before. I mean one that talked back. I don't mean talked back as in sassiness. I mean talked back out loud."

"You need not be nervous. What is your name?"

"Hollee from the Starling Forest."

"I spent some of my youth in your forest."

Hollee heard something crinkling, and as her eyes adjusted to the dazzling light, she saw that Sage was moving. Every time he shifted his body, his reddish skin rumpled and made a scrunching noise. She was surprised he was so small. Small for a dragon. His size matched that of a draft horse, but his skin hung on him in a baggy sort of way, and he didn't look nearly as majestic as one of the huge horses.

"Welcome, Wizard Fenworth."

"Thank you. May I have permission to use your name?"

"You may, and I am delighted that you remember dragon protocol. I also appreciate that you have worn your formal attire into my humble and humid home."

Fenworth bowed. "Sage, I come to reveal that I have trespassed under your valley. I ask your pardon and hope to enlist your aid. May I tell you more of the importance of our project?"

"Yes, you may, and have a seat. I apologize that I have no refreshments to offer you."

"But I have the Arbaneous Topicalee. May I place some before you?"

"Certainly."

Fenworth opened his robe and delved within one of the hollows. He pulled out a thick purple slab that looked like a giant beast's dried tongue.

"What is that?" Hollee asked with her nose wrinkled. She caught a whiff of a pleasant odor, and her face relaxed.

"It is Bane bark, pulverized, mixed with a bit of pica, and dried. It is sweet, from the pica, and filled with vitamins and minerals. Arbaneous is said to redden your blood, and Topicalee provides relief from old bones creaking and joints groaning."

He placed the Arbaneous Topicalee in Sage's outstretched forepaw. The old dragon nibbled off a piece, closed his eyes, and hummed.

Wizard Fenworth winked at Hollee, then perched on one of the many boulders. Hollee sat on a smaller one. They waited until Sage had swallowed a few bites.

When he opened his eyes again, his face wore an expression of bliss. "So good, so good, and so hard to come across in these mountains. Tell me of your project."

Wizard Fenworth recounted the history of the three stone statues.

"I know some of this tale from Sir Beccaroon. How does this relate to my territory?"

"Since the statues are powerful, safe sanctuary is imperative. I've built a chapel of sorts in the salt and crystal cavern below the floor of this valley."

"A place of worship?"

"And meditation."

"To your god?"

"To the God of the Universe."

"His name?"

"Wulder."

Sage nodded. "Wulder. My generation called Him Wulder Aldor.

"He Spoke the Truth. Yes, that is one of His names."

"I am honored to have under my care the Chapel of Wulder Aldor." Sage chortled. "I may even choose to live a few more years to see how Chiril responds to the Call of Wulder Aldor."

He sobered and looked at his wizard visitor. "Tell me of this invasion."

44

Hospital

Tipper stood on the roof of Byrdschopen, looking out over the peaceful countryside. The war seemed far away. In the rooms below, two dozen wounded soldiers slept in beds instead of cots. Their presence testified to the bloody battle that still maimed and killed her countrymen. The Byrdschopen hospital offered peace and rest for soldiers regaining their strength.

Gladyme provided good food. Several women from the village had moved to Tipper's home to aid in nursing the men. Others helped in the kitchen.

Lady Peg had found her niche. Tipper's mother became a tyrant of cleanliness. She kept more villagers busy washing clothes and linens, and those who could understand her scattered directions scrubbed floors and anything else that might become the least bit grubby. Tipper suspected Bar Besta's talents included organization. The minor dragon accompanied Lady Peg everywhere.

In the distant sky, a black spot took on colors, and as it came closer, Tipper recognized her former guardian. Sir Beccaroon had been ordered back to his forest to coordinate efforts in supplying the army with food from his district. Verrin Schope had provided grains and vegetable seeds that grew unnaturally fast.

The colorful parrot landed beside Tipper. "Still chafing that you aren't at the edge of the battle?"

"I was of use there."

"You're of use here. There's another ambulance wagon coming. You'll need six more beds."

"I'll tell Lipphil." Tipper turned to enter the stairway to the floors below.

"Wait."

"What?"

"I have a message from your father."

Tipper hurried back to the grand parrot's side. "For me or Mother?"

"One for you and one for Lady Peg." Sir Beccaroon cocked his head to look up at Tipper. "He's proud of you. The king is still fuming and saying that you and your mother have no business dirtying your hands in this business. If he had any men to spare, he'd send them to roust you out of your own home and take you to the Amber Palace."

"Then I'm glad he has the good sense to keep his men where they will do some good instead of interfering with our hospital." She shook her head. "But it was really Mother who caused the upheaval. She pothered on like a peahen sighting a snake when she saw the inside of the hospital tent."

"Her point is valid. Men on the road to recovery but not able-bodied yet will heal quicker here than on the front." Sir Beccaroon's forehead scrunched down over his eyes. "They aren't moved every time we have to retreat, and the tent is less crowded without these men taking up space for the newly wounded."

Tipper turned away, pressing her fist to her lips. She'd almost cried out. Instead, she batted back tears. "My grandfather wouldn't even let me leave the healing dragons. Those men—"

Sir Beccaroon said nothing as she fought to get her emotions under control. She sniffed and turned back to her friend.

Bec wiped a tear from her cheek with the tip of his wing. "Paladin brought in another watch of healing dragons. They are working very well for the tumanhofer couple who took over the wounded."

Tipper stared at the tiles on the mansion's roof.

"Ah," said the parrot. "Another reason for your dissatisfaction. You don't get to see Paladin."

Tipper didn't answer.

Bec used his wing to turn Tipper toward the staircase. "Yes." He cleared his throat. "Well now…then, um, the main point of your father's message is that he's proud of you. And might I add, King Yellat has finally agreed to allow Verrin Schope to help with strategies." He lifted his wingtip to the sky as if marking an important point. "Since then, there have been some less catastrophic engagements with the enemy."

"Less catastrophic?"

"We aren't being beaten at every encounter. We've actually won a skirmish or two."

They descended the stairs. Sir Beccaroon left Tipper's side to find Lady Peg and deliver her message from Verrin Schope. Tipper found Lipphil and asked that another room be opened for a ward and that new beds be erected. She hurried off to gather sheets.

Local men who worked in the fields aided in building beds. These older fellows did their best to tend the needs at home while younger men went to fight. They had slow hands but willing hearts. Tipper had grown fond of the men who answered Byrdschopen's bugle call. Lipphil's blast from the veranda had no tune, but between him and the other men, they'd made up a code they all understood.

It took the rest of the morning to tend to her duties with the healing dragons and the recovering soldiers. With the new beds made and noonmeal distributed among all those gathered—wounded, elderly, and the womenfolk—Lady Peg blessed their gathering and the food.

Rayn sat on Tipper's lap. The other dragons preferred to forage, but the undersized minor dragon took any opportunity he could to be with the emerlindian he loved above all others.

Sir Beccaroon ate a small amount, then bid Lady Peg and Tipper good-bye. "I've got rounds of my own to make. The seeds Verrin Schope gave us are sprouting and growing faster than anything I've ever seen. I must check which field will need harvesting tomorrow."

The arrival of the ambulance wagon interrupted the cleanup after the meal. Lady Peg didn't seem to notice six more men at the door plus the driver and attendant. She focused in her absent-minded way on the scrubbing of kitchen, dining room, trays, and dishes.

Several hours passed while Tipper made the men comfortable, saw that they were fed, and supervised more healing with the dragons. Rayn stayed with her, even when she urged him to stay on a soldier with a cramp in his leg.

"What is the matter with you?" she asked.

Rayn didn't have an answer but called another dragon over to sit on the poor man's leg. Tipper scolded him twice for being nervous and more in the way than a help.

Just as Tipper sat down on the veranda to have a cup of tea, Rayn announced that Sir Beccaroon was returning.

"Why would he do that?" Tipper stood to see her friend flying in low over the Indigo Forest. His speed alarmed her.

He landed on the stone balustrade that surrounded the extended terrace. "There's a squad of enemy soldiers approaching. They must have followed the ambulance. I'll take care of the offensive, but you must have everyone lie down. Anyone standing will be attacked by my warriors. Those in a prone position will be spared. These are the instructions I've given them, and if you do as I say, you will be safe." He flapped his wings. "Go, my girl. Spread the word. The minor dragons must be lying flat as well. Go."

Tipper ran into the house, leaving the teapot and cup on the glass table outside.

She ran to the kitchen first. "Everyone must find someplace to lie down," she instructed the women who prepared the evening meal. "Use the empty guest rooms upstairs. Some of you who live nearby can run home."

"Why, princess?" asked one of the farm girls.

"Sir Beccaroon has spotted enemy soldiers, and he's bringing in animals, I imagine." She winced at stating as fact what she had assumed. "To be his warriors. Yes, that must be it. They will attack anyone standing and leave those lying down alone."

She pulled one girl out of her chair. "Quick, go spread the word to everyone in Byrdschopen. Everyone, go, and then lie down. I'll find Mother."

Tipper found Lady Peg in the library, supervising a thorough dusting and the selection of books to be read to the wounded.

Out of breath from running, Tipper panted as she relayed Bec's instructions. "Everyone, go lie down. Enemy soldiers are coming. Sir Beccaroon has devised a way to keep us safe. But you must be lying down."

The girls scattered, but Lady Peg stood with her hand on her hip and a stubborn look on her face.

"Mother, we must go upstairs and go to bed."

"It's not time for my nap, Tipper. And since we have become useful, I have found I do not need my naps as often as before."

"Where's Junkit?"

The dragon crawled out from behind a drapery at the mention of his name. He yawned and stretched.

"Mother, Junkit needs a nap. You must go upstairs and lie down. You'll be safe up there." Tipper took her mother's arm and steered her toward the door. "We're going to go upstairs, you and I, before those soldiers get here."

"But, Tipper, you must be down here to make our guests comfortable. You haven't forgotten your duties as a hostess, have you? That would really be a shame. We've been making those poor soldiers feel at home for weeks now."

"Not our soldiers, Mother. These are enemy soldiers. Enemy soldiers are coming."

Tipper got her mother through the door and into the hallway. Junkit and Bar Besta flew ahead of them toward the grand staircase.

"Are these soldiers wounded?" Lady Peg asked.

"No, I don't think so."

"Then why are they coming here?"

"Probably to steal supplies, food, and other things."

"What other things?"

"I don't know, Mother. Please hurry."

"Do they steal valuables like jewelry and paintings?"

"They might."

"Then I'm staying here." Lady Peg resisted the tug on her arm.

"Mother, you must come up and be safe. Sir Bec has it all figured out, and we must be out of the way."

"Well, I shall stay here and explain to these enemy soldiers that they cannot take things. Stealing is not acceptable. If I offer them a meal, they may reconsider such bad manners and behave themselves."

"I doubt it. Mother, please. Father would want us to do as Sir Beccaroon instructed."

Lady Peg said nothing for a moment, then she hiked up her long skirts and headed for the stairs. "You're right, Tipper. Hurry up."

Instead of lying down on her own bed, Tipper chose to stay with her mother. They crawled under the covers and kept Junkit and Rayn with them. The minor dragons had no problem with hiding under the bedspread. Rayn shivered with fear.

Tipper listened for any sound that might be the marauders entering the house. Were they marauders? Probably. Would Bec's strategy thwart their evil plans? Probably.

Her heart raced, and she deliberately listened to her mother's breathing. She matched the steady in and out as Lady Peg relaxed. Soon soft snoring replaced her mother's breathing.

Although she could hardly believe her mother had fallen asleep, Tipper decided it was for the best. She didn't have to keep her mother from going downstairs to greet the company of soldiers or answer any more of her questions.

Junkit fell asleep, and his snoring rattled in between her mother's nasal clatter.

The bedroom door opened. Tipper hadn't heard any footsteps. She held her breath and stared at the opening. Movement caught her attention and brought her eyes lower. A sleek mountain cat's head appeared. Dark brown spots decorated the tawny fur on its head, neck, and shoulders. The blotches elongated as they covered its back until the markings resembled stripes on its hindquarters.

The big cat padded forward on silent feet, jumped up on the reclining sofa her mother often used for naps, and proceeded to lick one of his forepaws.

The draperies moved aside at the open window. A long, thick snake slithered into the room and disappeared behind the dresser. Tipper wondered what other friends from the Indigo Forest had been commandeered by Sir Beccaroon to protect the house.

"Tipper," her mother whispered.

"You woke up."

"Nonsense. I wasn't asleep."

Tipper didn't argue. Her eyes followed the big cat's every movement as it continued its grooming.

"Tipper," her mother whispered again.

"Hmm?"

"There's a cat on my daybed."

"Yes."

"We don't own a cat, do we? I mean not one that big."

"It's one of Sir Beccaroon's friends."

"Does it have a name?"

"I don't know."

"Do you think it's housebroken? We don't have a litter box, do we?"

"No, I don't think so."

"What do you suppose it eats?"

The cat stopped licking its chest and looked at the two women in the bed.

Through stiff lips, Tipper answered as quietly as she could. "Mice."

Lady Peg heaved a sigh of relief. "Oh, good."

The cat jumped down from the reclining sofa and sprang up to the end of the mattress. It tilted its head and regarded Tipper and her mother.

"Are you sure?" asked Lady Peg.

"Sure?"

"About the mice."

"Yes."

The cat's ears perked up, and it turned its head toward the open door. A few seconds later, Tipper heard the creaking of leather and the stomping of feet. The cat growled low in its throat.

"Is that purring?" asked Lady Peg.

"I don't think so."

"Our company has arrived."

"Yes."

"I think Sir Beccaroon can handle greeting them. I just don't feel like getting up right now."

45

Intrusion

Under the covers, Lady Peg found Tipper's hand and squeezed it. Tipper grinned and turned her head to reassure her mother. The cat kept watching the door.

"It's all right, Mother."

A loud bang and a crash interrupted her. The cat leaped from the bed and went to stand by the door, staring into the hall.

"What was that?" whispered Lady Peg.

"I think it was the front door banging against the large vase with the dried fronds in it."

Her mother stirred, shifting her legs toward the side of the bed. Tipper held her hand.

"No, Mother. You can't go see."

"Why not? It's my house. I'll send those ruffians out the way they came in and slam the door behind them."

"Have you forgotten the cat?"

"Oh!" Lady Peg fell back against the cushy mattress. "I had." She lay still for a moment. "I can't see it from here. What's it doing?"

"Staring into the hallway."

"What do you suppose it's thinking?"

Tipper's eyes opened wide as she shook her head in tight, jerky movements. "I don't know. I suppose it's watching for anything that's walking around instead of lying down."

"Shh!" Lady Peg tightened her grip on Tipper's hand. "Someone's coming up the grand staircase."

Bar Besta, Rayn, and Junkit shivered under the blankets. They rested against Tipper's leg, and the bump in the bed looked suspicious. Tipper raised her knee to make a little tent to disguise their presence.

Rough voices from downstairs shouted various orders.

"Find the owner!"

"Kill anyone who gives you trouble."

"Yarrah, raid the kitchen. We won't starve tonight!"

"Capture one of those healing dragons."

Through all the shouts, clatter, and bangs, Tipper heard clunking footsteps as someone big and burly reached the landing. She watched the cat tense, rippling muscles ready for a grand pounce. Holding her breath, she waited.

The cat charged, and from the hallway, a high-pitched scream silenced every other noise in the house. The thud of heavy boots coming up the stairs had sounded like a march. Going down the steps, the same feet reverberated like a rapid cadence on a drum. The panicked screech provided the tenor, and the growl of the cat, the bass.

Both Tipper and her mother sat up in bed. Rayn and Junkit fussed at Tipper for disturbing them. She mindspoke an apology. Bar Besta slipped out to curl around Lady Peg's neck.

"Oh my," said Lady Peg, "I hope he runs fast."

"The cat or the soldier?"

"The soldier, of course." She gave her daughter a disapproving glare. "Just because the man is ill-mannered doesn't mean our staff should stoop to the same coarse behavior."

"The cat isn't an employee, Mother."

"He's a friend of a friend, and our friends are considerate and polite."

Scales scraping across the wooden floor reminded the ladies that a snake also guarded Lady Peg's bedroom. They fell back against the pillows and drew the blanket up to their chins. Bar Besta moved to the pillow between mother and daughter.

"I suppose," said Lady Peg, "that being in bed, but sitting up, is not the same thing as lying down."

"I think you're right."

They listened as chaos clashed below.

Lady Peg pressed her lips together. Crashes and bangs, shouts and shrieks, almost lured Tipper out of bed.

"I wish I could see what is going on," she complained.

Her mother grasped her arm. "That snake is under the bed. I'm sure of it. We dare not put a foot to the floor."

"I'm not terribly afraid of snakes."

"I am."

In the distance, a man's strangled cry begged for help. "Get it off! Get-t-t it-t-t—awww—"

"That," said Lady Peg, "is a man with a snake around his neck. Squeezing. The snake is squeezing." She shuddered. "This is why I have told you so many times that your walks in the rain forest are dangerous. That could have been you with a snake around your neck. On another day, of course. Not today. But a day when you were ignoring my warnings and walking nonchalantly through Sir Beccaroon's Indigo Forest."

"The snakes in the forest are well-nourished. They don't need a skinny emerlindian to feed on."

"Tipper! You are not skinny. You are willowy and graceful."

The commotion moved from the floor below to the courtyard in front of the mansion. Below Lady Peg's bedroom window, someone ordered the soldiers to regroup and stand against the enemy.

"You men, circle around the wagon. Spears to the ready, men. Archers on the wagon, use the height to fend off this menagerie. We won't be trounced by brainless creatures."

"Brainless?" Lady Peg let out a most unladylike humph. "Even our pigs are smarter than these invaders."

Tipper had often heard her mother's theory that pigs were the smartest of the barnyard animals, but she couldn't fathom the connection to the soldiers. "How is that, Mother?"

"Have you ever heard of a pig getting into a battle with snakes and wildcats?"

The sounds from below gradually died away, making Tipper itch to get out of the bed and survey the damage done by Odidoddex's men. Bar Besta raised her head, listened, then darted under the covers.

"Do you think they're gone?" she asked her mother.

"No. I don't trust them to be gone when they should be."

"The lady is right."

Both women startled and looked at the door. A bisonbeck warrior filled the frame. One hand held a sword and the other a large knife. Tipper suspected the knife was from their kitchen.

"Remove yourself from my bedroom!" Lady Peg sat up and pointed a finger at the soldier. "I know you don't have proper manners, but even a lout knows not to intrude on a lady's boudoir."

Ignoring her, he stepped into the room. He looked around with narrowed eyes. He seemed too stoic to be the nervous type, but a twitching muscle in his hairy ear betrayed him.

Satisfied that no beast would pop out at him, he came to the bed.

"You are the owners of this estate?"

"My husband is."

"Where is your husband?"

"Experimenting with ways to exterminate vermin."

He pointed the sword at Lady Peg. "Where?"

"I don't really know." She waved a hand about. "Somewhere."

"Not here?"

Lady Peg looked carefully around the room. "No, not here."

"Do not rile me, woman. Your pets have caused enough havoc."

"Oh, most of the animals you encountered are friends of Sir Beccaroon, the local magistrate. We don't keep pets. We have farm animals and dragons."

The man jerked at the word "dragons." "Where are these dragons?"

"In bed with us." Lady Peg patted the covers.

Tipper watched the man's expressions change. He eyed the bed, then the older woman's face, and gave up on the idea of searching through the sheets. He opened his mouth to say something but grunted instead and fell over on his back.

"Whatever is the matter with him?" asked Lady Peg.

Tipper rolled over, apologized to the disturbed minor dragons, and peered over the edge of the bed.

"The snake's got him 'round the ankles."

The soldier thrashed, trying to sit up and reach his captor. Another snake slipped out from under the dresser. The quick, slim attacker wound around his throat. The bisonbeck dropped the sword and knife to grab the snake and tried to unwind it. His prying fingers couldn't get hold of the thin serpent.

The first snake, long and with massive muscles, dragged the bisonbeck toward the door.

Lady Peg sat up and leaned over her daughter. "There are two of them."

"Did you see two come in?"

"No, but I'm very happy to see two leave."

The snakes removed the intruder from the room and turned toward the stairs. In a few moments, the ladies heard the *thud, thud, thud* of the bulky soldier's uncomfortable descent.

"How long do you think we'll have to stay here?" asked Lady Peg.

"I'm not leaving until Bec gives the word."

"Me too," said Lady Peg. She leaned back. "I'm quite comfortable.

Hand me that book on the nightstand, dear. I'm at a very intriguing place where the villain is plotting to steal a necklace."

Tipper handed the book to her mother. "Isn't this the book you were reading last summer?"

"Yes, it is, and it seems to take the author a long time to get anything done. I'm glad your father, Bec, and Paladin are fighting our villains. They should have it all under control in a matter of a few weeks. It's taken months for this writer to get the necklace and the villain in the same room."

46

Encounter with Truth

Bealomondore gazed in the mirror and decided he looked infinitely better than when he'd arrived at the hotel the day before.

First, his complexion no longer held the tinge of green that overcame him every time he flew on the back of a dragon. He looked over his shoulder to where Laddin and Det rested on a pillow. He'd placed the cushion in the sun that streamed through the window. Both minor dragons were stretched out, totally relaxed and soaking up the luxury of the sun and the peace of not being on a battlefield.

Another change in his appearance resulted from a long, long soak in a tub of hot water. He was clean, really clean. He'd sent a hotel employee out to buy him some new clothes, and everything from his undergarments to his cravat smelled fresh and new. Being in Greeston helped. He'd sent the young man to his favorite haberdashery with a list. The clerks sent back clothing that not only suited his needs but also matched his style. They also sent a personal note saying they were delighted he had returned to the city.

The mirror reflected the old Bealomondore, the one who visited society's matrons, ingratiating himself with his wit, charm, and talent. The tumanhofer examined his image more critically. He had changed. He looked more…robust. A wry grin twisted his lips. Who would have predicted that Graddapotmorphit Bealomondore would one day have hardened muscles?

He wondered if his father would notice the difference. Hardly! He hoped his father recognized him as his younger son and didn't have him thrown out of his office when he realized this man was the boy he disliked so.

Bealomondore reached for his sword and began to buckle the belt around his waist. He stopped. *Force of habit.* He didn't need to wear a weapon to meet with his father.

Putting the sword aside, he spoke to his dragon friends. "I'm off now, on the king's errand. This shouldn't take long."

Det and Laddin lifted their heads, and Bealomondore felt a wave of reassurance pass to him.

"Right," he said. "Thanks."

His room was at the end of a hallway on the third floor. He counted the room numbers backward as he strolled toward the stairs. Stopping at the top step, he gazed downward. His breath caught in his throat, the staircase undulated, and he turned away, rushing back the way he'd come.

The dragons flew to him as soon as he banged open the door to his room. He collapsed on the only chair, covered his face with his hands, and planted his elbows on his knees.

Det sat on his shoulder while Laddin squirmed into the triangular space between Bealomondore's arms and chest. The tumanhofer straightened, pulling the healing dragon closer, nestling him in his arms.

"I don't know exactly what happened," he explained. "I got dizzy, then I was compelled to come back for the Sword of Valor."

He took several deep breaths, then stood. He put Laddin down on the bed, picked up the sword, and pulled it from its scabbard.

He chortled, not really amused at the script on the hilt. "A new message, 'Reconciliation slices away drivel.' And that is supposed to be comforting? Encouraging? Bah!"

He rammed the sword back in the sheath, noting how plain the hilt looked compared to the fancy lettering.

"I'm going," he announced as he strapped on the Sword of Valor. "Hopefully I'll get farther than the top of the stairs. You can come if you wish."

Det and Laddin flew to him and perched on his shoulders.

"You'll have to hide when we go in to see my father. He wouldn't approve."

Bealomondore grinned at the spectacle his father's face brought up in his imagination. His father would be utterly shocked by the sight of minor dragons in his office. "That's rather reassuring, makes our errand pale in comparison to the revelation that I've befriended dragons. No offense to you two, but my father is sensible to the extreme and doesn't have a regard for friendship. He wouldn't understand how valuable you are to me."

He'd sought out a hotel in the business district of Greeston, so he had very little time on the short cab trip to worry about how this interview would go. Having the dragons and the sword reminded him that his life had changed considerably, and he had changed along with it.

He introduced himself to the secretary, who seemed unaware that Master Bealomondore had two sons.

Irritation strengthened the tumanhofer artist's resolve.

After receiving permission from within the spacious office, the secretary formally announced him. His father remained seated as Bealomondore came in. He waited a moment, expecting his father to gesture toward a seat in front of the massive desk, but when he didn't even look up, Bealomondore walked across the expanse of the room.

"Good afternoon, Father."

The elder man replied, "Doubtful."

"King Yellat has asked me to relay a message."

His father threw down his pen and leaned back in his chair, glaring at his son. "So my dandy son has wormed his way into the castle."

"Actually, the king made his request in the strategy tent a few miles from the front line. We are at war, Father."

"I'm aware of that. Business is good."

"And that is why the king has asked me to deliver this message. You must refrain from selling ore from Bealomondore Mine to anyone other than our country's industry. The metal must go to making weapons for our forces."

"I've had this message before."

"Perhaps King Yellat believes you will respond more positively to an edict delivered by a person rather than on paper."

His father pushed back his chair and jumped to his feet. His red face and clenched fists signaled the need for a hasty retreat on his son's part, but the younger Bealomondore stood his ground.

The older man clasped his hands behind his back and paced. "The king can't interfere in a man's private business."

"He could charge you with treason, Father."

Master Bealomondore stopped, eyes popping and face even redder than before. "I'm a businessman seeing to his business. I sell to whoever offers the highest bid. The king would have me turn over the ore on the promise of payment?"

"Yes, that was his offer."

Master Bealomondore strode to the window and peered out. His next comment came in a lower volume. "A man must take into account many factors when determining a course of action."

"Exactly. The money you acquire will be worth nothing if you are hauled off to prison."

"We are fighting a superior force, Graddapotmorphit. There is no guarantee that Chiril will repulse the invasion. When the dust settles, a wise man will have forged an allegiance with the victor."

A principle Bealomondore had read in Wulder's Tomes came to mind, but he couldn't think how to phrase it so that his father wouldn't explode upon hearing it. Silence invaded the room except for the ticking of the clock on the desk.

Bealomondore quit trying to rephrase the words to a more palatable form. " 'An allegiance to evil is an alliance with despair.' "

His father whipped around. The glower on his face would have melted candle wax.

"Don't you think I know that?" He crossed to his desk and stood with clenched fists pressing down on the wood. "How dare you come in here and tell me what is right and wrong. I know." The bluster went out of him, and he crumpled, falling into his chair. His ashen face startled his son.

"Father!" Bealomondore came around to stand beside him. He felt the cold, clammy skin of his father's face, then pressed his fingers to the pulse at his neck. "You're ill."

"I'm sick of myself."

Bealomondore unbuttoned his coat. Laddin scrambled out, already aware of the emergency. He leaped to the elder man's chest.

"What!" Master Bealomondore tried to sit up. "Get this beast off me!"

Bealomondore pushed his father's shoulders back against the chair. "Calm yourself. This is a healing dragon. Let him work."

"Healing dragon? That's absurd."

"Let's see if you think so after he's done his job. Sit back and relax."

Bealomondore suspected that weakness supplied the cooperation from his father in the next few minutes. A natural color returned to his cheeks, and his breathing steadied.

"Laddin says you'll be fine."

"Laddin?"

"The dragon."

"He didn't say anything."

"He spoke directly from his mind to mine."

"Preposterous. You're an even bigger fool than when you left home years ago."

Bealomondore pressed his lips against the words in his throat. He hadn't left. He'd been thrown out. His father didn't appreciate his artistic abilities. Adding a column of figures and charming a customer brought praise for his older brother. Bealomondore could charm aristocratic hostesses, but they did not buy ore.

"You're feeling better?" Bealomondore took Laddin from his father's chest and held him.

Stubbornness crossed his father's features, but he reluctantly admitted, "I do."

"Father, you must not deal with enemies of the crown. In the end, the whole family will suffer."

"I know that."

His tone remained gruff, but Bealomondore glimpsed something different in the old man's expression. Fear, maybe? He remembered the paralyzing fear that had almost gotten him killed in his first sword fight. Someone else had come alongside him to help him not only endure the terror but also survive the experience. He deemed it too soon to introduce Wulder, but perhaps his father needed his wastrel son to bolster his courage.

The thought made Bealomondore laugh scornfully at himself, but he managed to keep his ill-timed humor to himself.

"What can I do to help, Father? What is at the heart of this dilemma?"

Master Bealomondore sighed and sank deeper into the leather cushions of his chair. "Humiliation. Dishonor. Death."

47

Encounter with Evil

Bealomondore studied his father's despondent expression. "I think if you just quit selling to the enemy, the king will not act against you. You can stop and avoid this humiliation."

Anger replaced his father's dejection. "You don't know anything!"

"I've been on the battlegrounds. I've spoken to the king. I believe I know a little more than nothing."

"I'm dealing with tumanhofers loyal to King Odidoddex. Just like their king, they are willing to kill anyone who opposes them. I'm trapped."

"Tell them there's no more ore for them."

"And have one of your sisters or your mother die in an 'accident'?"

A ball of ice filled Bealomondore's stomach. His mind shouted that his family could not be in danger over this business, but the look on his father's face said they were.

Bealomondore withdrew to the other side of the desk. He sat in one of the large leather chairs where henchmen of the Baardack king had sat and threatened his family.

"How many do you deal with?" he asked.

"What?"

"How many Baardackians have come to this office? How many do we have to convince that you will no longer do business with them?"

"Aren't you listening to me? I can't say no to these people."

"We'll figure this out, Father."

"You're insane. What are we going to do? Bargain for who they'll kill, one of your sisters or your mother?"

"Of course not. How many?"

The look from his father scorched Bealomondore's heart, but the older man answered. "Four."

"One in charge? Three ruffians?"

"Exactly. Mernantottencat is the leader, with another tumanhofer and two mariones to back him up."

"We can handle them."

"You *are* insane."

"I'll stand beside you."

"And what? Fight them off with that piece of jewelry you call a sword?"

Bealomondore frowned and looked down to his side. The Sword of Valor had sprouted gems, big gaudy jewels of red, green, yellow, and blue.

He gasped and pulled the sword from its scabbard. The blade looked the same, but the inscription had changed. He tilted it to the light and read, " 'Look past the luster.' "

Master Bealomondore scowled. "What does that mean?"

"I don't always know."

"And what does *that* mean?"

"This is the Sword of Valor, given to me by the Wizard Fenworth. It increases my skill in battle, gives me messages I assume are from Wulder's Tomes, although I haven't had a chance to look them up, and apparently changes appearance. The jewels were not there before."

"Poppycock. All poppycock."

Years of experience with his parent gave Bealomondore no hope of winning a verbal contest. No sense in arguing. "Even so, I am prepared to stand beside you should you decide to cease dealing with the enemy."

Master Bealomondore sighed, closed his eyes, and leaned back in his chair. His son waited.

"As I said, Graddapotmorphit, I am sick of myself. I feel that I should be humiliated. It's what I deserve, but I fear the dishonor. The Bealomondore name has always stood with right and justice. I've let my family down. But I would rather die myself than have harm come to your sisters or mother."

"And where does my brother stand?"

His father breathed deeply. No answer. He sat limply in the chair of authority, where he ruled the family business. Was he asleep? Had he had another spell that rendered him unconscious?

"Father?"

"Your brother has abandoned the problem. It was too big to tackle, so he has taken a trip. Ostensibly to secure land in Brodgenican or Shalmar, but really to be out of harm's way."

"Now that is something I would never have expected."

"Nor I." His father sat up. "I should send for the king's men and have them here to arrest Mernantottencat and his men."

"That sounds like a good plan."

"It means that the whole city—the whole country—will know of my betrayal."

"You were doing business with Baardackians before the war. It took time to realize they were using our ore to make weapons."

He shook his head. "No, if I am to do the honorable thing, I shall not add dishonorable to the mix. I will not pretend that I did not know how low I had fallen."

"Yes sir."

"Call my secretary. I will send for the king's men."

"Yes sir. Are you expecting Mernantottencat?"

"No, but we shall make arrangements."

With the decision made, the older man relaxed. His whole demeanor changed to one of patience.

His son breathed a sigh of relief and went to have the king's men summoned. Bealomondore also asked for the secretary to bring a restorative tea and a light repast.

She objected. "Master Bealomondore never eats in his office and rarely takes tea during business hours."

"My father's energy has been tasked by our discussion."

She looked into the office and spotted the dragons. "My word." Her eyes popped. "Should I call for someone to catch and remove those beasts?"

"The dragons are with me. They stay."

Giving him a disapproving glare, she nonetheless went off to do his bidding.

Bealomondore sat with his father and tried to start a conversation, asking about news of his sisters and mother and aunt. Master Bealomondore did not respond with more than a word or two, and the tumanhofer artist soon gave up. He decided to go by the house after he'd finished with the business at hand.

The tea, miniature cakes, and tiny sandwiches arrived. Master Bealomondore made disparaging remarks about the fancy display of delicacies but took a few bites. Evidently the food pleased him. He helped himself to more and ate heartily until only crumbs remained on the tray.

The secretary removed the remnants, and before she finished, four men walked in. She scurried to leave the room and close the door.

Bealomondore cringed. These men dressed well, but not in the uniforms of King Yellat's men.

Master Bealomondore came to his feet, and Bealomondore took his cue from his father. He stood off to one side as the men approached the desk.

"Greetings, Master Bealomondore," said the tumanhofer in a business suit. "We have good news. A ship has become available, and we will take possession of our purchase tomorrow."

His father assumed a familiar posture. He leaned over his desk with fists planted firmly on the wood. "I will return your money. I cannot sell to your 'company' any longer. I must give the ore into the hands of my king."

All pretense of congeniality dropped from Mernantottencat's manner. "That is not a wise decision, sir. I believe we've discussed the repercussions of such a move before."

"Even so, I refuse your business."

Mernantottencat studied Master Bealomondore and then turned his gaze upon the other gentleman in the room. "And who is this?"

Bealomondore gave the slightest of nods, not anything like the respect that would be given an honored customer. "I am Graddapotmorphit Bealomondore, second son."

"Have you been advising your father to take this foolish course?"

"I back his decision but did not make it for him."

"This is entirely unfortunate." Mernantottencat gestured to his henchmen and then toward the tumanhofer son. "Seize him."

Bealomondore leaped backward and drew his sword. Instead of the whisper of metal against leather, the sword sang a clear note of challenge. Bealomondore's eyebrows rose at the unexpected sound, but he didn't have time to marvel.

The shorter marione sprang at him. With one thrust, the tumanhofer stopped him on the point of the Sword of Valor. He pulled back, removing the blade and allowing the man to fall.

The shock of his ready defense held the other two henchmen back.

"Get him, you fools," ordered Mernantottencat.

The two men pulled knives with long, wicked blades. They brandished the intimidating weapons in front of them. Moving in sidesteps, they widened the distance between them, making Bealomondore's chances of defending himself harder.

The tactic didn't overly alarm Bealomondore. He'd been in battle, surrounded by dozens of the enemy. He jumped to the back of a stuffed chair, and as the chair fell, he used it to launch a somersault over the other marione. As Bealomondore came down behind him, he sliced the man's jacket from collar to hem. The tip of his sword penetrated the cloth and left a deep, red line on his skin.

The man yelled and put his hands behind him as if to examine his wound. Bealomondore deftly carved two small circles on each hand.

He whirled just in time to see the other tumanhofer thug throw his knife. He deflected it with his sword and pointed his weapon at the now unarmed man. The wounded man dropped to his knees, but Bealomondore didn't trust him. He still held a knife.

Bealomondore stepped sideways, taking the attention of the three men away from where his father stood, dumbstruck, behind his desk.

The downed man shouted, "Here!" and threw his knife to the one who stood between Mernantottencat and Bealomondore.

Deftly snatching the knife by its handle, the thug feinted a charge from the left, shifted, and dived from the right. Bealomondore jumped to the side and kicked the man in the stomach as he roared past. The enemy fell on his knife but only wounded his leg. He hobbled up, ready to charge again. If Bealomondore turned, he would face this charging bull but have his back to the treacherous Mernantottencat. Instead, he whirled back a few steps to end up behind the leader of this unsavory pack.

Grinning, Bealomondore grabbed Mernantottencat. With one arm bent to the breaking point behind his back and a stinging blade pressed against his throat, Mernantottencat didn't move.

Bealomondore smiled at the brutish tumanhofer. "Stay where you are, and drop your knife."

The knife thudded on the carpet.

"Move over to the wall, next to the dead man."

He complied.

"You!" Bealomondore indicated the other man with a chin thrust. "Crawl over to the other side of your fallen mate."

He went on his knees, cradling his injured hands.

"Not too close. You aren't going to need his knife, so just forget about it." Bealomondore spoke without taking his eyes off the villains. "Father?"

"Yes, son."

"Open the door, and let King Yellat's men in. They're coming into the outer office now."

"You heard them?"

"No, Det heard them and told me." He smiled a more cheerful grin than the one he'd used on the rogues. "His hearing is better than mine."

Mernantottencat growled, "No one told me you have a warrior son, Master Bealomondore."

"I don't," said the father. "This is my son, the artist. You should see his paintings." The old man chuckled. "His art is better than his fighting, which is better than his hearing." He laughed out loud as he went to the door. "And his hearing is better than your scheming. You've lost this battle, Mernantottencat. And I think I've won more than this skirmish."

48

Hollee

Meeting people topped Hollee's Happy Things to Do list. Being down in the cavern with her wizard and his librarian had made her right palm itch. In Prince Jayrus's valley, she could shake hands all day long and still have more people to meet the next day. Coming up out of the hole and talking to Sage had changed life for the better.

And now company abounded in the cavern, and the new tunnels were being built. Dragons roamed beneath the ground, guarding the statues and watching for intruders. Tumanhofers had been recruited from outside the valley to construct the Halls of Sanctuary, a new project of Wizard Fenworth's. The suggestion had come from Sage. He thought the statue chapel and the related halls would be a good retreat for those seeking more information about Wulder. The big surprise had been that Sage remembered Wulder from his youth.

Singing and dancing came right below meeting people on the Happy Things to Do list. The kimens in the valley liked singing and dancing just as much as the ones in the Starling Forest. Every night they taught Hollee new songs and new steps, and she shared those she knew from home. And, oh my, they all laughed when they came across songs and hops they all knew because the music came from so very long ago in kimen tradition.

Today had been just as fun as yesterday. Tonight, the weight of good food aplenty would make the tables groan at the one-towered castle. Ah, food belonged on the list as well.

Hollee skipped and jumped, turned flips and cartwheels. She sang and stopped to giggle when she came to the strange words the kimens of the valley sang. The proper words of this song were:

I've plenty of tin to make my ship
Plenty of rootygin to take many a sip.
And my friends all hold hands as we dance a bit
In the night, by the stars, and for the fun of it.

The kimens here had forgotten the words and sang:

I've plenty of magpie trumpet hats
Plenty of room-a-ring to do acrobats,
And my kin sing loud like all your kin
In the night, by the stars, and let's start again.

If the tune hadn't been so similar, and if the singing dragons hadn't said it was so, they might never have believed it was the same song. Hollee couldn't wait to go home and sing the funny words to her friends in the Starling Forest.

Playing with dragons held a slot near the top of her Happy Things to Do list. Playing with dragons hadn't even been on the list until she and Wizard Fenworth came to the valley.

Paladin showed up with two dozen emerlindian and marione volunteers. He set about training both the men and the dragons to survive in battle. Most of it looked like fun to Hollee, and she got to help. The men sometimes needed kimen assistance in communicating through mindspeak to the dragons they rode. Most of the warriors quickly developed a bond with their mounts and could now mindspeak on their own.

Hollee took pride in the emerlindian and dragon she had played with, even though the librarian said she tutored them. All the time, Librettowit insisted they *worked* with dragons. They did not play.

Hollee said, "If it's fun, why do we have to call it work?"

He said, "If it's work, why are you having fun?"

Hollee knew there had to be a retort to that cynical question, but she hadn't thought of one yet. Probably because she hadn't thought much about Librettowit's question, his philosophy, or the definition of *work*. Having fun doing the things on her Happy Things to Do list had kept her too busy to fret.

She stopped at the end of a complicated skip-jump-twirl pattern she often used for forward movement and stood stock-still. Closing her eyes, she took care to identify every sensation and thoroughly appreciate it. She tasted the breeze, as well as luxuriated in the brush of its warm breathlike wisps on her skin. She smelled flowers, wood smoke, and the rich loam of the earth at her feet. She heard the soft swish of the giant anamar butterfly and opened her eyes to watch the brilliant orange, red, and black wings fold and unfold in a slow, graceful homage to a wonderful day.

Movement above the distant mountains caught her attention. She scrambled up an incline of broken rocks, wondering how the huge boulders had managed to accumulate in the middle of a grassy field, how long it was until dinner, how many kimens lived in the valley if you counted the ones she hadn't met yet, and what was flying into the valley over the northern ridge. With patience, she figured she would find out about dinner and the flying thing. She could ask Librettowit about the hill of rocks and probably get a good story out of him. And she didn't really care how many kimens there were as long as some of them showed up for food, song, and dance.

She sat to watch the approach of the flier and soon decided it was a dragon. Occasionally she spotted large birds soaring over the valley.

But the wings on birds of prey extended more from the sides of the body, and dragons' wings sprouted higher on the torso and closer to the head. She also could tell from the stroke of the wings whether this was a feathered flier or one with scales.

She sprang to her feet. "Maxon!"

The dragon carried Bealomondore, Maxon, and two minor dragons. Maxon's voice sent a greeting to her mind. She jumped up and down. It would be good to see her friends and meet the new dragons, but visitors also meant news. She longed to hear someone say that Chiril had finally gotten the upper hand and was beating the enemy back to where they belonged.

Racing to the meadow near the castle where they were surely to land, Hollee called out the tidings to all she passed.

"Bealomondore and Maxon are here!"

The rolling hill and grassy field outside Prince Jayrus's garden swarmed with onlookers as Bealomondore's dragon set down. Maxon hopped off and ran to give Hollee a hug. The tumanhofer artist looked around as if trying to decide who was being welcomed in such a grand manner.

Paladin strode out of the gate and up the hill. The crowd of kimens, dragons, mariones, tumanhofers, and emerlindians parted and let him through.

Bealomondore spoke to the dragon and patted his flank, then went to greet Paladin.

"You're a sight cleaner than the last time I saw you," said the young ruler. "Did your business go well in Greeston?"

The artist beamed. "Yes. My father decided on his own that he should break business ties with a tumanhofer named Mernantottencat, and I was available to help convince the representatives of that enterprise that the decision was final."

Paladin looked pleased, and Hollee scooted forward to see if she could find out more of what had happened in Greeston. Bealomondore had not spoken of his early life often.

"And your family?" asked Paladin. "Did you get a chance to visit?"

"For an evening. My brother is abroad, but it was wonderful to see my sisters and aunt. My mother and father were with us for a short time, and then they had a social obligation to attend."

Paladin laughed out loud. "So your evening was very pleasurable indeed."

Bealomondore's head bobbed in agreement, and his face relaxed into a satisfied grin.

After a look of mutual understanding, Paladin gestured to those around them. He sobered. "We are rather isolated, and all are anxious to hear whatever news you can tell of the war."

Hollee held her breath. Each tidbit of information they received of late had been discouraging. The king and his army retreated farther into the center of the country. Casualties numbered in the thousands, and the encroaching army ravaged the country as they marched forward, taking what they wanted and burning the rest. Many Chirilians had lost much.

"It is not good," said Bealomondore. "Not only has the army pushed all the way to Ragar, but Odidoddex has backed up his warriors with an occupying force. The towns and villages that have fallen are now under the authority of soldiers who supervise rebuilding. It is clear that the new businesses erected are the property of Baardack, even though Chirilians are permitted to reopen their shops and live in new houses. Schools have reopened, but Baardackian teachers run them."

Hollee gasped. "Now that's bad."

Maxon still had his arm around her, and he squeezed. "Some of the people are relieved. When they do as the invaders order, our people are left in peace. After the devastation of their homes, they are willing to bend a little to avoid any more strife. And as long as they cooperate, the Baardackians are more than friendly."

"But the children are being taught by outsiders."

"Well, you know that won't happen in the kimen villages. None of our homes have been found and destroyed."

"Why not?"

"It would seem that we do not produce anything that Odidoddex deems valuable." Maxon half-laughed. "And I believe their soldiers are a bit superstitious when it comes to our people."

"What about The Grawl?"

"They say he went home. He hasn't been seen in Chiril for months."

"I hope he stays at home."

"Me too."

Bealomondore declared that he would never be a dragonback warrior. "Give me the land beneath my feet," he told Hollee and Maxon.

They sat on a knoll, watching the daredevil riders performing stunts that should aid them when engaged in fighting the enemy. Maxon busied himself sharpening Bealomondore's weapons, the Sword of Valor and several knives. The tumanhofer artist whittled a slingshot from a fork in a branch.

Bealomondore shook his head slowly from side to side. "I can't tell you how many times I've fallen during combat. And now that I think about it, I'm very glad the distance to the ground was short."

Hollee grinned. "You are the best sword fighter I know."

"Swordsman," said Maxon. "And he is good, but Paladin is better."

Hollee scowled at her friend. "I was trying to make him feel better. You know, boost his confidence."

Maxon laughed. "You don't have to do that anymore. He's good, and he works at getting better. And Paladin asked him to help in training the volunteers." Maxon laughed louder. "It is a good thing Paladin brought the men here first." His laugh died and the smile fell from his face. "Too many of our men went to the front lines with no preparation. They died."

Bealomondore agreed, but he kept his thoughts to himself. If King Yellat had chosen his counselors wisely, the status of the war would be different. He'd shunned Paladin, and two of his generals who dared to contradict the favorite advisors had been sent away from the front lines. King Yellat had been pushed back until he'd been forced to take refuge in Amber Palace at Ragar. The city was under siege.

One could say the war was at an end. All that was needed was a formal surrender, but if they could trust their king to do one thing, it would be to refuse to admit defeat.

Paladin had a plan, and Bealomondore wanted to be there when he put it into action. Whether they could turn the tide remained to be seen. The artist-turned-soldier wanted to swoop in and save his country. The heroics of such a feat appealed to his romantic side.

But more to the heart of the matter, an impossible victory sounded just like something Wulder would appreciate. The stories in the Tomes often talked about Wulder's sympathy for the least valuable person in the crowd. He found worth in the downtrodden. He elevated the lowly by recognizing significance in each soul.

The king's army was war-weary, tattered in clothing and spirit, and crushed by rampant slaughter. Their morale hung as rags torn by the conquering army. Their thoughts of the future conformed to the quelling presence of King Odidoddex as ruler. They had all but given up.

Except for the men in this valley. Paladin shaped hope in each individual.

The time was ripe for miracles.

49

The Grawl Makes Plans

The Grawl sat in the shadow of a crag overlooking a high mountain valley. This place had been the home of Prince Jayrus, now Paladin. In the air, dragonriders practiced flying in formation, passing off supplies, and targeting bales of hay. On the ground, the tumanhofer with the fascinating sword demonstrated swordsmanship and hand-to-hand combat. The old librarian, Librettowit, also gave instructions.

Along the southern wall, tumanhofers went in and out of an entrance to the mountain. Perhaps they were mining, but The Grawl had seen no evidence of ore being processed. The cut stone brought to the surface outlined a large square. A building of some sort would rise there. Since the tumanhofers concentrated on getting the stone out of the hole rather than building on the foundation, The Grawl assumed the outside structure was secondary to a more urgent job taking place within.

A lake with an island sat at the east end of the big valley. Very little activity took place on this sparsely wooded lump of land.

Every night, in the meadow outside the castle garden, the people gathered to eat and enjoy each other's company. But the long days of training meant the merriment ended early. The company turned in soon after the sun fell behind the western mountain ridge. Guards kept watch.

Where was the wizard? The bits of information The Grawl had collected on the long journey to this valley didn't help in his search. He had learned a lot of places where the wizard was not, but no definite clues as to where the old man hid.

This valley offered the most likely spot. The Grawl shifted, using the sharp edge of a boulder to scratch the itch between his shoulder blades. Several people had mentioned the possibility that the three statues had been taken to Prince Jayrus's castle for protection. The wizard knew the secrets of the stones, and the new songs said that Paladin stood as defender at the powerful gate they formed.

So where were the statues? Where was their protector?

The castle?

The island?

The mine?

Clouds drifted over the sun. A chill wind whistled through cracks in the rocks. For one moment, the sound resembled hooting owls, hundreds of hooting owls. The Grawl frowned.

Easing out of his blind, he headed back to the camp where he'd imprisoned his not-so-willing helpers. The schoergats weren't bound by any chains, but The Grawl had cunningly worked to elevate their fear of him. Every day they'd been in his company, he'd impressed them with his power, his cold wrath, and the swift death he administered with no show of emotion. The schoergats stayed where he told them to stay and jumped when he told them to jump.

His only problem with them had been when their superstition overwhelmed their terror of his fury. But even then, they didn't run off. They knew he could track them.

They also believed that his presence would deter any attack by fiends. They stayed with him lest some bogeyman jump out of this land their ancestors had cleared of dragons. The fear of the unfamiliar worked well to keep them in line. The Grawl, the monster in their midst, could out-thunder any creature of the night, of the deep, of the dark, of the unseen.

They didn't like the cold, so when he returned to the camp, he lit fires under the over-cropping shelves of stone. His technique in starting these fires further proved his awesome powers. He had matches. They didn't know about matches. He held one in his hand and flicked a rough fingernail over the red tip. Very impressive magic.

As the day grew colder, windier, and wetter, The Grawl contemplated the things he knew that he doubted those in the valley knew.

King Yellat's army had been split. The bigger part had hunkered down in Ragar and the forts that supposedly guarded the city. A smaller band had been cut off and forced to run in another direction. That group of a hundred or so men was headed for this valley.

A ship of Chirilian sailors had barely made it to shore. Damage inflicted by the superior Baardackian navy had crippled King Yellat's finest ship in a showy but hardly practical fleet. Those thirty men also headed this way. Loyalty to the king did not drive these men. The desire to find sanctuary and hide brought them to the valley.

The Grawl had decided to take this refuge and all its occupants. He would be sure that King Odidoddex knew of his cunning rout of the last stronghold. There would be a reward. He'd kill the wizard. It wouldn't hurt to add to his fame and his wealth at the same time.

The Grawl kills wizards.

The Grawl commands wild schoergats.

The Grawl wipes out fortified havens.

The Grawl is the victor of all enemies.

Yes, it all sounded good in The Grawl's ear.

50

In the Night

Bealomondore sat under the starlit sky and marveled at the colors he could see. In the city, all the stars looked white. Occasionally a red, blue, or green planet could be picked out. Here, in the high mountain valley, the planets looked the same, though brighter, but the twinkling stars shone in hues of yellow, orange, red, and white. He'd never seen that in Greeston. Tonight the moon only showed a sliver of its pearly white orb.

Chilly breezes whispered among huddled bushes. A shiver of pleasure reawakened Bealomondore's senses. His turn at night watch felt more like moments of meditation rather than an arduous chore.

He pulled his moonbeam cloak closer. Sealed in against the cold, he also blended into his surroundings. He watched small creatures of the night forage for food. A mouse skittered to a halt under a bush as an owl swooped close to the ground and veered up into the sky again.

His artist fingers itched to pick up a pencil and sketch. That surprised Bealomondore. He clenched his fists under the cloak. A lot of time had passed since his last drawing.

When he'd come to the valley, he'd been bone weary and content to teach the recruits how to use a sword, how to stay alive in battle.

Perhaps he should say he was soul weary. As he taught, he accepted that rather than teaching these men to kill, he taught them to live. And beyond keeping themselves alive, they were standing against evil with the hope of keeping their friends, family, and fellow countrymen alive.

A small, choked laugh escaped his lips. Just when he felt he could face the front line again, just when he felt ready to lead these men into bedlam, the urge to create blazed in his soul. To record beauty. To prove order by detailing the feathers of a wing on paper. To verify the Creator in simple art.

Why the sudden urge to create? Because he had reestablished why he fought. His art now had a purpose, and he was too busy to paint.

The rustle of wings and a slight nudge of a thought not his own brought him to his feet. Det flew in from surveying the valley. He reported men marching through the gap, the easiest entry to Prince Jayrus's isolated domain.

"Go tell Paladin," said Bealomondore. "I'll rouse our troops and get them ready to set up defense."

But before the small dragon took flight for the castle, Paladin ran out of the gate leading to his garden and charged up the hill. The ruler's dragon, Caesannede, swooped in to land a few feet from Bealomondore.

"Never mind, Det. Paladin is aware that company is arriving."

The young ruler barely panted as he reached the top of the hill. He gestured to Bealomondore and then to the waiting dragon. "Do you want to come with me?"

The tumanhofer looked at the huge beast quivering with excitement and the vacant place on his back between the outstretched wings. No saddle. His stomach clenched.

"No, thank you. I'll make ready here."

"Good." Paladin ran up the eager dragon's tail and dropped into the place where a sensible man would have a saddle secured. "I'll scout... find out who they are and how many of them are coming."

The dragon stamped his feet, impatient to take off.

Bealomondore held up a hand to keep them from flying away before he voiced his thought. "This could be our army or even the sailors I told you about when I first came."

"It won't hurt us to respond as if we anticipate an attack. A good drill for if the enemy does find us. I'll send word of what I discover."

Paladin's mount trotted a few yards, then lifted into the air.

Bealomondore turned to Det. "Wake the dragons and send them to the camp. I'll wake the men."

Det took off, and Bealomondore headed toward the flatland, where rows of tents housed their small force. Maxon sped out to meet him.

"We're awake," he called. "The men are gearing up now."

Bealomondore continued to stomp across the meadow. "It would seem I'm not much needed."

"What?" Maxon reached his side and spun to head back with him. "Who will lead the men if you aren't in charge?"

"Never mind me, Max. I'm out of sorts, wondering if I'm an artist, a warrior, or a failure."

"I wouldn't call you a warrior, sir." A ripple of colors passed through the light clothing Maxon wore. When the hues blended together to make a vibrant yellow, he continued. "You're an artist who's been trapped in a war. And because you're in the habit of mastering what is before you, you've become a good swordsman. But your heart will always wish to create and not destroy."

Bealomondore mulled the kimen's words. "'The habit that enables one to dig a hole three feet deep will sustain the building of a fence six feet tall.'"

"Exactly," said Maxon. "You're learning Wulder's principles? Where did you get the Tomes?"

"From Librettowit."

"I should like to have a look at it."

"Somehow I thought your people had copies."

The kimen's wild hair flew about his head as he shook it. "We have discovered that the principles are in some of our ancient songs. We sang the lyrics without knowing they came from Wulder's Tomes."

"Does that mean that many generations ago, your people knew of Wulder?"

"We think it does, and our elders are chagrined that we let the knowledge of the Most High Wulder Aldor slip from our memory."

"The disassociation must have taken many, many years."

Again the small man's head shook, and to Bealomondore, it looked like drops of light splattered the air like water from a wet dog. "The elders say it would take only two generations. If parents don't teach their children, and they become grandparents and don't teach their grandchildren, the knowledge is lost. Truth is relegated to legend. Legend becomes myth. Myth becomes fairy tale."

Bealomondore marveled over the experience he'd had while on watch. What a fragile thread bound them to the reality of a spiritual realm. He connected and grew stronger by acknowledging Wulder. A race lost the bond through lack of testimony.

At the camp, Bealomondore found the men he'd been training ready to go. They marched away from the peace of their tents and toward the unknown with their artist leader at the front.

The Grawl slipped into the cover of trees. A dragon flew toward him, coming from the one-towered castle, and headed toward the southeast corner of the valley. The crescent moon shed little light with its mocking smile, but relying on his keen eyesight, The Grawl felt certain he had seen only one rider. He remained where he was for the time being. He did not want to be spotted.

Thirty minutes later, a hundred or so men marched over the hill, heading the same direction. Patience and curiosity warred within The Grawl's mind. He scanned the starry sky, noting clouds gathering over the mountains to the west. Better yet, he saw no dragons in the air to see him and sound an alarm.

Through his nightly exploration of the potential battlefield, he'd become very familiar with the topography of the valley. He guessed the destination of dragon and soldiers. With no more hesitation, he hurried through the wooded area and came to a ravine with a trickle of a stream at the bottom. He lowered himself over the edge and loped toward the gap.

The dragon and rider had reached the overlook before him, but the soldiers wouldn't appear for more than an hour. He moved faster and knew a shorter route. Being careful to keep out of sight, The Grawl crept to the opposite side of the gap. From there he watched the man called Paladin as he watched the canyon floor below.

The Grawl smelled the men before he heard them. Their half-hearted effort to steal into the valley made him laugh. Finally, fewer than forty men came into sight, a ragtag group of sea dogs. Tattered uniforms proclaimed them sailors.

Fighting men, they were not. Unused to walking great distances, they limped as they trudged through the gap. They looked malnourished, worn to the point of collapse, and unfocused. The Grawl's nose twitched. They smelled unclean. Pitiful. An enemy force of four could have wiped them all out.

The scene no longer interested him. He turned his back and renewed his quest—finding the wizard.

51

Trouble

Hollee watched Wizard Fenworth carefully. He looked like he merely stood in the sunshine, soaking up the warm rays, but he'd been odd the last several days. After all the days underground, now he craved the open air. Well, she did too. And maybe his constant twitching and muttering would stop. She found it hard to live with a nervous wizard.

Fenworth had spent his days supervising the building of tunnels, not that the tumanhofers appreciated his suggestions. He also trained medium-sized dragons to roam the underground halls and guard the entire network of meditation rooms and the main cathedral. Paladin hinted that the dragons did not want to be trained and would do a superior job if left to operate in their own way. Wizard Fenworth bullied the dragons, and much to Hollee's surprise, the dragons took a liking to the old man and humored him. She learned from Librettowit that dragons have a lively sense of the absurd, a reverence for the elderly, and a strict code of courtesy.

Hollee did a twirly dance through the late autumn mumfers, gathering blooms to make a chain. Wizard Fenworth tilted his face up to catch the brilliance of the day. The satisfied expression on his face shifted to horror, and the old man dragged the sleeves of his wizard's garb up off his wrists to expose scrawny white arms.

"Look at that, Hollee," he cried. "The hairs are standing up. Trouble!"

He let the sleeves fall before she got a good look. He scoured the immediate area with steely eyes. Then he lifted one hand to shield against the bright sun and surveyed the rising mountains all around.

"Trouble!"

"What kind of trouble?" she asked.

He sniffed the air. "The Grawl, and something I daresay I've never smelled." He stuck his tongue out and wiggled it in the open air. "Tastes like trouble too."

"Are we going to go look for it?"

The twinkle left the old man's eyes. "No, it's coming to us."

Hollee swallowed to keep her voice from coming out in a squeak. "The Grawl?"

The wizard stood for a moment with his head tilted and an expression of deep concentration on his face. "Yes, I'm afraid so, but do not worry. The Grawl is not the only one coming and might very well get lost in the crowd."

"Reinforcements?"

"For us? No." He untangled a grasshopper from his beard and let it go. "Odidoddex's army is only about a half day's march to the east."

Hollee quivered so violently that her dress made of light blinked on and off. "Why shouldn't I worry?"

"Oh dear, oh dear. I don't like this business of war." He pointed to a dragon cresting the northern ridge. "Here comes the first of our bad news."

"What? What? What's happening?"

"Patience," said the wizard and placed a hand on her head, mashing down her unruly spikes of wispy hair.

The dragon landed next to the castle. A marione slipped off its back and ran in. A second rider, a kimen, came to Fenworth and Hollee.

"Tut, tut," said the wizard. "I wish I could be with Lady Peg and Tipper."

"Why?" Hollee watched the approaching messenger. "What's happened?"

"The city of Ragar has fallen."

The kimen reached them as Fenworth dropped down on a log. His hat wiggled and fell off in his lap. A bird flew away from his head.

"Oh dear, oh dear. I don't like war." Fenworth leaned forward, propping his elbows on his knees and putting his face in his hands.

Hollee spoke to the kimen. "There's more bad news, isn't there?"

The messenger nodded, his long hair falling into his eyes and his face distraught. "The king fought with his soldiers to defend Amber Palace and was killed."

"Oh no!"

"Verrin Schope rescued the queen and is taking her to Byrdschopen."

"That means Princess Tipper will be queen."

Wizard Fenworth lifted his head. "Why?"

"In Chiril," explained the messenger, "the crown goes to the second generation, second child."

"Lady Peg and her sister are the first generation," said Hollee, "and Princess Tipper is the second child."

Fenworth shook his head. "She has no older sibling."

Hollee hopped from one foot to the other. "No, but she has one older cousin." She stood on tiptoe. "I'm sorry the king is dead, but this is so exciting. Princess Tipper will be a great queen."

"Interesting." Fenworth nodded. "Unusual." He stood. "Odd." He sat again. "Is there a reason for this second generation, second child tradition?"

"Oh yes." Hollee used her hands to gesture, emphasizing the importance of the custom with wide, sweeping motions. "Royalty stopped killing each other to get the throne. The spouse cannot inherit the crown, and the royal children can't either. It makes plotting to overthrow the king useless. You see, the oldest child is supposed to guard the second child from harm. And if anything happens to the successor, the oldest child loses his citizenship and must go abroad. Banished, in other words."

"So where is this cousin?"

"Banished. He was never good at his job. Actually he never even tried to watch over Tipper. He doesn't believe in tradition. He mostly likes to have grand parties. So now he goes to grand parties somewhere else. Maybe even in Baardack. That's why Verrin Schope left Sir Beccaroon in charge of Tipper."

Wizard Fenworth nodded to the visitor. "Suppose you tell us the rest of your bad news."

"Odidoddex's army has secured Ragar, and their general has dispatched a battalion to conquer this valley."

"I suppose," said Wizard Fenworth as he stood, "there are thousands of them to our mere two hundred or so."

The messenger looked very gloomy. "Yes sir."

"And I have ascertained that they are quite near."

"Yes sir."

"I seem to remember something about a part of the army that was not trapped inside Ragar. They were cut off from the main forces and were headed this way."

"Were," said the kimen without looking up.

"Oh no!" Hollee froze. "They were all killed? Ambushed?"

"No." The kimen sighed. "They went home."

"Understandable," said Fenworth. "They probably considered the war lost. Only the official surrender needed to make it final. Oh dear." He turned back to the cave opening. "Hollee, you can stay aboveground if you wish to help. I shall tell Librettowit and make a last-minute check on our statues. I am so glad we had time to make all the preparations so that they will not fall into Odidoddex's hands."

<hr/>

The wizard came out of the same opening the tumanhofers used for their mining operation. After some time, he went back in.

The Grawl grinned and noticed the schoergat he called Torn Shirt shiver. He made the schoergats nervous. Even his satisfied smile caused alarm among these fierce allies. The time had come to reward their patience and set them free.

He raked his eyes over his three companions and watched them squirm. The Grawl appreciated beauty. The schoergats reeked of sweat and rancid food. They looked like stone ogres, smaller than grawligs and smarter. His association with them grew out of necessity, and soon they would not be needed.

The Grawl would go into the mine, come out the victor, and go home. He placed a hand on the pocket that held his silver box. His fingers outlined the square. Soon this tedious journey would be done.

"Tonight," he said to the three he'd brought with him, "we will invade their valley. I'll show you exactly where the dragons are most likely to be. You take care of them, and I will take care of the wizard."

52

Battle Cry

The people of the valley skipped the songfest after their evening meal. They also omitted turning in for the night. Instead of posting guards, Paladin dispersed all the men to cover entry points in the mountain walls. Dragons perched at intervals where they could observe the enemy and communicate their movement.

Hollee had chosen to stay with the commander of this small Chirilian force and run messages to the wizard in his cave. When Wizard Fenworth walked up behind Paladin, he startled both the young man and the kimen.

"I've been out and about, doing a few things," he said. "I thought I might help a bit before I return to sentry duty over the statues."

"Any help is appreciated," said Paladin. "We're vastly outnumbered."

Hollee gritted her teeth and scrunched her eyes. From experience, she knew that, at times, some help from the wizard was not worthy of appreciation. Things generally worked out in the end, but his contributions to a cause could be disconcerting. She opened her eyes to peek at the men.

Fenworth winked at her. "I am providing a disguise for your people and dragons, a masking non-sheen."

Paladin focused on the older man. "Non-sheen?"

"Yes." He began pulling jar after jar out of his hollows. "While the tumanhofers were busy, and on occasions when they didn't need my direct supervision, Librettowit and I brewed up this substance. You can have your kimen friends deliver it. Have them instruct the men and the dragons to rub it all over, including hair, clothes, and boots as well as skin. The more they buff the cream, the more unseeable they will become. That is why it is a non-sheen. Instead of becoming shinier, they will become less seeable."

"Invisible?" asked Paladin. He opened a jar and sniffed the contents. "No smell."

"Well," said Fenworth, "that would defeat the purpose, wouldn't it? If it smelled like something, your men and dragons would be unseeable but smellable. Not a very good plan to hide reeking soldiers all around."

"I agree," said Paladin. He motioned several dozen kimens to come closer and directed them to deliver the jars and instructions to the men. "You will have to help spread the non-sheen substance on the dragons."

They grabbed jars and raced off to do his bidding.

Paladin dipped into the cream and spread it on his face and through his hair. "It might have been better to give this to the men while they were still here in camp."

Fenworth frowned at him. "Right. Might have." He clapped his hands together. "But now the soldiers have something to do other than sit and worry about the coming engagement." He turned away, then back. "Oh, I forgot. I've put up sheening devices at intervals along the edge of the valley rim."

"And a sheening device…" Paladin stopped to give Fenworth an opportunity to explain.

"A sheening device, of course, does the opposite of a non-sheen cream."

"I see."

"Oh yes, you'll be able to see them. Folly to attack at night when the valley is equipped with sheening devices. But then, how would they know a wizard backs all your endeavors?"

The old man marched off, waving nonchalantly over his shoulder and humming a cheerful tune.

Paladin caught Hollee's eye and held it. "I suppose the enemy will shine."

"Glow," said Hollee and giggled.

A dragon screech scraped through the quiet night. Paladin's head jerked around as the noise continued to declare a dragon in trouble.

Hollee spotted the wounded dragon first and pointed to the sky over the lake. "A dragon and something else. They're fighting."

The two combatants charged each other.

"I'm going up there," said Paladin as Caesannede flew in. "I can't tell what that creature is."

"Can I go with you?"

"Of course." Paladin shook his head. "That thing must not have walked through Wizard Fenworth's sheening device."

"I was thinking the same thing. Doesn't glow. Flew over, most likely."

Caesannede landed. Paladin and Hollee scrambled aboard.

"All right," said Paladin. "Go to the weapons first."

Hollee assumed the dragon fussed at his rider. "He has a point. That thing looks fierce."

"Schoergats! He says they're schoergats."

The dragon fighting the creature shrieked again. Pain emanated through the harsh cry. Hollee whipped her head around to see the dragon fall from the air. "Oh no! Paladin, I think the dragon is dead."

"We must mobilize before too many dragons are in the air."

Caesannede landed nearer the castle, in the field where weapons were kept.

"A saddle!" Paladin shouted, and two marione soldiers appeared from a shed, lugging the many-strapped leather contraption between them. Hollee almost asked why he called for a saddle but realized he needed the many sheaths that held weapons. She and Paladin jumped off and gathered spears, a bow and arrow, and a slingshot.

Dragon battle cries announced the response to one of their own being killed. The sky filled with beasts of all sizes. Many of the dragons had launched the counterattack without waiting for the men who'd been trained to ride them.

"We have to hurry." Paladin dropped his armload of weapons and aided the two men fastening leather straps around Caesannede. "Dragons lose all sense when battling schoergats, and they usually lose the fight."

Hollee ran from the pile of weapons to the back of the dragon, loading the saddle with their supplies. "What are schoergats?"

"A low race, dragonkillers. Their greatest pleasure is to kill and then eat dragons. They were driven out of this valley by my predecessor but only after they had slain enough of the population that some claimed the dragons were extinct."

Several men barreled into the field in front of the armory.

"Sir," called one of the soldiers. "Our dragons took flight without us."

"I know," said Paladin. "Gather 'round."

More soldiers arrived. They formed a tight knot in front of their commander. Hollee smelled fear as they waited for orders.

"You must intercept your dragons. They will die if you're not on their backs, helping to strategize. Schoergats affect their minds with frenzy. Find someone with a mount that has not been crazed. Probably one of the older, steadier dragons. Use that dragon to take you up and transfer to your own steed. You must reach them and temper their mania. This will be a wild ride, but once you are on their backs, you'll calm them."

The men shifted, eager to be away, but Paladin had not dismissed them. None of their training had taken in the possibility of fighting these schoergats.

Paladin paused, inspecting his men and choosing his words. "The only way to kill this enemy is to fly over them and instruct your dragon

to use its tail to smack the schoergat to the ground. They carry a pultah, a spear. Sometimes the head is painted with poison. Make passes
to the side first. Try to knock the pultah out of the schoergats' hands.
Then go in for the kill from above. Any questions?"

A negative murmur rose from the soldiers.

Paladin studied them for a moment, then gave the order. "Go!"

53

Two Baardackians

Bealomondore stopped to catch his breath. His men were outnumbered by five to one, but Fenworth had done them a favor. The enemy shone like polished silver as they walked through the gap. He and his men could barely be seen, even by each other. The kimens toned down their light clothing, and all the others were smeared from head to toe with Fenworth's non-sheen cream.

Maxon stood at the tumanhofer's side on the rocky hillside. They'd taken refuge in a copse of bramblewood trees. Even with the advantage of being almost unseen, fighting as many as four enemy soldiers at once was tiring.

Two of Odidoddex's men, a marione and an emerlindian, approached. They crept through the bushes, crouching low and jerking at every little noise.

The marione stopped and whispered. "I'm for getting out of here, Cahn. We're fighting ghosts."

"Desert? You're crazy."

"What punishment could they deal out that would be worse than fighting phantoms?"

"Giving us over to The Grawl."

The enemy warriors stopped moving. Bealomondore imagined they were contemplating their fate in the hands of The Grawl. He shivered in sympathy.

At last the marione sighed. "We can see The Grawl. Whatever we're fighting in this valley cannot be seen."

"That's not strictly true. You gotta admit, you can see something move. It's just hard to see what it is that moved."

"And how do we fight something we can almost see?"

"Calculate."

The marione lowered himself to sit on the ground, his back to a boulder. "You're crazy."

"No, smarter than you."

The marione grunted.

"Listen to me, Demdar." Cahn's voice rose.

Demdar gestured wildly. "Shh!"

Cahn heeded and whispered so quietly that Bealomondore had to move closer to hear. A twig snapped under his foot.

"What was that?" asked the marione.

The men remained silent and still for a minute. Bealomondore held his breath.

"Nothing," said the emerlindian. "Listen. When the something moves, you get a general impression of its size. Then you calculate. You can calculate where the heart and head are."

"Yeah, but you can't figure where the weapon is. The weapon is what I want to calculate. Let's just go back through the gap a ways."

"That's likely to get us caught. I don't want to desert. I just want to stay alive. Deserting will lead to death, Demdar. Remember, I'm the smart one."

Demdar snorted. "Then calculate us staying alive."

"We can duck into that cave we saw and be out of sight. When the fighting is over, we'll come out and pretend we were in the battle but away from everyone else. You lie for me. I lie for you."

"What if someone sees us?" The marione gestured to his face and clothing. "We stand out, you know."

"Then we'll say that someone told us those statues were in the cave. You know how much Groddenmitersay wants those statues."

"If they're real. Even the mighty Groddenmitersay isn't sure. He has that 'if they're real' in the promise to reward the finder." Demdar thought for a minute. "Who told us the statues might be in the cave?"

"Some Chirilian we were about to kill."

"Where is he?"

"We killed him."

"Where's the body?"

"We killed so many Chirilians that we don't know where that one is."

"All right. Let's go."

The two Baardackians stole away. Bealomondore and Maxon followed.

As they passed his second in command, Bealomondore told him to let the men rest thirty minutes, then start chasing the Baardackians out of the valley again.

"Maxon and I are going to follow these two. But we'll be back before you reengage. If we're not, just go on without us."

"Why are you following them?"

"Dragons are supposed to be guarding the statues." Bealomondore pointed up. "I'm afraid most of the dragons are fighting schoergats. I'm just going to make sure the cavern chapel is secure."

"And if it's not?"

"I've got Maxon with me, and he'll come back for reinforcements."

They left the others behind and stalked the two Baardackians. Cahn and Demdar had moved ahead of them, but Maxon easily followed their trail. Bealomondore and Maxon caught up and watched them enter the cave.

The roar of a schoergat pivoted their attention to the sky. A large spear clattered on the rocks near them. Bealomondore traced the movement of a dragon with some difficulty. This rider had been able to cover his steed with the non-sheen cream. The schoergat flew away from the fray, doubled back, and came toward Bealomondore and Maxon.

"I bet he's coming back for his weapon," said Maxon.

"Then we'll move it." Bealomondore dashed forward, grabbed the pole with its deadly point, and raced back. He heard the flap of the schoergat's wings, heard the low-throated growl, and smelled its horrid, hot breath.

He dove between the rocks. "I'm glad those creatures don't breathe fire." He panted. "I'd have singed clothing."

"He probably didn't even see you." Maxon took the spear and poked it far into the bushes between two rocks. "I could barely follow your movements, and I knew what you were doing."

A dragon trumpeted a challenge above. The tumanhofer and kimen looked up in time to see the schoergat batted from the sky with the blow from a powerful tail.

"Come on," said Bealomondore. "We need to catch up to those two Baardackians."

They scrambled down a rocky incline, covered the open area quickly, and stopped just outside the entrance. "Hear anything?" whispered Maxon.

Bealomondore shook his head. He used all his senses. Nothing smelled, tasted, or looked out of place. He didn't want the men they were following to have a chance to set a trap. He especially didn't want to fall into any trap. He signaled to Maxon, and they crept into the darkness.

54

Confrontation

About thirty feet into the passageway, Bealomondore spotted a blue light up ahead. He and Maxon picked up the pace, knowing lightrocks waited for them at the first junction of two tunnels. Each armed with a glowing stone, they walked even faster, the kimen leading the way.

Maxon stopped and whispered. "I smell blood."

Bealomondore sniffed the air. "Yes. We'd better proceed with a bit more caution."

The scent grew stronger as they made their way to the underground chapel. Maxon slowed to a stop again.

"Up ahead," he said. "Do you see that?"

A mound of some kind glowed.

Bealomondore stooped so that he was closer to Maxon's ear. "It's the same color as Odidoddex's soldiers."

He pulled his sword, and they crept forward. Cahn and Demdar lay in a heap, in a pool of blood. Maxon turned away.

Bealomondore made sure no one was hiding in the shadow, then examined the bodies. "Their throats were ripped out."

"That's not the way dragons kill," said Maxon, keeping his back to the victims.

"And we haven't seen any dragons guarding the passageways."

"The Grawl?"

"Yes, I think The Grawl is here." Bealomondore stood. "Go back and get ten to fifteen men. I'll go on. Fenworth and Librettowit may need some help."

"I think the wizard can take care of The Grawl."

"You're probably right."

"But you're going anyway?"

"Yes."

Maxon took off. Bealomondore straightened his shoulders, gripped the Sword of Valor, and stepped around the dark red puddle on the floor. As he followed the tunnels down to the cavern, he inspected each meditation room.

He stopped just inside the opening to the chapel. Wizard Fenworth and his librarian were nowhere in sight, but The Grawl stood next to the display of the three statues. Bealomondore recognized the rapt expression on the big man's face. Verrin Schope's art often profoundly moved him. He'd spent time just gazing at a painting, marveling at all an artist's brush could reveal.

He took a few steps into the large cavern. The wizard had provided lighting that enhanced the natural beauty of salt and crystals. During the day, special lights accented the carvings formed by the wizard's hands. In the night, only the three statues were illuminated.

"I have a collection." The Grawl's comment startled Bealomondore. He hadn't realized the creature had noticed him.

"Of art?"

"Yes, but more than just art. Things of beauty. Anything that strikes me as exquisite. Anything exceptional."

"Verrin Schope's work always astounds people."

The Grawl looked over his shoulder, pinning the tumanhofer with a glare. "I will take these."

Bealomondore blinked. He took a deep breath and let it out slowly. "The *Trio of Elements* is necessary for the health of my friend and my country. I cannot allow you to take them."

"Then I shall kill you." The Grawl pulled a sword from its scabbard.

Bealomondore raised the Sword of Valor. It seemed suddenly heavier. He glanced down and saw that the hilt had enlarged and covered his hand, and the blade itself looked longer and thicker. He swished it in front of him. The balance seemed the same. The comfort of his grip felt the same. The sword had changed, but not the way he would use it. With just an ounce more confidence, Bealomondore came down the ramp that led to the expanse of stone floor.

The Grawl approached from the other direction.

The tumanhofer didn't like the patronizing grin on the creature. He didn't like that his head probably came no higher than the taller man's thigh. He didn't like fighting a superior force when he was tired from a night of skirmishes. His previous experience with The Grawl had ended in the river. He'd nearly died from a crushed skull and drowning. He steered his thoughts from that memory. He didn't need to undermine his own confidence.

He stopped at the proper distance for two swordsmen to face off for a fight.

Nerves sent a tremor through his body. *I will need more than my own power to defeat this foe. The sword will help. I will need more than that to even stay alive. Wulder. What does Wulder give in circumstances such as this? Enough bravery so that I won't turn and run? Enough skill to match my opponent? Enough strength to deflect his blows? Enough stamina to finish the fight? I ask for enough, Wulder, and just a little bit more.*

They crossed swords, and the battle began.

To Bealomondore's surprise, his size actually gave him an advantage in this battle. The Grawl miscalculated the distance between them. Bealomondore ducked under many swipes. He moved with the agility learned from his kimen instructors. He used the moves the sturdier librarian had taught him. The Grawl fought in a straightforward manner, but Bealomondore twirled, somersaulted, flipped, and leaped into the air.

They both attacked with determination. Bealomondore realized

The Grawl had not expected his expertise to be tested. Instead of dispatching Bealomondore after a moment's match, the combat lasted. The Grawl's anger increased. His moves sharpened. His eyes flamed. His jaw clenched.

Bealomondore prayed he would live. Maxon should return with soldiers, and then the tumanhofer artist would make no valiant effort to finish this battle alone. Let all those men run in and tackle The Grawl. His pride would stand up under such blatant effrontery to his fighting abilities.

The struggle dragged on, and The Grawl abandoned the finesse of sword fighting and threw his weight into sly moves. He moved behind a five-foot-tall column and shoved it down. Bealomondore jumped to keep his legs out of danger. The monster picked up a lantern and threw it at his opponent. The glass shattered and flaming oil splashed across the floor, but again, the tumanhofer avoided serious injury. They fought until both men dripped with sweat and panted for breath.

Finally, Bealomondore knocked The Grawl's sword from his hand, tripped him with a move Taeda Bel had shown him, and ended up standing on The Grawl's chest, heel pressed against his throat and blade pointed at his eye.

"No, no, no," Fenworth's voice echoed a bit in the chamber.

Some force lifted Bealomondore off his adversary and set him down a few feet away. He saw that The Grawl had been covered with a coarse net. The creature thrashed about, trying to extricate himself.

"You can't kill someone in the chapel, Bealomondore. It just isn't the thing to do."

A wave of relief flowed through Bealomondore, followed by a crash of anger. "Where have you been?"

"Here and there," said the wizard, "watching how our battle for the valley was ending. Dragons took the schoergats. Paladin and crew captured the rooks, knights, and all fighting on the ground. And you've cornered The Grawl. I'd say these hostilities only need an emissary to that odious King Odidoddex to inform him he's lost. You know, the kind of protocol carried on as peace is established."

Librettowit walked out of the shadows from a passageway that led to the library. He held an open book. "What are you saying, Fen?"

"They've done it, Wit. We've defended our sanctuary. Now this tiny force can go out and take back the rest of Chiril."

"Just like that? No problems with the greater force of Odidoddex's army?"

"Not much. After all, it's the determination of the people that matters, and now they know that defeating the invaders is possible."

"Now that's good news." Librettowit shrugged and turned his attention to the netted beast on the floor. "Why do we have The Grawl trussed up in the chapel?"

"Bealomondore defeated him with that sword."

Librettowit beamed at the other tumanhofer. "Good work, young man."

Bealomondore could only nod. He collapsed on a stone bench, suddenly feeling that all of his bones were made of sculpting clay.

Fenworth circled The Grawl as he spoke. "There will be some cleaning up to do. Shame this continent doesn't boast a urohm population. They're mighty handy at putting things straight."

Maxon charged into the chapel with soldiers at his back.

"Too late," said Fenworth. "Except for the tidying."

55

Tidying Up

The Grawl squatted in the corner of his cell. If he showed any interest in what the wizard said, the old man would talk forever. By not responding, The Grawl felt he had some control. And his taciturn refusal to engage in conversation meant the o'rant would give up and go away.

Fenworth had insisted on keeping The Grawl in the sanctuary. He gave him a room, provided some minimal comforts, and visited him daily. He shared with the captured beast each bit of news that came in from the resistance fighters beyond the rim of their valley.

"Ah." The old wizard would sigh in satisfaction. "We should have known the people of Chiril would do much better as a defiant underground alliance than an organized army."

The Grawl fumed.

"Now look at this." The wizard, another time, waved a map at his prisoner. "Three more towns liberated from the occupation."

The Grawl turned his back on the cheerful wizard.

A few days later, the wizard came to The Grawl's cell with more information. "You never liked that Groddenmitersay, did you? Good news for you then. He's been captured and will be tried for war crimes."

The Grawl flinched. He thought about the man who had respectfully requested him to perform deeds of war. Groddenmitersay understood that he was superior to the rest of the soldiers. Still, he deserved to be punished. He had surrounded himself with inferior warriors. The Grawl let his eyes roam around his small quarters. His imprisonment was an insult.

Bealomondore returned to the valley with good news. In just three months, the Chiril Alliance had taken back all the lost territory and had the enemy forces scrambling for the hills that led to Baardack. The people of Chiril rejoiced and celebrated Wizard Verrin Schope, Warrior Prince Jayrus, also known as Paladin, and the brave swordsman, Graddapotmorphit Bealomondore. The three men had rallied the underground troops and strategized a successful campaign. Chiril had beaten Baardack.

The three honored men came themselves to tell Fenworth and Librettowit. A band of the alliance came with them to meet the Amarans and see the now famous cathedral cavern.

The old wizard from Amara willingly undertook giving advice as to how they should proceed.

Bealomondore sat back and watched with amusement as the visitors from Amara concocted a scheme for Chiril's handling of the evil neighbor to the north.

"I believe Paladin should go to Baardack and deliver the bad news to King Odidoddex," Fenworth said. "As the official emissary for Chiril, he can list the things we won't do and King Odidoddex won't do."

Librettowit sat down and pulled out a pen and paper. "I'm ready."

Fenworth began his list. "Baardack will not attack Chiril again.

"Chiril will not return Odidoddex's army.

"Baardack will not withhold payment for damages to Chirilian crops and sundry property.

"Chiril will not plunder Baardack for compensation.

"Baardack will not abuse any Chirilian citizen doing business within Baardack borders."

Librettowit looked up. "That's three 'Baardack won'ts' to two 'Chiril won'ts.'"

"Well, we won after all. We shouldn't have to even up."

Librettowit agreed, wrote something more at the top of the page, and put it away. "I think the first order of business should be to send The Grawl home."

"Good idea."

The wizard scurried down one of the corridors and soon came back with The Grawl, walking sedately in front of him.

"Don't worry," he told the men in the room who had reached for their weapons as soon as they spotted the huge man. "He's confined, but you can't see the restraints."

The Grawl's deeds were well known. Most of the soldiers in the room knew someone who had disappeared, never to be found. As many as his crimes were, any malicious act that went unexplained was also blamed on the man-beast.

One of the men stepped forward. "He killed two in my family. Five altogether in my village. Is there a punishment vile enough to match his crimes?"

Another man's cold voice asked the question on all their minds. "What shall we do with him? How do we get rid of something that depraved?"

The wizard pulled a silver box from his robe and handed it to The Grawl.

"This is yours." He addressed the soldiers. "He has his silver box. Let him use it." Fenworth gestured toward the men standing around the wall of the chapel. "We'll send him on his way."

"What is it?" asked one of the men.

"It is a transport device. It will take him away."

Bealomondore thought of all the people this prisoner had murdered and started to object. Fenworth sent him a stern glare, and then his face altered to mischief that included a wink and immediately transformed back to the stone-faced wizard of judgment.

Every man in the room, including Bealomondore, stood ready lest The Grawl make a wrong move.

The creature stared at the wizard.

"You have the means to leave us. Do it," said Fenworth.

The Grawl turned the box over and over again in one huge hand. He looked around the room.

Bealomondore shivered when The Grawl's gaze passed over him. This "man" should not be given his freedom. Many would suffer from his hands if he was allowed to use the box. He started to object again and heard Fenworth's voice in his mind. *"Steady. Silence."*

The Grawl reluctantly opened the silver box. Threads of light streamed out and formed a gateway. The noises made by many of the men indicated they'd never seen such a thing. Momentarily distracted, Bealomondore glanced at them, observing their wide-eyed wonder.

"Keep alert, men." The tumanhofer's commanding voice pulled his soldiers back to the danger still in the room.

"Go on, Grawl," urged Fenworth.

The creature threw the silver box through the opening. Fenworth smiled. "We won't keep you from your destiny."

The Grawl stepped into the gateway, promptly immersed in the varying colors of the passage, just as Bealomondore had expected, given his limited knowledge of this wizardry means of travel.

However, the creature's shape did not disappear. Instead, his shoulder reappeared as if he'd turned to come back. Bealomondore saw his face. The snarl left, and a look of astonishment took its place.

A sudden *pop* startled the observers. The gateway, with its muddled colors and strands of light, rose into the air with a *swoosh*. It seemed to be pulled together into one shining spot. When completely concentrated, it gleamed with a silver light. Then a *snap* cut off the glow, and the silver box fell from the air to hit the stone floor with a clatter.

Fenworth strolled forward and picked up the box. He held it in his hand, turned it over several times, then smiled at the men watching him. "A suitable prison for an incorrigible villain."

He held it out to examine it again. "I really should label it 'Do Not Open.' Yes." He patted his pockets. "Bealomondore, do you have some paints? We could paint a warning on the outside."

"Not on me, sir."

"Oh, never mind." Fenworth tucked the slim silver box into a pocket. "I'll do it later." He gestured to the soldiers. "Come closer. I'm sure you would like to admire the amazing art of Verrin Schope. Come and I'll tell you a tale of adventure and glory. Actually, Librettowit will because he is so much better at not forgetting things and not adding things. I'll fix refreshments. Pleased to do it. Always willing to serve. Come, sit down, relax. You've had a hard night."

56

Past, Present, Future

Tipper stood in the driveway and waved to the last three wounded soldiers as they left Byrdschopen. For nine months the mansion had been a hospital. Slowly, as the men got well, fewer rooms were used for wards. They hadn't had a new patient in seven weeks, a sign that the war was truly over. The resistance had smashed the occupation forces and sent them home.

With a last wave, she turned toward the house. Her parents stood on the bottom step, her father's arm wrapped around her mother's shoulders. Lady Peg beamed, her happiness glowing through her gentle and confused soul. Verrin Schope kissed the top of her head, squeezed her closer, then whirled her to face the other direction. They mounted the three steps and entered by the massive front door. Several of the servants who'd come out to bid farewell followed them in.

For a moment, Tipper stood with her arms wrapped around her middle, feeling alone. A flutter of bright colors caught her eye, and she bolted toward the side of the mansion, following Sir Beccaroon.

"Wait," she called as she rounded the corner. "Wait for me."

The big parrot stopped and turned, waiting for her to catch up. "What is it, Tipper?"

"Can't you stay for a bit?"

"Not this afternoon. I still haven't found someone to help the Marrost family bring their harvest in." He glanced up at the gray sky. "I hope the rain holds off a few more days."

She nodded. The shortage of men made all aspects of life difficult. Too many husbands, fathers, sons, and brothers had been lost in the war.

Beccaroon spread his wings, and she quickly said, "Well, good luck then."

From the veranda across the back of the mansion, she surveyed her home. Her father had been fixing it up. He came back to find Byrdschopen in a sorry state, thanks to his daughter's ineptitude at running a household and farm. Now they wanted her to run a country. She was the next queen.

Tipper picked up her skirts and ran to one of the back doors. She zipped through the first floor and rushed up the stairs to the second floor and then the third and up to the top of the house to burst out on the flat roof.

She walked more calmly to the balustrade that edged the tiled outdoor dance floor. The balls held under starry nights had taken place long before her father inherited this home. She'd never danced with her true love while a small orchestra provided the music and liveried servants served delicate sandwiches and daggarts.

Maybe Byrdschopen didn't feel like a home to those who had dwelled here under such ostentatious wealth. But the now shabby house with two loyal servants and her besotted mother at the helm had always been a place of peace for her. She'd grown up under trying circumstances but nonetheless happy.

Now her father occupied all her mother's time. Tipper had been unwittingly crowded out. She was supposed to go to Ragar, reside in the Amber Palace, and take up the scepter of queen. Her future was set before her. The past, the scrimping and saving and conniving past, held more allure.

In the past, she'd had no money, but she'd had purpose. Now she had money but no purpose. Once queen, she would have money and purpose. Where was the elusive contentment?

Footsteps pounded against the stairs, echoing through the cupola that covered the door to the main house.

"Tipper!" Paladin's voice brought a smile to her face, pulling her out of the introspective doldrums that had plagued her all morning.

"I'm here."

"Finally!" He appeared in the door, and just as he stepped out of the shadow, the sun peeked from behind a cloud. He wore white and seemed to reflect sunbeams of soft light.

"I'm looking over my life from the vantage point of the very tiptop of the place I've always lived."

He came to stand beside her and put an arm around her waist, tugging her a bit closer. "I've been talking to your father."

"I thought he was with Mother."

"He was. She contributed quite a bit to our discussion."

Tipper giggled and leaned her head against his upper arm. The top of her head just barely reached his shoulder.

"She assured me that after I asked my question, you would be properly befuddled and it was high time as well."

Tipper leaned back and looked up at his mischievous grin.

"What question?" Her eyes grew wide as she deciphered her mother's remark. "Betrothed? Properly betrothed and high time."

"Don't leap ahead of me." He let her go and dug in his pockets, found the item he sought, and pulled it out.

Diamonds and sapphires sparkled in the sun.

He leaned forward and kissed her lips with a quick peck. "Stay right there. Continue to look ravishingly lovely. Don't interrupt once I get started."

He dropped to one knee before her. "Princess Tipper, I have grown to love you. I admire your spirit, your generosity, your tender heart, your practical approach to problems."

"That last one wasn't very romantic."

"You aren't supposed to interrupt."

"Right."

"I love your easy smile, your beautiful laugh, your singing, your cooking, your—"

"Hurry up. Get to the good part."

"Your impatience and your bossiness."

She arched her eyebrows but did not interrupt.

"Will you do me the honor of becoming my wife?"

She held back the explosive yes and watched him as he waited. He was confident and amused. She still waited.

"My knee is getting sore."

"Stand up."

He stood and brushed his pant leg with his hand.

"Well?"

She grasped his forearms and looked deep into his sky blue eyes. Her heart grew exceedingly calm as she saw peace, maturity, wisdom, and love in the very depth of the man who stood before her. She'd found contentment.

A bubble of joy rose to the surface and burst as she stopped holding back her response.

"Yes!"

Epilogue

Hollee worried. She couldn't help it. Her wizard said he was making fresh brain soup to celebrate. He'd gone for a walk and come back to the one-towered castle with a huge, lumpy bag. Then he'd taken over the kitchen, shooing everyone out except one kimen who would not go. The chief cook would not desert his domain, leaving his precious pots and ovens to an old man who shed bugs whenever he moved.

Verrin Schope sat with Lady Peg and Queen Venmarie in the main room by a roaring fire. Paladin and Princess Tipper stared at each other a lot. Since he'd asked her to marry him, the two had become boring. The wedding would be exciting, and immediately after that, the coronation would be fun. But for now, they were a dreary couple and they had hardly noticed her when she said Fenworth was cooking something strange.

No one would be interested in her concern. Still she searched for Librettowit. Perhaps he would know more about brain soup.

She found him in the chapel library. Bealomondore sat with him, looking at huge books of art from different countries.

As soon as the librarian looked at her, Hollee blurted out her reason for coming. "Wizard Fenworth is making brain soup."

Librettowit took the news in stride. "In celebration, I suppose."

"Yes. For ousting the Baardackians."

"Humph! It's more likely in celebration of finding the right plant."

"A brain plant?" Hollee hoped she was wrong. "We don't grow a brain plant in Chiril."

"We don't grow one in Amara either. But Fenworth finds this short vegetable that produces a clump of white florets so close together as to be almost solid. You pick off the head and boil it, though some people eat it raw. Fenworth says it looks like a pure brain, one that belongs to someone who doesn't bother to think that much."

Bealomondore laughed. "I think brain soup is a significant contribution to a celebration feast. Our countrymen will now have time to cultivate things of the mind instead of physically wrestling with an invading army." He winked at Hollee. "We can return to a life of ease, nothing more exciting than a new shade of green coming into fashion in time for the winter balls."

"This country has periods of leisure?" asked Librettowit. "I never would have suspected. But I'm in favor of returning to Amara. Fenworth and I have been gone a long time."

Hollee made a face.

"What's wrong?" asked Bealomondore.

"I like it with all of us here in one spot. But you and Paladin are going to negotiate a treaty with Odidoddex. Lady Peg, the queen, and Princess Tipper are going to Ragar to prepare for the wedding and the coronation. My wizard is going back to Amara. There just won't be any fun anymore."

Both tumanhofers raised their eyebrows and exchanged a look of incredulity.

"This has been fun?" asked Librettowit.

"Yes, all the bits between battles."

"Perhaps you can ask Fenworth if you may return with us through the gateway to Amara."

Hollee nearly passed her own record for consecutive flips.

When she stopped, Librettowit glared at her. "He'll teach you to cook brain soup, you know."

"Brain soup will be wonderful."

"Go off and ask him then."

Hollee did cartwheels out the door, singing a song she made up as she turned head down, then feet down, then head down, then feet down. It contained the words "grand adventure," some "*too-lee, too-las*," and a chorus of "Fenworth and me."

Appendix

Things

admitriol
Ointment made from an herb with healing properties.

amaloot
A warm soothing beverage, usually sweet.

Amber Palace
In Ragar, home of the reigning royalty.

Arbaneous Topicalee
Bane Bark pulverized, mixed with a bit of pica, and dried.

astain
A scrubby, tough bush with deep roots.

awdenberry
A sleep-inducing tea is made from the leaves, berries make refreshing juice.

Baardack
Country north of Chiril.

bellringer bird
A forest bird who is named more for his call than his looks.

bentleaf tree
A deciduous tree having long, slender, drooping branches and narrow leaves.

bogswart bark
A plant with pungent bark, found along streams.

bossvetch
A creeping vine with small round green leaves and delicate pink and white cluster blooms.

bramblewood trees
Small trees with gnarly branches and very rough bark.

Cheap Cheep
A diner in Ragar that serves only chicken and eggs and is open only for breakfast and noonmeal.

chukkajoop
A soup made with beets, onions, and carrots.

croomulite
A mineral that many believe revitalizes the blood.

daggart
A baked treat in the form of a small crunchy cake.

dopper
A cherrylike fruit.

drummerbug
A small brown beetle that makes a loud snapping sound with its wings when not in flight.

fibbird
A tiny, brightly colored bird with a long slender bill for sipping nectar and narrow, rapidly beating wings for hovering over flowers.

First Speatus
Rank in Baardackian army, similar to first lieutenant.

hollow
A nondimensional space captured by a wizard to use for storage.

Icardia
A land bridge from one continent to another, made of very tall mountains.

Insect Emporium
Shop selling insects and insect compounds for medicinal purposes.

jimmin
Young tender meat—chicken, veal, lamb.

krupant
A porridge heavily laced with fruit.

losibird
A large black bird that sends up a noisy clamor when disturbed.

Misken Minstrels
Traveling troupe of acrobats, jugglers, and dramatists.

monger
A long black aggressive snake, very poisonous.

moonflower
Large white blossoms found on a three- to four-foot moonbeam plant having large shiny leaves.

mullytawny tree
A tree that sprouts round bronze-toned green leaves that resemble burnished coins.

mumfer
A plant known for its showy flower heads of profuse petals and brilliant colors.

oubotis ivy
A very strong vine that clings stubbornly to brick walls.

parnot
A green fruit like a pear.

Perchant Crags
A landmark on the northern side of the Hanson Valley.

platter tree
A deciduous tree with large platterlike leaves.

pultah
A lance used by schoergats for hunting and battle.

Rat Tail
A card game involving collecting cards in sequence to make the longest "rat tail."

Round Baker Inn
The tavern/inn where Verrin Schope bases his spying operation.

schoergats
Flying beasts that favor dragon meat above any other; said to be a mutation of schoergs, one of the low races.

sparkle bug
A night-flying insect that generates a sparkling light.

spinet tree
Bears long leaves so green, from a distance they look black. The bark is white with scar marks of dark brown.

tangonut crème pie
Tangonuts taste a lot like butterscotch, so a créme pie would have the puddinglike base in a pie shell with a whipped cream covering.

tincture of trussell
A medicine for headaches.

torleo
A medicine made into a plaster and applied to sore muscles.

wild cascade
A flowering bush on which smaller branches of tiny leaves cascade off of larger, sturdier branches. Bears clusters of purple flowers that also appear to be cascading.

yumber
Dried fruit, nuts, and grain ground into a paste and shaped into a bar.

Seven High Races

doneels

These people are furry with bulging eyes, thin black lips, and ears at the top and front of their skulls. A flap of skin covers the ears and twitches. Small in stature, they are rarely over three feet tall.

emerlindians

Emerlindians are born pale with white hair and pale gray eyes. As they age, they darken. They are tall and slender.

kimens

Smallest of the seven high races. Elusive, tiny, and fast, under two feet tall, musical, and merry.

mariones

Excellent farmers and warriors. They are short and broad, usually muscle-bound rather than corpulent.

o'rants

Five to six feet tall with no distinguishing characteristics except that they are most likely to become wizards because they are most likely to hold Wulder in esteem.

tumanhofers

Short, squat, powerful fighters, though for the most part, they prefer to use their intellect.

urohms

Largest of the seven high races. Gentle giants, well proportioned, and very intelligent.

Seven Low Races

bisonbecks

Most intelligent of the low races. They are often enlisted as fighters.

blimmets

Burrowing creatures that swarm out of the ground for periodic feeding frenzies.

grawligs

Mountain ogres with clunky features and low intelligence; strong and clumsy.

mordakleeps

A shadowy creature with a long tail. Appear as black globs and must stay close to a water source.

quiss

These creatures are extremely slippery, live in water, and have enormous appetites. Every three years they develop the capacity to breathe air for six weeks and forage along the seacoast, creating havoc.

ropmas

These half-men, half-animals are useful in herding and caring for beasts. Low intelligence, basically docile, easily manipulated by other races.

schoergs

Black fur, skinny arms and legs, bulbous body; they tend to dwell in caves.

Characters

Graddapotmorphit Bealomondore

Tumanhofer artist.

Sir Beccaroon

Grand parrot, magistrate over the Indigo Forest; former guardian to Tipper.

Trader Bount

A sea trader who is tried and executed in Baardack.

Brox

Bisonbeck warrior under Kulson.

General Commert

One of the commanding officers of the Chiril army.

Advisor Cornagin

An o'rant on King Yellat's council.

Door

Ropma who helps rescue Tipper.

Wizard Fenworth

Ancient o'rant wizard from Amara.

General Fitz

The third commander on the war council.

Gladyme

Housekeeper at Byrdschopen.

Gorse

Bisonbeck warrior under Kulson.

The Grawl

Huntsman, ruthless killer for hire, procurer of collectibles; from a mysterious background.

Doremattris Groddenmitersay

The tumanhofer chief of Odidoddex's intelligence, head of spying forces in

Chiril, commander of tactical forces deployed to Chiril.

Hollee
Kimen assigned to Wizard Fenworth.

Hopdin
A magistrate from Selkskin.

Prince Jayrus, Paladin
The newly appointed champion of the people and communicator of Wulder's truth to the Chirilian people.

Kulson
First Speatus in charge of sabotage, following orders of Groddenmitersay.

Trevithick Librettowit
Friend and librarian to Wizard Fenworth.

Chief Advisor Likens
Emerlindian member of King Yellat's council.

Lipphil
Butler at Byrdschopen.

Advisor Malidore
A marione on King Yellat's council.

Maxon
Kimen assigned to Bealomondore.

Mernantottencat
A tumanhofer thug who runs the gang forcing merchants to deal only with Baardack.

King Odidoddex
Tyrant king of Baardack.

General Orchin
One of the top commanders of the Chiril army.

Roof
Ropma who helped rescue Tipper.

Runan
Evil wizard who attempted to overtake Chiril.

Lady Peg Schope
Wife of Verrin Schope, mother of Tipper, daughter of King Yellat and Queen Venmarie.

Taeda Bel
Kimen assigned to Tipper.

Tipper
Princess and heir apparent.

Queen Venmarie
Queen of Chiril.

Winkel
Elder in kimen village.

King Yellat
King of Chiril.

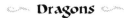 **Dragons**

Bar Besta
Pale blue minor dragon with faint purple markings, gifted in organization and logical thinking; serves Lady Peg.

Bevlo, Pennek, Sheran, and Trincum
Green minor dragons charged to help Tipper heal wounded soldiers.

Caesannede
Prince Jayrus's white and gold riding dragon.

Det
Map dragon helping Bealomondore as leader of his troops.

Grandur
Healing dragon Verrin Schope brought back from Amara.

Gus
Riding dragon.

Hue
Purple minor dragon.

Junkit
Family minor dragon from Byrdschopen.

Kelsi
Purple riding dragon.

Laddin
Healing dragon serving Bealomondore.

Merry
Blue riding dragon.

Rayn
Chameleon dragon given to Tipper by Paladin.

Sage
Oldest living dragon.

Printed in the United States
by Baker & Taylor Publisher Services